PRAISE FOR
The Year of the Witching

"If *The Handmaid's Tale* were set in a religious, Puritanical cult during the Salem witch trials, with a heavy dose of horror . . . [A] surreal and feminist historical fantasy."   —BuzzFeed

"A masterpiece of Puritan-esque dark fantasy, filled with an air of delirium. Alexis Henderson has created a full, believable world populated with living, breathing people, and nestled within it is the vital lesson to be wary of who we hand power over to."   —San Francisco Book Review

"Has a classic setup but updates the olde puritanical tale to deal with issues of racism and sexism."   —*The Washington Post*

"*The Year of the Witching* is Alexis Henderson's debut novel, but you'd never know it. . . . The story is enchanting, enticing, enthralling, enigmatic."
—Tor.com

"A thrillingly brisk and bracing tale of magic and power. I loved this book. It takes the best tropes of horror and witchcraft and gives them a refreshingly feminist twist."   —S. A. Chakraborty,
national bestselling author of The Daevabad Trilogy

"A dark, dramatic tale of oppression and rebellion, ideology and morality, with a complicated, appealing protagonist caught in a *Handmaid's Tale* nightmare."   —Louisa Morgan, author of *The Age of Witches*

"Creepy, compelling, and compulsively readable . . . blends the terror of the supernatural with the all-too-recognizable human evils of power and dogma."   —Fonda Lee, award-winning author of the Green Bone Saga

"Bone-chilling and breathtakingly beautiful. . . . Storytelling at its finest."
—Rena Barron, author of *Kingdom of Souls*

"A brutal tale of religion, witchcraft, & patriarchy. The perfect read for fans of *The Handmaid's Tale*."   —amanda lovelace,
national bestselling author of *the princess saves herself in this one*

NOVELS BY ALEXIS HENDERSON

The Year of the Witching

The

YEAR

of the

WITCHING

ALEXIS HENDERSON

ACE
New York

ACE

Published by Berkley

An imprint of Penguin Random House LLC

penguinrandomhouse.com

Copyright © 2020 by Alexis Henderson
Readers Guide copyright © 2021 by Alexis Henderson
Penguin Random House supports copyright. Copyright fuels
creativity, encourages diverse voices, promotes free speech, and
creates a vibrant culture. Thank you for buying an authorized edition
of this book and for complying with copyright laws by not reproducing,
scanning, or distributing any part of it in any form without permission.
You are supporting writers and allowing Penguin Random House to
continue to publish books for every reader.

ACE is a registered trademark and the A colophon is a trademark of
Penguin Random House LLC.

ISBN: 9780593099612

THE LIBRARY OF CONGRESS HAS CATALOGED THE ACE HARDCOVER
EDITION OF THIS BOOK AS FOLLOWS:

Names: Henderson, Alexis, author.
Title: The year of the witching / Alexis Henderson.
Description: First edition. | New York : Ace, 2020.
Identifiers: LCCN 2019050966 (print) | LCCN 2019050967 (ebook) |
ISBN 9780593099605 (hardcover) | ISBN 9780593099629 (ebook)
Subjects: GSAFD: Fantasy fiction. | Occult fiction.
Classification: LCC PS3608.E52548 Y43 2020 (print) |
LCC PS3608.E52548
(ebook) | DDC 813/.6—dc23
LC record available at https://lccn.loc.gov/2019050966
LC ebook record available at https://lccn.loc.gov/2019050967

Ace hardcover edition / July 2020
Ace trade paperback edition / June 2021

Printed in the United States of America
6th Printing

For my mom,

to whom I owe everything.

The Beast

SHE WAS BORN breech, in the deep of night. The midwife, Martha, had to seize her by the ankles and drag her from the womb. She slipped out easy, dropped limp into Martha's arms, and lay still as stone.

The midwife's daughter gave a low groan that bubbled up from her belly. She grasped at the folds of her nightdress, its hem soaked black with blood, but she made no move to reach for her child. Instead, she turned her head, cheek pressed to the tabletop, and stared across the kitchen to the window above the sink, gazing into the woods.

"Her name," she demanded, eyes sharp with moonlight. "Give me her name."

The midwife took the babe, cut her cord, and swaddled her in a scrap of burlap. The child was cold against her breast, and she would have thought her dead if it weren't for the name that rattled at the back of her throat, its flavor bitter as bile, and yet sweet as wine. The taste of the name the Father had chosen for her. But she didn't want to say it—not out loud.

With the last of her strength, the girl twisted to face her. "The name. I want her name."

"Immanuelle," she finally bit it out like a curse. "She will be called Immanuelle."

At that the girl on the table smiled, blue lips stretching taut. Then she laughed, an ugly, gargling sound that echoed through the kitchen, spilling out to the parlor, where the rest of the family sat waiting, listening.

"A curse," she whispered, still smiling to herself. "A little curse, just as she said. Just as she told me."

The midwife clutched the child close, locking her fingers to still their shaking. She gazed down at her daughter, lying limp on the table, a dark pool of blood between her thighs. "Just as who told you?"

"The woman in the woods," the dying girl whispered, barely breathing. "The witch. The Beast."

PART I

Blood

CHAPTER ONE

*From the light came the Father. From the darkness, the
Mother. That is both the beginning and the end.*

—THE HOLY SCRIPTURES

IMMANUELLE MOORE KNELT at the foot of the altar, palms
pressed together in prayer, mouth open. Above her, the Prophet
loomed in robes of black velvet, his head shaved bristly, his bloodied hands outstretched.

She peered up at him—tracing the path of the long, jagged scar
that carved down the side of his neck—and thought of her mother.

In a fluid motion, the Prophet turned from her, robes rustling
as he faced the altar, where a lamb lay gutted. He put a hand to its
head, then slipped his fingers deep into the wound. As he turned
to face Immanuelle again, blood trickled down his wrist and disappeared into the shadows of his sleeve, a few of the droplets falling to the stained floorboards at his feet. He painted her with the
blood, his fingers warm and firm as they trailed from the dip of
her upper lip down to her chin. He lingered for a moment, as if to
catch his breath, and when he spoke his voice was ragged. "Blood
of the flock."

Immanuelle licked it away, tasting brine and iron as she pressed
to her feet. "For the glory of the Father."

On her way back to her pew, she was careful not to spare a

glance at the lamb. An offering from her grandfather's flock, she'd brought it as a tribute the night before, when the cathedral was empty and dark. She had not witnessed the slaughter; she'd excused herself and retreated outside long before the apostles raised their blades. But she'd heard it, the prayers and murmurs drowned out by the cries of the lamb, like those of a newborn baby.

Immanuelle watched as the rest of her family moved through the procession, each of them receiving the blood in turn. Her sister Glory went first, dipping to her knees and obliging the Prophet with a smile. Glory's mother Anna, the younger of the two Moore wives, took the blessing in a hurry, herding her other daughter, Honor, who licked the blood off her lips like it was honey. Lastly, Martha, the first wife and Immanuelle's grandmother, accepted the Prophet's blessing with her arms raised, fingers shaking, her body seized by the power of the Father's light.

Immanuelle wished she could feel the way her grandmother did, but sitting there in the pew, all she felt was the residual warmth of the lamb's blood on her lips and the incessant drone of her heartbeat. No angels roosted at her shoulders. No spirit or god stirred in her.

When the last of the congregation was seated, the Prophet raised his arms to the rafters and began to pray. "Father, we come to Thee as servants and followers eager to do Thy work."

Immanuelle quickly bowed her head and squeezed her eyes shut.

"There may be those among us who are distant from the faith of our ancestors, numb to the Father's touch and deaf to His voice. On their behalves, I pray for His mercy. I ask that they find solace not in the Mother's darkness but in the light of the Father."

At that, Immanuelle cracked one eye open, and for a moment, she could have sworn the Prophet's gaze was on her. His eyes were wide open at the height of his prayer, staring at her in the gaps between bowed heads and shaking shoulders. Their eyes met, and his flicked away. "May the Father's kingdom reign."

The Prophet's flock spoke as one: *"Now and forevermore."*

IMMANUELLE LAY BY the river's edge with her friend, Leah, shoulder to shoulder, both of them drunk off the warmth of the midday sun. Yards away, the rest of the congregation gathered in fellowship. For most, the shadow of the Sabbath slaughter had already faded to a distant memory. All was peaceful and the congregation was content to abide in that.

At Immanuelle's side, Leah shifted onto her back, peering into the thick banks of the clouds that loomed overhead. She was a vision, dressed in sky-blue chiffon, her skirts billowing gently with the breeze. "It's a good day," she said, smiling as the wind snatched her hair.

In the Scriptures and the stories, in the stained-glass windows of the cathedral or the paintings that hung from its stone walls, the angels always looked like Leah: golden-haired and blue-eyed, dressed in fine silks and satins, with full cheeks and skin as pale as river pearls.

As for the girls like Immanuelle—the ones from the Outskirts, with dark skin and raven-black curls, cheekbones as keen as cut stone—well, the Scriptures never mentioned them at all. There were no statues or paintings rendered in their likeness, no poems or stories penned in their honor. They went unmentioned, unseen.

Immanuelle tried to push these thoughts from her mind. She didn't want to be jealous of her friend. If there was anyone in the world who deserved to be loved and admired, it was Leah. Leah with her patience and virtue. Leah, who, when all the other children at school had scorned Immanuelle as a child of sin, marched across the courtyard, took her firmly by the hand, and wiped her tears away with her sleeve.

Leah, her friend. The only one she had.

And Leah was right: It *was* a good day. It would have been nearly a perfect day, if not for the fact that it was one of the last of its kind, one of the last Sabbaths they would have together.

For years, every Sabbath, the two of them had met after the service ended. In the winter months, they'd huddle together in an empty pew at the back of the cathedral and gossip to pass the time. But in the warm seasons, Leah would bring a big picnic basket stuffed with pastries from her family's bakery in the village. On good days, there'd be an assortment of biscuits and sweet breads, scones and cookies, and on the very best days, a bit of honeycomb or jam to go with them. Together, they'd find a spot by the stream and eat and gossip and giggle until their families called them home. Such had been their custom, as though on those long afternoons in the meadow, the world began and ended there at the riverside. But, like most good things Immanuelle knew, their custom was not made to last. In two weeks' time, Leah was to marry the Prophet. On that day, once she was cut, she would no longer be Immanuelle's companion, but his.

"I'll miss days like this," said Leah, breaking the silence. "I'll miss the sweets and the Sabbath and being here with you."

Immanuelle shrugged, plucking at blades of grass. Her gaze followed the path of the river down the sloping plains and through the reeds, until it spilled into the distant forest and disappeared, devoured by the shadows. There was something about the way the water trickled through the trees that made her want to get up and follow it. "Good things end."

"Nothing's ending," Leah corrected her. "Everything's just beginning. We're growing up."

"Growing up?" Immanuelle scoffed. "I haven't even bled yet."

It was true. She was nearly seventeen years old and she'd never once had her flow. All of the other girls her age had bled years ago, but not Immanuelle. Never Immanuelle. Martha had all but declared her barren months ago. She was not to bleed or be a wife or bear children. She would remain as she was now, and everyone else would grow up, pass her by, and leave her behind, as Leah would in a few short weeks. It was only a matter of time.

"You'll bleed one day," said Leah firmly, as though by declaring it she could make it so. "Just give it time. The sickness will pass."

"It's not sickness," said Immanuelle, tasting the tang of lamb's blood on her lips. "It's sin."

What sin specifically, Immanuelle couldn't be certain. She had wandered astray too many times—reading in secret, in breach of Holy Protocol, or forgetting to say her evening prayers and falling asleep unblessed. Maybe she had spent too many mornings daydreaming in the pastures when she should have been herding her sheep. Or perhaps she hadn't demonstrated a spirit of gratitude when being served a bowl of cold dinner gruel. But Immanuelle knew this much: She had far too many sins to count. It was no wonder she hadn't received the Father's blood blessing.

If Leah was aware of Immanuelle's many transgressions, she made no mention of them. Instead, she waved her off with a flourish of the hand. "Sins can be forgiven. When the Good Father sees fit, you will bleed. And after you bleed, a man will take you up, then you will be his and he will be yours, and everything will be as it should be."

To this, Immanuelle said nothing. She narrowed her eyes against the sun and stared across the field to where the Prophet stood among his wives, offering his blessings and counsel to the gathered faithful. All his wives wore identical dull yellow dresses, the color of daffodil petals, and they all bore the holy seal, an eight-pointed star cut between their eyebrows that all the women of Bethel were marked with on their wedding day.

"I'd rather tend to my sheep," said Immanuelle.

"And what about when you're old?" Leah demanded. "What then?"

"Then I'll be an old shepherdess," Immanuelle declared. "I'll be an old sheep hag."

Leah laughed, a loud, pretty sound that drew gazes. She had a way of doing that. "And what if a man offers his hand?"

Immanuelle smirked. "No good man with any good sense would want anything to do with me."

"Rubbish."

Immanuelle's gaze shifted over to a group of young men and women about her age, maybe a little older. She watched as they laughed and flirted, making spectacles of themselves. The boys puffed out their chests, while the girls played in the shallows of the creek, hiking their skirts high above their knees in the streaming current, careful to avoid drifting too far for fear of the devils that lurked in the depths of the water.

"You know I'll still come visit you," said Leah, as though sensing Immanuelle's fears. "You'll see me on the Sabbath, and after my confinement I'll come to you in the pasture, every week if I can."

Immanuelle turned her attention to the food in front of them. She picked up a hunk of bread from the picnic basket and slathered it with fresh-churned butter and a bloody smear of raspberry marmalade. She took a big bite, speaking thickly through the mouthful. "The Holy Grounds are a long way from the Glades."

"I'll find a way."

"It won't be the same," said Immanuelle, with a petulant edge to her voice that made her hate herself.

Leah ducked her head, looking hurt. She twisted the ring on

her right hand with her thumb, a nervous tic she'd adopted in the days following her engagement. It was a pretty thing, a gold band set with a small river pearl, likely some heirloom passed down from the wives of prophets past.

"It'll be enough," said Leah hollowly. Then, more firmly, as though she was trying to convince herself: "It will have to be enough. Even if I'm forced to ride the roads on the Prophet's own horse, I'll find a way to see you. I won't let things change. I swear."

Immanuelle wanted to believe her, but she was too good at spotting lies, and she could tell there was some falsity in Leah's voice. Still, she made no mention of it. No good would come of it anyway: Leah was bound to the Prophet, and had been since the day he first laid eyes on her two summers prior. The ring she wore was merely a placeholder, a promise wrought in gold. In due time, that promise would take the form of the seed he'd plant in her. Leah would birth a child, and the Prophet would plant his seed again, and again, as he did with all his wives while they were still young enough to bear its fruit.

"Leah!"

Immanuelle looked up to see that the group that had been playing in the river shallows was now drawing near, waving as they approached. There were four of them. Two girls, a pretty blonde Immanuelle knew only in passing from classes at the schoolhouse, and Judith Chambers, the Prophet's newest bride. Then there were the boys. Peter, a hulking farmhand as thick-shouldered as an ox, and about as intelligent, the son of the first apostle. Next to him, with eyes narrowed against the sun, was Ezra, the Prophet's son and successor.

Ezra was tall and dark-haired, with ink-black eyes. He was handsome too, almost wickedly so, drawing the stares of even the most pious wives and daughters. Although he was scarcely more than nineteen, he wore one of the twelve golden apostle's daggers on a chain around his neck, an honor that most men of Bethel, despite their best efforts, went a lifetime without achieving.

The blond girl, Hope, who had called to Leah, piped up first. "You two look like you're making the most of your day."

Leah raised a hand to her brow to shade her eyes from the sun, smiling as she peered up at them. "Will you join us?"

Immanuelle cursed silently as the four sat down in the grass beside them. The ox boy, Peter, began rummaging through the contents of the picnic basket, helping himself to a hearty serving of bread and jam. Hope wedged herself between Immanuelle and Leah and immediately began prattling on about the latest gossip of the town, which largely centered on some poor girl who had been sent to the market stocks for tempting a local farmer into adultery. Ezra claimed the spot across from Immanuelle, and Judith flanked him, sitting so close that their shoulders touched.

As the conversation wore on, Immanuelle did her best to make herself small and unassuming, willing herself invisible. Unlike Leah, she didn't have a stomach for socialities. In comparison to the grace and charm of Hope, Leah, and Judith, she suspected she looked about as dull as one of her sister's corn-husk dolls.

Across the picnic basket, Ezra also sat in silence, his ceremonial dagger glinting in the sun. He seemed distracted, almost bored, not even bothering to nod along to the conversation as his gaze scanned the distant plains, east to west, then back again. He watched the horizon like he was looking for something, and Immanuelle couldn't help but wonder what. Ezra hadn't had his First Vision yet and wouldn't until his father's life was coming to an end. Such was the way of succession—a young prophet's rise to power always meant the demise of his senior.

Beside Ezra, Judith sucked a bit of butter off the tips of her fingers, squinting at Immanuelle through the thick fringe of her lashes. She wore a yellow dress like the rest of the Prophet's wives, but the fit was a little too snug to be modest. Her skirts tangled about her legs, and her bodice was cinched tight, nipping her waist and accentuating the sweeping dip of her hips beneath the folds of her underskirts. The seal between her eyebrows was still pink, and a little swollen, but scarring well enough.

Immanuelle remembered the day Judith had gotten her first blood. The three of them, Leah, Immanuelle, and Judith, had been out in the schoolyard together, plucking mushrooms from a fairy patch, when Judith began to cry. She'd lifted her skirts high above her knees, revealing a single thread of blood trickling down her right leg and disappearing into the shadow of her boot. Their teacher had been quick to whisk her away, but not before Immanuelle heard her whisper in Judith's ear: "You're a woman. You're a woman now."

And so she was.

Judith had been quick to forsake her girlhood. She unbound her braids and piled her hair atop her head, traded smocks and pinafores for corsets and bodices, and adopted all the graces and finery of womanhood in a way that made it seem like she'd been born to them.

Judith licked the last of the butter from her fingertips and leaned closer to Immanuelle, so close she caught the sweet balm of her perfume. "Is it true what they say about you?"

The question took Immanuelle by surprise, though it shouldn't have. It was the same one she saw on the lips of every loose-tongued telltale in Bethel. They'd all been saying the same thing since the night her mother turned the Prophet's blade against him, nearly slitting his throat before fleeing to the Darkwood. They held her name in their mouths like a foul thing that was relished nonetheless.

"That depends," said Immanuelle, feigning ignorance. "What do they say?"

Judith shrugged, smirking. "Well, I suppose if you don't know already, it must not be true."

"I suppose not," she ground out through gritted teeth.

Judith cocked her head to the side. "So, you don't have a Gift?"

Immanuelle shook her head.

There was a time when Gifts hadn't been a rarity. Long ago, in the Age of Light, the Father had blessed multitudes with the power to wield wonders and work miracles. But ever since the Holy War, and the dark ages that followed, Gifts had become scarce. With every passing year, there were fewer of them, as the saints of old went to their graves and took their powers with them. Now Martha was one of the few midwives in Bethel with the Gift of Naming, and only prophets possessed the Gift of Sight. Even the apostles were limited to a select few with the power of Discernment—a Gift that allowed one to tell truth from falsehood—or the Healing Touch. In Immanuelle's generation, Gifts had been bestowed upon only a handful of the Father's most favored—and as a bastard by birth, she was anything but.

"Pity," said Judith, leveling her gaze. "I was hoping there was *something* remarkable about you. Considering."

Immanuelle stiffened. "Considering what?"

Judith arched a perfect brow and a cruel smile played over her lips. "Well, your mother, of course."

Immanuelle had known the mention of her mother was coming. It always did. But something about the way Judith said it now doubled the insult, making it sting more than usual.

For a long moment there was silence, save for the babbling of the river and the drone of the wasps lurking among the wildflowers. Even the distant chatter of the other churchgoers seemed to quiet, lost to the rush of wind in the woodland. Then . . .

"You know," said Immanuelle. "Now that I consider it . . . I *do* have a knack for dancing naked in the woods—with the beasts and devils, of course. It's hard to find the time, what with all the sheep I shepherd, but when the full moon rises, I do what I can." She smiled brightly at Judith. "Like mother, like daughter, I suppose."

There was a pause, the hiss of breath drawn. Leah winced as the group fell once again into complete and utter silence.

For the first time since he'd sat down the Prophet's son, Ezra, turned his attention from the horizon. His eyes fixed on Immanuelle.

She knew then that she'd made a mistake. A sinful, foolish mistake made in the heat of anger. A mistake that she would no doubt pay for with a scolding or lashing, or perhaps even a day in the market stocks.

But then, to her surprise, Ezra's lips skewed into a lopsided grin and he began to laugh. It wasn't a mean laugh, but the boisterous kind that comes deep from the belly. His shoulders shook, and his black hair fell across his eyes. After a moment, Peter joined him, with a barking bellow that carried across the churchyard and drew stares from the kinfolk standing in the shadow of the cathedral. This, in turn, made Ezra laugh even harder. In a matter of seconds, Leah and Hope joined in, and then at last, even Immanuelle cracked a small smile. Before she knew it, all of them were cackling together like a band of old friends.

All except Judith, who did little more than choke out a scandalized cough as she stood. She tugged Ezra up with her, pulling on his arm, but as he rose to his feet, he offered Immanuelle that crooked smile of his again.

"Until the next Sabbath," he called over his shoulder as Judith ushered him back to the cathedral, back to his father, the Prophet, and away from Immanuelle. But as he entered the waves of swaying high grass, he paused, turning back to look at her. Something flickered through his eyes, and in that moment, she could have sworn he saw the truth of her.

CHAPTER TWO

For the Father is good, and His goodness is everlasting. He smiles down from the heavens to bestow His flock with blessings, that they might find contentment in His light.

—THE HOLY SCRIPTURES

THAT EVENING, THE Moores gathered for their usual Sabbath dinner. Martha tended a bubbling vat of chicken stew that hung on an iron hook above the crackling fire, mopping sweat from her brow with the back of her hand. While she hunched over the hearth, Anna mixed batter bread with both hands, folding in fistfuls of flaxseeds and crushed walnuts, singing hymns as she worked. Immanuelle ducked between the two of them, taking on different tasks and trying her best to be of help. She was clumsy in the kitchen, but she did what she could to aid them.

Anna, ever cheerful, was the first to break the silence. "It was a good service this morning, wasn't it?"

Immanuelle set a pewter plate down at the head of the table, before her grandfather's empty chair. "That it was."

Martha said nothing.

Anna plunged her fists into the bread dough again. "When the Prophet spoke, I felt like the air had been sucked right out of me. He's a true man of the Father, that one. More so than other prophets, even. We're lucky to have him."

Immanuelle set one spoon beside Martha's plate and another

beside Honor's bowl, a little wooden thing she'd carved and poli-shed some three summers ago, when the child had been no bigger than a minnow in Anna's womb. For Anna's eldest, Glory, she re-served the brass spoon she liked best, an antique Martha had bought from a market peddler years ago.

Glory, like her mother, had an appetite for pretty things: rib-bons and lace and sweets and other delights the Moores couldn't afford. But when she could, Immanuelle tried her best to oblige the girl with little tokens. There were so few pretty things left in the house. Most of their treasures and trinkets had been sold dur-ing the thick of the winter in an attempt to make up for the bad reap and all the livestock they'd lost to sickness the past summer. But if Immanuelle had anything to say about it, Glory would have her spoon, a small token to offset their world of lack.

When the meal was prepared, Martha carried the vat of stew to the table and set it down with a loud thump that carried through the house. At the sound, Honor and Glory raced into the dining room, eager to fill their seats and eat. The wives sat next, Imman-uelle's grandmother, Martha, claiming her place at the opposite end of the table, as was custom, and Anna, second wife of Im-manuelle's grandfather, claiming the seat beside her husband's empty chair.

After a few long moments, there was the groan of hinges, the sound of a door opening, then the pained and shuffling racket of Abram making his way down the stairs. Her grandfather was having a bad day; Immanuelle could tell by the sound of his gait, the way his stiff foot dragged across the groaning floorboards as he moved toward the table. He had skipped church again that morning, making it the third Sabbath he'd missed in a month.

Once, long ago, Abram had been an apostle—and a powerful one too. He had been the right hand of Simon Chambers, the prophet who served before the current prophet, Grant Chambers, had been chosen and ordained. As such, Abram had once owned one of the seven estates in the sacred Holy Grounds, and he had wielded the Father's Gift of Discernment. At age nineteen, he married Martha. The two of them were well yoked, both in age and in status, but despite this, the Father did not bless them with children for a long time. In fact, after years of trying, Abram and Martha were only able to conceive Miriam, and her birth was succeeded by a series of stillborns, all of them sons. Many later claimed that Miriam's birth damned the children who were born after her, said that her very existence was a plague to the good Moore name.

On account of Miriam's crimes, Abram had been stripped of his title as apostle, and all the lands that went with it. The Moore stead, which had once been a rolling range so big it rivaled the Prophet's, was divided up among the other apostles and nearby farmers, who picked it apart like vultures do a carcass. Abram had been left with a small fragment of the land he once owned, shadowed by the same rambling forest to which he'd lost his daughter. Such was the life he lived now, in ridicule and squalor, scraping together an existence from the meager reap of pastures and blighted cornfields that were his only claim.

It had been nothing short of a miracle that Anna agreed to follow Abram to the altar eighteen years ago despite the shame of Miriam's fall from grace. Immanuelle suspected that her loyalty stemmed from the fact that Abram had used his Healing Touch to save her when she was dying of fever as a young girl. It was as though she owed him a kind of life debt and was steadfast in her resolve to fulfill it. Perhaps that was why her love for Abram seemed more akin to the way the apostles revered the Holy Father than to the common affections between husband and wife.

As Abram entered the dining room, Anna broke into a wide smile, the way she always did. But Abram paid her no mind as he limped past the threshold. He paused to catch his breath, bracing his hands on the back of a broken chair. The right side of his body was clenched, his fingers twisted to near bone-breaking angles, his arm bent and drawn to his chest as if held by some invisible sling. He limped with his left leg thrown out to one side, and he had to brace himself on the wall to keep from falling as he dragged his way around the dining room to his seat at the head of the table.

He settled himself roughly in his chair, then began the prayer, struggling with the words. When it was finished, Abram raised his fork with his good hand and set into his food. The rest of them followed suit, the children eagerly spooning up the stew, as though they worried it would disappear before they'd have the chance to finish it. The sad truth was it was less a chicken stew and more a watery bone broth with a bit of parsnip, a few stray cabbage leaves, and the grisly scraps of the chicken. Even so, Immanuelle took pains to eat slowly, savoring every bite.

Anna took another stab at kindling conversation, but her attempts were futile. Martha kept her eyes on her stew and the girls were smart enough to stay silent, fearing their father's wrath.

In turn, Abram didn't say much. He rarely did on his bad days. Immanuelle could tell it pained him, to have once been the voice of the Prophet and now, in the years since her mother's death, to be reduced to little more than the village pariah, cursed by the Father for his leniency. Or so the rumors went.

Really, Immanuelle knew little of what had happened to Abram after her mother died. All she knew were the scant morsels that Martha offered her, the fragments of a story too vile to be told in full.

Seventeen years ago, her mother, Miriam, newly betrothed to the Prophet, had taken up illicit relations with a farm boy from the Outskirts. Months later, after their affair was uncovered, that same farm boy had died on the pyre as punishment for his crimes against the Prophet and Church.

But Miriam was spared, shown mercy by the Prophet on account of their betrothal.

Then, on the night before her wedding, Miriam—grief-mad and desperate to avenge her lover's death—had stolen into the Prophet's bedroom while he slept and tried to slit his throat with his own sacred dagger. But the Prophet had woken and fought her off, thwarting the attack.

Before the Prophet's Guard had the chance to apprehend her, Miriam had fled into the forbidden Darkwood—the home of Lilith and her coven of witches—where she disappeared without a trace. Miriam claimed that she spent those brutal winter months alone in a cabin at the heart of the wilderness. But given the violence of that winter and the fact that the cabin was never found, no one in Bethel believed her.

Months passed with no sign of Miriam. Then one night, in the midst of a violent snowstorm, she emerged from the Darkwood, heavy with child—the sinful issue of her lover, who had died on the pyre. Mere days after her return, Miriam gave birth to Immanuelle.

While his daughter screamed in the midst of labor, Abram was struck by a stroke so violent it remade him, twisting his limbs and warping his bones and muscles, stripping him of his strength and stature, as well as the power of his Holy Gifts. And as Miriam struggled and labored and slipped into the afterlife, so nearly did he. It was only a miracle of the Father that saved him, dragging him back from the cusp of death.

But Abram had suffered for Miriam's sins, and he would continue to suffer for them until the day he died. Perhaps he would have suffered less if he'd had the strength to shun Immanuelle for the sins of her mother. Or if he had simply shunned Miriam after she'd returned pregnant from the woods, he may have found the Prophet's favor once more.

But he hadn't. And for that, Immanuelle was grateful.

"You'll go . . . to the market . . . in the morning," said Abram across the table, grinding the words between his teeth as he spoke, every syllable a struggle. "Sell the black yearling."

"I'll do my best," Immanuelle said with a nod. If he was intent upon selling the yearling, their need must be dire. It had been a bad month, a bad month at the end of a string of terrible months. They desperately needed the money. Abram's sickness had worsened in the winter after a bad bout of fever, and the steep costs of his medicines had pushed the family to the brink of ruin. It was vital that Immanuelle did her part to ease the burden, as they all did.

Everyone in the Moore house had some job or trade. Martha was a midwife blessed with Father's Tongue and through it the power to call down Names from the heavens. Anna was a seamstress with a hand so gentle and an eye so keen she could darn even the finest lace. Abram, once a carpenter, had in the years after his stroke taken to whittling crude little figures that they sometimes peddled at the market. Even Glory, a talented artist despite the fact that she was barely twelve, painted little portraits on woodcuts she then sold to her friends at school. Honor, who was too young to take up a craft, helped around the farm as best she could.

And then there was Immanuelle, the shepherdess, who tended a flock of sheep with the help of a hired farm boy. Every morning, save for the Sabbath or the odd occasion when Martha called her along for a particularly risky birthing, Immanuelle would take to the pastures to watch over her sheep. Crook in hand, she'd lead them to the western range, where the flock would spend its day grazing in the shadows of the Darkwood.

Immanuelle had always felt a strange affinity for the Dark-wood, a kind of stirring whenever she neared it. It was almost as though the forbidden wood sang a song that only she could hear, as though it was daring her to come closer.

But despite the temptation, Immanuelle never did.

On market days, Immanuelle took a selection of her wares—be it wool or meat or a ram—to the town market for peddling. There, she would spend the whole of her day in the square, haggling and selling her goods. If she was lucky, she'd return home after sun-down with enough coppers to cover their weekly tithes. If she wasn't, the family would go hungry, and their tithes and debts to Abram's healers would remain unpaid.

Abram forced down another mouthful of stew, swallowing with some effort. "Sell him . . . for a good bit. Don't settle for less than what he's worth."

Immanuelle nodded. "I'll go early. If I take the path that cuts through the Darkwood, I'll make it to the market before the other merchants."

The conversation died into the clatter of forks and knives strik-ing plates. Even Honor, young as she was, knew to mind her tongue. There was silence, save for the rhythmic *drip, drip, drip* of the leak in the corner of the kitchen.

Martha's cheeks all but drained of color and her lips were bloodless. "You never go into those woods, you hear? There's evil in them."

Immanuelle frowned. The way she saw it, sin wasn't a plague you could catch if you ventured too close. And she wasn't sure she believed all the legends about the evils in the womb of the Dark-wood. In truth, Immanuelle wasn't sure what she believed, but she was fairly certain a brief shortcut through the forest wouldn't be her undoing.

Still, no good would come from an argument, and she knew

that in a battle of wills, she couldn't win. Martha had a heart of iron and the kind of unwavering faith that could make stones tremor. It was futile to provoke her.

And so, Immanuelle bit her tongue, bowed her head, and re-signed herself to obey.

THAT NIGHT, IMMANUELLE dreamed of beasts: a girl with a gap-ing mouth and the yellowed teeth of a coyote; a woman with moth wings who howled at the rising moon. She woke in the early morning to the echo of that cry, the sound slapping back and forth between the walls of her skull.

Bleary-eyed and drunk with exhaustion, Immanuelle dressed clumsily, trying to push the twisted images of the woodland ghouls from her mind as she fumbled into her button-down dress and readied herself for a day at the market.

Slipping out of the sleeping household, Immanuelle strode toward the far pastures. She began most every morning like this—tending to the sheep by the light of dawn. On the rare occasion when she couldn't—like the week she caught whooping cough a few summers prior—a hired farmhand by the name of Josiah Clark stepped in to fill her role.

Immanuelle found her flock huddled together in the eastern pastures, just beyond the woodland's shadow. Crows roosted in the branches of the oaks and birches in the nearby forest, though they sang no songs. The silence was as thick as the morning's fog, and it was broken only by the sound of Immanuelle's lullaby, which echoed through the foothills and distant fields like a dirge.

It wasn't a normal lullaby, like the folk songs or nursery rhymes that mothers sing to their children, but rather a rendition of an old mourning hymn she had once heard at a funeral. Her song carried across the pastures, and at the sound her flock moved east, sweeping like a tide across the rolling hills. They were upon her in moments, bleating and trotting happily, pressing up against her skirts. But the yearling ram, Judas, hung back from the rest, his hooves firmly planted and his head hanging low. Despite his age, he was a large and fearsome thing with a shaggy black coat and two sets of horns: the first set jutting like daggers from the crown of his skull, the second curling back behind his ears and piercing along the harsh cut of his jaw.

"Judas," Immanuelle called above the hiss of wind in the high grass. "Come now, it's time to go to the market."

The ram struck the dirt with his hooves, his eyes squinted thin. As he stepped forward, the sheep stirred and parted, the little lambs tripping over their hooves to make way for him. He stopped just a few feet from Immanuelle, his head turned slightly to the side so he could stare at her through the twisted crook of his horn.

"We're going to the market." She raised the lead rope for him to see, the slack dangling above the ground. "I'll need to tether you."

The ram didn't move.

Stooping to one knee, Immanuelle eased the loop of the knot over his horns, tugging the rope taut to tighten it. The ram fought her, kicking and bucking and throwing his head, striking the earth with his hooves. But she held fast, bracing her legs and tightening her grip, the rope chafing across her palms as Judas reared and struggled.

"Easy," she said, never raising her voice above a murmur. "Easy there."

The ram threw his head a final time and huffed hard, a cloud of steam billowing from his nostrils, thick as pipe smoke on the cold morning air.

"Come on, you old grump." She urged him along with another tug on the lead rope. "We've got to get you to the market."

The walk through the Glades was long, and despite the initial chill of the morning, the sun was hot. Trails of sweat slipped down Immanuelle's spine as she trudged along the winding path to town. Had she taken the shortcut through the woodland—instead of the long way around the forest's edge—she would have been in town already. But she'd promised Martha she'd stay clear of the woods, and she was determined to keep her word.

So Immanuelle trudged on, her knapsack weighing heavy on her shoulders as she went. Her feet ached in her boots, which were a size and a half too small and pinched her heels so badly they blistered. It often seemed like everything she owned was either too big or too small, like she wasn't fit for the world she was born to.

Halfway to the market, Immanuelle stopped for breakfast. She found a cool spot in the shadow beneath a birch tree and rummaged through the contents of her knapsack for the wedge of cheese and brick-hard brown bread Anna had baked the night prior. She ate quickly, tossed the bread crusts to Judas, who snapped them up and bucked his head, tugging the lead rope so hard she had to seize him by the horns to keep him from bolting.

In the distance, the Darkwood stirred. It almost seemed to call to her as the wind breathed through the branches, like a hissing, secret tongue.

According to legends and the Holy Scriptures, the Darkwood, like all of the cursed and wretched things of the world, had been spawned by the Dark Mother, goddess of the hells. While the Good Father wrought the world with light and flame, breathing life into the dust, She summoned Her evils from the shadows, birthing legions of beasts and demons, mangled creatures and crawling things that lurked in the festering half-world between the living and the dead.

And it was from that half-world, from the corridors of the

cursed forest, that the first witches—Lilith, Delilah, and the two Lovers, Jael and Mercy—had first emerged. The Unholy Four (as they were later called) found a place among Bethel's early settlers, who accepted them as refugees and offered them sanctuary. The women took husbands and birthed children, lived among the Father's flock as allies and friends. But while the four witches wore the skin of human women, their souls were made in their Mother's image, and like Her, they sought to destroy the Good Father's creations, choking His light with their darkness and shadow.

The four witches planted seeds of discord in the hearts of good Bethelan men, tempting them and leading their souls astray. The roots of their deceit ran deep, and it wasn't long before the rule of the land shifted into their hands. It was only by the Father's grace that a young man by the name of David Ford—the first prophet— had rallied a brave army of holy crusaders to overthrow the four witches with fire and purging in a bloody rebellion, banishing their souls to the cursed woods from whence they came.

But the power of the witches and the dark Goddess they served remained long after the Holy War had ended. Even now, their ghosts still haunted the Darkwood, hungry for the souls of those who dared to enter their realm.

Or so the stories said.

Once Immanuelle had finished her breakfast, she rose to continue her journey through the Glades. The main road snaked closer to the Darkwood now, and she could see the memorials dotting the distant tree line. There were wreaths of wildflowers, tokens and tributes, even a small pair of children's shoes hanging from a fence post by the laces—as though someone believed the child they belonged to might one day emerge from the trees to claim them. These relics were all that remained of those who were lost to the Darkwood. For what the forest took it rarely returned.

Immanuelle and her mother were exceptions to this—miracles, some said. But in her weakest moments, when the wind stirred through the pines and the crows sang their songs, Immanuelle felt as though the Darkwood still had a hold on her, as if it was calling her home again.

With a shiver, Immanuelle walked on, past the shacks and cabins and rolling cornfields, making her way along the forest's edge, following the path of the stream. Overhead, the sun shifted, and the air grew thick and heavy. The sprawling pasture of the Glades gave way to the stone-paved streets of Amas—the village at the heart of Bethel. Here, barns and homesteads were replaced with a clutter of cobblestone cottages and slate-roofed town houses, stone buildings with stained-glass windows that glared brilliantly in the light of the noonday sun. In the distance, looming high above the rooftops, was one of the tallest structures in all of Bethel, surpassed only by the cathedral's steeple. It was called the Hallowed Gate, and it was a wrought iron wonder built by the first prophet, David Ford.

Beyond the gate was a wide cobblestone road flanked by ever-burning streetlamps that was called the Pilgrim's Way. If Bethel was an island in the vast sea of the forest, that road was a bridge to the foreign territories far beyond its borders. But as far as Immanuelle knew, only the Prophet's Guard, apostles, and a selection of esteemed evangelists were allowed to leave Bethel, and only on rare occasions. And never—in all of Immanuelle's sixteen years—had a single foreigner entered through the gate.

Sometimes Immanuelle wondered if the cities beyond the Bethelan territories were nothing more than myths. Or perhaps the ever-encroaching woodland had devoured them entirely, the way it might have Bethel if the Father's light hadn't forced its darkness back. But Immanuelle knew those ponderings were far above her station. The complexities of the world beyond the Hallowed Gate were better left to the apostles and Prophet, who had the knowledge and discernment to parse them.

Tightening her grip on Judas' lead rope, Immanuelle shouldered her way through the ever-thickening market crowds. As usual, the square was thronged with stalls. There were candle stands and a butcher with fly-swarmed meats on melting ice slabs. Next to the butcher, a large stall that sold fabric by the bolt, displaying an array of brocades and velvets, twills and soft silks. As Immanuelle passed the perfumer's tent, she caught the scent of fine oil, brewed from flowers and myrrh musk.

The watchmaker had a stall just outside his cottage. On a long oak table, he peddled his clocks and timepieces to the fine men who dressed like they could afford them. Just a few paces from that, a shoe shop offered leather boots with buckles that were finer than anything Immanuelle had ever owned. Finer than anything she likely *would* ever own.

But she didn't dwell on that. She made a point to hold her head high, never straying from the main road or even so much as breaking her pace to examine the wares. Judas trotted alongside her, his black hooves skittering across the cobbles. His ears quirked this way and that, nostrils flaring as he took in the sights and sounds of the marketplace. Sometimes he wandered, but Immanuelle kept the lead rope short so that he was never farther than a pace's length from her hip.

At intervals along the road, crouching at the cobbled corners with bowls and coin cups, were beggars from the Outskirts. Many of them walked barefoot, rising to collect coins from the passersby who were kind enough to offer them. But most of the marketgoers ignored the beggars entirely. The Outskirters were exiles, after all, dismissed as the lower, less-favored children of the Father. A few of the more radical members of the flock suggested that their very appearance was a punishment, claimed that the rich ebony of their skin was an outward sign of their inner allegiance to the Dark Mother, who bore their likeness.

There were many stories about how the Outskirters first came to Bethel, but the general understanding was that they were the descendants of refugees who fled there in the ancient days. There were many rumors about what they were fleeing. Some said it was a drought that turned the earth to ash. Others told stories of a sky that wept fire and brimstone. Still more claimed that a hungry sea had flooded their homeland, the tide swelling so high it drowned mountains and forced them to flee to the wilds.

A saint called Abdiah ruled the Church at that time. He said that the Father had punished these refugees for their allegiance to the Mother. Claimed that the plagues that drove them from their home were a form of divine retribution. He determined that it was the Father's will to lead those in the Outskirts to Bethel, that they might continue the process of their sanctification through service to the Church. And so, at Abdiah's bidding, for the first time in its centuries-long history, Bethel opened its gate to outsiders.

To prevent what Abdiah called the spread of fallacies, Outskirters were contained to a settlement on the southern cusp of Bethel. There, servants of the Church ministered to them—spreading the word of the Father, turning heathen to believer one soul at a time in what was later called the Great Evangelism. Over the passing decades, those in the Outskirts assimilated to the ways of Bethel. They adopted its faith and common tongue, continued their process of contrition through service to the Church. Gradually, as the generations passed, those in the Outskirts turned their back on their history, until they became more Bethelan than not. But it was clear to Immanuelle that they weren't treated as such. *She* wasn't treated as such.

Never mind the fact that most modern Outskirters bore the

blood of Bethelan settlers or that they fought against Lilith's armies in the Holy War. Shared or spilled, it seemed that blood did not matter as much as appearance did. And so, no matter how many centuries passed, no matter what they rendered in service of Bethel's betterment, it seemed the Outskirters would always be consigned to the fringes.

On that day, there were around a dozen beggars on the main road. As Immanuelle neared them, they turned to her as they always did, though none extended their bowls or cups, or even greeted her with more than a cold stare. Instead, they seemed to study her, their expressions she would describe as a mix of curiosity and contempt.

She didn't blame them.

While on the outside she shared their features—the dark skin, the firm nose, the wide black eyes—she was not *of* them, not really. She had never known the poverty of a life beyond the Glades or walked the roads through the Outskirts, nor had she met the kin she likely had there. For all Immanuelle knew, those who lurked on the roads may well have been her blood—relatives of her father, uncles or cousins perhaps—but she didn't claim them as such, and they in turn didn't claim her either.

Immanuelle walked a little faster, staring down at her shoes, trying to shrug off the lingering gazes of the Outskirters as she made her way to the livestock sector. She was nearly there when she spotted the best shop of all: the peddler's bookstall.

In comparison to the other shops, with their painted signs and elaborate displays, it wasn't much. Its tent was small, just a sheet of burlap stretched across three wooden stakes. Beneath it were five rows of shelves, all of them taller than Immanuelle and crowded with books—real books—not like the decorative tomes and hymnals that sat above the mantel at the Moore house, untouched and unread. These were books on botany and medicine, books of poetry and lore, atlases and histories of Bethel and the settlements beyond it, even little pamphlets that taught things like grammar and arithmetic. It was a wonder they had been approved by the Prophet's Guard at all.

After tethering Judas to a nearby lamppost, Immanuelle drifted toward the stall. Despite knowing she was supposed to be well on her way to the livestock district, she lingered between the shelves, opening the books to smell the musk of their bindings and run her fingers along the pages. Although she had stopped her formal schooling at age twelve, as all girls in Bethel did to observe the Prophet's Holy Protocol, Immanuelle was a strong reader. As a matter of fact, reading was one of the few things she felt she was truly good at, one of the few things she prided herself on. She sometimes thought that if she had any Gift at all, it was that. Books were to her what faith was to Martha; she never felt closer to the Father than she did in those moments under the shadow of the book tent, reading the stories of a stranger she'd never met.

The first book she selected was thick and bound in pale gray cloth. There was no title, only the word *Elegy* stamped along its spine in golden ink. Immanuelle opened it and read the first few lines of a poem about a storm sweeping over the ocean. She had never seen the ocean before, or known anyone who had seen it, but as she read the verses aloud, she could hear the bellow of the waves, taste the brine of the waters, and feel the wind snatching at her curls.

"Back again, I see." Immanuelle looked up to find the shopkeeper, Tobis, watching her. Beside him, to her surprise, stood Ezra, the Prophet's son, who'd sat with her and Leah by the riverside the day before.

He was dressed in plain clothes, same as the farmers who'd come fresh from the fields, except for the apostle's sacred dagger, which still hung from the chain around his neck. He was holding two books in one hand. The first was a thick copy of the Holy Scriptures bound in brown leather; the second was slim, cloth-bound, and titleless. He smiled at her in greeting, and she dipped her head in response, slipping the book back into its place on the shelf. She couldn't afford it anyway. The Moores barely had enough to put food on the table and pay tithes to the Prophet and his Church; there were no coppers to waste on frivolous things like stories and paper and poetry. Such privileges were reserved for apostles and men who had money to spare. Men like Ezra.

"Take your time," said Tobis, strolling closer, the spiced scent of his pipe smoke wafting through the shelves. "Don't let us trouble you."

"You're not troubling me at all," Immanuelle murmured, stepping toward the street. She motioned toward Judas, who stood beneath the shadow of a lamppost, striking the cobbles with his hooves. "I was just leaving. I'm not here to shop, only to peddle."

"Nonsense," the shopkeeper spoke around the stem of his pipe. "There's a book for everyone. There must be something that catches your eye."

Immanuelle's gaze went to Ezra—to his fine wool coat and polished boots, to the leather-bound books tucked beneath his arm, so well made she imagined the price of one would be enough to cover Abram's medicines for weeks to come. She flushed. "I have no money."

The shopkeeper smiled, his teeth riddled with steel and copper. "Then how about a bargain? I'll trade you a book in exchange for the ram."

For a split moment, she hesitated.

Some foolish part of her was willing to do it, willing to sell Judas for a few scraps of poetry. But then she thought of Honor with wads of cloth packed into the toes of her shoes to fill the holes and stop the wet from seeping through, of Glory in her hand-me-down dress, hanging off her shoulders like an old grain sack. She thought of Abram and his barking cough, thought of all the medicines he'd need to cure it. She swallowed, then shook her head. "I can't."

"What about that?" The shopkeeper jabbed his thumb toward her mother's necklace—the polished river stone strung on a leather cord. It was a crude token, nothing like the pearls and jewels that some of the Bethelan girls wore, but it was one of the only things Immanuelle had inherited from her and she treasured it more than anything. "That stone sits prettily on your chest."

Immanuelle raised a hand to it on impulse. "I—"

"She said no," Ezra cut in harshly, surprising her. "She doesn't want the book. Leave her be."

The shopkeeper had the good sense to mind him. He bobbed his head like a hen as he backed away. "As you say, sir, as you say."

Ezra watched the peddler return to his books, mouth set, eyes narrowed. Something in his gaze reminded Immanuelle of the way he'd looked at her on the Sabbath, the way he'd faltered, as if he'd seen something in her he hadn't meant to. Now he turned back to her. "You read?"

Immanuelle flushed despite herself, more than a little proud he'd taken notice. So many of her peers—Leah and Judith and the others—could scarcely read at all, knowing no more than their own names and a few of the Scripture's most important verses. If it hadn't been for Abram's insistence that Immanuelle learn to read and manage the Moore farm in his stead, she might have ended up like most other girls she knew, barely able to sign her own name, not knowing a book of stories from a collection of poetry. "I read well enough."

Ezra raised an eyebrow. "And you're here alone? You don't have a chaperone?"

"I don't need a chaperone," she said, knowing it was a bending of

Protocol at best and a breach at worst, but she didn't take Ezra for a snitch. She freed Judas from the lamppost and led him into the street. "I know the roads well enough to make the trip on my own."

To her surprise, Ezra followed at her side, the crowds parting as he walked. "That's a long way to travel alone. The Moore land is what? Nine miles away?"

"Ten." Immanuelle was surprised he knew their land at all. Most didn't. "And it's no trouble at all. I leave after sunup and I'm here before noon."

"And you don't mind?" he asked.

Immanuelle shook her head, her grasp tightening on the lead rope as they crossed into the livestock sector. Even if she did, it wouldn't matter. Her complaints and annoyances wouldn't put food in her belly; they wouldn't pay tithes or thatch the roof or cover the debts that were due in the fall. Only the wealthy had the luxury of minding things; the rest simply ducked their heads, bit their tongues, and did what needed to be done. Ezra obviously fell into the former category, and she the latter.

In truth, it was a surprise to find him in the market at all. As the Prophet's successor, she imagined he'd have more important responsibilities than buying and bartering. Tasks like that were far beneath him. And yet, there he was, walking with her as if he was taking a Sabbath stroll, carrying books like the Prophet had sent him out on a servant's errand.

Ezra caught her staring and extended one of his books, the bigger of the two, with the words *The Holy Scriptures* embossed in gold across the cover. "Here. Have a look."

Immanuelle shook her head, tugging Judas away from a pen of chickens. "We have our own copy of the Scriptures at home."

Ezra cracked a half smile and glanced over his shoulder, slipping Judas' lead rope from her hand. "These aren't scriptures."

Immanuelle took the book gingerly. On the outside, it looked just like the Scriptures, but when she flipped it open, there were no verses or psalms, but rather pictures, sketches and pressed ink prints of strange animals and looming trees, mountains, birds, and insects the likes of which she had never seen before. A few of the pages were etched with drawings of great kingdoms and temples, heathen cities in realms far beyond Bethel's gate.

Just then, a loud jeering sounded above the din of the marketplace. Immanuelle raised her eyes to a break in the crowds and caught a glimpse of the lashing stocks. There, bound and muzzled and swaying on her feet, was a young blond woman, the same one whom Judith and her friend had gossiped about on the Sabbath— the poor girl who'd lured a local farmer into sin with seduction and harlotry.

At the sight of her, Immanuelle snapped Ezra's book shut so fast and so hard, she almost dropped it in the muck of the street. She shoved it to his chest. "Take it back. Please."

Ezra rolled his eyes, handing her Judas' lead rope. "And here I thought a girl with the gall to dance with devils wouldn't be frightened by such things."

"I'm not frightened," she lied, ears ringing with the shouts of the crowd. "But that book, it's—"

"An encyclopedia," he said. "A book of knowledge."

Immanuelle knew full well there was only one book of knowledge, and it had no pictures. "It's forbidden. A sin."

Ezra studied her silently for a moment; then his gaze tracked across the market to the girl in the stocks, weeping and struggling against her chains. "Isn't it strange how reading a book is a sin, but locking a girl in the stocks and leaving her to the dogs is another day of the Good Father's work?"

Immanuelle stared at him, startled. "What?" She would have

never thought the Prophet's own son—and the heir to the Church, no less—would say such a thing, even if it was true.

Ezra flashed that lopsided grin of his, but his gaze was dark. "I'll see you on the Sabbath," he said, and then, without so much as a nod, he took his leave.

CHAPTER THREE

The dead walk among the living. This is the first truth, and the most important.

— THE HOLY SCRIPTURES

IMMANUELLE DID NOT sell the yearling that day. She bargained, she haggled, she called to the passing townsfolk and did all she could to be rid of the ram, but no one wanted him. There would be no new dress for Glory, no shoes for Honor or tithes to pay the Prophet.

She'd failed.

The main road was almost empty when Immanuelle abandoned her market post and began the long journey back to the Glades. As she walked, her thoughts went to that harlot in the stocks. The memory of the girl—shackled and weak-kneed and so young, mumbling pleas through her muzzle—haunted her, even as she tried to force it from her mind and focus on her journey home.

She walked on. The sun sank low to the horizon and a black storm swept across the plains. Rain slashed down from the clouds, and the wind howled about her like something alive.

Immanuelle picked up her pace, pulling the strap of her knapsack higher and tugging Judas along. He fought her at every step, black hooves tripping over the cobblestones, eyes rolling. She tried to talk him down above the thunder, but he wouldn't heed her.

As they crossed from the main road to the dirt path that cut across the Glades, a bolt of lightning cleaved the clouds. Judas reared with such force that Immanuelle lost her footing and slipped on the rain-slick cobbles. A bone-bruising bolt of pain split between her ribs and kicked the air from her lungs. She gasped, squatting in the muck as Judas shook his head about wildly.

"Easy," she wheezed, struggling to get back on her feet. "Easy there."

The ram reared again, hooves cutting deep into the soil as he landed on the other side of the road. He turned to look Immanuelle in the eye; then he lowered his head and charged her.

Immanuelle leaped right. Judas veered left, the point of his horn clipping the edge of her mouth, splitting her bottom lip. She hit the ground on her knees again, scraping them raw.

The enraged ram gave another mighty pull, and the lead rope snapped in two. Freed, Judas bucked once more, then tore toward the forest, disappearing into the trees.

Immanuelle snatched a ragged breath and screamed: *"Judas!"*

She pushed to her feet, staggering to the curb, where half the road diverged toward the distant woodland. The path through the forest was leagues shorter than the long way around, and if Immanuelle took it she was certain she would make it home sooner.

But Martha's warning trailed through her mind: *There is evil in the woods.*

But then she thought of the coming tithes and their leaking roof and the holes in Glory's shoes. She thought of bad harvests, gruel suppers, and waning winter stores. She thought of everything they needed, and everything they lacked, and she took a step toward the tree line. Then another.

At the forest's border, it was quieter, the wind dying down. Immanuelle called for Judas once again, hands cupped around her mouth, staring into the shadows between the trees. But there was nothing, just the whisper of the wind threading through the pines and seething through the high grass. *Come hither, come hither,* it seemed to say.

Immanuelle felt something stir in the pit of her belly. She felt her heart quicken, beating as fast as a hummingbird's wings. She glanced back toward the road, toward town. The sun was still partially obscured by storm clouds, but by the way it sat in the sky she knew she had close to an hour before it set fully. An hour to search for Judas, then. An hour to right her wrongs.

She could do it, if she hurried. She knew she could fix her mistake yet, with no one—not even Martha—the wiser.

Immanuelle took one halting step into the trees, and then another, her legs suddenly leaden, her feet numb in her boots.

The wind flowed through the tree branches, beckoning her onward: *Come hither. Come hither.*

All at once, she was running, breaking between the elms and oak trees. The air smelled of rain and sap, loam and the sweet decay of forest rot. Thunder sounded and the wind picked up again. Brambles snagged her dress and caught on the straps of her knapsack as she tore through the woodland.

"Judas!" she shrieked, wading through the underbrush, tripping over tree roots and knots of tangled bramble. On and on she went, running through the forest as fast as her legs would carry her.

But the ram was gone.

And the sun was setting.

And Immanuelle soon realized she was lost.

Squinting through the rain, she turned, trying to retrace her footsteps. But the Darkwood seemed to shift as she moved, and she couldn't find the path again. She was cold and alone and hungry. Her knees were weak and her knapsack felt heavy, as though it was weighted with stones. Ruefully she realized Martha had been right to warn her against the woods, and she had been foolish to disobey.

Gazing up to the treetops, Immanuelle saw that the last of the storm clouds were thinning. The wind still rattled the branches, but the pelting rain had died down to a drizzle, and the dull glow of the setting sun filtered through the pines. She followed its light, breaking west, running as fast as her numb feet would carry her. But the shadows were faster still, and night fell quick around her.

As the last rays of sunlight died into darkness, Immanuelle's knees buckled beneath her. She staggered, collapsing into a muddy nook between an oak tree's roots. There, cowering in the muck, she drew her knees to her chest and tried to catch her breath. As the wind howled through the trees, she clutched her mother's pendant for good luck.

But she didn't pray. She didn't have the gall to do that.

Overhead, the last of the storm died away, leaving only a scattering of stars and a gibbous moon that hung, low-slung, in the evening sky. As Immanuelle peered up into the distant heavens, a calm settled over her like the soft folds of a blanket, and she began to feel less alone, less afraid. There was something gentle about the way the moonlight licked the leaves and wind moved through the treetops. It was as though the Darkwood was singing her a lullaby, one she'd heard before: *Come hither, Immanuelle. Come hither.*

As the wind's voice seeped through the trees, the shadows blurred before her eyes, moonlight and darkness smearing together like paint. A kind of alertness came over her, and she tasted metal at the back of her throat. But somehow, she felt no fear. It had been stripped from her, as though she'd become a little less than whole, a half a girl existing between what is and isn't.

She wasn't just Immanuelle now. She was more. And she was less.

She was in the Darkwood. And the Darkwood was in her too.

Bracing a hand against the trunk of the oak tree, she rose, knees still weak beneath her, feet still numb. The whisper on the wind grew louder, and she stumbled blindly through the darkness after it, hoping it might lead her to the forest's edge.

Gradually, the trees thinned, and for a moment, Immanuelle thought she'd found its end. But her hope faded as she crossed into a small clearing, a circle cut into the thick of the forest all aglow with the light of the moon. Around its perimeter grew a wide fairy ring of morel mushrooms, the biggest Immanuelle had ever seen.

And at the very center of that ring, two women lay twined and naked, their bare legs tangled together, lips split apart. The bigger of the two, a black-haired woman with the build of a spider, lay on top of the other, her spine contorted, shoulders tensed so tightly Immanuelle could see the corded muscles strain and spasm beneath her skin, which was as thin and gray as a corpse's. The second woman writhed under her lover, moving her mouth to her neck.

Immanuelle's knapsack slipped off her shoulder and struck the ground.

The women stopped, seized, and detangled themselves from each other, rising from the ground. One of them clawed for something in the shadows of the high grass, a dark object Immanuelle couldn't see from where she stood. They turned to face her in unison.

Standing upright, the women were a foot taller than she. Both wore the same slack expression: mouths agape, lips red and slick, like the flaps of an open wound. Cut between their eyebrows was what appeared to be a bride's seal, only the star in the middle was slightly different, less elaborate, perhaps. Though the women stood motionless, their bones seemed to shift and move, as though their skeletons were fighting to be free of them. Their eyes were dead white, the color of sun-bleached bone. No pupils, no irises, and yet, somehow, their gazes were fixed on Immanuelle.

Chapter Four

It is an odd love between the Father and the Mother, between the light and the darkness. Neither can exist without the other. And yet they can never be one.

—THE HOLY SCRIPTURES

THE BLOND WOMAN stepped forward first, her hand slithering free of her lover's grasp. She crossed the glade in a few long strides and stopped just short of where Immanuelle stood. Up close, she could see that the woman's features were mangled— her nose was badly broken, the bone at the bridge protruding into a sharp joint. Her lips were full, if a little swollen, and Immanuelle saw that the bottom one was split down the middle. Her breasts hung heavy and bare, and her head lolled to one side, as if her neck lacked the strength to hold her skull upright.

The black-haired woman eased forward after her, wading through the grass and bracken. She was the taller and more beautiful of the two and she walked with the tentative grace of a doe. She stopped just short of her lover and slid a hand around her waist, as if to draw her back. But the woman brushed her off and stepped forward anyway, slowly extending a hand to Immanuelle, as if in greeting. Her fingers were pale and crooked—as mangled as Abram's—and they were folded around something small and black.

A leather-bound book.

The pale woman pressed the tome to Immanuelle's chest and she staggered back, falling into the trunk of a nearby pine. The woman's mouth wrenched into something like a smile.

Take it. The words were on the wind, seething through the branches of the trees. Immanuelle's knees went weak at the sound. *It's yours.*

Her hands trembled as she accepted the woman's gift. The book was heavy, and strangely warm to the touch, as though blood flowed through its binding. As she grasped it, Immanuelle felt no fear at the presence of the women, no shame at their nakedness. The strangest sensation settled over her. It was a kind of unmooring, as if her soul wasn't bound to her body anymore.

A strangled scream split through the forest, breaking her trance. *Judas.*

Immanuelle snapped to attention and turned back to the trees. She managed to stagger forward a few steps, snatch her knapsack from the ground, and shove the book into its front pocket before she broke into a full run.

Branches snagged her dress and lashed her cheeks. She couldn't tell if it was the wind wailing in her ears, or the women calling her back to the clearing. But with every step, every lunge, the forest seemed to swallow her. The brush thickened; the treetops pressed lower; the shadows churned like stirred ink.

She didn't care. She ran on.

Immanuelle's boot caught the hook of a tree root, and she fell, striking the dirt with a *thud*. She pushed herself from the ground, gasping for air, and saw a familiar face peering back at her from the shadows: Judas.

But it wasn't *all* of Judas—just his head, severed, bleeding, perched atop a nearby tree stump.

She shoved a hand to her mouth at the sight of him, biting back a shriek and the bile that clawed up her throat. She began to shake, great shudders that racked her so violently she could barely stay on her feet.

She started running again, even faster this time, cutting through the thicket and between the pines, desperate to escape. And, by the Father's grace, she did.

The trees began to thin, and the shadows retreated, and gradually the woodland gave way to the Bethelan plains, and she could at last see the winding path that would lead her home again. She collapsed there on the edge of the woodland, crawling from the shadows of the trees on her hands and knees as she struggled to catch her breath. She managed to force herself to her feet, weak-kneed and heaving as she limped the rest of the way home to the Glades, staggering down the path as if she had weights chained to her ankles. As she neared the Moore land, she saw Martha, Anna, and Glory walking the high pastures and the dead cornfields, all of them grasping lanterns and calling her name.

Immanuelle shouted to them and they turned. Glory broke forward first, the hem of her nightgown lashing around her ankles as she sprinted. She caught Immanuelle around the waist in a fierce hug.

Anna came next, praising the heavens as she raised a hand to Immanuelle's cheek to run her fingers along the bleeding scratches where the brambles had cut her, her split lip and bruised chin. "What happened?"

Immanuelle opened her mouth to answer, but no words came out. She raised her gaze to Martha, who was standing a few yards back, her lantern lowered, eyes narrowed. Without a word, she dipped her head, motioning the three of them back to the farmhouse. Glory loosened her grip around Immanuelle's waist and Anna backed away, and the four of them walked across the pastures in utter silence.

After they entered the house, Anna ushered Glory up the stairs, pausing only to wish the two of them good night. It was only after they disappeared into their respective bedrooms that Martha turned to Immanuelle and spoke: "Follow me."

Martha led her through the parlor and into the kitchen, which was dark save for the warm glow of the hearth. She took an iron poker from its hook and stoked the fire. Then she leaned the handle against the side of the hearth, propped up on the bricks so its iron point remained in the thick of the flames. "Did you sell the ram?"

Immanuelle shook her head.

"Then where is he?"

Immanuelle closed her eyes, and she could still see Judas' head perched atop that stump. "I lost him. I lost him in the woods."

"You went into the Darkwood? At *night*?"

"I didn't mean to," Immanuelle said softly, her split lip throbbing as she spoke. "Judas broke free of his tether and ran into the trees. I thought I could find him, but there was a storm and I got lost, and then night fell. I'm so sorry. It was dangerous and foolish. I should have known better. I should have listened to you."

Martha pressed a hand to her brow. She looked old in that moment, withered, like the happenings of the night had drained what little youth she had left. Abram was not the only one who had wasted over the passing years. Immanuelle had watched Martha suffer too. She knew her grandmother clung to her doctrines and her scriptures not out of faith, but out of fear. For though Martha never so much as muttered her daughter's name, Immanuelle knew she lived in Miriam's shadow. Everything Martha did—from her prayers to her charity—was just a futile attempt to escape the curse of her daughter's death.

"I saw something," Immanuelle said, and her own voice sounded distant and foreign, like some stranger was speaking from another room.

"What?" A terrible light came to Martha's eyes. "What did you see?"

"Women. Two women in the woods, alone." Immanuelle folded her fingers around the strap of her pack. The strange book felt as heavy as a stone at the bottom of it. She knew she ought to surrender it to Martha. But she didn't; she couldn't. The women's words in the wind traced through her mind: *It's yours.* Immanuelle had never owned much of anything. Sometimes she felt like she barely belonged to herself. The idea of parting with one of the few things in the world that was hers to claim was almost unbearable, worse than a lashing. No, she couldn't give it up.

"And what were these women doing in the woods?"

Immanuelle swallowed thickly. For a moment, she remembered how she had felt back at her first confession: sitting at the edge of her chair in the shadows of the kitchen, the apostle Amos seated opposite her, Scriptures in hand, frowning. He'd asked her if she'd ever indulged in the sins of the flesh, or if, in the night, her hands had wandered where they ought not go.

Martha huffed, and Immanuelle returned to the present. "They were together, holding hands. And their eyes were odd, glazed, all white. They looked sick. Almost, well . . . dead."

Martha's lips twitched, then twisted so violently that, in the dull glow of the hearth, she almost favored Abram. Her hand shook as she reached for the poker again, grasping its iron hilt as she drew it from the coals, hot and red and smoking. "Hold out your hand."

Immanuelle took a half step backward. Try as she might, she couldn't bring herself to unfurl her fingers. Her nails cut deep into the soft of her palms.

Martha's gaze darkened. "It's either your hand or your cheek. Choose."

Gritting her teeth, Immanuelle raised her arm and extended her hand into the bloody glow of the fire's light.

In turn, Martha uttered the sinner's prayer. "Mind thine eye and heart's desire. Still thy tongue and stop thy ear. Heed the call of thy Father's whisper. Linger not with devils near. Turn thy heart from sin's temptation, and when thy soul is cast astray, seek solace through true confession, in atonement find thy way."

Martha's grasp tightened around the poker's hilt, and she lowered its glowing point to the flat of Immanuelle's palm. "For the glory of the Father."

The scorching pain of the burn brought Immanuelle to her knees. She cut a scream through gritted teeth and collapsed, weeping, clutching her hand to her chest.

Her vision went for a moment, and when her eyes focused again, she found herself leaning against the kitchen cabinets, Martha on the floor beside her. The faint smell of flesh char hung on the air.

"Evil is sickness, and sickness is pain," said Martha, looking ready to weep herself, as if the act of delivering the punishment was as bad as the punishment itself. "Do you hear me, child?"

Immanuelle bobbed her head, choking back a sob. With her good hand, she drew the knapsack close, fearing her grandmother would search it and find the book within.

"Tell me you understand. Promise me."

Immanuelle dragged the words up from the pit of her belly. The lie tasted bitter as it skimmed across her tongue. "I promise."

CHAPTER FIVE

*The Father loves those who serve Him faithfully. But those
who stray from the path of righteousness—the heathen and
the witch, the lecher and the heretic—will feel the heat of His
heavenly flames.*

—THE HOLY SCRIPTURES

THAT NIGHT, AFTER Anna bandaged her hand and the rest of
the Moores were asleep in their beds, Immanuelle slipped
the forbidden book from her knapsack and raised it to the candlelight. It was well-made, she realized upon closer inspection. Its
front and back covers were cut from scraps of leather, as soft as
the muzzle of a newborn calf. A silk bookmark stuck out from
between its pages, so light it fluttered a little when Immanuelle
breathed.

She peeled open the front cover, the spine cracking with the
motion, and caught the mingling perfume of aged paper and horse
glue. There was a scribbled signature at the bottom of the first
page: *Miriam Elizabeth Moore.*

Immanuelle's hands shook so violently she almost dropped the
book. That was her mother's name and signature. The book had
belonged to her. But why would those women in the Darkwood
have a book that was once her mother's? What business did they
have with her?

Below the signature, to Immanuelle's shock, was a small ink
sketch. Its edges were ragged as if it'd been ripped from some

other book and pasted into the pages of this one, but the details were so well rendered that Immanuelle immediately recognized her mother's features from the paintings that hung in the parlor. In the sketch, Miriam was young, perhaps seventeen or eighteen, barely older than Immanuelle herself. She wore a long dress, colorless in the drawing, but Immanuelle knew it to be wine red, as it was the same one that lay folded at the bottom of her hope chest. In the portrait, the woods were behind her, and she was smiling.

On the following page, an illustration of a young man who favored Immanuelle. His hair was a tight cap of corkscrew curls, and a few of the loosest ringlets fell over his brow. He had a cut jaw and dark eyes fringed with thick lashes, and his skin was just a few shades deeper than Immanuelle's. His expression was rather stern, but his eyes weren't unkind. There was no date beneath that portrait, just his name, the first time it had ever appeared in the pages of the book: *Daniel Lewis Ward*. The portrait was accompanied by a series of writings that read like love poems:

Sometimes I think we share a soul. His pain has become mine. And mine his.

A few pages later . . .

I love him. He taught me how. I don't think I knew how to choose to love until I met him.

The following entries were shorter, the handwriting a bit sloppier than it had been before, as if the words were written in great haste. Most of them detailed brief encounters Miriam had with Daniel under cover of night or stolen moments after church on Sabbath days. In all of these entries, of which there were dozens, Miriam never once mentioned the Prophet. Still, Immanuelle could sense his presence in the pages, a shadow in the margins, a stain behind the words. And while Immanuelle knew that this story could only ever end in tragedy, she found herself hoping in vain for a different outcome. Miriam's entries turned from glee to hope to trepidation to outright despair . . . and after the despair came a kind of helplessness.

There was a months' long gap between entries and Immanuelle could only assume it accounted for the time Miriam was detained in the Prophet's Haven. Then: *They took him from me. They put him on the pyre. The flames burned high. They made me watch the fire take him.*

Immanuelle tried to blink back her tears, but a few fell anyway. She forced herself to turn the page. The next entry was dated *Summer in the Year of Omega*. It read: *I am with child.*

The tears flowed freely then, and Immanuelle paused to wipe them away on the sleeve of her nightdress. The following entry was dated *Winter of Omega*—a full eight months after the one that preceded it. It read: *I have seen the evils of this world, and I have loved them.*

The entries that followed were progressively stranger. Instead of the sweeping calligraphy Immanuelle had come to know as her mother's hand, these entries were sloppy, as if she had written them in the dark. The drawings, too, were different. The portraits and landscapes had become frantic scribbles, ink-stained abstractions so mangled Immanuelle could barely decipher them. One depicted a woman bent double, appearing to vomit tree branches. Another was a self-portrait of Miriam standing naked, one arm folded around her breasts, her hair hanging loose down her back. Her pregnant belly was swollen and painted with a crude symbol that reminded Immanuelle of the seals brides wore cut between their eyebrows, only this mark was much larger.

On the opposing page, an image of two twisted figures. They were naked like the other women, and their hands were joined. Both of them bore what Immanuelle initially mistook for the Prophet's seal between their brows. But upon closer inspection, she noticed the star in the middle of their seal had only seven points, instead of the customary eight. Etched into the corner of the drawing was a title and date: *The Lovers, Winter in the Year of Omega*. They were the women Immanuelle had seen in the woods. The women who had given her the journal. And they weren't just *any* women. They were the Lovers, Jael and Mercy, witches and servants of the Dark Mother who'd died in the fires of the Holy War, purged on account of their sin and lechery.

Somehow, defying all logic, they were alive in the Darkwood and her mother had *known* them. Dwelled with them perhaps. Why else would the witches have given Immanuelle the book? Why else would the book have sketches of the witches? Had the Lovers considered themselves doing Miriam's bidding when they gave it to Immanuelle? Was this meant to be a kind of inheritance? The fulfillment of a promise they'd made to Miriam long ago?

Shaken, Immanuelle read on. The entries became shorter, fewer, and farther between. Just crude sketches mostly, punctuated here and there by the odd illegible entry. One sketch depicted two oak trees, their trunks carved with strange forked symbols. Just behind the trees, an idyllic little cabin, standing in a small dell in the midst of the forest. It took her a moment to realize what she was looking at. That cabin was the place where Miriam claimed she spent the months of winter after fleeing into the Darkwood.

Immanuelle continued skimming through these strange writings—it seemed odd to call them entries, given how incoherent they'd become. But one drawing caught her eye. In the foreground, there was a face—a hatched line for a mouth, two narrow eyes, full lips, and a crude, long nose that looked broken. In the background, lurking above her shoulder, was the twisted contour of a woman's naked form. Mounted on her neck was not a head, but something that Immanuelle could only describe as a buck's skull, crowned with a sprawling rack of antlers.

Lilith.

The name rose to Immanuelle's mind unbidden, the fragment of a story told only around bonfires or whispered behind cupped hands. Lilith, daughter of the Dark Mother. The Mistress of Sins. Witch Queen of the Woodland. Immanuelle would have known her anywhere.

On the following page, a sketch of a woman emerging from what appeared to be a lake. Like the Lovers, she was naked, and her long black hair hung limp about her shoulders. The image was titled *Delilah the Witch of the Water*. Beside the drawing, a note: *I have seen the Beast and her maidens again. I hear their cries in the woods at night. They call to me, and I call to them. There is no love as pure as that.*

A bitter seed formed in the pit of Immanuelle's belly. Her hands shook as she turned the journal's final pages. Of everything she'd seen thus far, these scribbled drawings were the most troublesome. The accompanying words were so tangled it was almost impossible to decipher them. But Immanuelle was able to parse one phrase that appeared and reappeared over and over again in the backgrounds of drawings, crushed into the margins of scribbled entries: *Her blood begets blood. Her blood begets blood. Her blood begets blood.*

Immanuelle read on, and as she did, the drawings became progressively more abstract. Some pages were just spattered with ink, others with a series of dashes inflicted so violently the marks ripped the pages to shreds. Of these final illustrations, if you could even call them that, there was only one that Immanuelle could distinguish. It, no, *she*—because, for some unfathomable reason, Immanuelle was sure it was a she—was a maelstrom. A mangle of teeth and eyes and rendered flesh. The tulip folds of what might have been the creature's groin or perhaps an open mouth. Broken fingers and disembodied eyes with slits for pupils. Inexplicably, the ink still looked wet, and it rippled toward the edges of the paper as if threatening to spill onto the bed, soak the sheets black.

The final entry of the journal was unlike any of those that came before it. Every inch of those two pages was covered with the same four words: *Blood. Blight. Darkness. Slaughter. Blood. Blight. Darkness. Slaughter. Blood. Blight. Darkness. Slaughter. Blood. Blight. Darkness. Slaughter* . . .

On and on it went.

Just below the storm of those words, a scribbled footnote at the bottom of the journal's final page: *Father help them. Father help us all.*

CHAPTER SIX

I first saw you by the riverside. There was sun on your cheeks and wind in your curls, and you sat with your feet in the water, smiling at me. I don't think I'd felt real fear until that moment, but Father as my witness, I feared you.

—FROM THE FINAL LETTERS OF DANIEL WARD

EIGHT DAYS PASSED without event. In the mornings, Immanuelle sent the sheep to pasture. Sometimes she walked the children to school. She sold her wool at the market and avoided the temptations of the book tent and the woods. On the Sabbath, she went to the cathedral and laid her sins at the feet of the Prophet. She closed her eyes in prayer and did not open them. She sang her hymns with so much vigor she went hoarse halfway through the service and had to whisper her way through the remaining hours of worship. At home, she did not disobey Martha or bicker with Glory.

She kept to the creeds and commandments.

But in the nights, after the rest of the Moores had retired to their bedrooms and the children were asleep, Immanuelle slipped her mother's journal from beneath her pillow and read it with reverence, the way Martha pored over the pages of the Prophet's Holy Scriptures.

In her dreams, she saw the women of the woods. Their tangled legs and grasping fingers. The dead gazes that stared, unseeing, into the black of the forest's corridors, their lips split apart as if they'd been caught in the midst of a kiss. And in the morning, when Immanuelle woke from those wretched dreams—sweating cold, her legs tangled in her sheets—she thought only of the Darkwood and her growing desire to return to it once more.

THE MORNING OF Leah's cutting and her binding to the Prophet, Immanuelle woke with her mother's journal beneath her cheek. She sat up with a start, smoothing the pages before she snapped it shut and slipped it under her mattress.

After forcing her feet into her muck boots, she trudged downstairs and out the back door, crossing through the farmyard and down into the paddock to let the sheep out to pasture. Then, in preparation for the buggy ride to the cathedral, she took the old mule from his shack and brushed him down, then fed and bridled him.

Across the fields and pastures was the black of the woods, the trees cast into shadow by the light of the rising sun. Immanuelle found herself looking for faces among the branches, the Lovers she'd seen in the woods that night, the figures sketched in her mother's journal.

But she saw nothing. The distant woods were still.

By the time Immanuelle returned to the farmhouse, the Moore daughters were eating breakfast in the dining room. Honor sat at the table, spooning up the last of her gruel, and Glory studied her reflection in the bottom of a polished pot, tugging at her braids and frowning.

Anna wore her Sabbath best. Her hair was heaped atop her head and adorned with wildflowers. She was beaming; she always beamed on cutting days.

"To think it's Leah who drew the Prophet's eye," she said, almost singing the words.

Martha rounded the corner of the kitchen, bringing Abram with her. He leaned heavily on her shoulder, his mangled foot sliding across the floorboards. Martha stared at Immanuelle pointedly, a frown creasing the seal between her brows. "It speaks to her virtue."

Immanuelle's cheeks burned with shame at the subtle slight. "That it does."

With that, she dismissed herself to the washroom, tripping on the hem of her nightdress as she went. She set about the task of readying herself. There was little she could do but wash the dirt off her hands and wet her curls in a sad attempt to tame them. She tried to pile her hair atop her head the way Anna did, but her ringlets tangled, devouring pins and snaring the teeth of her comb.

So she let her hair hang long, the thick curls sweeping the base of her neck. She pinched her cheeks to give them color, bit her lips and wet them.

She frowned at her reflection in the mirror above the sink. The longer she stared into her own eyes, the more her face warped and changed. Her skin paled. Her eyes gaped wider. Her mouth twisted into a sneer.

All at once, it was not her face in the mirror at all, but that of one of the Lovers. The same ghoul that had given her the journal. Her lips twisted apart. A strange and warbling voice echoed through her mind: *"Blood. Blight. Darkness. Slaughter."*

Immanuelle staggered back from the sink so fast she crashed into the tub and hit the floor. Upon scrambling to her feet, she fled the washroom and scaled the iron stairs up to her attic bedroom, kicking the door shut behind her.

She snatched a few long breaths in an attempt to still her racing heart. Her hands shook as she pressed them to her face, squeezing her eyes shut as if the dark was enough to keep her memories at bay. But there was no forgetting the woodland women. And worse yet, Immanuelle wasn't sure she wanted to forget. Surely if she did, she would have abandoned her sin and turned over the journal. Or better yet, cast it into the hearth fire to burn. But she hadn't. She couldn't. She would sooner take a branding iron to the cheek than watch what little she had left of her mother turn to ashes.

But the witches who had given her the journal, and the evil they wrought, were a different matter entirely. She refused to fall prey to their torments the way her mother had. She wouldn't abandon her faith so quickly. She resolved to keep the journal, if only as a reminder of what sin could do to someone weak enough to succumb to it.

Lowering her hands, Immanuelle found the dress she had worn to Judith's cutting stretched across the foot of her bed. It was a faded sable color with a thin skirt, long puff sleeves, and a string of rusty copper buttons that stopped just short of the bosom. A child's dress, better suited to a girl of Glory's age than Immanuelle's.

She sighed. There was no help to be had for it. She certainly couldn't wear her Sabbath attire. It was far too informal for such an important occasion. But then she remembered the drawing of her mother she'd found in the back of the journal a few days prior. The sketch of her standing in front of the forbidden woods.

Immanuelle dropped to her knees in front of the hope chest and rifled through her belongings. Most were just keepsakes, quilts and bits of ribbon, dried bouquets and other tokens she'd collected over the passing years. Nothing as important as the journal, nothing forbidden. But at the bottom of the chest, wrapped in parchment paper, was her mother's dress, the same one she had worn in the portrait.

It was nothing special like the gown Leah would wear to her cutting, but it was a well-sewn Sabbath dress, wine red with copper buttons at the throat. On the odd occasion when Immanuelle wore it—in her attic bedroom when all of the others had fallen asleep—she felt perfectly presentable, pretty even, like the girls she often saw wandering the shops of the market with their gloves and silken shawls.

She stripped out of her nightgown and slipped into the dress. It wasn't a perfect fit, the waist was cut too wide and the hips were perhaps a little tighter than what Martha would deem wholesome, but it was a better fit than Anna's hand-me-downs and much finer. Plus, its hem fell low to the floor so it would easily cover the tops of her boots, which were too scuffed to be suitable for any occasion more formal than a romp across the pastures.

Once dressed, Immanuelle took a wreath of wildflowers from the top of her wardrobe. The blossoms had dried nicely in the week after she'd picked them with Leah, and the band of the crown—a twisted web-work of braided stems—held fast. Gingerly, she set it atop her head, pinned it in place, and turned to peer at her reflection in the bedroom window.

She couldn't call herself a vision; her lip was still badly split and bruised from her tussle with Judas days before. But she thought that, alongside Judith and Leah and the rest of the girls who would attend the cutting, she wouldn't look so out of place. The color of the dress complemented the rich tan of her skin and pulled the color from her eyes, and with the flowers in her hair, her curls looked rather nice.

Immanuelle slipped into the hallway, her skirts rustling around her ankles. She took the stairs slowly and entered the kitchen. Honor was dressed in a dusk-colored smock, her plump feet stuffed into tiny leather boots. She was the first to spot Immanuelle, and she shrieked with glee at the sight of her.

"Let me wear the crown!" she pleaded, laughing and clawing at the air. With a wry smile, Immanuelle obliged her, balancing the wreath atop the child's ginger curls.

"That's Miriam's dress." Martha stood at the threshold, grasping a damp dishrag.

Immanuelle couldn't remember the last time Martha had said her daughter's name. It sounded strange in her mouth, foreign.

Immanuelle took the wreath off Honor's head and placed it on her own again, quickly adjusting the pins. "I found it at the bottom of my hope chest. I thought I might wear it to the cutting, if you think it fitting."

"Fitting?" Martha's lips twisted. "Aye, it is that."

Immanuelle stalled, unsure of what to say and wondering if she ought to return to her bedroom and put on the dress Anna had laid out for her. But she couldn't bring herself to move.

To her surprise, Martha's gaze softened, not with affection, but with what Immanuelle could only describe as resignation. "You wear it like your mother," she said.

THE MOORE BROOD took the buggy to the cathedral, the mule dragging the lot of them across the plains. It was a bright day. The sun was a hot kiss on the back of Immanuelle's neck and the air smelled of summer, all sweat and honey and apple blooms.

As they rode, she was careful to keep her eyes off the Darkwood. Martha had been watching her ever since the night she'd returned from the forest. Her eye was keen, and Immanuelle knew that the punishment would be swift and painful if she was ever caught wandering the woods again. So she kept her gaze trained on the floor of the wagon, her hands clasped in her lap.

By the time they arrived at the cathedral, most of the congregation was already gathered in fellowship on its lawn. Immanuelle hopped out of the buggy and scanned the crowds for Leah, but instead her gaze found Ezra, who stood with a few boys his age and a gaggle of girls, including Hope, Judith, and a few of the Prophet's other wives.

At the sight of Immanuelle, he nodded by way of greeting. She waved in turn—conscious of the way Judith and the rest of the girls studied her as she did—and escaped into the shadows of the cathedral. There she found Leah kneeling at the foot of the altar in prayer. At the echo of Immanuelle's footsteps, she opened her eyes and turned to face her.

Leah was a vision, draped in white, her hair hanging so long it touched the small of her back. She broke into a smile and sprinted down the aisle, catching Immanuelle in a fierce hug.

They held on to each other in silence for a long time.

This was to be the end of them, the end of what they'd shared in girlhood. Somewhere amidst the passing years, Leah had become a woman and Immanuelle had not, and now the two of them would be split apart.

"You look like the bride of a prophet," said Immanuelle, trying not to sound as sad as she felt.

Leah beamed and gave a little twirl, the pale skirts of her cutting gown billowing, light as fog. She'd hand sewn them from chiffon months before her wedding, working through the night by candlelight, stitching the verses of the Prophet's Scriptures into her underskirts, as was custom for young brides. Her feet were bare and clean, her hair parted down the middle. About her neck was a new golden holy dagger much like the ones the apostles wore, though its blade was dull and much shorter. She toyed with it a bit as she spoke. "I thought you'd never come. I was worried."

"Our mule took his time," said Immanuelle.

"Well, I'm glad you're here now. I need you. For strength."

"You have me. Always."

Leah reached out to grasp Immanuelle's hand, her fingers

cold. She studied the bandages. "Are you going to tell me what happened?"

"I wasn't planning to."

"Well, I want to know and you can't refuse me because it's my cutting day. Out with it."

Immanuelle gazed down at her boots. "I was burned as a punishment."

"It was Martha's doing, wasn't it?"

Immanuelle nodded, not looking at her.

"She's too hard on you. Always has been."

"This time, the punishment was warranted. Believe me."

Leah frowned. "What did you do?"

Immanuelle stalled, half ashamed, half afraid to tell her. "I went into the Darkwood. My ram broke free of his tether, fled for the trees. I tried to follow him, but night fell fast and I got lost. I was going to give up, wait until morning to find my way home again . . . but then I heard voices."

"And what did the voices say?"

Immanuelle faltered. "They weren't saying anything I could understand."

"So they were . . . *foreigners*?"

"No. I don't think so. It's just that the sounds they were making, they weren't words at all. It was just whimpers and moaning."

Leah looked very pale and very sick. "What did they look like?"

"They were tall, very thin. Too thin. And they were lying together in a glen in the woods, embracing the way a husband and wife might."

Leah's eyes went wide. "What did they do when they saw you?"

Immanuelle opened her mouth to tell her about her mother's journal but stopped short. It was better for the both of them if she bit her tongue. She feared she'd said too much already. After all, in a short while Leah would be the Prophet's wife, bound to him by the sacred seal. Immanuelle knew there was power in a promise like that, and while she trusted Leah as her friend, as a prophet's bride she wouldn't belong to herself anymore. "They didn't do anything. They just stood there. I ran before they had the chance to come closer."

Leah was quiet for a long time, as if trying to decide whether or not she believed her. Then: "What on earth were you thinking? The woods are dangerous. There's a reason we're taught to stay clear of them."

A flare of anger licked up the back of Immanuelle's neck. "You think I don't know that?"

Leah caught her by the shoulder, gripping so hard she winced. "Knowing isn't enough, Immanuelle. You have to promise me you'll never go into the Darkwood again."

"I won't."

"Good," said Leah, and her grip slackened. "I hope those women you saw go back to the hell they came from. There's no place for them here."

"But they weren't here," said Immanuelle quietly. "They were in the Darkwood."

"And does the Father not have power over the woods as well?"

Immanuelle thought of her mother's journal, the four words at the end of her final entry: *Blood. Blight. Darkness. Slaughter.* "Maybe the Father turned His back on the forest," she said, careful to keep her voice low. "He has His kingdom, and the Dark Mother has Hers."

"Yet you passed through the Darkwood's corridors unharmed. That has to mean something."

Before Immanuelle had the chance to respond, the church bell tolled and the front doors swung open. The Prophet entered in a slant of sunlight. He wore plain clothes, no robes or stoles as he did on Sabbath days. Somehow, his common wear made him all the more intimidating. Immanuelle could not help but notice how sallow he looked. His eyes were shadowed with dark bags and she could have sworn there was blood crusting in the corners of his lips.

The Prophet's gaze went to Immanuelle first, falling to her dress, and something like recognition stirred in his eyes. He seemed to stare through her, to a lost time when Miriam was still alive. She had never fully understood what the Prophet had seen in her mother. Some said it was love, others lust, but most believed that Miriam had seduced the Prophet with her witchery. There were so many stories and secrets, tangled threads and loose ends, but Immanuelle wondered if the truth lay somewhere in the intersections between them all.

After a long beat, the Prophet turned and nodded to Leah, as if he'd only just remembered she was there. He walked to the altar in silence, only pausing to cough into his sleeve. The rest of the congregation spilled in after him, filing into the pews. The apostles walked around the perimeter of the room, Ezra among them.

Immanuelle tried her best not to look at him.

In turn, Leah's gaze fell to the Prophet. "It's time."

Immanuelle nodded, giving Leah's hand a final squeeze before she slipped toward the altar. As Immanuelle went to find her place in the pews, the apostles lifted an invocation and Leah climbed up onto the altar, careful to gather her skirts in such a way that her knees didn't show. And there she lay, motionless, in wait of the blade.

The Prophet placed his hand to her belly. "I bless you with the seed of the Father." His hand shifted to her chest. "The heart of the lamb."

Leah gave a tremulous smile. Tears slipped down her cheeks.

The Prophet lifted the chain of his dagger and slipped it over

his head. "May the power of the Father move through you, hence-
forth and forevermore."

The flock spoke in unison. *"Blessings forevermore."*

With that, he lowered the blade to Leah's forehead and cut her,
carving the first line of the holy seal. She did not scream or struggle, even as the blood slipped down her temples and pooled in the
hollows of her ears.

The flock watched in silence. Immanuelle gripped the pew
white-knuckled to keep herself from bolting as the cutting ritual
dragged on.

What felt like hours later, the Prophet placed a hand to the top
of Leah's head and stroked her, gently, his fingers lingering in the
locks of her hair, mussing her curls.

At his touch, Leah sat up slowly, a trickle of blood skimming
down the slope of her nose and slicking her lips. With a wavering
smile and tear-filled eyes, she turned to face the congregation and
licked the blood away.

CHAPTER SEVEN

Lilith with her crown of bone
Is mother of the beasts
Delilah with her tender smile
Swims in waters deep

Jael and Mercy sing their songs
to moon and stars above
Telling tales of mortal sin
And their unholy love

But those that venture to the wood
after the sun sinks low
Will never see the morning's light
Or live to learn and grow
—BETHELAN NURSERY RHYME

A FEAST FOLLOWED the cutting, one of the biggest since the autumn harvest. There were nine tables to accommodate the guests of Leah and the Prophet, each so long they stretched from one end of the churchyard to the other. Every one was crowded with an assortment of platters and dishes. There was braised beef and potatoes, roasted corn, and an assortment of breads and cheeses. To drink, apple cider and barley wine, which the men guzzled from big, wooden mugs, their beards rimmed with lather. For dessert, poached plums with cream and sugar.

Overhead, the moon hung round and full and the sky was spangled with stars. The guests partook in abundance, dining and chatting and laughing, drunk off the power of the cutting. Families gathered in fellowship and the Prophet's wives moved between tables, tending to the guests and taking the time to greet each person in turn.

At the head of all of this—at a small table set for two—sat Leah and her husband, the Prophet. She was smiling despite the pain of her new wound, which had since been cleaned and bandaged. When she saw Immanuelle, sitting with the Moores in the back of the churchyard, Leah's smile grew wider still. Her eyes were ablaze with the light of the bonfires, her cheeks flushed from the heat and perhaps a few too many sips of barley wine. At her side sat the Prophet, his elbows propped up on the table, fingers laced. He followed his new wife's gaze to Immanuelle, and she got the distinct impression that he was studying her.

A chill cut down Immanuelle's spine at the thought, but before she had the chance to look away, the Prophet stood up, and at once, his flock fell silent. His gaze shifted away from her as he rounded the table to address the congregation. "Tonight is a joyous occasion," he said, his voice a little hoarse. "I have joined myself in holy union with a true daughter of the Father, and for that, I am grateful."

The flock applauded.

"The Father, in His divine providence, has seen fit to offer me many wives who embody the virtues of our faith. Because of that, I would like to honor our Father in celebration for His infinite grace and generosity." He paused to cough into the crook of his shirtsleeve, then recovered himself with a smile. "Call forth the witches."

The congregation cheered. Men raised their cups and wives clattered their plates against the tabletop; children slapped their knees and bellies. At the sound of the fanfare, the apostles emerged from the cathedral, bearing scarecrows fashioned into the shape of women. Each of the figures was mounted on an iron cross so that her wooden arms were outstretched, her neck and body bound.

Upon their arrival, the congregation erupted into applause. Men raised their fists, shouting curses to the wind.

The first apostle stepped forward with the first witch, a small wicker figure barely bigger than Honor.

"That's Mercy," said Anna, taking time to school her daughters in the particulars of the faith.

The next apostle held his witch high above his head, so her nightgown lashed and fluttered on the wind. When her skirt flapped up, exposing what would be her modesty, a few of the bolder men jeered. *"Harlot! Whore!"*

"And who might she be?" Anna pointed as the apostle carried the figure toward the roaring flames.

"That's Jael," said Immanuelle, and she shuddered when she said the name, remembering the wretched creature she'd encountered in the Darkwood days before. "The second Lover."

"Aye," said Anna, and her lip curled in disgust. "That's her. And she's a mean one too. Wicked and cunning like the Dark Mother Herself." She snaked out a hand to tickle Honor's belly. The girl shrieked and giggled, kicking her legs beneath the table, the plates and cups jumping a bit when her boot struck its leg.

The third witch followed. She wore a dress not so unlike Immanuelle's, only her bodice was stuffed with straw to emulate the swell of a pregnant woman's belly.

"Delilah," said Martha. "Witch of the Water. Hell's own whore."

It was Ezra who carried the last witch, bearing her on an iron cross. The figure was twice the size of the others, and she was naked, her body a thatch-work of birch branches. The arms of a sapling twisted from either side of her head, forming a rack of antlers.

Anna didn't say her name out loud, though she cheered when Ezra carried her near. But Glory and Honor fell silent in her wake, cringing a little as the shadow of the last witch slipped past them.

Her name surfaced from the depths of Immanuelle's mind: Lilith. First daughter of the Dark Mother. Witch Queen of the Woodland who reigned in wrath, slaying any and all who opposed her.

Each of the apostles raised his witch overhead and staked her deep into the soil, so that the figures stood upright on their iron crosses. The Prophet raised his torch, a flaming branch nearly as long as Immanuelle was tall. Then he moved it to the witches, lighting each of them in turn. The Lovers, Jael and Mercy, first, then the Witch of the Water, Delilah.

Immanuelle tasted something sour at the back of her throat, and her stomach twisted. The sound of blood pounding through her ears briefly drowned out the jeering crowds.

Lilith was the last witch to burn that night, and the Prophet made the most of the moment. He raised his blazing branch high above his head and thrust it between her horns, the way one might wield a sword. His eyes held the glow of the torch flame, the embers seeming to spark in the pits of his pupils.

In silence, Immanuelle watched Lilith burn, watched the flames chew her up and swallow her, even as the rest of the guests returned to their food and chatter. She watched the witches burn until the fires died and Lilith's blackened bones were the only thing that remained, smoking on the arms of the iron cross.

IMMANUELLE FLED THE feast, her belly warmed by barley wine, her head thick. She passed children running rings around the charred remains of the witch pyres, hollering hymns above the music of the fiddler. She passed Leah and the Prophet and the throng of his other wives. She passed the Moores unseen.

Immanuelle staggered around the cathedral to the graveyard behind it. There, she broke to her knees and heaved, retching barley wine into the thicket. She pushed to her feet, dizzy, took a few steps forward, and heaved again. Her sick splattered a nearby tombstone and seeped, reeking, into the dirt.

Shaking despite the summer heat, Immanuelle breathed deeply to steady herself and wiped her mouth on her sleeve.

She had been foolish to think she could banish the memory of the witches. What she'd seen in the woods that day was real. The Lovers weren't passing figments. They'd been flesh and blood, as real as she was. The journal, the letters, the forbidden forest—none of it would leave her, and she couldn't leave it. No amount of prayer or penance would banish it.

What she'd seen in the woods had become a part of her . . . and it was a part of her that she knew she needed to kill, and quickly.

Pushing herself off the ground, Immanuelle wandered the cemetery, weaving between the headstones, reading epitaphs in an attempt to clear her head. Some of them belonged to prophets and apostles of ages past, but most marked the resting places of the crusader soldiers who died in the civil war to overthrow the witches. A few were mass graves, and the stones that marked these simply read: *In remembrance of the Father's Men and the dark they purged.* As for the witches, there were no monuments to mark their graves. Their bones and memories lay within the Darkwood.

At the center of the cemetery was a thick slab of marble, nearly two stories tall, hewn into a pinnacle that jutted from the soil like a half-buried bone. Immanuelle knelt to read the inscription at the foot of the monument, though she didn't have to. Like most everyone in Bethel, she knew it by heart.

It read: *Here lies the Father's first prophet, David Ford, Spring in the Year of the Flame to Winter in the Year of the Wake.* Below that, words gouged deep into the stone read: *Blood for blood.*

Immanuelle shivered. Buried beneath her feet were the bones

of the Witch Killer, the prophet who'd purged and burned and cleansed Bethel of evil. For it was David Ford who'd ordered Lilith and the rest of her coven to the pyre, who'd set the fire and stoked the flames. Every purge began with him and the war he'd waged during the Dark Days.

Immanuelle pressed off the ground and stood. As she did, she heard a soft cry on the wind. Easing between the tombstones, she walked to the edge of the graveyard, which stopped just short of the forest. An iron fence ran along the edge of the cemetery, separating it from the encroaching woodland just beyond the Holy Grounds. And it was there that she spotted them, Ezra and Judith together in the darkness just a few paces from the memorial she cowered behind. They stood close to one another, and Judith was holding him by his shirt, the cloth balled up in both of her fists.

"Enough," said Ezra, and he pulled at her fingers, trying to pry them open.

Judith only clutched him tighter. "You can't make me want him."

"You made a vow," Ezra snapped. "You were cut same as Leah, and you'd do well to remember that."

He started to push her off him, and that was when Judith rushed forward, forcing her lips to his. She fit her hands beneath his shirt, shifting her hips against him. "Please." She mumbled into his mouth, his neck. "Please, Ezra."

He seized her by the shoulders, shoving her back. "I said no."

Tears filled Judith's eyes. She strained forward again, catching him by the hilt of his dagger, and she pulled it so violently the chain that held it snapped. Silver chain links skittered into the darkness, a few flying so far they hit the ground at Immanuelle's feet.

Her heart stumbled, then skipped a beat. She turned to leave, tripping over the skirts of her mother's dress as she went, desperate to get away, when one of the children playing by the fire screamed.

Ezra snapped to attention, spotting Immanuelle as he turned his head. He called her name and she fled, running as fast through the graveyard as she had in the woods the night of the storm.

CHAPTER EIGHT

Father help them. Father help us all.
—MIRIAM MOORE

THAT NIGHT, IMMANUELLE dreamed of the forest. In sleep, she conjured visions of the Dark Mother wandering the corridors of the woodland, cradling a slaughtered lamb in Her arms, Her black veil trailing through the brush. She dreamed of scarecrow witches burning like torches in the night, tangled limbs and stolen kisses. In her nightmares, she saw the Lovers toiling in the dirt, grasping at each other, teeth bared, pale eyes sharp with moonlight.

When she woke, she was sweating cold, the back of her nightdress damp, clinging to her shoulders like a second skin. She sat up, dizzied, her heart tapping a sharp rhythm against her ribs. Her ears rang with a plaintive bleating.

At first, she thought it was the echo of a dream. But when it sounded again, her mind went to her flock, the shadows of her nightmares fading as she sprang to her feet and took her cloak off its hook on the door. She shoved her feet into her muck boots, snatched her lamp off the bedside table, and eased down the attic stairs and into the hall.

The farmhouse was silent, save for the wheeze of Abram's

snores. She knew he'd taken Anna's bed because of how close he sounded. He took Anna's bed often those days, rarely, if ever, haunting Martha's.

Immanuelle was glad of it. On the nights that Abram did go to Martha, she didn't sleep, and often Immanuelle would hear her pacing through the halls. Once, years ago, near midnight, Immanuelle had caught her grandmother in the kitchen with a mug full of Abram's whiskey, staring out into the black of the forest while her husband slept in her bed.

Another cry cut the silence, and Immanuelle's thoughts returned to her flock. She dashed downstairs as quietly as she could. Her lamp swung as she hurried, throwing light and shadow. The wailing continued, a hollow, keening sound that seemed to slip through the bones of the house. As Immanuelle crossed into the back pasture, she realized—with a cold twist in her belly—that it was coming from the Darkwood.

Stepping off the back porch, Immanuelle crossed into the pastures, the glow of her oil lamp a spot of warmth in the black tide of the night.

Another cry, this one sharper than the last, and louder.

Immanuelle broke toward the pastures in a full run, only to find her flock clutched together against the midnight cold, still and silent and entirely unharmed. She did a quick head count. Twenty-seven in total, every lamb and ewe accounted for. But the crying continued, now more a howl than a wail.

Then, something else: a scream, ripped straight from a woman's throat.

At the sound, a sharp pain shot through Immanuelle. She doubled over, the lamp slipping from her hand. She snatched it from the ground before the oil could spill and the grass catch fire, her teeth set against the pain in her stomach.

The cries became more frenzied, until Immanuelle realized

that they weren't cries at all, but rather a kind of song. She knew she ought to go back to the house, return to her bed where it was safe and leave the wood to its own evils. But she didn't.

It was as if someone had tied a thread around her sternum and pulled, drawing her closer. As if something, or someone, was leading her to the Darkwood. Perhaps she could fight it if she really tried. She could listen to every instinct urging her to turn around and return to the farmhouse. She could keep her promises.

But she didn't do any of those things.

Instead, she took a step toward the tree line, wading through the swaying grass of the pasture, climbing over the fence that encircled it, lured by the forest's cries. Lamp in hand, Immanuelle picked through the thick of the underbrush, following the woodland call through the trees. She didn't know where she walked, or what she walked toward, but she knew—without really knowing—that she wasn't lost.

On and on she went. Brambles snatched at her nightdress, and the cold breathed down the back of her neck. The cries seemed to slither between the trees, though they were softer, dying into gasps and whispers that lost themselves in the hissing wind. She could hear her name now in the chorus: *Immanuelle. Immanuelle.*

But she didn't feel afraid. She didn't feel anything but dizzy and light, as though she wasn't walking as much as she was skimming between the trees, as weightless as the shadows themselves.

A branch snapped. Her hand tightened around the lantern's handle, and she winced a little, her burnt hand chafing beneath her bandages.

She smelled something wet and heady on the air, and as the cries quieted, she heard the soft lapping of moving water.

On instinct, she followed the sound, raising her lamp high to illuminate the trees. Shouldering through the brush, she entered a small clearing. At its center was a pond, its water as black as oil.

Like a mirror, it reflected the moon's face back at itself. She paused by the water's edge, her hand tightening around the handle of her lantern.

"Hello?" she called out into the night, but the forest swallowed the sound. Despite the silence, there was no echo. The cries died. The trees were still.

Immanuelle knew then that she should have run, retraced her steps and fled back to the farmhouse. But instead, she squared her shoulders and braced her feet, finding a scrap of strength to cling to. "If there's anyone out here, show yourselves. I know your kind lurks in the Darkwood. I know you knew my mother, and you call to me like you called to her." Whatever evil they sought with her, Immanuelle needed it to be known now and done with.

A great, rippling ring formed at the center of the pond. The waves licked the shore and Immanuelle's lantern sputtered as if the oil was running low.

In the flickering light, a woman emerged from the shallows. Immanuelle staggered back a half step and raised her lantern. "Who's there?"

The woman didn't answer. She skimmed through the shallows like a minnow, her limbs tangling in the reeds. As she drew closer, Immanuelle saw that she was beautiful, with the kind of face that could turn a prophet's head or snatch a man's heart from behind his ribs. And then Immanuelle recognized her from the pages of her mother's journal. She had the same harsh mouth as one of the women in the drawings, which would have been almost comically wide if her lips weren't so full and beautiful. Her hair was dark and slick, the same color as the pond scum that clung to the rocks in the shallows. Her skin was as pale as a corpse's, the same as the skin of the Lovers, and like them, she bore a mark between her brows, a seven-pointed star in the middle of a circle.

Immanuelle knew then: This was Delilah, the Witch of the Water.

The woman slid her belly along the slope of the shore and dragged herself to her feet. The black mud covered her naked breasts and modesty, but in the warmth of the lamplight, Immanuelle could distinguish her every cut and contour. As the witch drew nearer, she realized she was not a woman at all but rather a girl of about her age, no more than sixteen or seventeen, eighteen at the very oldest.

Delilah drew so close, Immanuelle could smell her. She reeked of dead things, all lichen and leaves and pond rot. It was then—by the moonlight—that Immanuelle saw her bruises, black splotches as dark as ink stains marring her cheeks. Her right eye was slightly swollen, and both of her lips were split.

The witch extended a hand, fingers folding around Immanuelle's wrist. In one swift movement, she shredded the bandages, exposing Immanuelle's burn to the cold night air. Despite all of Anna's ointments and tending, it hadn't healed well. It was red and angry and weeping pus, likely to leave an ugly scar once the scabs flaked away.

Gingerly, the way a mother holds a child, the woman brought Immanuelle's palm to her mouth and licked it. Her lips radiated a numbing cold.

Then Delilah kissed her: first the meat of her palm, then her wrist, the witch's lips trailing along her tendons to the tips of her fingers. She kept her dark eyes on Immanuelle's as she did this, never breaking her gaze.

Fear flooded through Immanuelle's chest and her vision blurred. She caught snatches of the pages of her mother's journal transposed with the woman's face—her slim, pale, dead face. The lantern slipped from her grasp and struck the dirt with a dull *thud*.

Delilah tugged on her hand. Immanuelle took a half step forward, then another, slipping out of her boots as she walked. She entered the water barefoot. She felt the waves rise around her, up to her ankles, her calves, her thighs, licking at the curve of her crotch, the swell of her breasts, until her feet skimmed the bottom and the water kissed her chin.

Delilah led her on, deeper and deeper, wading backward so that she could look at her. Those dead, swollen eyes fixed on Immanuelle's.

And then they were under, lost to the black and the cold and the shadow. The witch's grip slackened, her fingers slipping from Immanuelle's wrist as she slithered into the dark depths of the pond.

Immanuelle tried to follow her, but her legs were dead beneath her, so leaden she had to fight for every step. The cold rose from the depths of the pond, and she was sinking like she had bricks chained to her ankles. Her chest seized as she slipped down into the dark.

She saw faces, passing figments, in the cold blackness: the flash of her mother's smile, the moon-pale portraits of the Lovers, the wicker corpse of a witch burning on a cross, a baby girl, a woman with her hair shorn as short as a boy's.

Immanuelle reached to them and tried to call out, her voice warbling, lost to the waters.

And then—just as she was surrendering to the darkness—she ascended again, breaking the surface with a gasp. Across the waters of the pond the distant tree line blurred and doubled. The witch was gone. She was alone.

In Bethel, it was a sin to swim. It was not modest or prudent to enter the water, for it was deemed the demons' domain. But Leah had taught Immanuelle in secret one summer, when they were both young and bold. The two of them had bobbed up and down in the shallows of the stream, plugging their noses and paddling until Immanuelle learned to breathe between strokes.

And it was Leah whom Immanuelle thought of now, as she paddled and kicked, following the glow of her lantern back to the pond's shore. A deep-moving current pulled at her ankles, and every stroke was a struggle. When she finally made it back to the shallows, she crawled up the bank on her hands and knees and collapsed, retching sludge into the shore.

Her sin had saved her.

As she pressed off her belly, arms shaking, she glimpsed two bare feet stride through the shadows of the underbrush and step into the pale halo of the lamplight. Pushing wet curls from her eyes, she peered up to see a form that was feminine—yet bestial—looming over her.

She—for Immanuelle was certain it was a "she"—had a tall, crude shape. Her legs were long and slender, her arms low-slung, fingertips skimming her knees. And she was naked, so much so that not even a fur of modesty covered her groin. But it was not her nakedness that drew Immanuelle's eye so much as the deer skull that perched atop her thin, pale neck. A crown of bone.

Her name rose to Immanuelle's lips like a curse. "Lilith."

The Beast huffed hard. Steam churned through the cracks of her skull, coiling around her antlers.

Immanuelle squatted low to the mud. Even in her terror, she had the good sense to know a queen when she saw one. She dropped her gaze, her heart pounding so hard within her chest it hurt. And there she lay, prostrate in the muck and shadow, her breath hitching, her tears cutting tracks through the grime and pond sludge on her cheeks.

She was going to die there; she was sure of it. She was going to die like the others who'd been fool enough to cross into the woods at night. She had no faith that she would reach the heavens—not after all of her sins and folly—but she prayed anyway.

The Beast's feet shifted. Her bare toes clutched the mud as she lowered herself to a crouch. Immanuelle risked a glance upward. That great skull head angled to the side, a motion so human, even girlish, that for a fleeting moment, Immanuelle was reminded of Glory.

The Beast raised a hand that looked only loosely human. With fingers that were long and impossibly thin, she skimmed along the bridge of Immanuelle's nose, then slipped down to the dip of her cupid's bow.

Transfixed, Immanuelle searched for Lilith's eyes, staring into the fearsome skull's black, empty sockets. But she found nothing within them but steam and swirling shadows.

Her knees went weak beneath her.

Lilith wrapped a giant, cold hand around her wrist and dragged her to her feet. The wind shuddered through the forest, and the trees seemed to bow and tremble in her wake. The waters of the pond churned and surged, and fog flooded the clearing, swirling around her ankles. As the creature raised a hand to tuck a curl behind Immanuelle's ear, something like a sob broke from her lips.

Then pain pierced through her stomach once more, and Immanuelle doubled over, barely staying on her feet. Again, she begged for salvation—this time out loud—calling to the Father, then to the Mother, and finally to Lilith herself, whatever gods might deign to listen.

But there was no response, nothing. Nothing but the burning pain in her belly.

And as Immanuelle's knees weakened beneath her, a trail of blood slicked down her leg, threading along the slope of her calf and slipping down to her ankle, where it disappeared into the water pooling at her feet.

All at once, the pond stilled.

The wind calmed, and the trees ceased their thrashing.

Lilith retreated slowly into the shadows, dipping her skull low to avoid catching the branches with her antlers. As she did so, Immanuelle could have sworn she saw something briefly flicker in the blacks of her sockets. And then the witch was gone.

IMMANUELLE RAN. BUT with every step, every lunge she took through brush and bracken, the pain in her stomach grew sharper, and the darkness grew thicker, and the forest seemed to swallow her up, dragging her back ten feet for every five she sprinted. Overhead, the branches arched into a strange kaleidoscope, moonlight splintering, shadows smearing, stars flickering in the black.

But she ran onward, even as the darkness dragged at her ankles, drawing her back to the forest's heart. She saw a distant light in the darkness. The dull glow of candle-warmed windows. The Moore farmhouse peered through the gaps between trees.

Pain carved through her belly and a great roaring filled her ears as the shadows rose around her. The last thing Immanuelle saw, before the night swallowed her, was the bright eye of the moon, winking through the trees.

CHAPTER NINE

With the bloodletting comes the power of the heavens and hells. For an iron offering buys atonement, in all of its many forms.

—THE HOLY SCRIPTURES

IMMANUELLE WOKE SPRAWLED across the floor. It took her a few seconds to realize she was not in the deep of the Darkwood, but in her own house, in her own kitchen, lying facedown at the foot of the sink. Across the room, her wet and muddied cloak lay in a heap beside the back door, which was slightly ajar.

All at once, the memories of the night came flooding back to her. There was Delilah slithering through the reeds and shallows, Lilith slipping back into the shadows of the Darkwood as silently as she arrived, the branches closing in around her, the darkness falling. She remembered running through the woods, the pain in her belly, the bleeding, collapsing at the forest's edge, the moon's face peering down at her through the breaks between trees.

She might have thought it was all a dream, if not for the black sludge caked beneath her nails, her wet hair and muddy nightdress.

No, it had happened. *All* of it had happened.

From the blue light seeping in through the kitchen window, she knew it was nearing sunup, though as far as she could tell the rest of the household had yet to wake. She was grateful for that.

She could only imagine the thrashing Martha would inflict if she knew Immanuelle had been in the forest again.

Immanuelle pushed the thought from her mind, tasting bile at the back of her throat. Dull pain split through her belly again and she winced. Squinting, she peered down between her legs to see that there was a small, cold puddle of blood beneath her. She was flowing freely, the red wet seeping through her underskirts and staining the floorboards.

Her first bleed.

IMMANUELLE SCRAMBLED TO clean the kitchen, sopping up the blood with an old dish towel, wiping the mud away. When the floor was scrubbed clean, she crept upstairs to the washroom, snatched a fistful of rags from the basket by the sink, and struggled to fit them into her bloomers, feeling less like a woman and more like a toddler trying to change its own soiling cloths. Her bleed should have been a moment of celebration, relief—against all odds, she was a woman at last—but all she felt was small and wounded and a little sick.

Immanuelle shared the news with Anna first, then Martha after her. There was a flurry of excitement, someone sat her down in a dining room chair, provided her with a steaming cup of raspberry-leaf tea and a plate of eggs and fry cake, which she felt far too ill to eat. But despite Anna's insistence that she remain in bed, by sunup Immanuelle was on her way to the pastures, crook in hand. Herding the flock was a difficult task. She was slow and tired from her night in the woods, and her belly ached with the pains of bleeding. The flock seemed to sense her disquiet. The rams were restless, the ewes skittish. The lambs bleated at every passing breeze as if they feared the wind would snatch the meat off their bones. It took everything Immanuelle had to herd them to the western pastures, and when the deed was finally done, she collapsed into the high grass, spent, her stomach aching.

Just beyond the pasture's edge, the Darkwood loomed, the forest's shadow clawing across the plains as the sun shifted. A few vultures circled the pines, riding the wind, but there was no sign of the witches. No women of the wood. No writhing Lovers. Delilah didn't lurk among the trees and she saw no sign of Lilith.

The woods were silent.

As the light of the rising sun shifted through the trees, Immanuelle's thoughts went to the final entry in Miriam's journal: *Blood. Blight. Darkness. Slaughter. Father help them.*

What had Miriam seen in the woods that inspired those writings? What did she know that Immanuelle didn't? And perhaps most importantly, what was the carnal urge that compelled Immanuelle to return to the forest again and again despite the danger?

Why did the Darkwood call to her?

Immanuelle might have sat there all day, staring at the trees and struggling with the truth, if she hadn't been distracted by the sound of someone calling her name.

She turned, squinting against the light of the rising sun, and saw Ezra coming toward her, a package in his hand. "Good morning," he said.

With a pang, Immanuelle remembered seeing him the previous night, on the edge of the woods, wrapped in Judith's embrace.

Immanuelle shifted her gaze back to her sheep. In the distance, their farmhand, Josiah, herded the flock away from the Darkwood. "May the Father will it so."

Ezra stopped just short of her, but the breeze carried the scent of him—fresh-cut hay and cedar. A beat of silence. He slipped his hands into his pockets. "I'm here to apologize."

Immanuelle faltered, unsure of what to say. Officials of the

Church rarely offered apologies, on account of the fact that they rarely sinned. "Apologize for what?"

Ezra sat down in the grass beside her, so close their shoulders almost touched. He watched the pasture in silence, then turned to her. "For what you saw last night, after the feast. I didn't behave in a way that was worthy of my name. It was low of me, and it was also selfish to make you privy to my sins."

His sins weren't her concern. Immanuelle's gaze moved to the tree line. She hugged her knees to her chest and stayed silent. Without waiting for her reply, Ezra pushed the package he had been carrying into her hands.

Immanuelle was of a mind to refuse his gift, until she felt the weight and shape of it. It was a book.

"It's the one you were reading in the market," he said as she ripped the paper away. A little color came to his cheeks and he almost looked embarrassed, though she knew that wasn't possible. There was no way someone like her could provoke that reaction from the likes of him. "The same exact, nearly."

Immanuelle flipped to the middle of the book until she found the poem she had read that day. He was right, it was the same, though the binding on the outside was different, and most every page was marked with the seal of the Church. He must have searched the Prophet's own private library for it, she realized with a start. It would have been a kind gesture, if not for the fact that it was a bribe.

"I don't need a book to keep quiet." She snapped the book closed and held it out to him. "Your business is yours. I won't tell anyone. You needn't worry."

"I'm not worried. I . . . just feel guilty for asking you to keep my secrets."

"Then don't ask," said Immanuelle, still holding the book out to him. "It's no trouble."

"But it is a sin." Ezra was right about that much. It was a sin, and a grave one at that. The same crime that put her father, Daniel, on the pyre. But in light of what she'd seen in the woods the night before, it seemed almost trite.

"Sins can be forgiven," she said, echoing Leah's words from a few Sabbaths prior.

"Aye," said Ezra. "But guilt's a hard thing to ease."

"And that's why you want me to have the book? To ease your guilt?"

"If it's not too much to ask." Ezra shrugged. "Besides, I'd rather like to have someone to chat with."

"About poetry?"

He nodded. "There's more of it in the library. I can check the shelves, bring you more books."

"No," said Immanuelle. "This will do, thank you. Even if you are trying to buy my silence."

She cringed, anxious that yet again she'd gone too far and said too much, but Ezra only smiled.

For the first time, she noticed he had a light dusting of freckles across his nose, which was slightly crooked, as if he'd taken a bad punch in a schoolyard fight. And perhaps he had. Rumors about Ezra spread about as quickly as the rumors about her. He was known to be wickedly smart, always reading or studying, the kind of person who knew how to ask the right questions. He was also strong, with his father's stubborn will, and like him, Ezra had the respect of most men in Bethel, and if not that, then fear—fear of the Prophet's power that burned in him like holy fire, though he hadn't even witnessed his First Vision yet.

"What happened to your lip?" Ezra's question pulled her from her thoughts, and she realized he was watching her. She raised a hand to touch the spot where Judas had struck her. Though her split lip had long since scabbed over, the edge of her mouth was still bruised and swollen. "I lost a fight with an angry ram."

"The one you had at the market?"

"Yes." She thought of Judas' bleeding head, left on the stump like a present, then blurted out, "He's dead."

"A sacrifice?" His gaze shifted back to the pasture.

She started to shake her head but stopped herself. "Maybe."

Ezra pressed to his feet and stretched, rolling his shoulders. "Tell me how you like that book. There's more where that came from. There's a library in the Haven; I can get you what you want."

Immanuelle opened her mouth to reply, to tell him that a girl like her had no business with the Prophet's books no matter how much she wanted to read them, when a scream broke across the pastures. She recognized the voice: Glory.

There was a moment's pause; then a second scream rang out.

Immanuelle was on her feet in an instant. Ezra angled himself in front of her as she moved, as if he meant to shield her from whatever harm was coming their way. But Immanuelle had no time to humor his chivalry. She pushed past him, sprinting toward the echo of Glory's cries. And as she ran, all she could think of were the women of the woods—the dead-eyed witches.

She found Glory by the well at the end of the pastures, a few yards from the forest's edge, a bucket capsized at her feet.

"Are you hurt?" Immanuelle asked, slowing to a stop.

Glory shook her head, mouth open, blond curls sticking to her lips. Her gaze flickered to Ezra, as if she was as shocked to see him as she was by whatever had startled her. But the moment passed, and she snapped to her senses. Words seemed to catch in her throat as she pointed to the bucket with a shaking finger.

Ezra stooped to pick it up. It was then Immanuelle caught the scent of rot on the air, wet and fetid. Something black seeped into the soil, slicking the walls of the bucket.

Immanuelle swallowed dry, her stomach roiling, as Ezra put the bucket on its hook and lowered it into the depths of the well again. He twisted the crank, and the bucket descended, disappearing into the deep. When the sound of the bucket's rim breaking water echoed up the shaft, he began to crank the lever again, working fast, his shoulders straining with the effort.

Slowly, the bucket climbed above the stones of the well's wall. Ezra took it off its hook and Glory staggered back, as though he'd reeled a viper from the water.

He lowered the bucket to the ground, and to Immanuelle's horror, she saw it was filled to the brim with a thick, dark liquid that sloshed over the rim and blackened the soil below. Immanuelle dropped to her knees beside it and dipped her fingers into the bucket. When she removed her hand her fingertips were slick red.

"Blood," she whispered, and with those words, a kind of dreadful déjà vu settled over her, so powerful it seemed to tear her soul from her body. It took her a moment to come back to herself. "Where is Martha?"

"She left for the Holy Grounds with Mother for a birthing," said Glory, stumbling over the words. "Apostle Isaac's sixth wife went into—"

"What of Abram? Where is he?"

"I-in his workshop."

"Fetch him," she said, and when the girl didn't move, she gave her a little shove in the right direction. *"Now!"*

Ezra stepped forward then, frowning down at her. "Are you all right?"

Immanuelle nodded, tried to answer him, but trailed off into silence as she stared down at her bloodstained hand. She felt that pull again, the phantom force that had dragged her from her body mere moments before—not at all unlike the lure of the woods. "I'm . . ."

Blood. Blight. Darkness. Slaughter. Blood. Blight. Darkness. Slaughter. Blood.

Blood.

"Immanuelle—"

"Thank you for the book." With that, Immanuelle turned and broke toward the farmhouse, cutting through the pastures in a full run. It was empty, as Glory had said it would be, and Immanuelle rushed through the parlor and bounded upstairs to her bedroom. At the foot of her bed, she dropped to her knees, slipped a hand beneath her mattress, and withdrew the journal. She opened it there on the floor, smearing the pages with blood as she tore past them to the final entry: *Blood. Blight. Darkness. Slaughter. Blood. Blight. Darkness. Slaughter. Blood. Blight. Darkness. Slaughter. Blood. Blight. Darkness. Slaughter. Blood—*

Blood.

Of course.

Shock turned to dread, and dread turned to horror as Immanuelle read the words, realizing their significance for the first time. The journal. The list. The drawings of the forest and their witches. Miriam's words weren't the ramblings of a madwoman. They were warnings of what was yet to come.

Four warnings. Four witches. Four plagues, and the first had come upon them.

"Immanuelle, what the—" Ezra stepped into her bedroom, dropped to a crouch at her side. His gaze went from her to the journal lying open in her lap. "What's that?"

Immanuelle snapped the journal shut, tossed it back into her hope chest, and closed it. She turned to offer Ezra some passing excuse, but the sound of church bells cut her short. Twelve tolls in quick succession, a pause, and then more bells ringing across Bethel as others took up the alarm call. And so, the first of the plagues began.

Chapter Ten

Love is an act of loyalty.
—The Holy Scriptures

Immanuelle sat on the mule cart alongside Martha, staring out across the dying plains as they rolled down the main road toward the Holy Grounds. The air was thick with the stench of gore, and the drone of blood-fat mosquitoes was so loud it almost drowned the sound of the cart's wheels rattling.

In the ancient times—when the daughters of the Dark Mother had waged war against the Father's flock—there had been battles on the plains. Immanuelle recalled the stories her teachers told at school, tales of wounded men and blood-soaked battlefields that stretched as far as the eye could see.

Immanuelle thought of those stories as they rode toward the cathedral, crossing through the dying farmsteads of the Glades and past miles of gore-blackened cornfields. In the weeks since the blood plague had struck, the tainted waters had seeped into the soil, infecting the earth and killing the crops.

The whole world had gone red and rotten.

Immanuelle's throat ached. She hadn't had a sip to drink since sunup. The Moore household rationed water now—everyone did—but still, there wasn't enough to go around. Clean water could not be found anywhere within Bethel's borders, and rumor had it that the Church's stores were all but depleted.

To Immanuelle's surprise, Martha tugged at the reins, steering the mule toward the Outskirts, a sprawling shanty village that cowered in the shadow of the southern wood. Most Bethelans avoided the Outskirts, for fear of the sinners who dwelled there in shame and squalor.

"Blood flooding in the Holy Grounds," said Martha, to explain why she'd decided to take the long way to the cathedral. "The roads there are impassable."

The cart pulled past a series of shacks so bowed and decrepit they looked as if they were one good gust away from collapsing into a heap of sticks. As they drew toward the center of the village, Immanuelle spotted the small, dilapidated church where those in the Outskirts gathered to worship on the Sabbath when the rest of Bethel assembled at the cathedral. The building had a short, crooked steeple and a single stained-glass window that depicted a woman in a black veil, who Immanuelle assumed was a saint or angel, though she wore no diadem. It wasn't until the cart drew nearer that she recognized the woman for who she was: the Dark Mother.

In the frescoes painted across the cathedral's vaulted ceilings, the Goddess was always depicted as a wretch, all twisted limbs and clawed fingers, lips smeared with the blood of crusaders she'd devoured in battle. But in this portrait, the Dark Mother looked beautiful, even gentle. Her skin was a deep shade of ebony, almost as dark as Her veil, but Her eyes were moon pale and wide. She didn't look like the damned Goddess of witches and hells. No, in this depiction, She appeared more mortal than monster . . . and somehow, that was worse.

The cart rattled on. A few shirtless boys ran barefoot through the muck of the streets. As Martha and Immanuelle approached, they stopped their games and froze, owl-eyed and silent as the mule cart rumbled past.

Lurking in the distance was the shadow of the western Darkwood. The deeper they ventured into the village, the closer the Darkwood crept. While the forests of the Glades in the east were lush and thick, they were nothing in comparison to the wilds that bordered the Outskirts. Somehow, the woods of the west seemed more alive. The treetops crawled with life—fox squirrels as big as cats ran the branches of the trees, and crows roosted in the canopy of oaks and dogwoods, sunning their wings and cawing their evening songs. Overhead, a white-bellied hawk circled the sprawling woodland and a powerful wind stirred through the trees, carrying the scent of loam and slaughter.

Running the length of the wood were tributes and sacrifices—a bushel of corn tucked into a nook between tree roots, a sheepskin slung over the low bough of an oak, a basket of eggs atop a tree stump, wreaths of what appeared to be dried rosemary, dead chickens and rabbits strung by the legs and hanging from the branches of pine trees.

Immanuelle craned out of her seat to get a better view of the strange assortment. "What is that?"

Martha kept her eyes on the road. "They're offerings."

The wagon rumbled past what appeared to be a kind of altar—an intricate thatch-work of twigs and branches upon which a goat lay gutted. "Offerings to who?"

"The woods," said Martha, and she seemed to spit the words. "In these parts, they worship them. The Prophet ought to cast them to the wilds for such a sin. If they love the woods so much, let them return to it."

"Why doesn't he?"

"It's an act of mercy, I assume. But I don't presume the ways of the Prophet and neither should you." She cast Immanuelle a firm glance before returning her gaze to the road. "Besides, those in the Outskirts have their station—as we do ours. Even the sinner has a place in this world. And even the heretic can exalt the Father in his or her own way."

As they crossed into the heart of the shanty village, a young woman with mahogany skin emerged from the ruins of a crumbling cottage and wandered into the middle of the road. Her feet were bare and bruised, and there was a squalling infant bound to her chest with a sling. She threw her arms out as they approached, her parched lips parted, eyes wild. "Water for the baby, please. Spare us a drop to drink."

Martha muttered a prayer and flicked the reins. The wheels of the cart broke through a puddle, splashing the woman with blood. She staggered back, clutching her child, and stumbled on the hem of her dress as she retreated.

Immanuelle turned to say something, but Martha caught her by the wrist. "Leave her to her sins."

But Immanuelle couldn't pull her eyes from the woman. She watched her, crouched and weeping on the side of the road, until she shrank to no more than a mote on the horizon, and then disappeared.

They journeyed on. As they turned south toward the Holy Grounds, the drone of flies and mosquitoes grew louder. The shanty village gave way to open plains and blood-flooded meadows that were drowned by the overflow of contaminated groundwater. In the distance, the sprawling estates that belonged to the apostles of the Church, cornfields and cattle ranges so large they stretched well past the western horizon. They were filled with the rotting, fly-swarmed corpses of cows, horses, and other animals that had died of thirst in the early days of the plague.

"Miriam used to ride these hills," said Martha, her hands still tight around the reins. She smiled faintly, and Immanuelle caught a glimpse of the woman she might have been before her daughter's death. Someone kind, warm even. "Abram bought her a pony the summer of her thirteenth birthday. She rode it most every day, up and down these paths—going fast as the devils themselves—until one day she ran it too hard. That mare tripped over a stray stone in the road and snapped its leg at the knee. I watched it happen. She fell right there." Martha pointed to a copse of dead apple trees along the shoulder of the road.

"What happened to the horse?" Immanuelle asked, and when she spoke her chapped lips split open. She tried to wet them, but her tongue was dry.

"Miriam put it down," said Martha, in this flat dead tone, as if she was merely remarking on the weather. "Abram was going to do it, but she wouldn't let him. She fired the rifle herself, shot that pony clean through the eye."

Immanuelle processed this in silence, a chill carving down her spine. The cart shuddered down the road to the cathedral, the shadows pressing in as the sun set. It was just her and Martha that evening. Anna had stayed home to tend to the rest of the family.

"Go in peace," she'd told them as they left, and Immanuelle could tell she was worried. Anyone with the sense the Father gave them was. The earth beneath their feet was bleeding, and despite their best prayers and efforts, they couldn't make it stop. It was just as Miriam had prophesied in her journal.

If the Prophet and apostles knew the cause of the blood plague or a way to stop it, they had not shared their findings with the flock. They simply urged the people to pray and fast, in the hope of winning the Father's favor. Until then, they were told to ration their resources—harvest fruits and vegetables for juicing, collect rainwater and what little they could from dewfall every night and morning. But these meager efforts weren't enough. Immanuelle had already lost six of her sheep to thirst or poisoning.

But despite these dire straits, there was some hope. Days after the blood plague, rainstorms swept through Bethel. And, owing to coordinated efforts by the farmers and Church, a fair amount of water was collected. In addition to that, the ice reserves in the catacombs of the Prophet's Haven proved useful, as did its extensive wine cellars. There was even talk of importing fresh water from settlements beyond the Hallowed Gate. Still, despite these provisions, resources were dwindling rapidly, and with no rain for several days, the panic was beginning to mount again. Cattle and livestock were dying by the day, and more losses, *human* losses, were expected to follow if the blood plague didn't end soon.

After a long, meandering ride, they approached the cathedral to find it full. It was a weekday, but the farmers had left their fields early and all of the apostles had assembled.

Immanuelle hopped out of the cart. The crowds shifted, the yard full of men and boys dressed in sweaty shirts and bloodstained slacks, their clothes reeking of the fields.

In the distance, Immanuelle saw the stream where she and Leah used to meet after church, reduced now to little more than a bleeding gash carved into the hills. The jutting river rocks were smeared with gore. The whole ravine looked like the scene of a slaughter, and Immanuelle caught the stench of rot from where she stood.

"This way." Martha urged her on. Together, they ducked through the gathering crowds, dodging carts and carriages. In comparison to their Sabbath fellowships, this was a solemn affair. Everyone seemed to be speaking in low murmurs as if they feared they'd provoke the Father Himself if they talked any louder.

Martha and Immanuelle made their way up the steps and into

the cathedral. Indoors, the air was thick with the tang of blood and sweat. People crammed the pews and spilled into the adjacent aisles. Up front, standing in a row behind the altar, were the apostles and other high-ranking saints of the Church, but Ezra wasn't among them. He was on the cathedral floor, walking from pew to pew with a bucket of milk and an iron ladle. He stooped in front of an old man and put the ladle to his lips. A few moments later, when a little girl wandered to his side, he lowered his bucket to the floor, dropped to one knee, and whispered something that made her laugh. After she drank her fill, he dried her mouth with his shirtsleeve, picked up his bucket, and walked on.

When he crossed into the center aisle, his eyes met Immanuelle's. He faltered for a moment, as if embarrassed to be caught in the midst of his ministry. But then he recovered and started toward her, crossing through the crowds to her side.

He raised the ladle to her lips. "Here," he said, his voice ragged. He sounded as if he could use a drink himself.

Immanuelle leaned forward, the cold rim of the ladle pressed against her bottom lip. She took a small swallow. Then another. The milk was warm and sweet. As she drank, it soothed her chapped lips and eased the burning in her throat. She drained the ladle dry, and Ezra was dipping it into the bucket again to offer her a second drink, when Martha called her name.

The woman's hand closed around Immanuelle's shoulder in a tight grip. Her eyes flickered from Immanuelle to Ezra, then back to Immanuelle again. "Come now, we ought to find a place to sit before we're made to stand."

"She's welcome to sit with us," said Ezra, and he nodded to a pew a few feet away, crowded with his friends and half siblings. His invitation seemed to pique their interest. As the rising heir, Ezra was a prize among Bethel's young bachelors and was known to court girls when it suited him. But if their shocked expressions were any indication, Immanuelle was quite certain his friends had never seen him entertain a girl who looked like her.

Martha seemed aware of this too, and Immanuelle could tell that she scorned the attention. "Immanuelle will remain where she belongs, with me."

"Very well," said Ezra, perhaps realizing that his will was no match for Martha's. Gingerly, he took the ladle from Immanuelle's hand and returned to his friends. In turn, she started after Martha, acutely aware of the gazes that followed her as she went.

Shortly after they were seated, the First Apostle, Isaac, stepped up to the altar. He was a tall man, pale and hawkish, with a dour mouth and a hard chin. Immanuelle imagined he might have been quite handsome in his day, and she knew he had the wives to prove it. His voice bore the rich timbre of a well-tuned organ, and it reverberated through the cathedral as he spoke. "We gather today to address a grave sickness. I'm here on behalf of the Prophet, who has—in the wake of this great evil—retired to his sanctuary, for a period of prayer and supplication."

This declaration was met with a chorus of murmurs. In the past year alone, the Prophet had spent weeks locked in the Haven, engaged in fasting and meditation. But there were growing concerns that his abrupt sabbaticals were actually due to his failing health.

"Our lands have been tainted," said the apostle, pacing at the foot of the altar. "A great evil moves through our waters. Our rivers run with it. I know that you fear for your families, crops, and land. You're right to do so. This plague is not the work of nature, as we know it. It's more than happenstance. Someone among us, maybe even someone sitting in the pews tonight, brought this curse upon us."

Gasps echoed through the cathedral, and the whispers began, a great hissing like the sound of cicadas in the summertime.

Apostle Isaac raised his voice to a near yell. "The Prophet is certain that someone convened with the forces of the dark to wake this once-dormant evil."

Immanuelle's breath hitched. She thought of Delilah wading through the shallows of the pond, of the Lovers writhing in the dirt of the meadow, the glimpse of Lilith's bare feet as she emerged from the shadows of the Darkwood. Was it possible those brief exchanges were the start of something far greater and more horrible than she'd realized at the time? Was it possible that *she* had some part in this?

"Tell me, how was this evil conjured?" A voice echoed from the back of the cathedral, thin and warbling. An old woman stepped forward, and Immanuelle instantly recognized her. It was Hagar, the first wife of the previous prophet, and one of the last still living. Leaning heavily on her cane, Hagar limped into the aisle and glared up at Isaac. "You say this sinner must have convened with forces in the Darkwood, but it must've been more than that. Many fools have walked the wood and borne witness to its horrors without spawning plagues like this one. We haven't seen power like this since the days of David Ford. Why would such a grave evil awaken now, of all times?"

"The Prophet believes there was some sort of . . . *incentive* made," said Apostle Isaac haltingly. "The Father is not the only one who receives blood offerings. If someone among us performed a ritual, made a blood sacrifice to the Mother, it may have been enough to awaken this evil."

Immanuelle's breath slackened a bit at that. She may have sinned when she entered the Darkwood, witnessed things she shouldn't have, but she hadn't stooped so low as to make an offer-

ing to the Mother. The plague must have been the work of someone else.

Still, it seemed like Apostle Isaac spoke only to Immanuelle
when he said, "If any among you has offered yourself to the Dark,
I ask that you confess your sins now—that you might spare your
soul from the fires of the pyre and the holy flames of purging."

CHAPTER ELEVEN

For it is in the fires of purging that the souls of men find faith.

—THE HOLY SCRIPTURES

THERE WAS FIRE on every tongue when the meeting adjourned. Burning was the traditional punishment for witchcraft or heresy in Bethel, but it had been years since the last purging. Some spoke of it like a blessing, others a thrill, recalling the great pyres that had burned atop the hills in purgings of the past. While it seemed everyone was badly shaken by Apostle Isaac's proclamation that a curse had been cast deliberately, Immanuelle couldn't tell what frightened them more: the blood plague or the threat of the holy flames.

"Immanuelle." She turned at the sound of her name to find that Leah had escaped the clutches of the Prophet's other brides.

It was the first Immanuelle had seen of her friend since the night of her cutting. The seal between her brows was healing well, though the bruise-dark bags beneath her eyes had deepened, if only slightly.

"You look well." Immanuelle allowed herself this small fib as they embraced. "Are the others kind to you?"

"They treat me as they will," Leah said, then glanced over her shoulder. A few yards off, the Prophet's other wives clustered together, their mouths pressed into thin lines as they studied the crowd. She took Immanuelle by the elbow and guided her a few paces away, where listening ears wouldn't hear them. "Most of them aren't cruel, but they're not kind either. Esther—Ezra's mother—is the only one who's truly good to me."

"And what of your husband? Is he good to you?"

Leah blushed, but her eyes didn't warm. "He summons me often."

He beds her often. Immanuelle cringed at the thought. "And . . . does that please you?"

Leah stared down at her hands, and Immanuelle saw that they were shaking, ever so slightly. She grasped her fingers in an attempt to still them, squeezing so hard they went bloodless. "It pleases me to do the Father's will."

"I'm not asking about the Father's will. I'm asking about yours." She angled a little closer to her friend, lowered her voice. "Does he please you? Are you happy?"

"What pleases me is being here with you."

"Leah—"

"Don't," she said, a firm rebuke. "Please, Immanuelle. Can we just talk of something, anything, else? It's been weeks since I last saw you. How have you fared?"

"Well enough," said Immanuelle, reluctant to change the subject but knowing she didn't have a choice. "The flock is doing well, considering, though I've lost a few lambs and one of my best breeding ewes to the plague—"

"But what of *you*, Immanuelle? How are you?"

"I . . . well. I bled." Something locked into place when Immanuelle said those words.

She *bled*.

Somehow she'd almost forgotten. That night in the Darkwood, as Lilith stood over her and Delilah moved through the shadows of the deep, her first blood began. Her flow was steady by the time she woke the following morning, on the floor of the kitchen, but she'd first begun bleeding that night in the pond with the witches.

Immanuelle's hands began to shake. Her heartbeat quickened to a fast and brutal rhythm.

What if her monthly bleed was the blood sacrifice Apostle Isaac spoke of? What if she had spawned all this evil? Was it possible that she'd been some unknowing accomplice in Lilith's plot? The very idea made her want to vomit, but she couldn't deny the growing suspicion that whatever had occurred in the Darkwood that night was far greater than a chance encounter.

A horrible thought occurred to her then, the answer to a question she'd been asking herself ever since she first entered the forest. What if the journal was bait? All those weeks ago, when the witches first gave her the gift of her mother's words, she'd assumed their motive had been some sort of kinship or affinity toward Miriam. But what if that wasn't it? What if the real reason they gave her the journal was to ensure that she'd come back to bleed there? What if the journal was just a lure, a tie to the woods?

Immanuelle's legs went weak with dread as the full truth dawned on her. That night in the Darkwood, she'd been baited and manipulated into making the blood sacrifice the witches needed to spawn the plague. She'd set something in motion. Opened a door that she didn't know how to close, and now all of Bethel was suffering for her sin and naivete.

She had done this.

Leah reached for her hand. "Immanuelle? What's wrong?"

Immanuelle didn't answer. Her thoughts were reeling so quickly it was impossible to form words. If she were a better person, she would have confessed to everything then and there. She would have gone to Apostle Isaac, told him what she knew about the plague—how it started, where, and the fact that she suspected there were more to come. She would have turned in her mother's journal. But Immanuelle knew that if she did that, there was a strong chance she'd be sent to the pyre on charges of witchcraft. To inform the Church was to damn herself—she was certain of it. And the thought of rendering Miriam's journal to the Church was unbearable. It might have been used to bait her, but it was still a piece of her mother, and more than that, it was the locus of her knowledge about the witches and the woods they roamed. Perhaps it could still be of some use to her.

Something dawned on her then, a dangerous idea . . . What if there was another way? A way to stop the blood plague without involving the Church, without incriminating herself. What if she could end the plague the same way she started it: with her blood?

It wasn't such a strange idea. It stood to reason that if a sacrifice unleashed all this evil upon Bethel, another sacrifice could draw it back. Perhaps if she returned to the forest, she could undo what was done. After all, it was her blood that spawned this plague; maybe her blood could end it too.

But if she entered the woods again—no, *when* she entered the woods again, she would need to be prepared. This was no time for instincts and deductions; she needed facts. She knew that breaking the plague couldn't be as simple as going to the Darkwood and bleeding. There had to be something more, some ritual to how an offering was made. But there was no way for her to access that information on her own. Immanuelle was going to need an accomplice—someone with the keys to the Prophet's library—and she knew exactly whom to turn to.

"I need to speak with Ezra," said Immanuelle, craning to peer through the thinning crowds. "Do you know where he is?"

Leah frowned, clearly confused. "Why do you need to speak to him?"

"He owes me a favor," she said, thinking back to their conversation in the pasture. Ezra had told her that the Prophet's library was an extensive collection. If there was any information on the practices of witches and how they cast and broke their plagues, it would have to be there.

"Perhaps we should just go outside," said Leah, in the gentle way you'd talk down a spooked horse. "Take some air. You look like you're about to faint."

Immanuelle spotted Ezra then, standing at the foot of the altar where Apostle Isaac had delivered his speech just a few minutes before. He was chatting with a group of friends, but to Immanuelle's surprise it wasn't a challenge to catch his eye. When she gestured toward a dark corridor on the eastern wing of the cathedral, he was quick to dismiss himself, shouldering through his friends with barely a parting word.

"Wait—" said Leah, almost frantic in her concern.

Immanuelle waved her off. "I'll only be a moment."

And with that, she started after Ezra, wading through the crowd until she reached the empty pew where he stood waiting.

"I thought your grandmother was going to slit my throat. Is she always that intimidating or . . . ?" He faltered, reading her expression. "What's wrong? I didn't get you into any trouble, did I?"

"Not at all. I just need a moment of your time, if you have it to spare."

Ezra's eyes narrowed but he nodded and led her to a small apse off the main cathedral. Here, there were two prayer benches standing side by side before a stone effigy of the Holy Father. On a low altar were dozens of candles, most of them lit and flickering. In a ceramic platter, incense burned and the fragrant smoke hung on the air like threads of spider silk.

Ezra and Immanuelle knelt on the bench, shoulder to shoulder, and lit candles, as was custom, one for each of them. Immanuelle clasped her hands and bowed her head. "The last time we talked, you mentioned the Prophet's library. You said there were all sorts of books there. Even books of knowledge, like the one you showed me in the market that day."

He nodded. "If there's a book you want, give me the title and I'll fetch it for you."

"That's just it, I don't know exactly what I'm looking for. I'd have to be there, in the flesh, sort through the books myself in order to find what I want, what I need."

"And what is that, exactly?"

"A way to stop the blood plague."

Ezra blinked at her, and with no small measure of satisfaction, she realized she'd caught him off guard. His expression went from contemplative to troubled. "Shouldn't you leave the business of breaking plagues to the Church?"

"Why should I when the men of the Church are clearly no more informed than I am?" Of course it wasn't just that; she'd hidden the truth about her own role in the blood plague, and the way the witches had used her to spawn it. But she couldn't trust Ezra with such things. He might be a rebel in his own way, skeptical of the very Church he served, but he was still the Prophet's heir. "I want to help, and I don't see why I shouldn't be able to."

Ezra watched the candles in silence for a long time, rubbing the back of his neck. "It's forbidden for women to walk the halls of the library."

"I know. I wouldn't ask if it wasn't important, but—"

"I've made you stomach my sin, so now you want me to shoulder yours?"

Immanuelle hadn't wanted it to come to that, but she nodded. "I'd have something on you, and you'd have something on me. We'd be even. A secret for a secret."

Ezra considered this for a moment. Then: "When do you need access?"

"Tomorrow afternoon, preferably, while our farmhand can tend to the flock." When she'd have the time to slip away unnoticed.

He pushed to his feet. "Tomorrow, then. I'll meet you by the gates of the Haven at noon."

CHAPTER TWELVE

We are the consecrated, the Father's chosen. And what be-
longs to Him is His, forevermore.

—THE HOLY SCRIPTURES

THE PROPHET'S HAVEN was the oldest building in all of Bethel, built in the Dark Days before their faith had scriptures or a proper doctrine. It stood on a lone hill that overlooked a stretch of rolling cattle fields. It was a tall, looming structure, comprised of the main quarters—a collapsing stone cathedral where the first of the faith had once worshipped—and a series of expansions, some of them constructed as recently as a month prior.

The entire estate was ringed by a wrought iron wall that stood some nine feet tall. It was said that during the Holy War, the severed heads of the four witches and their allies had been mounted upon its spikes. According to those same legends, Lilith's headless corpse had also been strung from the wall's gate and, on the orders of David Ford, crowned with a deer skull diadem to make a mockery of her reign and slaughter. Walking toward the gate, Immanuelle could almost picture it: the severed heads of the sinners gawking down at her, their jaws nailed shut by the wall's iron spires; beside them, the witch queen's skull-crowned corpse strung from the archway, swaying with the wind. Immanuelle shook her head to clear it of the ghastly image and continued on through the entryway.

She found Ezra waiting for her just behind the Haven's entrance. He sat beneath the branches of a tall cottonwood, back pressed to its trunk and legs crossed at the ankles, reading a palm-size book.

There were a great many people wandering the yard—mainly servants and the farmhands who tended the Prophet's sprawling ranges—but Ezra still raised his head at her approach, as if he knew her from the sound of her footsteps. He slipped his book into the back pocket of his trousers as he stood, nodding toward the doors of the Haven. "Right this way."

IF THE PROPHET'S Haven appeared grand on the outside, its interior was nothing short of immaculate. The entry hall was almost as big as the cathedral itself, with ceilings arching high overhead. Each of the hall's windows was ten feet tall, and every casing was fitted with panes of stained glass so the sunlight shafting through them tinted the walls and floor with the colors of the rainbow. The air smelled of spices, a good, heady stink that brought to mind harvest feasts and meat roasting on bonfires in the wintertime.

Ezra led her down a series of long corridors, their footsteps echoing as they went. He distanced himself by a few paces whenever others passed them, but when they were alone, he took the time to point out little details about the house. Among these were the paintings that hung from the walls (mostly portraits of the first prophets who'd reigned in the days after the Holy War), and the corridors that led to places like the Haven's kitchen or the confinement wards, where new brides were housed.

Immanuelle wondered, in passing, which hall led to the room where her mother had stabbed the Prophet, but she didn't dare ask.

They rounded another corner, entering into a small, bright hallway. Here, a series of thin windows lined the walls, each less than a half a pace apart from the next. Opposite the windows was a row of doors, each with a name painted on the cross rails in golden ink: *Hannah, Charlotte, Sarah, Charity, Naomi, Esther, Judith, Bethany, Justice, Dinah, Ruth, Tilda.* These were the wives' chambers. Immanuelle read each name in turn, looking for Leah's.

"Ezra, is that you?" A voice seeped out from an open door down the corridor. It was thin and graced by a faint accent Immanuelle had never heard on the tongue of any Bethelan native.

Ezra stopped short, breathing a low curse. Then he composed himself and strode to the doorway. "Yes, Mother?"

Immanuelle slowed to a stop at his heels, gazed into the room just behind her. There, standing at its center, was Ezra's mother, Esther Chambers. Immanuelle had only ever caught passing glimpses of her—from across the cathedral or on the other side of the churchyard—but those brief encounters were enough to distinguish her as one of the most beautiful women she had ever seen. Esther was tall like Ezra, if a little slight. Pale veins threaded along her neck and skimmed up to her temples. Her hair, which was the raven-black color of her son's, was heaped atop her head and held by a single golden pin. As she neared, Immanuelle caught a whiff of jasmine on the air.

The woman surveyed her, and a thin smile crossed her lips and disappeared within the span of an instant. "Who is your friend, my son?" she asked, her gaze returning to Ezra.

"This is Miss Immanuelle Moore." He sidestepped to give his mother a better view of her. "Miss Moore, may I present my mother, Esther Chambers."

"Ah," said the woman, and that smile crossed her mouth again, a subtle twin to Ezra's. "Miriam's daughter."

"Yes, ma'am," Immanuelle murmured, staring at her boots.

The woman who stood before her now was widely known to be the Prophet's favorite wife.

"Please, call me Esther." She slid her cold hand into Immanuelle's. "It's a pleasure to make your acquaintance."

Immanuelle managed a nod and a smile. She expected the woman to slip her hand away as Protocol would dictate, but she didn't. She held on to Immanuelle's fingers, her verdant green eyes skimming over her in cold appraisal. "And what brings you to the Haven?"

Ezra stepped in. "She's here to see Leah."

"I believe Leah's in the west wing," said Esther, speaking softly now. Up close, Immanuelle noticed something she'd missed before. At the edge of Esther's mouth was a bruise made faint by what appeared to be an application of pale face powder. "She's at the Prophet's side. He's been . . . rather troubled today. It would probably be best to call on her at a later date."

Ezra went quiet for a beat too long as he searched his mother's face. "I'll have a word with him."

"You will do no such thing," said Esther with sudden sharpness, but she recovered herself before she spoke again, forcing that gentle smile. "Don't forget you have a guest. It would be rude of you to abandon her. Please, be on your way and may the Father bless your steps."

Ezra fell quiet after his mother retired to her parlor, closing and locking the door behind her. He walked away in silence, hands in his pockets, gaze on his boots, lost to a kind of brooding that Immanuelle didn't know how to breach, though she felt she should.

She didn't fully understand what had occurred with Esther in the hall—but she suspected it had something to do with the Prophet and the bruise at the corner of Esther's mouth. The thought of Leah being with the Prophet in the midst of his dark mood turned Immanuelle's stomach. Prophets were merely men and men were fallible creatures, prone to the passions of the flesh, tempted to violence, even, when their anger spilled over.

After all, a prophet was nothing more than a vessel of the Father, and the Father was not always the benevolent god of light. He was also wrath and fire, brimstone and storm, and He often used His almighty power to smite the witch and the heathen alike. Immanuelle could only imagine how dangerous a man might become when filled with a holy wrath like that.

After a short walk through a series of dim, lamplit halls, they came upon a wide gallery. At its end was a pair of black double doors almost twice as tall as Immanuelle. This had to be part of the Haven's original structure, she realized, where the first of the faith had worshipped.

Ezra slipped a key from his back pocket and fit it into the door's lock. There was a soft click as the bolt slipped out of place. Both doors swung open and they entered the library within.

Immanuelle had never seen so many books in one place at one time, and she was sure she never would again. This was not some one-room study tucked into the back of a schoolhouse. It was a full cathedral, but in place of the pews, there were bookshelves, rows and rows of them, from the altar to the threshold where she stood. On the right wall was a spiral staircase that twisted up to what ought to have been the organ deck, but instead of an organ, there were just a few rusted pipes with crooked shelves wedged between them. The front half of the deck was caged off by a wrought iron gate, a twin to the one that fenced the Haven itself.

"This is it," said Ezra with a wave of his hand. "The Prophet's library."

"It's huge."

"I suppose it is," said Ezra, as though he hadn't considered it that way before. And perhaps he hadn't. After all, the grandeur of

the Haven was all he had ever known. He motioned for Immanuelle to follow him through the shelves to the stairway that twisted
down from the organ deck. Gathering her skirts, Immanuelle
climbed after him, and Ezra, ever the gentleman, offered her his
hand.

"This is the restricted section," he said as they ascended. "All
texts relating to the dark craft are kept here. If you're seeking information about the plagues, this is where you'll find it."

Immanuelle risked a glance down to the ground floor, far below. The drop was so far it was almost dizzying. "I don't think
I've ever been this high up."

"One day I'll have to take you up to the cathedral's bell tower.
That view is far better than this one." Ezra scaled the last of the
stairs, stopped in front of the gate, and unlocked it with a small
rusty key he produced from his pocket. He held it open for her
and ushered her through with a pass of his hand.

Immanuelle stepped past him onto the overhang. It was larger
than she'd expected, but most of the floor space was taken up by a
series of nine tall shelves that stretched from the stairs to the far
wall. Almost all the books housed there were chained to the
shelves they sat on.

Ezra immediately began to comb through the collection. Clouds
of dust, as thick as smoke, bloomed in the air as he slid books off
the shelves, their rusty chains rattling.

"Do you often come up here to read?" Immanuelle asked, trailing after him down the aisles.

"No," said Ezra. "The last time I was up here, I was nine years
old. I didn't have my dagger then, so I scaled the gate to get in.
Broke my elbow when I landed on the other side, but I still managed to flip through a few books before I was found."

"Were they worth the pain?"

Ezra smiled ruefully and shook his head. "No, but the expression on my father's face when he realized I'd managed to success-fully break into one of the most restricted places in all of Bethel certainly was."

Immanuelle tried to hide her smile by turning to the bookcase nearest her. Many of the books shelved there were so old, Imman-uelle feared they might collapse into a pile of dust if she touched them. Some were little more than a few sheets of crumbling paper strung together with bits of twine. Others were just journals like her mother's, penned by prophets of the past.

It was these collections that Immanuelle and Ezra began to sort through, searching for references to the plagues. It was slow and at times painstaking work, but Immanuelle found she didn't mind it. At first, it was rather exhilarating, to read the words of men who'd died so long ago. But her enthusiasm waned when she realized the immensity of the task that lay before her. There were hundreds of books in the overhang alone, and thousands more below. It would take years to sort through them all.

For hours they combed through the collection, with little to show for it, and Immanuelle was close to giving up on her search when she spotted a lone book on an empty shelf in the far corner of the organ deck. Cradling the tome in her arms, Immanuelle scraped a frosting of dust away with a pass of her fingers and flipped open the cover. The title page read: *The Unholy Four: A Compendium* and was dated the *Year of the Harrow*. There was no author cited.

What followed was a history of the witches and their crimes—from the dawn of the coven's rebellion to their defeat at the hands of David Ford seven years later. At first, Immanuelle assumed the book was limited to the events of the Holy War, but as she flipped through its pages she realized it delved deep into the practice of witchcraft and the heathen power Lilith's coven wielded against the Bethelan armies. Among these accounts one practice, specifi-cally, caught Immanuelle's eye—*the feeding of the Mother.*

It described, in broad terms, a ritualistic offering that took place in a lake at the heart of the woods, known only as the Mother's Belly. While the book had many redactions—pages that were ripped out or painted with black ink to block the words—Immanuelle was able to gather the gist of the practice. The book claimed that those who made blood offerings to the Mother in this unholy place were often rewarded with dark power.

According to the account, there were rumors that Lilith and her ilk made sacrifices at the Mother's Belly in order to win power and favor. There were reports of witches who cut their wrists in the middle of the lake, let their blood flow into the water to sate the Mother's hunger. Some claimed that Lilith tossed the severed heads of crusader war captives into the water's depths. One passage described witches who squatted in the shallows with their skirts raised to their knees, allowing their monthly bleed to flow into the water. The book also noted that in the wake of the war—when Lilith and her coven were defeated—David Ford and his army of crusaders executed witches in the pond, drowning them for their sins against the Church.

The following passage noted that all these offerings were preceded by a kind of prayer or call that the Darkwood hearkened to. The witches sang an incantation that sounded like the hiss and hush of wind in the forest's trees. Others waded into the depths of the pond, whispering their most earnest wishes to the wood as they went. But it was apparent to Immanuelle that the Darkwood demanded a prayer before an offering was made, and she got the impression that it was not so much what one said but rather the act of saying it that mattered most. Bleeding wasn't enough. The Darkwood wanted the souls that came seeking its power to beg for it first.

Below these gruesome accounts was a detailed illustration of a pond in the middle of the woods. Immanuelle's hands began to shake violently, trembling across the page. It was a near-perfect rendering of the pond where she'd first encountered Lilith and Delilah. Every detail of that drawing aligned with her memory.

This was all the confirmation that Immanuelle needed. That pond, where she'd first encountered Lilith, was the Dark Mother's altar, and Immanuelle's first blood was the sacrifice. It was plain to her that if she wanted to end the plague, she would have to return to that pond and make a second offering to reverse the first.

But there was a problem with her plan: Immanuelle had not the slightest idea how to get back to the pond. The forest was vast and disorienting. It would take her days, if not weeks, to locate the pond, if she was able to locate it at all.

Immanuelle closed the book, scrambled to her feet, and went to Ezra. "I need to see a map of Bethel. Can you find one for me?"

Ezra raised an eyebrow, but to Immanuelle's immense relief, he didn't question her. He just nodded toward the stairway as if to say, *After you*. Upon descending, he disappeared down a long aisle of bookshelves. After a few long moments, he returned with a massive tome, its front cover about as wide as Immanuelle's shoulders were broad.

"This way." He nodded toward the front of the chapel. Immanuelle followed him to a cracked stone slab with a single wooden chair pulled up to it. It took her a moment to realize it was an altar, where the first of the faith must have made their sacrifices.

Behind it was a stained-glass window that stretched from the cathedral floor to its vaulted ceiling some twenty feet overhead. On the left-hand side of the pane were depictions of holy crusaders on horseback, surging across the plains, their swords blazing with the Father's fire. And upon closer inspection, Immanuelle saw His face in the great eye of the sun, watching as His children charged into battle.

On the opposite side of the pane was a maelstrom of the hells, a legion of beasts and witches fleeing the Father's flames. Looming above her spawn in a veil of night was the Dark Mother. She wore the moon as a crown, and she was weeping tears of blood.

An iron plaque beneath the window read: *The Holy War.*

"It's something, isn't it?" said Ezra, staring up at the panes of stained glass, his cheeks washed red by the sunlight casting in through the fire's flames. "An entire legion turned to ash, all on a whim."

Immanuelle stared at him, stunned quiet. His words came close to outright blasphemy, a sin that might provoke a public lashing if Ezra were anything less than the Prophet's successor. Her gaze tracked to the left corner of the window, where a small, dark-skinned boy cowered as the Father's flames devoured a woman that might have been his mother.

"But it wasn't a whim," she said at last, finding her voice. "The crusaders called upon the Good Father to deliver them from the witches, and He answered their prayers with holy fire. He saved them all from ruin, from damnation at the hands of the Dark Mother. Those flames were His blessing."

Ezra's eyes narrowed, and he gazed up at that window with obvious contempt. "So the Scriptures say."

"You don't believe them?"

"All I'm saying is that if I was an all-powerful god who could do as I pleased, I would have found another way to end the war." He looked back at Immanuelle. "Wouldn't you?"

"I'm not a god, so I couldn't say. I can't presume to know the Father's will. And if I did know it, I'm certain there would be no cause for doubts or questions."

"Spoken like a true believer," said Ezra, but he made it sound like an insult.

After a few moments of searching, he found the right page and motioned to it with a pass of his hand. There, inked into what appeared to be vellum, was a map. It outlined the boundaries of Bethel: the western wall, the village and market square, the sprawling Holy Grounds, and the rolling pastures of the Glades beyond them. In the far left-hand corner of the map, reduced to little more than a scribble, were the Outskirts. And encircling it all were wide swathes of shadow, marked with a simple footnote: *The Darkwood.*

"Did you find what you were looking for?" Ezra's voice echoed in the quiet.

Immanuelle shook her head. The pond where she'd encountered Lilith wasn't marked anywhere. "Would the library have something more specific? Like a map of the Darkwood?"

Ezra frowned. Once again, she wondered if she'd gone too far, or trusted him too easily. "As far as I know, there's no map of the forest," he said, and he closed the book. "But I might be able to help you. I used to play in the Darkwood when I was younger, and I still know the area well enough. There's a good chance that if you know where you want to go, I can get you there."

Immanuelle gaped. "You went into the woods as . . . *a child*?"

"Sometimes, when I found a way to sneak out of the Haven." Ezra shrugged like it was nothing, but he looked a little proud. "Of course, I never stayed after sundown. I wasn't too keen on the idea of the woodland witches ripping the flesh off my bones."

Immanuelle shivered, thinking back to the witches, with their hungry eyes and hooked fingers. "You'd have been lucky if that's all they did."

He scoffed, like it was a joke, like all the legends of the Darkwood were merely fodder for wives' tales.

"You don't believe the stories?" she asked, incredulous. "You don't believe the witches are real?"

"It isn't a question of belief."

"Then what is it?"

He took his time to think over his answer. At last, he said, "It's a question of who's being creative with the truth."

Immanuelle wasn't entirely sure what he meant by that, but it felt close to blasphemy. "Creative truths don't explain away centuries of disappearances in the woods."

"People don't disappear in the woods. They escape. That's why they never return: because they don't want to."

Immanuelle couldn't imagine anyone intentionally leaving Bethel. After all, where would they go? To the godless, heathen cities in the west? To the lifeless ruins in the east? No one would seek solace in places like those. Beyond Bethel, there was nothing. There was no other place to go. "And all the missing children? What happened to all of them?"

Ezra shrugged. "The Darkwood is a dangerous place. Predators have to eat, and out there a defenseless child is just food for the wolves."

"Then where are all the bodies? The bones?"

"Nature has a way of cleaning up its messes. My guess is the animals get to the corpses before anyone else has the chance to."

"And what about the blood plague?"

"What about it?"

"Well, if it didn't come from the forest, then what's the source of it all? Is it really so hard for you to believe that there could be something in the Darkwood that wants its due? That the legends are true, and the witches who died never left, and now they want . . ." She traced her fingers across the carvings on the altar, recognizing the words from David Ford's tombstone: *Blood for blood.* "Vengeance."

Ezra started to reply, but before he had the chance to speak, there was the jangle of keys and the sharp *click* of a lock's bolt slipping out of place. He twisted to face her, his expression panicked. "There's a door at the back of the library, behind the shelves of the medical section. It leads to a flight of stairs that feeds into the cellars. Go down the hall, through the doors at its end. I'll meet you by the front gate." The doors opened with a resounding groan. *"Go, now!"*

Immanuelle broke for the two nearest shelves, ducking behind them as a lone man crossed into the center aisle. "Back in the library again?"

Although the voice was hoarse, Immanuelle immediately recognized it from past Sabbaths and feasts.

It belonged to the Prophet.

"I thought I might do some research," said Ezra.

The Prophet nodded, doubling back so he stood by a shelf that was only a few feet from Immanuelle. She retreated, trying her best to step lightly on the cobbles.

The Prophet lingered, nothing but a few books between them. Up close, Immanuelle was certain she didn't mistake the poorly veiled contempt in his expression when he regarded Ezra. His upper lip curled a bit when he spoke. "Research on what?"

Ezra's eyes went to Immanuelle. *Go,* his gaze seemed to say. But she crouched, frozen, behind the shelf, afraid she'd be caught by the Prophet if she moved so much as an inch.

Ezra shifted his attention back to his father, his expression unreadable. "Mother is suffering from her . . . *bruising affliction* yet again. I was looking for a way to ease her pain, but I'm beginning to think I won't find a cure behind these walls."

The Prophet flinched at the veiled threat, his composure failing him for a moment. But he regained himself quickly, slid a book off the shelf nearest to him, a thick tome with no title, and thumbed slowly through the pages. "If your mother is ailing, have her call upon a physician. I have more important work for you."

Ezra went very still, as if he feared he'd say something he'd regret. When he spoke, his voice was strained. "What would you have me do?"

The Prophet turned to place his book back on the shelf, and Immanuelle ducked down an adjacent aisle to avoid being seen. There, she found the door. It was small, a good half a foot shorter than she, as if it was made for a child. She was reaching for the handle when she heard the Prophet say, "I need the census accounts of all the women in Bethel."

A chill raked down Immanuelle's spine. Hastily, she slipped through the door and began to draw it shut behind her. The creaking of the hinges echoed through the library.

"Did you hear that?" The Prophet's voice was sharp.

Immanuelle froze, her hand still on the latch. She peered through the crack between the door and its frame. She knew she ought to retreat down the corridor as instructed, but she couldn't pull her eyes from the scene unfolding before her.

The Prophet coughed, harshly, into the crook of his elbow. When he spoke again, his voice was just a thin rasp. "I could have sworn I heard something."

Ezra pushed off the altar and strode down the center aisle. "Just the stones settling, most likely. The Haven has old bones."

"That it does." The Prophet's voice echoed as he moved down the aisle where Immanuelle had hidden just moments before. She could have sworn he was limping a bit, but perhaps it only looked that way because of her odd vantage point.

She held her breath as the Prophet drew nearer still, and she cowered behind the door now, knowing she ought to leave. But she needed to know about the names of Bethel's women. What did the Prophet want with them? What if he had seen something in a vision, or he suspected one of them was behind the plague? What if he suspected *her*?

The Prophet's heavy footsteps were mere paces from the door now.

"Father, the names," Ezra called out, drawing his attention away. "If I'm to pull the records of all the women in Bethel, that must be at least eight or nine thousand."

"Likely more than that." The Prophet walked on past the door, much to Immanuelle's relief. She risked another peek through the crack. "Make the selections from the census and send the records to my quarters. I want all of the accounts on my desk by the week's end. Have the scribes help you, if necessary. I don't care if they have to work through the night to see it through. I want it done. Am I understood?"

Ezra dipped his head. "Is that all you require of me?"

The Prophet mulled this, gazing at Ezra with something akin to disgust. It was a known fact that the Prophet's chosen son was not often his favorite. Immanuelle imagined it was not an easy thing for a man to stare into the face of his own undoing. The Holy Scriptures were filled with stories of prophets who had tried to kill their heirs in order to extend their own lives and reigns. In turn, several heirs had tried to kill their predecessors to hasten their rise to power.

Watching the Prophet and Ezra then, Immanuelle was reminded of those horrible histories—of violence against son and father, master and apprentice, schisms that threatened to tear the Church apart. The tension between the two of them was as sinister as it was palpable. In that moment, Ezra and the Prophet were enemies before they were kin. One the ruination of the other. Immanuelle could not help but think it was a horrible thing to behold, regardless of whether the Father had ordained it.

"There is one more thing." The Prophet moved to stand before his son. He drew something from the back pocket of his trousers. Squinting, Immanuelle could see that it was a dagger.

Ezra's dagger.

The chain was broken, the latch badly bent, as if it'd been ripped from around Ezra's neck—and Immanuelle realized, with a start, that it had. It was the same blade that Judith had snatched in the midst of her fight with Ezra, the night of Leah's cutting.

The Prophet let it dangle now between him and his son, the blade catching the sunlight as it swung back and forth. "I found this in Judith's quarters. Tell me, how did it come into her possession?"

By some miracle, Ezra maintained his composure. "I lost my dagger the night of Leah's cutting."

"You *lost* it?"

"I was distracted."

"By my wife?"

"No," said Ezra, and Immanuelle marveled at the way he could make a lie sound just like the truth. "Not Judith. By something . . . someone else. When I returned to the place I thought I dropped my dagger, it was gone. Judith must have found it. I'm sure she intended to return it to me."

"But it was under her pillows," said the Prophet in a hoarse whisper. "Why would my wife keep my son's holy dagger beneath her pillows while she slept at night?"

Immanuelle wanted more than anything now to run—to flee and leave the Haven far behind her—but she found herself unable to move; her feet stayed pinned to the floor.

The Prophet took Ezra by the wrist and pressed the dagger deep into the center of his palm, folding Ezra's fingers over the blade so he was forced to grip it barehanded. The older man paused, his hand resting lightly over his son's, and he peered into his eyes. Then he squeezed, so suddenly and so hard that his knuckles popped.

Immanuelle watched in breathless horror as blood streamed

through the cracks between Ezra's fingers. He worked his jaw, but he didn't flinch, didn't break his father's gaze, even as the blood trickled down his wrist and the blade bit deeper.

"What you do in the shadows comes out in the light." The Prophet leaned closer to his son. "I thought I raised you to understand that. Perhaps I was mistaken."

"You weren't." Ezra's expression remained unchanged, but there was something cold and defiant in his eyes, as though his father was the one who had amends to make, not he.

The Prophet released him abruptly. He looked startled, almost sick, at the sight of what he'd done—at the dagger and his own hands, both smeared with his son's blood. "The Father's mercy is one matter," he said as he tried to recover his composure. "But mine is another. You'd do well to remember that."

The Prophet turned to depart then, but Ezra didn't let go of the dagger. In fact, Immanuelle could see he gripped it even tighter, and she gasped as a fresh stream of blood trickled down his wrist. He watched silently as his father walked to the library doors.

Blood dappled the cobbles at Ezra's feet, but still he kept his hand clenched around the dagger's blade. It was only after his father departed the chamber that he answered, his voice soft: "I will remember, Father."

CHAPTER THIRTEEN

I tried to love him, and I tried to put you from my mind. But it isn't an easy thing to turn your back on a home, and that's what I found in you.

—FROM THE LETTERS OF MIRIAM MOORE

THE CELLARS BENEATH the Prophet's Haven reminded Immanuelle strangely of the corridors of the Darkwood. The shadows were thick and wet, and they seemed to cling to her clothes as she made her way through the halls. The air smelled of iron and decay, and by the light of the flickering torches she could see that the stone walls were weeping blood.

She wandered, disoriented and cold, one hand slipping along the gore-slick wall to guide her. Alone, there was nothing to keep her from replaying the scene in the library in her head: the Prophet's paranoia; his sudden, vicious malice; blood spattering the cobbles; and Ezra's blank stare. With every step, the corridors closed in around her, and the shadows seemed to fill her lungs so that she had to gasp and struggle for every breath.

By the time she finally reached the first floor, her heart was beating so fast it ached. She stumbled through the doorway, out of the wet shadows and into a narrow hall with arched ceilings.

A door opened and closed, and Immanuelle turned to see Judith standing a few paces away. She wore a dress of pale blue, and in her hand was a fraying scrap of embroidery that was still far better than anything Immanuelle had ever sewn.

"What are you doing here?" Judith demanded, and her gaze traced over her, taking in every flaw—the patched holes at the tops of her boots, her bloodstained skirts, the unkempt riot of her curls. "Shouldn't you be in the fields with your flock . . . or in the Outskirts?"

Immanuelle flinched. She raised a hand to fix her hair, but then thought better of it and stopped. No amount of preening would satisfy Judith's spite. She would always find some fault to fixate on, or some cruel barb to make Immanuelle feel like less than she was. "Good morrow to you, Judith."

The girl offered no greeting in return. Her gaze drifted from Immanuelle to the door behind her. "Where did you just come from?"

Immanuelle took a step past her. "I lost my way."

Judith caught her by the arm, her grasp tight enough to leave bruises behind, but when she spoke her voice was still thin and sweet. "You smell of blood. Were you wandering the catacombs?"

"No. I'm here on business," said Immanuelle, keeping her voice steady.

"Whose?"

"That's my concern."

Judith angled her head to the side. A smile played over her lips, but there was no kindness in it. Her hand slipped away. "I know that you saw us that night."

That should have been the end of it, but Immanuelle stalled a beat, lingering in the center of the hall.

"You think you're so clever, don't you? Holding little threats above my head."

"I don't know what you're talking about."

"Don't insult my intelligence. I know you saw us that night. You were snooping around then just like you are now, sticking your nose where it doesn't belong."

"I'm not here to snoop."

Judith scoffed, then laughed outright, and somehow she looked more cruel smiling than she did scowling. "You wear a lie about as well as a toddler does a corset," said Judith, and she plucked at one of her own bodice strings. "Deception doesn't become you, and that's all right if you're pocketing taffy at the market or fibbing to your father about some boy you kissed behind the schoolhouse. But I don't think those are the kinds of secrets you're keeping. I think the sins you're hiding could send you to the pyre if you're not careful."

Judith must not know, Immanuelle realized, of the danger she was in, that the Prophet was aware of her dalliance with Ezra. There was no way Judith would be wasting time in the corridor with her if she knew how much trouble she was in. The spoiled girl was so used to always having her way, she couldn't imagine a day she might not. The idea that she'd be caught was so minor, so inconceivable, she hadn't even paused to consider it. "You're a fool if you think I'm the one in danger."

For the first time in recent memory—or perhaps in all the sixteen years Immanuelle had known her—Judith looked properly taken aback. A range of emotions passed over her face, like a series of shadows in quick succession, ranging from rage to fear to doubt. She parted her lips to respond to Immanuelle's warning, or perhaps demand an explanation, when a door opened down the hall. The two girls turned immediately and watched as a tall, pale man stepped past the threshold. He was a servant, if his dirtied boots and smock were any indication. Hanging from the loop of his belt was a holy dagger, as well as a small iron hammer just longer than Immanuelle's hand. The only mark of his station was the symbol of the Prophet's Guard, which was embroidered into the right-hand corner of his smock.

The man smiled at them, but the gesture lacked any pretense of warmth. "Pardon me, mistress. Your husband wants a word."

Judith's eyes went from the man to Immanuelle, then back to the man again.

"This way." He sounded impatient now.

Judith's eyes filled suddenly with tears, and she began to tremble. For one absurd moment, Immanuelle thought to reach for her, as if there was something she could do to stay whatever fate awaited her in the form of that strange, sneering man at the hall's end.

But then Judith started forward, each step slow and heavy, her velvet skirts trailing behind her as she went. Immanuelle saw the terror in her eyes as she brushed past the threshold to the man who stood waiting for her, rounded a corner, and disappeared.

※

Chapter Fourteen

*We have broken ourselves to be together. The fragments of
me fit with the fragments of you, and our remnants have
become greater than the sum of who we used to be.*
                    —From the Letters of Daniel Ward

IMMANUELLE FOUND EZRA just outside the front gate in the
eastern pastures, standing beside the same cottonwood he'd
been reading under when she first arrived. In his good hand, the
reins of a tall black steed. In his bad one, a stained rag he gripped
to staunch the bleeding. "What took you so long?" he demanded.

Immanuelle forced herself not to stare at his hand. "Your lovely
mistress caught me in the halls. She wanted to chat."

"Judith?"

"Yes, Judith," Immanuelle snapped, suddenly furious. "What,
do you have trouble remembering them all?"

Ezra frowned. He forced his good hand toward her and nodded to the cart. "Climb up. I'm taking you home."

Immanuelle didn't move. "What's between you two?"

"What?"

"You and Judith. What's between you?"

"There's nothing between us."

Immanuelle fought the urge to fold her arms over her chest. "I
saw her kiss you, and it didn't seem like it was your first time."

Ezra's hand tightened around the rag, and he worked his jaw. "No, it wasn't. But it was the last."

Immanuelle knew then that she ought to bite her tongue, leave Ezra to his sins. But then she thought of that strange, sneering man in the hall and the look of terror that had passed over Judith's face when she walked to meet him. Her rage bubbled over, and the words tumbled out before she had the chance to bite them back. "Why did you start in the first place? Girls have burned on the pyre for less than the sins you committed together. My own father burned for lesser crimes."

Ezra at least had the decency to look ashamed. "Immanuelle—"

"You knew the danger. You must have."

"I did. We both did."

"So why?" she demanded, motioning to his hand. "Why risk everything?"

"You wouldn't understand."

Immanuelle's thoughts went to her father. She imagined him with her mother, meeting in secret as Ezra had with Judith. She thought of all they'd risked for each other: their happiness, their faith, any chance they'd ever have at a future. "You're right," said Immanuelle tightly. "I'll never understand why people choose to hurt those they claim to love."

"I don't love Judith, and she doesn't love me. It's not like that. It never was."

"It didn't appear that way the other night."

"Well, everything isn't always the way it appears," he said, frustrated. "Look, Immanuelle, if you want a story about love and loss and heartbreak, you should've taken a book from the library. What Judith and I had was nothing like that."

"Then why bother with it in the first place?"

"We're done discussing this." He nodded toward the cart. "Now, come on."

"I'll walk."

"No, you won't," said Ezra, turning to harness his steed to the cart. He struggled with the buckles a bit, wincing every time he was forced to use his bad hand. "Look, I've answered all of your questions to the best of my knowledge. I lied to my father to get you into the library, breaking at least half the codes of Bethelan Protocol in the process. So if you would be so kind as to allow me to escort you home, I'd greatly appreciate it. Is that agreeable enough for you or would you prefer it if I grovel?"

She shouldered past him. "I'd prefer to walk."

"Goddamn it, Immanuelle."

She turned on him then, so fast her heel dug deep into the dirt. "Such a filthy tongue for a prophet's son."

"It's a filthy world," he snapped. "Which is exactly why I'd prefer it if you'd let me escort you home."

A low wind seethed through the high grass.

Immanuelle peered down again at Ezra's hand. The rag he was clutching was all but soaked through, and though he kept his expression stoic, she could tell he was in pain. He had to be, with a wound like that. And then there was the matter of deeper pains—the invisible ones that couldn't be nursed with bandages or salves.

"Is this about your father?" she asked quietly.

Ezra didn't look at her, but his grip on the rag tightened. "Climb up. The sun's setting fast."

"You didn't answer my question about you and Judith."

"And I don't intend to." He patted the cart bench. "Up. Now."

"Give me an answer and I'll consider it."

Ezra set his jaw again, and for a moment Immanuelle was quite certain they'd both stay there, rooted in place, until the night melted into dawn and their legs went weak beneath them. But to her surprise, Ezra broke first.

"People do foolish, reckless things when they're desperate to find ways to escape themselves." He sighed and hung his head. "As ugly as it is, sometimes the truth is nothing more than that."

Immanuelle studied him for a moment. Then she climbed onto the cart.

For a while, the two of them rode in silence, the sunset dying into darkness, shadows stretching between the trees as they crossed through the Holy Grounds. As they neared the Glades, Immanuelle took a roll of bandages from the pocket of her knapsack. With some coaxing, Ezra let her take his hand and peel the rag away from his wound. It was an ugly gash, deep enough to need stitching, but Immanuelle did the best she could to wrap the bandages tight and staunch the bleeding. As she tended him, she thought of the irony of it all. Just a few weeks ago, she had nursed a similar wound. Perhaps she and Ezra had more in common than she thought. Was that the source of the budding kinship she sensed between them? Shared pain?

A cold, bitter wind swept down from the north and blasted through the treetops. The steed spooked, sidestepping so Ezra had to drag on the reins and raise his voice above the roar to talk him down.

Immanuelle shivered and gripped her seat. Ezra, eyes still fixed on the distant darkness, took one hand off the reins and reached into the back of the cart, producing a blanket. "Here."

"Thank you," she said, drawing the quilt around her shoulders.

"It's nothing."

"Even still."

The path twisted east toward the Glades, cutting through Bethel's heartland. But as they neared the Darkwood's edge once again, its thrall grew stronger. Immanuelle wondered then if the Father's power called to Ezra in the same way that the forest did her. If he was as drawn to the light as she was to shadow.

Ezra glanced at her out of his periphery. "What is it?"

She blushed, embarrassed to be caught staring. "It's just that . . . well, I wondered if—"

He smirked, clearly amused by her stammering. "Out with it."

"Have you always felt called to the Prophethood?"

Ezra shook his head. "I never wanted to be heir. I wanted to travel, go beyond the wall."

"Why would you ever want to do that?"

"Because there's more to the world than Bethel. The wilds don't go on forever. There is life beyond them. There has to be."

"You mean the heathen cities?"

"That's one name for them. But before Ford built the wall, those heathen cities were Bethel's allies."

"But that was centuries ago."

"I know," said Ezra, his eyes on the horizon. "That's why I wanted to go—to figure out what happened, to know if we're alone out here."

She frowned, confused. As heir, Ezra was one of the only people in Bethel who had the jurisdiction to open the Hallowed Gate and grant passage through it. It seemed to Immanuelle that if he'd really wanted to leave Bethel, he would have been gone already. "Why don't you just go?"

Ezra slipped his dagger from his pocket by way of answer. He had yet to clean it, Immanuelle noticed, and the blade was still crusted with his blood. "I'm told my place is here."

They fell quiet once more. The wheels of the wagon rattled through potholes and bloody puddles as they entered the Glades. While the dark was far too thick to see through, Immanuelle could hear the gentle *hush hush* of the wind in the branches of the western forest.

"We should go up to the cathedral's bell tower tomorrow," said Ezra, breaking the silence between them. "I'll be in session with the apostles in the afternoon, but I'm free in the morning."

His proposal startled her, both in its boldness and in the fact that he suggested it at all. When he'd mentioned taking her to the bell tower, she had never—even for a moment—expected him to follow through on that promise. But even though a part of her was excited by the prospect, she shook her head. "I can't."

"You have other plans?" Ezra asked, and Immanuelle had the odd suspicion that there was something else, something more behind the question, though she couldn't say exactly what.

"I'm going to the Darkwood." The moment the truth was free of her, she wondered why she had offered it. She supposed a small, weak part of herself wanted to impress him . . . and she hated herself for it.

But to her surprise, Ezra seemed relatively unfazed by her confession. "I thought you were afraid of the woods."

"I am. Anyone with the good sense they were born with would be," said Immanuelle. And while this was true, she'd come to realize that fear wasn't a reasonable excuse not to do what needed to be done. It was a strange notion, as Immanuelle had never been particularly brave. But in the days that followed the onset of the blood plague, she'd begun growing into her own kind of courage. And she liked the feel of it. "Some things have to be done whether they scare me or not."

Ezra shifted closer, tipping his head toward hers, and she could tell he was struggling to read her, parse out the truth. "What does a girl like you need to do in the witches' wood?"

She didn't see the point in lying to him. "I want to stop the bleeding," she said simply. "And I think I know how to do it."

Immanuelle waited for his laughter, for his ridicule, but it didn't come. "I'll meet you by the well at daybreak."

It was her turn to be shocked. "You can't come with me."

"I can and will," said Ezra, as if the matter had been discussed and decided already. "There's no way I'm letting you go into the Darkwood alone."

"But it's dangerous for men to walk the woods," said Immanuelle, remembering the stories Martha had told her as a child, to warn her of the forest and its evils. She had often claimed that during the Dark Days, men who dared to enter the forest frequently returned rabid, bewitched into madness by the woodland coven.

Ezra waved her off. "That's superstition."

Immanuelle had once thought the same, but that was before she witnessed the witches of the woods. Now she knew the dangers of the Darkwood were real, and while she was willing to risk her own life to stop the plague she'd started, she wouldn't risk Ezra's too. "It's too dangerous. Believe me. Especially since you're a holy man, the wood is hostile toward the likes of you."

He rolled his eyes. "That's a lie pagans devised in the ancient times to keep Bethelan soldiers from crossing their borders."

"That's not true. Just because you haven't seen the horrors of the Darkwood firsthand doesn't mean they're not real. The forest is dangerous, and if you want to live, you should stay well clear of it."

Ezra opened his mouth to respond when the horse gave a loud shriek. The cart listed so far to the right that Immanuelle would have tumbled off headfirst if Ezra hadn't caught her by the waist.

Ahead of the horse, in the center of the road, was a hound. It was a hulking, mangy creature, and it was growling, its eyes reflecting the light of the cart's swinging lanterns. It snapped at the horse's hooves, its mouth blood-slick and frothing.

Ezra passed the reins to Immanuelle. "Hold these and stay here."

"But your hand—"

"I'm fine." He twisted to the back of the cart, where, from a heap of hay, he produced a long rifle.

"You're not going to—"

"It's rabid," he said as he hopped from the cart. Gun raised, he stalked toward the hound. It snarled at his approach, pressing itself low to the ground.

The horse bucked, and Immanuelle yanked the reins so hard her palms chafed.

Ezra raised the rifle to his shoulder.

The hound lunged.

The crack of the bullet breaking from the barrel split the darkness. The hound staggered, tripping over its own paws, and fell dead to the dust.

Bile rose in Immanuelle's throat, and she choked back the sick as Ezra returned to his seat, tilting the rifle against the bench. He took the reins from her shaking hands and snapped them twice, urging the horse past the hound's bleeding corpse. Neither he nor Immanuelle said a word.

After a few more minutes, the cart rounded a bend and started down the long, jagged road that led to the Moore land. The light of the farmhouse appeared in the distance, glowing through the rolling waves of wheatgrass.

As they neared, Ezra said, "In the morning, then? At daybreak?"

Immanuelle muttered something less than holy under her breath, but conceded, knowing it was futile to argue. "Yes, and bring that rifle of yours. You may well need it."

He snapped the reins, looking a little smug. "I'll meet you by the well."

Immanuelle nodded. Then something occurred to her. "Why did the Prophet want those names?"

"What?"

"In the Haven, your father asked you to compile all the names of the women and girls in Bethel. Why?"

Ezra's answer was halting. "It's said that a curse can only come from the mouth of a woman. From the mouth of a witch."

A curse. There it was, then. The truth out in the open. "That's what he thinks this is?"

"Well, it's certainly not a blessing," said Ezra. "What else could you call it?"

Immanuelle thought back to the cathedral, to the stained-glass window that depicted the Mother's legions being burned and slain. She thought of the muzzled girl, chained to the market stocks. She thought of jeering crowds and flaming pyres. She thought of Leah lying prone on the altar, blood pooling in the hollows of her ears, a blade at her brow. She thought of young girls married off to men old enough to be their grandfathers. She thought of starved beggars from the Outskirts squatting by the roadside with their coin cups. She thought of the Prophet's gaze and the way it moved over her, lingering where it shouldn't.

Immanuelle answered Ezra's question in a hoarse whisper: "A punishment."

*
—————— ✱ ——————

CHAPTER FIFTEEN

When the forest is hungry, feed it.
—FROM *THE UNHOLY FOUR: A COMPENDIUM*

THE FOLLOWING MORNING, Immanuelle woke before sunrise and went to Abram's empty workshop to fetch supplies. She sorted through the tools before making her selections: a thick coil of rope long enough to run the length of the farmhouse with slack to spare, a clean roll of gauze, and Abram's sharpest whittling knife. The rope was heavy enough to throw her off balance, but Immanuelle managed to sling it over her shoulder as she crossed through the fallow fields to the gated paddock where the sheep spent their nights. Hurriedly, she let them out to pasture, where they would remain under the watchful eye of the farmhand, Josiah, while she was away in the woods.

With the flock attended to, Immanuelle started toward the well on the eastern edge of the pastures, where she waited for Ezra to arrive. To pass the time, she flipped through the pages of her mother's journal, revisiting the sketches of the witches in preparation for what she was about to do. If all went according to plan, she would locate the pond, go into the water, and make her sacrifice, and by the time she emerged from the Darkwood again, the blood plague would be over. She just prayed that the daylight was enough to keep Lilith's coven at bay.

Several yards off, cresting a hill and crossing into the pasture, came Ezra. He wore work clothes and his hand was freshly bandaged with a few strips of clean white gauze. On a leather strap slung over his shoulder, his rifle.

Immanuelle frowned, peering up at the sun. It had already risen above the horizon. "You're late."

The sheep scattered as Ezra moved through the flock. He stopped just short of her. Up close he looked rather tired, perhaps from a night spent sorting through the census. "And you're reading forbidden literature."

Immanuelle snapped the journal shut and hastily shoved it into her knapsack. "How do you know it's forbidden?"

"You look guilty. No one looks guilty reading a book Protocol allows." He nodded toward the coil of rope by her side. "What's that for?"

"Fishing," she said, brushing the dirt off her skirts as she stood. "Shall we?"

Ezra started forward first, wading through the waves of high grass to the forest's edge. She followed him into the brush, hating herself for the way her heart eased the moment the trees closed in around her. The woods were as beautiful as she'd ever seen them. Sunlight filtered through the trees, dappling the narrow path that wended through the forest thicket.

Never had the woods seemed so gentle and alive. In comparison to Bethel—where everything was withered and dying—it was a stark juxtaposition. There, in the Darkwood, it almost seemed like the blood plague was some vague and distant nightmare. If not for the glimpses of the red river threading through the trees, or the blood-filled ruts in the path, Immanuelle might have believed the blood plague had been contained to Bethel alone.

But the truth was even more startling. Unlike Bethel, which had been ravaged by the horrors of the plague, the forest was thriving off it. As if the woods were glutted with blood. The trees bloomed out of season, their branches lush with new growth. The bramble thicket was so dense it encroached on the path, making it hard to follow at times. It almost seemed like the forest was expanding, growing past its designated limits.

Was that what this blood plague was all about? Was it some ploy of the witches to take dominion over Bethel? Was Lilith trying to claim what had been lost to her all those years ago?

Ezra glanced back at Immanuelle. "For someone who claims to fear the Darkwood, you certainly seem at ease."

He was right, at least in part. There was something about the Darkwood that made her feel as though she became more like herself when she entered it, and when she left it, less. But perhaps that was just the trickery of the witches. "You seem rather tense for someone who doesn't."

"If you're ready for the worst, then you won't have anything to fear in the first place."

"Is that what you expect to find out here?" Immanuelle asked, ducking beneath the bough of an oak. She felt a little pang of guilt for all the secrets she'd been keeping from him. "The worst?"

"Perhaps," he said. "I may not believe in witches and folktales, but I know enough to realize few good things come from the Darkwood."

The words stung, and it took her a moment to realize why: She was from the Darkwood, at least partially. It was the place where she'd grown in her mother's belly, her first home, whether she wanted to admit it or not.

Ezra turned to look at her. "You don't agree?"

"I don't know," she said, stepping closer, halving what little distance there was between them. "I guess I'm inclined to think good things can come from unexpected places."

Ezra reached above his head, grasping a branch with his good hand, leaning on it a bit. They were close to each other, too close to be considered proper by Bethelan Protocol. But they weren't in Bethel anymore, and the Darkwood was lawless.

It was Ezra who broke the silence, a ragged edge to his voice. "You're a bit of a puzzle, you know that?"

Immanuelle tilted her chin to peer up at him in full. Ezra's lips were parted, and the sunlight played over his face, painting shadows along his cheeks and jaw. Though there was barely a finger's length between them, all Immanuelle wanted to do was step closer. But she didn't dare let herself go. She couldn't. "So I've been told."

They walked in silence for a time after that. Immanuelle was all too conscious of the sudden quiet, and the careful distance between them. It seemed like hours had passed when Ezra finally stopped and motioned to a break in the trees. "We're here."

Immanuelle stepped in front of him. Sure enough, they were. There was the pond, a wide, bloody wound in the middle of the forest. The trees that encircled it were much taller than Immanuelle remembered, and their roots reached into the pond's depths, submerged in blood, glutting themselves on it. The sweet stench of decay was so cloying and thick, Immanuelle almost gagged at the smell of it.

She turned back to Ezra, slipped the coil of rope off her shoulder, and lowered her knapsack to the dirt. "Close your eyes and turn around."

"What are you—"

Immanuelle lifted the hem of her skirt up to her knees and looked at him over her shoulder. The forest's song turned taunting. It was in the quick rhythm of her heartbeat, in the hiss of the wind, in the dull *thud* of Ezra's boots on the dirt as he stepped a little closer.

"Eyes closed," she reminded him.

This time, Ezra obeyed, closing his eyes and tipping his face to the treetops. "Why do I feel like whatever you're up to is a bad, creed-breaking idea?"

"I don't know." She paused to kick off her boots. "Maybe because you're a bad, creed-breaking heir who has a taste for such ideas."

She wasn't looking at him, but she could hear the smile in his voice when he answered. "You think I'm a bad heir?"

"I think you're a devious one." She wiggled out of her dress, the fabric pooling at her ankles. She folded it quickly and retrieved the rope, knotting it around her waist. When it was secure, she walked to Ezra and slipped the slack into his good hand. "Hold this and don't let go."

Ezra turned to face her fully, and his eyes flashed as he traced the rope from his hand to her waist. Immanuelle's slip suddenly felt as thin as mist in the morning. "I told you to close your eyes."

Ezra's gaze went from her to the water, then back again. She could have sworn he looked almost . . . flustered. "You're not going to—"

"I have to. The blood plague won't end if I don't."

"This is ridiculous," said Ezra, shaking his head. He'd humored her antics thus far, but it was clear his patience was long spent. "If you're hell-bent on someone going into that pond, let it be me. You hold the rope."

Immanuelle shook her head. "It has to be me."

"Why?" he demanded, exasperated. Angry, even. "What does this pond have to do with ending the blood plague? I don't understand."

"I don't have time to explain it to you, and even if I did I'm not sure you'd believe me. But that doesn't matter now. You're here because you chose to be, so you can either help me or you can leave. I just ask that whatever you choose to do, you do it quickly and with discretion. I've kept your secrets, so you keep mine."

Ezra clenched his jaw, conflicted. "This is a fool's errand."

"Just keep hold of the rope," she said, stooping to take Abram's knife from her knapsack. "If you do that, then there's nothing to worry about."

"But the water's tainted."

"Well, I'm not going to drink it, am I? I'll make like a fish and swim. You've got the rope. If anything goes wrong—I'm under too long or I start to struggle—haul me back. No harm done."

Ezra's hand tightened around the slack. "Fine. But the instant that something goes wrong—you so much as splash too hard—and I'm reeling you back to shore."

"Fair enough."

Knife in hand, Immanuelle started down the shore. The cold, blood-black mud oozed between her toes and sucked at her feet, the brine making her blisters sting. Swallowing back a wave of nausea, she trudged in up to her ankles, her knees, her waist, cringing as the cold, bloody sludge lapped at her belly and seeped through her slip. Pausing to steel herself, she walked on, wading through the gore. When her bottom lip was barely above the water, she squeezed her eyes shut and whispered her prayer to the Darkwood.

"I'll not tell you my name, because you know it already. I've heard you call me before." She paused a beat, pushing up on her tiptoes, straining to keep her head above the surface. "I'm here on behalf of Bethel, to beg . . . no, to *plead* for an end to the plagues that were spawned here weeks ago. Accept this sacrifice. Please."

And with that, she raised the knife to her forearm and made a deep cut.

As her blood mixed with that of the pond, a great wind moved through the forest, so strong it bent the pine saplings double. Wide ripples radiated from the center of the pond, as though someone had dropped a boulder in its depths. Waves broke against the shore of the pond in quick succession, and Immanuelle had to root her feet in the muck to keep from being swept away.

Ezra gave the rope two sharp tugs, and she turned to look at him over her shoulder. He yanked on the rope again, harder this time, shouted her name above the roaring wind. But before Immanuelle had the chance to answer him, a cold hand wrapped around her ankle and dragged her under.

CHAPTER SIXTEEN

The woman is a cunning creature. Made in the likeness of
her Mother, she is at once the creator and the destroyer. She
is kind until she is cruel, meek until she is merciless.
—FROM THE EARLY WRITINGS OF DAVID FORD

THE WITCH OF the Water floated in the shadow of the deep.
She darted around Immanuelle, swift as a minnow, as she
flailed and struggled, trying not to drown. The witch cocked her
head to the side, ebbed closer, so they were nearly nose to nose.
Her expression twisted into a frown, lips ripped apart, and when
she wailed, the blood began to bubble, and great black shapes rose
from the shadows of the deep.

Immanuelle thrashed, so startled she nearly snatched a breath
and choked. The shapes were figures, women and girls. Some were
Honor's age, some even younger. As they drew closer, Immanuelle
could see they were all gravely wounded in one way or another,
little more than corpses caught in the current's grasp. One woman's throat was gashed open. Another wore a noose around her
neck. A third's face was so bruised and swollen she barely looked
human. A fourth cradled her severed head to her chest the way
you would a baby. More and more souls rose from the shadows of
the deep until the dead were near legion.

From the black came a bellow, like a cathedral bell was tolling in the deep. At the sound, the corpses stirred to life and floated back into the darkness.

Then, from the murk and shadow, a new face appeared.

The Prophet?

No. Not him.

This was a face Immanuelle recognized from the statue in the market square, from the portraits that hung from the walls of the Prophet's Cathedral and Haven.

He was the first prophet. The Witch Killer, David Ford.

Ford's lips stretched into a ghastly grin, his mouth yawning wide like he meant to swallow her whole. He took a deep breath, and a lone cry echoed through the pond.

And then, from the black, there was fire.

The flames stormed through the water and devoured the women. Their cries became a chorus, mixing with the deep, roaring laughter of David Ford. The women wept and thrashed, some pleading for their mothers, others for mercy. But the flames didn't relent.

Immanuelle strained forward, reaching for their hands, desperate to help them, but the rope around her jerked, the knot biting into her belly. She fought it, clawing forward, toward the women and girls, as the fire raged.

Another yank on the line knocked the wind right out of her. She gasped, and blood rushed in to fill her mouth. In the black depths of the pond, she could still hear Delilah screaming.

IMMANUELLE DIDN'T REMEMBER breaking the surface of the water or being pulled to the pond's bank. One moment she was in the bloody depths; the next she was lying on her back, staring at the treetops. She sat up—rolling to her knees—and vomited. Blood and bile spattered the shore. It wasn't until the second wave of sick subsided that she raised her head and squinted through the twilight shadows. She could swear it had been just past midday when Delilah dragged her under. How long had she floated in the depths?

The pond's conjurings flooded back to her: the figures, the pleas and shrieking, the fire. Those women and girls weren't all witches—some were too young to practice any faith at all. They were victims, innocents slaughtered by the likes of David Ford under the guise of a holy purging. He'd killed them in cold blood. The Holy Scriptures had always made those conflicts seem like battles and wars, but in actuality, it was just a massacre.

It was a horrible truth, but one Immanuelle was forced to push to the back of her mind. She needed to focus on the curses and the witches and getting back to Bethel and . . . Ezra.

Ezra.

She raised her head to look for him, knees buckling beneath her as she pushed to her feet. But he wasn't by the bank where she'd last seen him. And the rope around her waist was slack.

Immanuelle staggered forward, calling for him, but he didn't answer.

Then, as she scrambled up the bank, she spotted him lying in the reeds. She ran to him, stumbling up the shore, and fell to his side. Ezra lay limp, with his eyes wide open, his pupils swollen so large they nearly devoured his irises. His nose and mouth were smeared with blood, but she couldn't tell if it was the pond's or his. The gash on his bad hand was bleeding freely, the bandages ripped and the stitches split open by the friction of the rope, which he still had hold of in a vise grip. And his limbs . . . they were pinned to the forest floor, bound by a tangle of thorns and tree roots.

A few feet from where he lay was his rifle, lying useless in the reeds, the metal barrel twisted into a knot, as if it was nothing more than a bit of wire.

Immanuelle struggled to pry the growths away—bloodying

her hands as she tore at the brambles—but the forest's grip on Ezra held fast, and try as she might she couldn't free him. Desperate, she raised Abram's knife and began to hack at the tangle of thorns and tree roots, painstakingly cutting his arms free.

Ezra reached for her, his hand hovering in the air between them. He stared up at her with a kind of dazed awe, but his eyes were vacant and completely unfocused, as if he was seeing something more than just her. But the longer he stared at her, the more his expression changed—awe turning to confusion, confusion to dread, and dread to outright horror.

Something shifted in the woods.

The air went cold. The pond began to gurgle, small waves lapping against its gory shores. Overhead, a bank of dark clouds churned, and storm winds hissed through the treetops. A few crows winged to the sky, fleeing east, and the wind began to roar, blasting through the trees so hard it bent them double.

Immanuelle kept hacking at the vines with Abram's knife, working as fast as she could. She bloodied her own hands ripping at the brambles around his ankles. "You're going to be okay. I'm going to free you. Just hold on a little longer; you're almost . . . Ezra?"

He stared back at her like she was a stranger . . . no, worse than a stranger, an enemy. He stopped struggling against the vines and branches that bound him to the forest's floor and started to fight against her, lashing out and yelling, demanding that she stay away.

But Immanuelle refused to relent. She kept hacking at the branches, working to free him from the Darkwood's hold, even as he thrashed and struggled as though her touch was burning him. And when Immanuelle cut the last of the roots that pinned his legs to the ground, Ezra lashed out, locking a hand around her throat so quickly she didn't have the chance to scream.

His fingers—slick with gore and blood—bit deep into the hollows on either side of her throat, sealing it shut. Immanuelle tried to pry his fingers away, clawing at his hands, his arms, his shirt. But to no avail. Ezra's grip was unrelenting, and his hold on her only tightened. Her hearing went first, and her sight began to go after it, the black edging in from her periphery. She realized then that she was about to die, there in the woods, at the hands of a boy she would've called her friend.

In a last act of desperation, Immanuelle raised Abram's knife, forced it to Ezra's chest, and the tip of the blade bit into the hollow between his collarbones. For a moment they sat there, frozen in place—Ezra with a hand around Immanuelle's throat and Immanuelle with a blade to his.

Just as she began to lose consciousness, Ezra's eyes came into focus. There was a flash of recognition, then horror after it.

He let go.

Immanuelle kicked away from him, gasping for air, and raised the blade between them, ready to use it should he reach for her again.

But before Ezra had the chance to do anything more than mumble her name, his limbs twisted in a series of convulsions. He thrashed, his head snapping on its axis, back arched so severely Immanuelle feared his spine would snap in two. But somehow, despite the throes of those horrible seizures, Ezra was . . . speaking, spitting prayers and catechisms, psalms and proverbs, and strange Scriptures that Immanuelle had never heard before. It was then, and only then, that she realized what she was witnessing—a vision, Ezra's first.

Storm winds swept through the forest. Pines bowed low and the treetops churned. Immanuelle weighed her options as she fumbled into her dress. Her first thought was a selfish one: avoid the risk of a second attack and leave Ezra there in the woodland. Let him find his own way out. But as she stood to leave, her own guilt got the better of her. She turned back to Ezra, who lay motionless in the dirt, the worst of his vision now over.

Either they left the forest together, or not at all.

So she sat Ezra up, ducked under his arm, and stood, with no small amount of struggle, gritting her teeth as she pushed both of them to their feet and staggered toward the trees. Immanuelle tried to cry for help above the roaring winds, praying that some hunter or field hand would heed them, but her calls for help were lost to the tumult of the storm. Still, she pressed on, fighting for every step, lungs burning with the effort.

The Darkwood's edge seemed to retreat three steps farther for every two she took, so Immanuelle moved faster, even as the shadows rose around her like water. In the distance, she could just make out the bright line of the wood's edge, where sunlight spilled through the trees. But as strange and twisted as it was—despite her terror and her desperation, despite Ezra's dire state—there was still some wretched part of her that desperately wanted to stay.

But Immanuelle would not be so easily tempted.

Not now when Ezra's fate depended upon what she did next.

She forced herself onward, fighting for every step toward the sunlight. And then, with a final lunge, she cleared the woods and broke to her knees at the cusp of the tree line. Ezra went down with her, and they struck the dirt together with a bruising *thud*.

Immanuelle scrambled onto her hands and knees, rolling Ezra onto his back, pushing the hair from his eyes. She pressed a hand to his chest, but she couldn't feel his heartbeat.

Across the distant pastures, the farmhand, Josiah, broke toward them in a full run, scattering the flock as he approached. Immanuelle cradled Ezra's head between her hands, brushed the dirt from his cheeks, pleaded with him to come back to her.

But he didn't answer. He didn't stir.

Chapter Seventeen

The Father will pour His spirit into the flesh of His servant; and the flock will call him Prophet, for he will see the wonders of the heavens and speak in the tongues of angels. The secrets of earth and blood will be revealed to him and he will know his Father's voice.

—The Holy Scriptures

IT WAS NINE days before Immanuelle heard any news of Ezra. After Josiah rode to Amas for aid, he'd returned with what seemed like half of the Prophet's Guard on horseback. Immanuelle was still in the pasture with Ezra, his head cradled in her lap, Anna on her knees beside them, dabbing his brow with a bit of damp cloth in a vain attempt to ease the torment of his vision. Glory stood weeping a few yards away, waves of dead, high grass swaying at her waist. In the distance, the Prophet's Guard spilled down the rolling hills of the pasture.

The rest happened very quickly. At least, it seemed that way to Immanuelle.

One moment, Ezra's head was cradled in her lap, his hand grasping hers as he struggled through his second seizure. The next, he was gone, snatched away by some faceless members of the Prophet's Guard. A few of the guardsmen had stayed back to interrogate Immanuelle, there in the pasture. In turn, she'd supplied them with a few lies and half-truths. Just enough to lay their suspicions to rest without incriminating herself or revealing the true horror of what had really happened in the Darkwood that day.

Immanuelle could only hope that if Ezra woke—no, *when* Ezra woke, he wouldn't expose her lies. But she wouldn't have blamed him if he did. Not after all that he'd endured in the Darkwood.

When news of Ezra's condition finally arrived, it came in the form of a holy edict hand delivered by one of the Prophet's personal couriers. While the letter was addressed to Abram, he gave Immanuelle the honor of breaking the seal and reading the edict within. Her hands shook violently as she tore the wax seal in two. The letter read as follows:

> *With the utmost joy, we share the news that Ezra Chambers received his First Vision. After eight days of dwelling with the Father through the Gift of Sight, he has regained conscious-ness and is now recovering in the Haven, in preparation for the coming Sabbath. Long live Ezra Chambers, heir to the Holy Prophethood, and may the Father bless his predecessor, Grant Chambers, in his final days.*
>
> *In light alone,*
> *The Holy Assembly of the Prophet's Apostles*

THERE WAS A gutting on the following Sabbath to commemorate Ezra's First Vision. The Moores woke early, dressing in their best, taking care to iron the creases out of their skirts and polish their shoes in honor of the special occasion. They left at daybreak and arrived before the sun cleared the treetops.

The cathedral was as crowded as Immanuelle had ever seen it. A few paces from the churchyard, the river ran freely. Most of the gore on the rocks had been washed away and the water had cleared to a rusty hue. The taint of the blood plague was finally over. Many declared it a miracle—Ezra's first.

Immanuelle scanned the crowds in the churchyard, searching for Leah. But she noted her friend was not among the Prophet's brides who stood grimly at the cathedral's threshold, all of them dressed in identical gowns of black. A few held damp handkerchiefs to their swollen eyes, openly grieving what they stood to lose—a husband, a father, a leader. The Prophet wouldn't be long for this world now that Ezra had risen to power. If the rumors of his sickness were to be believed, he wouldn't live to see the New Year.

At the sound of the bell's toll, Immanuelle crossed the churchyard and trudged up the cathedral stairs. She shuffled into a pew that stood just a few feet from the altar.

It was hot with everyone crowded into the benches, standing shoulder to shoulder. The air was thick with the smell of sweat and burning incense.

The doors of the cathedral slammed shut. The apostles moved along the walls, shuttering the windows as they went. The Prophet came after them, dressed in formal robes, his bare feet shuffling across the floor. He had a pronounced limp and it seemed like he struggled more and more with each step. Several times he had to catch himself on the back of a pew to keep from falling. As he staggered closer, Immanuelle could hear his labored breathing, a deep wheeze that rattled in the pits of his lungs. It was clear that whatever illness plagued him—be it gout or fever or some unnamed affliction—was rapidly getting worse.

Ezra entered after his father, slowing his steps to keep from passing him by. They stepped up to the altar together and stood, shoulder to shoulder, facing the flock. There was a smattering of applause, but the Prophet ordered silence with a raised hand.

The cathedral doors swung open again. The sound of hooves on stone echoed through the cathedral as Apostle Isaac brought forth the sacrifice. It was a small calf, the buds of its horns piercing through its hide, its wide eyes brown and doe-like.

Honor grabbed a fistful of Immanuelle's skirts. She had never taken to the slaughters well.

"It's all right," Immanuelle whispered, running her fingers through her hair.

Apostle Isaac hauled the calf up onto the altar. It slipped a little on the stained stone stairs, hooves sliding out from underneath it, legs skewing as it found its footing. Isaac eased a hand down its side, collecting its legs so that it was forced to lie with its stomach pressed to the cold slate of the altar. The calf obeyed without a struggle, too young and too dense to catch the scent of death on the air.

The Prophet moved forward with Ezra at his side, his bare feet rasping across the floor. He raised the blade high above his head. "To Ezra."

The flock answered as one. *"Long may he reign!"*

A FEW HOURS after the Sabbath service and slaughter, Immanuelle left her family and took the bride's carriage back to the Haven with Leah. All eyes were on Immanuelle as she entered the gallery. Despite her initial fears, Ezra, Father bless him, had not betrayed her to the Church. Quite the opposite, in fact. Whatever lie he'd constructed to explain their presence in the Darkwood that day had cast her as the hero. And now it seemed that everyone wanted to know the story of the hapless shepherd girl who saved the Prophet's successor from the clutches of the Darkwood. But Immanuelle was tired of stories and lies. And she did all that she could to avoid wandering gazes as she settled into her place at the feasting table and picked through her food. She tried to keep up with the conversation at hand, but when the discussion turned to the laborious endeavors of childbirth, her attention waned and her gaze roamed about the room.

The gallery was immaculate. The tables were decorated with wreaths of roses, freshly cut and harvested from the Prophet's own conservatory. Candlesticks as tall as Abram stood at intervals along the walls, their light warming the faces of the guests, who sat chatting over heaping plates of roast and potato. With the blood plague now ended and the rations order revoked, wine and water flowed in abundance.

At the front of the gallery stood a long oak table where the Prophet was seated. To his left sat Esther in a gown of pale lilac, and to his right, Ezra, his eyes glazed and bloodshot.

The Prophet leaned forward in his seat, carving a bit of meat from the roasted goat on the platter in front of him. As he worked his blade between the bones, his gaze moved across the congregation and found its way to Immanuelle. Their eyes locked, and the Prophet set his knife down and, with some effort, raised his goblet to toast her, a motion that a few of his guests mirrored.

All Immanuelle managed in response to the gesture was a curt nod. She fixed her eyes on her plate, trying to swallow down the sickness that boiled at the back of her throat whenever the Prophet's gaze landed upon her.

And lately, that had been often.

Leah put a hand to her shoulder. "Are you all right?"

"Fine," said Immanuelle, tracing her fork through a puddle of gravy. "Why do you ask?"

"Because you look pale and frightened, as though you've seen the face of the Dark Mother herself. Are you sick?" Leah demanded.

"No."

"Tired, then?"

Immanuelle nodded. Of course she was. She was exhausted and annoyed, tired of telling the same stories again and again, answering the same questions, and entertaining the same people who, under typical circumstances, wouldn't want anything to do with her. She wanted nothing more than to go home and retreat to her bed. She couldn't remember the last time she'd felt so terribly out of place.

Typically, Immanuelle would have never attended such an esteemed celebration in the first place, but on account of the fact that it was she who had "rescued" Ezra, the Prophet had offered her a formal invitation to the celebratory feast. She should have been excited, but all she could summon in response to the invitation was a deep and ugly dread. She'd never been good with social events, and they were always harder to endure without her family by her side. She'd tried every excuse she could think of to avoid the occasion, but Martha had held firm, forcing her to accept the invitation lest she insult the Church. So, there she sat. "I'm sorry. I'm not myself today."

Leah rubbed her arm sympathetically. "It's all right. Patience was only asking if you'd tell us the story again."

A slight, pretty girl, who Immanuelle assumed was Patience, smiled coyly from down the table. Immanuelle could tell she was a new bride from the scab-flaked seal between her eyebrows. If her fine dress and poised air were any indication, she'd married well.

Immanuelle took a sip of mulled wine to buy herself some time, the drink so hot it stung her tongue. In fewer words, she recounted the same lie she'd told the apostles: "I was in the pastures and I found Ezra on the edge of the woods. I tried to wake him, but he didn't stir, so I called for help . . . and help came."

Hope let out a long sigh, her shoulders slumping. "It sounds like the beginning of a love story."

"Don't be ridiculous," said Patience, rolling her eyes. "Ezra Chambers has far more important things to do than romp in the Darkwood with"—her eyes traced over Immanuelle, taking in her curls, her dark skin, her full lips—"some girl from the Outskirts."

Immanuelle flinched. There was truth in those harsh words. Whatever kinship she and Ezra once shared had likely died the day of his First Vision. There were certain codes of conduct in Bethel that kept those on the Outskirts from venturing inward, and even if they went unwritten and unsaid, she knew she was expected to abide by them.

"Besides," Patience rambled on, "between Ezra's new title and what became of Judith, I daresay our heir will be keeping his distance."

At the mention of Judith's name, the table went quiet. Leah stared into her goblet, seemingly enamored by the depths of her wine, and the younger girls who'd sat giggling at the table's edge were now still.

"What happened to Judith?" Immanuelle tried to keep her voice light and even, but her heart beat faster as she thought back to that day at the Haven, when the strange man in the stained smock appeared at the corridor's end to escort Judith to the Prophet.

No one answered. Everyone seemed preoccupied with picking at their food or sipping wine.

At last, Leah said, "The night after Ezra's vision, Judith was taken from the confinement ward and sent to contrition."

Contrition. It was a punishment reserved for the grossest offenders of the Father's Holy Protocol. No one knew what contrition entailed exactly—apart from immediate excommunication or detainment. Some claimed it consisted of forced fasts to starve out sin and cleanse the soul. Others told tales of long imprisonments in the Haven's dungeons, where those paying penance were subjected to violent beatings to exorcise demons and sins from the body. But one thing was certain: Everyone who was sent to contrition returned . . . changed. It was the ultimate act of sanctification, if the soul in question was strong enough to see it through.

Immanuelle felt suddenly sick, as if she was in jeopardy of

bringing up every mouthful of roast she'd forced herself to swallow. She could barely get her words out. "What was Judith's sin?"

"They won't say." Patience raised her goblet to her lips, then added, "But if her whoring had anything to do with it, I assume she'll be held for some time."

Leah's brows knit together. "You shouldn't say such terrible things."

"Why shouldn't I? It's the truth." The girl's gaze slid back to Immanuelle. "One I daresay a few of us could learn from."

Immanuelle stiffened. With a pang, she stared across the gallery to the Prophet's table. Next to his father, Ezra sat slumped in his chair, downing the last dregs of his wine. He paused to wipe his mouth on the back of his hand, grabbed for the decanter, filled his goblet to the rim, and drank like he was trying to drown himself.

Immanuelle wondered if he felt responsible for Judith's punishment, if it was their tryst that had resulted in her detainment. If so, Immanuelle feared for her. She and Judith were far from friends, but if the horrors of holy contrition were all that Immanuelle believed them to be, then she couldn't help but pity her. And with that pity came a kind of rage, not at Judith or Ezra, but at the system that held one accountable for her sins while the other was lauded.

Ezra's gaze shifted, and he met Immanuelle's eyes for the first time that day. When she offered him a smile, he cast his gaze away and pushed back from the table so abruptly the cutlery rattled. Without a parting word, he staggered across the gallery to the doors at its opposing end. The gazes of the guests followed him, but no one pursued him. Esther attempted, but the Prophet put a firm hand to her wrist, pinning it to the table. Behind them, the Prophet's Guard stood taciturn, waiting for an order.

Never one to miss a beat, the Prophet pushed back from his chair and stood. He ordered the quartet to play a lively hymn, and with a flash of his hand, he summoned a fresh barrel of mead from the Haven's kitchens. The servants scurried from table to table, filling mugs and goblets to the brim. In a matter of moments, Ezra's departure was all but forgotten.

Immanuelle shoved back from the table, the feet of her chair scraping across the floor.

"Where are you going?" Leah asked. "We haven't even had dessert yet! I have it on good authority that the chefs are serving an apple tart with clotted cream."

"I don't have the stomach for sweets today," said Immanuelle, gazing through the crowd to the doors through which Ezra had disappeared. "I think I'll take some air."

Leah gazed at her, eyes narrowed. Then she shoved back from the table and grabbed Immanuelle's hand, locking their fingers. "I'll go with you."

As soon as they left, cutting down the aisles between tables, and exited into the corridor, Leah turned to her. "You're going after Ezra, aren't you?"

"What makes you think that?"

"He's been casting you furtive glances whenever your back is turned, and you've been doing the same to him. The two of you can't keep your eyes off each other."

Immanuelle flushed, but she didn't break pace. "It's not like that."

"Then what are you not telling me? Don't you trust me?"

"I do trust you. I just don't want to drag you into undue trouble."

"Trouble?" Leah caught her by the arm as a servant walked past, shouldering a tray of apple tarts. She lowered her voice to a whisper. "What do you mean by trouble? Did something happen in the woods that day? Did Ezra do something to you?"

"Of course not! Ezra would never."

But even as she spoke, Immanuelle knew it didn't matter

whether Ezra had done anything. The real danger was being near him at all, under the watchful eyes of Bethel. Judith was a prime example of this. And Immanuelle was ashamed to admit it, but she was selfishly relieved that it was Judith who was now paying the price in contrition, for it could have just as easily been her.

"If it's not Ezra, then what was it? What is all of this?" Leah demanded, motioning to her with a pass of her hand. "You look a fright, Immanuelle—all frail and quiet. It's not like you. Does this have something to do with those women you saw the night you went into the Darkwood?"

Immanuelle didn't want to lie to her, but she knew that in light of things, a lie was better than the truth. "No."

Leah studied her for a beat, trying to decide what she wanted to believe. Immanuelle braced herself for more questions, but they didn't come. With a smile, Leah hooked an arm through hers. "Good. I was a little afraid Ezra had turned you into a simpering harlot." Immanuelle elbowed her in the ribs and Leah laughed. "Of course, I wouldn't blame you if he had. For all of his Holy Gifts, he's got the eyes of a devil—and the tongue of one too. I don't trust him one bit."

"He's not as bad as he seems," said Immanuelle. "Now, quiet down. These corridors carry echoes, and he may hear you."

"Well, he won't hear anything he doesn't know already. I'm certain that boy's been scheming since the day we met at the riverside. I saw the way he looked at you."

"*Leah!*"

Leah smiled at Immanuelle, wiggling her eyebrows suggestively, and the two dissolved into a fit of giggles. By the time they arrived at the library, they were laughing and staggering, tripping over their own shoes, trading jokes and stories.

"Prudence tried to dye her hair red with beet juice," said Leah between giggles. "And her curls went as blue as a cornflower's petals. All that effort to catch the eye of *Joab Sidney*? I mean, the man's ancient. If you ask me, he's two steps from the grave."

"You're wretched."

"*We're* wretched. That's why we're a perfect fit. Always have been."

"And will be," said Immanuelle, starting down the hall toward the library, but before she could make it more than a few steps, Leah dragged her back.

"I have something to tell you," she said, suddenly grave.

"What is it?"

Leah hesitated. "Promise me you'll keep this to yourself. No matter how you feel, no matter how angry it makes you."

"I promise I won't tell a soul," said Immanuelle. "You have my word."

"All right," said Leah, and her chin trembled a bit. "Give me your hand."

Immanuelle obeyed without question, and Leah guided her hand past the layers of her gown, until Immanuelle could feel the shape of her belly, which was swollen into a pronounced bump.

"Are you . . . you're not . . . you *can't* be . . . ?"

"Pregnant."

Immanuelle's mouth gaped open. "How many months?"

Leah's brows knit together the way they always did when she was deciding whether or not she wanted to lie. At last she whispered, "Six. Give or take a few weeks."

Immanuelle went very still and very quiet.

"Say something," Leah pleaded, in a voice so soft and so young it didn't even sound like her own. "Say anything. Yell at me if you have to. I'd prefer that to your silence."

"Is it his?"

"Of course it's his," she snapped, with a harshness that didn't become her.

"But how is this possible? You've barely been married a month."

Leah stared down at her feet, ashamed. "We were betrothed soon after."

"Soon after *what*?"

Leah frowned, and she couldn't tell if it was anger she read in her eyes or hurt. "He came to me one night, before my cutting, while I was doing penance."

Penance. Of course.

Many girls in Bethel were invited to serve the Church as maidservants to the Prophet's wives or other inhabitants of the Haven. As a bastard by birth, Immanuelle was never enlisted, but Leah served often in the years before her engagement. Toward the end of her service, it seemed like she spent more nights at the Haven than she did in her own home. Now Immanuelle knew why. "When did it start?"

Leah looked sick with shame. "A few weeks before my first blood."

"So you were barely thirteen?" Immanuelle whispered, and it was so horrible that even as she said it, she could barely believe it was true. "Leah, you were . . . he was . . ."

Leah's chin trembled. "We all sin."

"But he's the Prophet—"

"He's just a man, Immanuelle. Men make mistakes."

"But you were a child. You were just a little girl."

Leah hung her head, trying to choke back tears.

"Why didn't you tell me?"

"Because you would have done what you're doing now."

"And what am I doing, Leah?"

"Baring your broken heart. Sharing in the shame of my sin like it's your burden too." Leah reached out to her then, took her by the hand, and pulled her close. "This pain is mine. I don't need you to carry it for me. One day you're going to have to learn that we can't share in everything. Sometimes we'll have to walk alone."

The words landed like a slap. Immanuelle opened her mouth to say something, anything, to fill the ugly silence that formed between them, fearing that it would lag on forever if she didn't, but Leah beat her to it.

"I'll leave you two to talk."

"What—"

A door slammed shut down the hall, and Immanuelle turned to see Ezra emerging from the library with an armful of books piled so high he had to balance the top of the stack with his chin. As he started toward them, a few of the larger tomes tumbled from his arms and struck the floor with a resounding *thud*. Immanuelle stepped forward to help him pick them up.

Ezra muttered something that sounded like a thank-you and snatched the book from her hand. Up close, he reeked of alcohol— something much, much stronger than the mulled wine that was served at the feast. Immanuelle turned back to Leah, torn between staying and going. But when Ezra staggered down the hall, she fell into step behind him. Just before she rounded the corner, she turned back to look at her friend. Leah stood motionless in the middle of the hall as if pinned in place. Immanuelle watched as she hung her head, wrapped both arms around her belly, and slowly turned away.

Chapter Eighteen

Sometimes I wonder if my secrets are better swallowed than spoken. Perhaps my truths have done enough harm. Perhaps I should take my memories to the grave and let the dead judge my sins.

—Miriam Moore

WE NEED TO talk," said Immanuelle, struggling to keep pace with Ezra's long strides.

"If you're worried I told someone what happened in the woods, don't be," he said gruffly, looking straight ahead. He spoke like he knew something more than what she'd told him, which begged the question . . . what? What did he think happened in the woods?

"I know you didn't tell anyone," said Immanuelle, double-stepping to keep up with him. "If you had, I'd likely be in contrition right now—"

"Or on a pyre." He paused, then said, "Come with me."

Gathering her skirts in one hand, Immanuelle followed Ezra down the hall and up a winding flight of stairs. At the top was an iron door which Ezra kicked open, nearly dropping his books in the process. He turned to look at her. "Are you coming in or not?"

Immanuelle had never entered a man's chambers before and she was certain Martha would skin her to the bone if she ever so much as suspected her of such a grave and salacious transgression. She stalled for a beat, then nodded.

As soon as she was past the threshold, Ezra dumped his books on a nearby table and drew the door shut. Overhead, the chandelier shivered, crystals rattling together. Immanuelle noticed that the ceiling was painted like the heavens, dotted with planets and stars and etched with the shapes of constellations, some so large they spanned the room from one end to the other. The stone walls were hung with tapestries and portraits of stern-looking saints and apostles of ages long past. On the right half of the room was a large iron bed draped with dark brocade and a few thick sheepskins. Just beyond it, a wooden desk built in the blunt fashion of a butcher's block, its surface strewn with quills and parchment paper.

Opposite the door was a hearth that ran the length of the wall. Above it, hand painted across the bricks, was a map of the world beyond the Bethelan territories. Immanuelle saw the names of all the heathen cities: Gall in the barren north, Hebron in the midlands, Sine in the mountains, Judah at the cusp of the desert, Shoan south where the raging sea licked the land, and the black stain of Valta—the Dark Mother's domain—in the far east.

All around the room, stacked in piles as tall as Immanuelle, were books. They were shoved into shelves, perched atop the hearth's mantel, even crammed beneath the bed. But it was only when Immanuelle drew near enough to read their titles that she realized almost all of them related to the history, study, and practice of witchcraft.

Her heart seized in her chest, as if some hand had closed around it and squeezed tight. She could think of only one reason Ezra would have developed a sudden taste for books of witchcraft, and it began with her and ended with what happened in the Darkwood. "What is this, Ezra? You're scaring me."

"Something dragged you under," said Ezra, and the weight of his gaze made her skin crawl.

"What?"

"Back in the woods, at the pond, something dragged you under, and it kept you there for a long time."

In spite of the blazing fire, a deep chill racked her. "What do you mean by a long time?"

"Twenty minutes. Maybe more."

"That's impossible," Immanuelle whispered, shaking her head. "You must be mistaken, I was barely under for more than a minute. I warned you, the Darkwood has a way of twisting the minds of men—"

"Don't patronize me," he snapped. "I know what I saw. You went into the water, something dragged you under, and it kept you there." His voice broke on the last word, and he hung his head. "I tried to dive in after you, but the forest caught hold of me, and I couldn't. I just had to stand there helpless, watching you drown with that damn rope in my hand. Toward the end, I was just hoping to reel your corpse ashore so your kin would have something to bury."

"Ezra . . . I'm sorry."

Immanuelle wasn't even sure he'd heard her. He kept his eyes locked on the fire as he spoke. "When I was young, my grandmother used to tell me stories of girls who floated inches above their beds while they slept at night. Girls who could talk a man into taking his own life or the life of someone else. Girls who were executed—tossed into a lake with millstones chained to their ankles—only to be reeled from the water alive an hour later. Girls who laughed when they burned on the pyre. I never used to give those stories credence, but you . . ." He lost his train of thought. Took a moment to collect himself. "What was your obsession with the blood plague? You said you just wanted to end it, but it was more than that, wasn't it? You know something the rest of us don't. What is it?"

So Ezra did know the truth, or at least enough of it to send her to the pyre. It was futile to lie, in light of that. "I went into the Darkwood, just before the blood plague began, and while I was there I had . . . an encounter."

"An encounter with what?"

"The witches of the woods. They're real. I was with them the night before the blood plague struck. I think that my presence in the woods unleashed something terrible. When I went back I was trying to undo it. And I would have told you sooner, I wanted to, but—"

"You couldn't trust me."

"You're the Prophet's son and heir. A word from you could've sent me to the pyre. I didn't know if I could trust you with my secrets. I still don't."

Ezra sidestepped past her, crossed the room to his desk, unlocked its top drawer with the blade of his holy dagger, withdrew a sheaf of papers, and extended them to her.

Immanuelle took them. "What is this?"

"Your entry in the census. I was supposed to surrender it to my father days ago."

"Why didn't you?"

"Read it yourself and find out." When she hesitated, Ezra nodded toward the chairs that stood by the hearth. Between them was a table that housed a glass decanter and goblet. "Go on."

Immanuelle took a seat on one of the chairs and Ezra settled himself opposite her. He poured himself some wine, watching her over the rim as he drank. The first page recounted the particulars of Immanuelle's personal history—her full name and the names of her parents, her date of birth. At the end of the account, a strange, muddled mark that Immanuelle initially mistook for an ink spot. But upon closer examination, she saw that it was some sort of strange symbol: a bride's seal, only the points of the star were longer, and there were seven of them instead of eight. The longer she studied that strange mark, the more certain she was that she'd seen it before.

Then the realization struck her.

That mark was the same one carved into the foreheads of Delilah and the Lovers.

Immanuelle's hand began to shake. She leaned out of her seat, pointed to the mark at the end of her census, and extended the page to Ezra for clarification. "Is this—"

He merely nodded, his gaze on the fire. "The Mother's mark. It's the symbol the cutting seal was derived from, years ago. David Ford sought a way to reclaim it, so he altered the mark and called it his."

"Then why does it appear unaltered here?"

Ezra downed the dregs of his wine, pressed to his feet, and set his glass on the mantel. "Normally, the Church uses the Mother's mark to identify those who were credibly accused of witchcraft. But sometimes, it's used to identify the direct descendants of witches and trace their bloodlines. Days ago, when my father asked me to go through the census files, that's what he was looking for."

"I don't understand."

Ezra rubbed the back of his neck like his muscles were paining him. He looked about as haggard and weak as he had at the pond, days ago. "The Mother's mark appears beside at least one of your ancestors, every other generation, on your father's side. The last being your grandmother, your father's mother, Vera Ward."

"Which means . . ."

Ezra just nodded, quiet and despondent. Neither of them spoke to the silent accusation that hung on the air between them like a pall of pyre smoke.

"When did you discover this?" Immanuelle whispered.

"The night before we entered the Darkwood. Your census was one of the first ones I read."

Her hands began to shake. "Have you told anyone?"

"Of course not."

"*Will* you tell anyone?"

Silence, then: "I'm not my father."

"And yet here I am, under an inquisition."

"Is that what you think this is?" Ezra demanded, looking almost betrayed.

"What else would you call it? From the moment I entered this room, all you've done is question me like I'm some sort of criminal on trial."

A long silence spanned between them, broken only by the crackling of the hearth fire. Outside, a rogue wind ripped across the plains, and the windowpanes rattled in their casings. A disembodied chorus of laughter and music floated up from downstairs, the sounds so distant they seemed almost spectral.

Ezra turned to Immanuelle, extended his hand. "Give it to me."

"What?"

"Your census account. Give it to me."

"Why?" Immanuelle whispered, stricken and perhaps more terrified than she had ever been before. "What are you going to do with it?"

Ezra didn't ask again. He stepped forward and snatched the papers so quickly Immanuelle didn't have the chance to grab them back.

"Ezra, please—"

He hurled the papers into the fire, and they both watched in silence as the hungry flames devoured them.

"We're going to keep this quiet," said Ezra in a hushed murmur. "I won't speak of what happened in the Darkwood that day and neither will you. No one need know the truth of your heritage. When we leave this room it'll be like it never happened—the woods, the witches, the census, all of it. We'll never speak of it again."

"But the plague—"

"Is over, Immanuelle. You ended it at the pond."

"You don't know that," she said, remembering her mother's journal, the words scrawled across its final pages: *Blood. Blight. Darkness. Slaughter.* "What if there's more to come?"

"More of what to come?"

"Plagues," said Immanuelle, treading carefully now. "What happens if it's more than just the blood?"

"What do you mean?"

"I mean what if this plague isn't the last one? What if there's more to come?"

"It ended with the blood," said Ezra, and he sounded so much like his father that Immanuelle cringed.

"Just because you want that to be true doesn't make it so. The Sight is formidable, yes, but it only allows you to see glimpses of the future. It doesn't give you the power to shape it. I know that you're afraid, Ezra. I am too. But that doesn't give us the right to close our eyes and pretend what scares us doesn't exist. If more plagues are coming—"

"For the sake of the Father, they're not."

"*If* they are, we have to be ready to face them."

Ezra returned to the seat beside her, looking exhausted. He hunched forward, arms braced against his kneecaps, head hanging low. "Listen to me, Immanuelle. It either ends here, with this, or it ends with you dead. There is no in-between. That's why I'm telling you—I'm *begging* you—to lay this to rest."

She faltered at that. It wasn't a threat, but the way Ezra spoke made it seem like the future was *immutable*, which was, of course, impossible. Unless . . . "Did you see that in one of your visions? Did you see me?"

He dodged the question. "I don't need the Sight to confirm what I already know to be true. Girls like you don't last long in Bethel. Which is why you need to keep your head down if you want to survive this. Promise me that you will."

"Why do you care what I do, Ezra?"

He kept his gaze fixed on the floor, like he couldn't bring himself to look at her. "You know why."

Immanuelle flushed. She didn't know what to say to that, or if she was meant to say anything at all. "You make me a promise too."

"Anything. Whatever you want."

"It's in regard to your father."

Ezra froze. A range of expressions passed over his face in quick succession, so fast she couldn't tell what he was feeling. "Did he hurt you?"

Immanuelle shook her head. "Not me. A friend. She was young when it happened, and I fear she's not the only victim of the Prophet's . . . *compulsions.*"

Ezra stood so fast the feet of the armchair scraped the floor with a screech. He half turned to the bedroom door.

"Don't," said Immanuelle, throwing out a hand. "He's dying. Some say he won't last the year. He'll never take another bride. He's too weak to raise a hand to anyone now."

"Then what would you have me do?" Ezra demanded, and she saw the rage in him then. "Nothing?"

"Nothing except promise me that when it's your turn to wear the Prophet's dagger, you'll protect those who can't protect themselves— from the plagues, from their husbands, from anyone or anything who might hurt them. Promise me you'll right the wrongs of the past."

"I promise," said Ezra, and at once she knew he meant it. "On my life."

Immanuelle nodded, satisfied that she'd done what little she could. For a farm girl from the Glades, she had certainly come far. It seemed surreal to her that she was cutting bargains with the Prophet's heir, reckoning with witches, making plans for the future of Bethel, when just weeks ago the extent of her responsibilities ended with the borders of the Moore land.

But the time for thrilling schemes and grandeur had come to an end. For now, and perhaps forever, the plagues were over. Ezra would go his way, and she hers. Whatever affinity they shared would quickly die. In fact, she doubted they would ever speak in such a candid way again. In due time, Ezra would rise to take his place as Prophet, and Immanuelle would recede into the shadows of his past. She should have been content with that. But she wasn't.

"Take care of yourself," said Ezra, and he, like she, seemed to sense this was goodbye. "Please."

She forced a smile as she pressed to her feet. "You do the same."

"And if you ever need anything—"

"I won't," said Immanuelle, striding to the door. She stalled a beat, her hand on the knob. "But thank you. For all of it. You were a friend to me when I sorely needed one, and I'll never forget it."

✤

Chapter Nineteen

From the Mother comes disease and fever, pestilence and blight. She curses the earth with rot and sickness, for sin was ushered from Her womb.

—THE HOLY SCRIPTURES

THREE WEEKS PASSED without any sign of the curses. The beasts of the Darkwood were dormant. No witches called to Immanuelle in the night or haunted her dreams. Had she not seen them firsthand—had she not felt Lilith's cold fingers lock around her wrist—she might have believed the plagues were over and been lulled into complacency like the rest of Bethel, convinced that whatever evil descended upon them had been purged by the Father's light.

But Immanuelle *had* seen, and despite her oath to Ezra, it wasn't easy to forget it.

That evening, Glory and Honor had retired to their beds early, sick with a summer flu. For a while, Immanuelle and the Moore wives stayed awake to tend to them. But after the girls drifted off into the fitful sleep of fever, they too retired to their respective chambers for the night.

With everyone asleep, and the farmhouse quiet, Immanuelle returned to the pages of her mother's book. This had been her ritual every night since Ezra's formal investiture as the Prophet's heir. She turned to her favorite drawing in the book—the portrait of her father, Daniel Ward, that Miriam had sketched all those years ago.

Now that the plague was over, she felt she had time to mourn her father in a way that she never had before. She'd always lived alongside Miriam's memory, having grown up in the house of her childhood, but it was different with Daniel. He had never been fully real to her in the way that Miriam was . . . until that evening, weeks ago, when she'd first read her census account at the Haven and seen the witch mark beside her name, the same one that denoted the accounts of so many Wards who'd come before her.

And while a part of her desperately wanted to keep her promise to Ezra and put the past behind her, an even greater part of her wanted to understand the truth of who and what she was. She wanted to know her kin in the Outskirts, and if they suffered from the same temptations she did. She wanted to understand why she was so compelled by the Darkwood, why the witches first gave her Miriam's journal, why they chose to use her blood as an offering to spawn that horrible plague. Perhaps it was just her pride, but try as she might, she couldn't resign herself to the life she'd led before. She wanted answers and she knew where to find them: in the Outskirts, with the kin she'd never known.

The only thing that kept her from pursuing answers was her oath to Ezra. Still, she couldn't help but feel that, of the two of them, she was the one made to sacrifice more. After all, Ezra knew who he was—son of the Prophet, heir of the Church—but the same couldn't be said about Immanuelle. The question of who and what she was remained, and unless she delved into the mysteries of her past, it always would.

With a sigh, Immanuelle shut the journal and padded across the room to the window, climbed to a perch on its ledge, and brushed back the curtains. The moon was a crescent cut into the night sky. In the distance, the Darkwood was black and motionless, and even though there was no wind to whisper her name, Immanuelle could still feel its call. The weeks of denial and repression still weren't enough to silence it. Staring at the trees, she wondered if she would ever be free of that temptation. Or if the Darkwood's thrall was as intrinsic to her as the Sight was to Ezra.

Maybe she didn't have a choice. Was it foolish of her to think that she did?

A dull ache throbbed in her stomach, and Immanuelle startled to attention. It took her a few long moments to realize what it was: the pains of her bleed. Sure enough, when she raised the skirts of her nightdress and checked her undergarments, she found them wet and red, stained through.

Slipping off the ledge of her windowsill, Immanuelle left her bedroom and climbed down the attic steps. She crept into the washroom and took her basket of rags from the cabinet beneath the sink. Anna had showed her how to cut them so they'd be comfortable to wear but also thick enough to staunch her flow.

She fit them into her undergarments, then washed her hands in the sink. As she did so, she was conscious of how tired she looked in the mirror, her bloodshot eyes shadowed by dark bags. She was walking back to her room when she heard a sharp rapping on the back door of the farmhouse. It was midnight, far too late for visitors. But the knocking continued, its rhythm steady as a heartbeat.

Moving a hand to the wall, she slipped into the hallway and down the stairs, entering the front parlor. There, she found Glory standing in front of Martha's armchair, her eyes closed.

Immanuelle relaxed then, as Glory had been known to stroll in her sleep. The girl wasn't adventurous in her waking hours, but at night it wasn't uncommon to find her roaming the halls in her dreams. The Moores locked the doors every evening, just to keep her from wandering into the woods.

"Glory." Immanuelle put her hands to the girl's shoulders, trying to shake her awake. She could feel the heat of fever burning through the fabric of her nightgown. "You're walking in your dreams again. Will we have to tether your wrists to your headboard to keep you from wandering awa—"

Another crack. This one struck with the hollow sound of a bone breaking—and it had come from the kitchen.

Immanuelle's hands fell from Glory's shoulders. Following the sound, she eased through the front room, pausing to lift a heavy bookend off the hearth's mantel. As she rounded the corner and entered the kitchen, she raised it high above her head, ready to strike whatever stranger had found their way into their home.

But there was no intruder.

Across the kitchen, standing in the shadow of the threshold, was Honor, her forehead pressed to the door. Her back arched as she threw herself forward, and her head struck the wood with a stomach-churning crunch. Blood streamed down the bridge of her nose.

Immanuelle broke forward, the bookend clattering to the floor.

Honor struck the door again, with so much force the windows rattled in their casings. Then Immanuelle was upon her, dragging the child away, crying for help. Honor lay in her arms, stiff and stoic, burning with fever, deaf to her cries.

And so, the second curse came upon them.

PART II

Blight

CHAPTER TWENTY

*A man who knows his past is a man with the power to choose
his future.*

—FROM *THE PARABLES OF THE PROPHET ZACHRIAS*

I N THE DAYS that followed, more than two hundred fell ill, suc-
cumbing first to the fever, then to the madness after it. Immanuelle heard stories of grown men clawing their eyes from
their sockets, chaste women of the faith who stripped off their
clothes and fled, naked, into the Darkwood, screaming as they
went. Others, mostly little children like Honor, suffered from a
different, but perhaps more sinister, affliction and succumbed to
the clutches of a sleep as deep as death. As far as Immanuelle
knew, none of the healers in Bethel were able to wake them.

Of those who fell ill in the early days of the contagion, sixty
died before the Sabbath. To keep the plague from spreading, the
dead were burned on purging pyres. But those who fled to the
Darkwood in fits of madness were never seen or heard from again.

By all accounts, it was the worst contagion in Bethel's thousand-
year history, and people called it many things—the affliction, the
fever, the manic flu—but Immanuelle only ever referred to it by
one name, the one written dozens of times in the final pages of
her mother's journal: *Blight*.

"More water," Martha demanded, mopping a sheen of sweat

from her forehead. Though all the windows were open, each breath of wind brought the hot smoke of the pyres that burned throughout the Glades. "And bring the yarrow." Under normal circumstances, burning the bodies of the blameless was a grave breach of Holy Protocol. But in a desperate attempt to stop the spread of the disease, the Church made a rare amendment to its sacred law.

Immanuelle obeyed, skirts sweeping around her ankles as she ducked into the kitchen, grabbing a basin of water and a bundle of dried yarrow flower from the herb box beneath the sink. She raced upstairs as fast as she could without tripping on the hem of her skirts and entered the children's room.

There, she found Anna tightening the knots around Glory's wrists, tethering her to the headboard to keep her from escaping, as she had tried to do six times since the night she first took ill. Anna tied the cloth cuffs so tight there were bruises around her daughter's wrists, but it couldn't be helped. Nearly half of those afflicted with the blight had maimed or even killed themselves in the throes of their madness, jumping out of windows or bashing their own heads in, as Honor had nearly done the night Immanuelle found her.

At her mother's touch, Glory thrashed and shrieked, legs tangling in her sheets, her cheeks bright with fever.

Immanuelle set the basin beside the bed, took the yarrow from her mouth, and grabbed the bowl on the nightstand. She crushed the blooms as best she could, mashing them into a paste. Then she added a little water—still faintly tinged by the last traces of the blood plague—and mixed the pulp with her fingers.

It was Martha who administered the draught, seizing Glory firmly by the base of her neck and thrusting her upright, the way one holds a squalling newborn. She forced the bowl to her mouth, and Glory thrashed and spat, dragging at her binds, her eyes rolling back in her skull as the draught dribbled between her lips and down her chin.

Honor lay across the room with her eyes closed, her blankets tucked beneath her chin. Immanuelle put a hand to her cheek and winced. The fever raged in her yet. The girl lay so still Immanuelle had to slip a finger beneath her nose just to see if she was breathing. She hadn't stirred once since the blight had arrived. That night, she'd struck herself into a deep slumber they feared she'd never wake from.

It went on like that for hours—Glory thrashing in her bed, Honor comatose, Anna weeping on a chair in the corner—until Immanuelle couldn't bear it anymore. She left the farmhouse for the pastures. Days ago, their farmhand, Josiah, had been called back to his own home in the distant Glades to tend to his blight-sick wife. So apart from Immanuelle, there was no one to keep watch over the grazing sheep.

As she crossed the pastures, crook in hand, she weighed the options available to her. Her darkest fears had become reality. The sacrifice she'd made at the pond hadn't worked after all. Blight was upon them, and if it didn't end soon, Immanuelle feared the lives of her sisters would be forfeit. But what could she do to stop it?

Her blood offering hadn't been enough to break the curse, and she had no one to turn to for aid. The Church seemed helpless in the face of such great evil. Immanuelle considered turning to Ezra for help, as she had done before, but decided against it. He'd made it plain that he wanted no part in plagues or witchcraft, no part of her. The last time she'd dragged him into her schemes he'd almost paid a mortal price. It seemed cruel to call upon him again.

But if not Ezra, whom could she turn to? There had to be someone, something. A cure or scheme to stop this. She had to believe that, on principle alone, because if she didn't, it meant that hope was lost and her sisters were going to die.

A memory surfaced at the back of her mind, an image of her

census papers, the witch mark below her name and the names of the Wards who came before her. Was it possible that the very answers she sought—about the plagues, and the witches and a way to defeat them—could be waiting for her in the Outskirts, in the form of the family she had never known? If the witch mark was any indication at all, they were versed in the magic of the Darkwood and the coven that walked its corridors. If there was any help to be found in Bethel, Immanuelle was certain she'd find it with them.

But how could she slip away to the Outskirts unnoticed, with Honor and Glory as sick as they were? There was no way she could excuse her absence for more than an hour, and she would need at least a day to find her kin in the Outskirts.

Immanuelle frowned, staring past the flock of grazing sheep, to the windows of Abram's workshop glowing in the distance. An idea took shape at the back of her mind.

Abram. Of course.

Immanuelle might not have been able to win Martha over . . . but perhaps Abram would be more sympathetic. He was kindhearted, gentler than Martha, and less pious than Anna. Perhaps he would see the merit in her desires to reach out to her kin in the Outskirts.

Emboldened by this idea, Immanuelle herded the last of the sheep into the corral where they spent their nights and started toward Abram's workshop. It was a humble space. The wood floors were dusted with a thick carpet of sawdust. As usual, a series of half-finished projects cluttered the workspace—a pair of tree-trunk side tables, a stool, and a dollhouse that was no doubt intended to be a gift for Honor's birthday.

Paintings adorned the walls, all of them her mother's. There were sweeping landscapes on wood panels, parchment painted with faint watercolor flowers, a few still lifes. There was even a

self-portrait, which featured Miriam, smiling, with her hair unbound.

Immanuelle peered over Abram's shoulder to see what he was
working on and stopped dead. There, on the table, was a small,
half-carved coffin. It was big enough for only one member of the
Moore family: Honor.

"She's still . . . with us," said Abram without looking up from
his work. "I just want to be ready . . . if the worst comes."

Immanuelle began to shake. "She's going to wake up."

"Perhaps. But if she doesn't . . . I have to be prepared . . . Always
promised myself . . . that if I had to . . . bury another child . . . I
would do it properly. In a coffin . . . of my own making. I missed
that chance . . . with your mother. I'll not . . . have it happen again.
Even if . . . I have to collect . . . her bones from the . . . pyre, I
intend . . . to give her . . . a proper burial. Should it . . . come to
that."

Immanuelle knew what he referred to. Bethelan custom man-
dated that the blameless were buried and the sinful were burned,
in the hopes that the flames of the pyre would purge them of their
sins and allow them passage into the realm of purgatory. On account of her crimes, Miriam had died in dishonor and, as a result,
she never had a proper coffin or burial plot in the graveyard where
her ancestors were laid to rest. "Do you miss her?"

"More than you know."

Immanuelle took a seat on the stool beside him. "And do you
regret breaking Protocol to hide her here, years ago?"

Abram's hand tightened around his chisel, but he shook his
head.

"Even though it was a sin?"

"Better to take sin upon . . . one's own shoulders . . . than allow
harm . . . to befall others. Sometimes a person . . . has an obligation . . .
to act in the interest of the . . . greater good."

This was her moment, and Immanuelle was quick to seize it. "During that time, did my mother ever speak of my father?"

Abram faltered, then lowered his tool. "More than she did . . . anyone else. When the madness . . . took her she used . . . to call for him. Claimed his ghost . . . was wandering the . . . halls. She'd say he was . . . calling her home. I like to think . . . that he did in the end."

Immanuelle's throat clenched so tightly she could barely speak. "I want to go to the Outskirts, Pa. I want to know the people that knew him. I want to meet his kin. *My* kin."

Abram remained expressionless. He returned to his work, scuffing a bit of sandpaper along the wall of the coffin. "Why now?"

"Because if I don't do it now, I may never get the chance to. What with the fever spreading."

"When do you . . . want to go?"

"Tomorrow, if possible. But I'd rather Martha not know. It would only trouble her."

"So you've come to ask for my blessing?"

"That and your help. Perhaps you could distract Martha."

"You mean lie . . . for you. Mislead her . . . into believing something that . . . isn't true."

Immanuelle flinched but nodded. "Like you said, sometimes a person has an obligation to act in the interest of the greater good even if it means they have to sin in order to do it. And is it not good for me to meet my kin while I still have the chance to?"

Abram offered her a rare smile. She could have sworn he looked almost proud of her. "Pity you weren't . . . born a boy. Would've made a . . . fine apostle with your penchant . . . for talking in circles."

"So you'll do it?" Immanuelle whispered, barely believing her good fortune. "You'll help me get to the Outskirts?"

Abram paused to blow sawdust from the inside of the coffin. "What won't I do . . . for you?"

Chapter Twenty-one

IMMANUELLE LEFT FOR the Outskirts at daybreak. The journey passed in a series of disembodied glimpses, as though she was so overwhelmed at the prospect of meeting her kin she couldn't process what she was looking at. There was the flash of a man in a mask like a crow's face, stoking a pyre's flames with a pitchfork, a shroud-wrapped body in the back of a wagon bouncing with every rut in the road. Blue smoke broke in waves above the treetops, so thick it stung her eyes, and the air rang with the cries of the blight sick.

There were women wandering in nothing more than their slips. Barefoot men shambling along the roads, a few of them shaking, others howling and scratching themselves bloody. As Immanuelle passed a neighboring farm, she saw a girl running through a dying cornfield, arms outstretched toward the Darkwood. She was wearing nothing but a long, bloodstained nightgown, and its skirts tangled around her ankles as she fled. A man tore after her, her father or husband perhaps; the distance made it hard to tell. He caught her around the waist and dragged her kicking and screaming to the dirt just a few feet from the forest's edge.

Immanuelle averted her eyes. The scene seemed like the sort of indignity that was wrong to bear witness to. Shaken, she walked on, traveling fast down the main road, until she saw the Outskirts emerge from a haze of pyre smoke.

Her heart kicked up to a fast rhythm, even as she slowed to a stop in the middle of the road.

After all of these years of pining, she was finally going to meet her kin.

Immanuelle started forward, noting that the Outskirts were strangely quiet. No children in the streets, no fever-struck fleeing for the forests. The roads were mostly empty, apart from the odd farmer or merchant steering a mule cart. The windows on the houses were shuttered. Dogs were tethered to lampposts and fences; a few of them barked at her as she passed them by. Every so often, a crow shrieked in the distance, but apart from that, the silence was near complete. For whatever reason—whether it be the small population, or some act of mercy on behalf of the witches—the Outskirts were spared the full wrath of the blight plague.

After a long walk through the winding streets, Immanuelle found the village center, where the chapel stood. It was an odd structure. Unlike the Prophet's Cathedral, which was built from slabs of slate, the Church of the Outskirts was comprised of a rustic thatching of woven branches and saplings. Its windows were set with stained-glassed portraits of strange dark-skinned saints that Immanuelle didn't know by name. Each of them held some sort of talisman—a lit candle, a cut branch, a red ribbon woven between their fingers, the twisted knob of a knucklebone.

In all her sixteen years, Immanuelle had never seen any saints or effigies in her own likeness. None of the statues and paintings housed in the Prophet's Cathedral bore any resemblance to her. But when she looked at those saints immortalized in stained glass, a kind of aching familiarity settled over her, as if something she'd forgotten she'd lost was finally being returned.

The front door was cut from a thick slab of oak, and it looked like it belonged on the hinges of a vault, not a church. Even though it was slightly ajar, Immanuelle had to throw her shoulder against it and heave her full weight into the effort of forcing it open. The room within was dim, cast in a haze of incense smoke so dense her eyes began to sting and fill with tears. There were no pews there, just long, narrow benches that ran half the length of the room, positioned in rows on either side of the aisle. Overhead, a balcony wrapped around the room's perimeter, where several women stood watching her.

At the aisle's end was a kind of altar. But unlike the one in the Prophet's Cathedral, this altar had a raised lip around its edges, creating a sort of shallow basin within, where a small fire burned. A man stood over the offering, his face bathed with smoke. As Immanuelle drew near, she saw that he wore a holy dagger—albeit an old and rusty one. He had a shaved head, and his eyes were the palest shade of amber, a sharp contrast to the rich ebony of his skin. If she had to guess, she'd say he was about Abram's age, perhaps a little younger. He wore simple robes cut from what appeared to be rough burlap, belted at the waist with a leather cord so long its tassels skimmed the floor. Approaching him, Immanuelle felt a certain gravitas that she had only ever experienced in the woods when Lilith first emerged from the tree line.

"My name is Immanuelle Moore—"

"No need," he said and turned back to the fire. Beside it, on a small stone pedestal, was a group of young chickens, bound together by their necks. The priest picked them up by the rope and released them into the flames with the mutter of something that might have been a prayer, but it was so brief Immanuelle couldn't tell. The scent of burnt feathers and seared meat mingled with the thick stench of the incense. "I know who you are."

"How?"

The priest chuckled, like she'd told a particularly witty joke. "There are few of us who don't. Tell me, what brings you to the Outskirts today?"

"I'm here for my family."

"And why do you seek them now?"

"Because I'm ready."

The priest raised an eyebrow. Appraised her through the rolling smoke. "You weren't before?"

Immanuelle squared her shoulders. "I was scared before. But I'm not anymore. So I'd like to see them, if you could point me in the right direction."

The priest's expression shifted from cold to pitying. "I'm afraid you've come to the wrong place, Ms. Moore. There are no Wards here."

The wind left her, as though she took a punch to the stomach. She leaned forward, braced herself on the back of a pew. "They're all gone? Dead?"

"No. Not all of them. As far as I know, your grandmother, Vera Ward, is the last of your living kin. But she left Bethel just days after your father was murdered."

So there was hope after all. Perhaps all wasn't lost. "Do you know where she is?"

The priest nodded to the right. Immanuelle followed him down a narrow aisle between two benches and into a little room off the chapel. It looked much like the adjoining apses and galleries of the Prophet's Cathedral, only this space was much smaller. Its walls were painted with the sprawling mural of Bethel and the territories beyond it. On the far wall were the Glades, Outskirts, and Holy Grounds, with the appropriate designations for famous landmarks like the tomb of the first prophet, the Haven, the Church of the Outskirts, and of course the Prophet's Cathedral. Surrounding it all was the Darkwood . . . only it wasn't painted that way. In the mural, the forest took the form of a naked woman, curled fetal around Bethel.

Immanuelle stared at the fresco for a long time in breathless silence, tracing the woman's form, trying and failing to parse its meaning. Eventually, her gaze fell to a short verse etched into a wooden plaque on the right side of the wall: *The forest is sentient in a way man is not. She sees with a thousand eyes and forgets nothing.*

"Is that from the Holy Scriptures?" she asked.

The priest shook his head. "Not one you'll find in your holy book. Consider it . . . an unsanctioned addendum."

"Is it meant to be a reference to the Mother or the forest?"

"Both," said the priest. "The Mother *is* the forest. She is the soul, and the Darkwood is Her body. To us, the two entities are intrinsic. One is the same as the other."

Immanuelle touched a spot toward the edge of the woodland, tracing the path of the tree line that ran along the Moore land. "I've never heard it explained that way before."

"That's because your people aren't schooled in the ways of the Mother."

Immanuelle didn't like the way he said "your people," as if to erase the blood tie that bound her to the Outskirts and the Wards. But she made no mention of that discrepancy. Instead, she turned her attention back to the mural, tilting her head to study the map above her. The ceiling loomed high, and it was painted with the faint outlines of maps, but the illustrations were far more abstract than the ones that depicted Bethel. She saw a few names she recognized—Hebron, Gall, Valta. "The heathen cities?"

"In the words of your Prophet, yes."

"Is that where I'll find my grandmother?"

The priest shook his head and tapped a small blank spot in the wilds just north of Bethel. The village was labeled Ishmel. To Immanuelle's immense surprise, it wasn't far from Bethel. Judging by the scale of the map, it was only a few leagues from the Hallowed Gate. She guessed that with a good horse, a trained scout could ride there in no more than a day or so.

"Is there any way to get word to her?"

The priest shook his head. "It's illegal to send letters past the gate, and even if you could get a letter through, there's no promise you'd receive a response. I doubt Vera would send a letter back to Bethel and risk the wrath of the Church. If you want to talk to her, you'll have to do it in the flesh. Find someone to smuggle you through the Hallowed Gate, and someone else to smuggle you back in again."

"Is that even possible?"

"Almost anything is possible if you ask the right questions to the right people and you're willing to pay the price."

Immanuelle mulled this for a moment. "How will I know if my grandmother's still in Ishmel?"

"You won't. There's no way to. Leaving Bethel is an act of faith. Vera used to say so herself before she left."

"You mean before she was exiled?"

He frowned at her as if she'd said something disrespectful or out of turn. "Vera turned her back on this place of her own accord. Left through the gate long before your Prophet had the chance to exile her formally. In fact, she left the night after her boy burned. His body was still on the pyre when she fled."

Immanuelle cringed at the image of her father, dead on the pyre. "Do you think she's still out there?"

"I do," said the priest. "That woman knew how to bleed for

what she wanted, and she always had a way with the woods. I'm sure the wilds were kind to her."

Immanuelle thought back to weeks ago, to the last time she was in the Outskirts. On that day, as she and Martha rode past in the wagon, she'd seen a multitude of tributes strewn along the forest's edge. Was that how the Outskirters were attempting to avoid the full wrath of the plagues? By feeding the Darkwood in order to win its favor? "You mean she made offerings to the forest in exchange for . . . safety?"

The priest laughed, a brash sound that echoed through the chapel. "The wood protects no one. If you want the dull comforts of safety, you make a blood sacrifice to the Father in the hopes of appeasing Him. But if it's power you want, you'd best leave your sacrifices at the Mother's feet."

"But how do you bleed to buy the Mother's power?" Immanuelle asked, growing more and more confused. "I imagine it has to be more difficult than nicking your thumb and saying a prayer."

The priest frowned, clearly growing suspicious. "Why would a girl from the Glades ask a question like that?"

"Passing curiosity," said Immanuelle, but she could tell the priest knew it was a lie.

He stepped past her, his robes rustling as he walked back to the chapel. "You know, Vera wanted to keep you. Always said that if Daniel and Miriam were to have children, they ought to be raised in the Outskirts."

"I didn't know," Immanuelle whispered, her voice thick with tears. All these years she'd been such a fool, assuming that her family in the Outskirts had no interest in her, that she was alone in the world, apart from the Moores. It was a strange and wonderful revelation, but there was pain in it too. It hurt to think that she'd been kept apart from someone she might have known and loved. Someone who might have loved her, too, and understood her in a way that the Moores simply could not.

"If the gate ever opens for you, then you should go to Vera. You're all the family she has left. It would do her good to see you."

Immanuelle turned to look at the small spot on the wall, Ishmel, an islet in the vast sea of the wilderness. "Perhaps I will."

The two meandered out of the apse, back into the chapel. The chickens were still burning on the altar, and a girl stood by it, feeding the fire with pine needles, moss, sprigs of dried rosemary, and other herbs Immanuelle didn't know by name.

"If you have no other questions, I really should be getting back to my work." The priest motioned to the burning altar.

"I do have one more request."

He raised a brow. "Hopefully not one that pertains to witch-craft and blood magic?"

Immanuelle flushed. "No. Nothing like that. I just wondered if it was possible for me to see the house where my father and grand-mother used to live."

The priest considered this for a moment, then nodded, call-ing over the girl who tended to the burning offering. She was stunning—tall and dark-skinned, with wide eyes and well-cut cheekbones. Her hair was a few shades darker than Immanuelle's, and it was carefully braided back into a series of four thick corn-rows and collected into a tight bun at the nape of her neck.

"Adrine, this is Immanuelle Moore," said the priest, and he nodded between the two of them. "You'll take her to the ruins of the Ward house."

Adrine appraised her, expressionless, nodded, then turned on her heel and stalked out of the chapel. Immanuelle turned to bid the priest farewell, but he was already praying over the altar, his face veiled by a haze of smoke.

---�֎---

CHAPTER TWENTY-TWO

The doors of the Father's house are always open to those who
serve him faithfully. But the sinner will be turned away.
—THE HOLY SCRIPTURES

IMMANUELLE AND ADRINE walked in silence through the empty streets. The village they passed through was so quiet, Immanuelle might have thought it long deserted. There were no children playing in the streets. No dogs barking. No signs of life at all, save for the vultures circling overhead.

"Everything is so still," Immanuelle whispered as they passed yet another shuttered house. There were bone wind chimes strung from the rafters of its porch, and they clattered together with a hollow sound when a breeze swept down the street. "The Glades are crawling with the blight sick."

Adrine wrinkled her nose. "Is that what you're calling it in the Glades? The blight?"

Immanuelle shook her head, embarrassed by her slip of the tongue. "It's just . . . my own colloquialism. I'm not sure it has a proper name."

"We call it an affliction of the soul," said Adrine. "Our ancestors passed down stories of witches and soothsayers that used to curse men with a similar sickness."

"So it was used as a kind of weapon?"

Adrine nodded. "In a sense."

"Do you think there's a cure for it?"

"I think the sickness is the cure," said Adrine.

"I'm afraid I don't understand your meaning."

"Sometimes the things that seem like they're hurting us are really a part of healing. When a child is sick and you bleed them, to them the bite of the knife seems like a punishment, when really it's the cure. When your people purge, you do great harm, but you see the violence and the fire as a cure for sins that are far worse. Maybe this sickness is much the same. Maybe it's a kind of purging, meant to root out a deeper evil."

Immanuelle mulled that theory as the two started down another path. This one diverged from the main road, weaving through a series of slums. Here, the stench of sewage was thick on the air. The streets were mostly packed earth and mud, and several times Immanuelle stepped into ruts so deep the muck reached the top of her boots. The main road that weaved through the slums was narrow, the houses so tightly packed that at times the alleys between them were little more than shoulder width. Most of the homes were far too modest to have luxuries like glass windows, but Immanuelle caught glimpses inside these strange abodes when the wind blew their curtains back. There were families huddled together in prayer, children playing with corn-husk dolls, a mother nursing her baby, a black cat sleeping peacefully at the foot of a long bed mat. It was clear to Immanuelle that despite their squalor, none of the inhabitants had been touched by the blight.

Immanuelle was relieved when the little outcrop of houses gave way, once again, to open grassland. In the Glades—where wealthy farmers coveted every spare scrap of land—these wild ranges would have been farmed and converted into capital. But here, the land was left entirely untouched, save for the lone road that cut through it.

In the distance, the Darkwood lurked, the trees so dense they seemed almost impenetrable. Here the forest's pull was far stronger than it was in the Glades, the trees sang to her when the wind moved through them, and it was a struggle for Immanuelle to keep to the path instead of drifting toward them.

"We're here," said Adrine, and she motioned to a wide plot of land, just beyond the reach of the forest where the grass grew waist-high. Immanuelle stepped off the road, into the meadow, and it was only as she drew closer that she saw the charred bones of the house's ruins and the cracked stones of what used to be its foundation.

By the wreckage alone, she could tell that the house was far larger than the ones in the shanty village they'd passed through. In fact, it may have rivaled the size of the Moore house in its day. It was clear that despite their residing in the Outskirts, the Wards had been of good standing. Only a family of consequence could afford such a large home.

Immanuelle lifted her skirts, stepped gingerly over a charred piece of timber that may have been a rafter. She walked the perimeter of the house once, stepping carefully through the debris, then stopped and dropped to a crouch beside one of the large slate foundation stones. Up close, she saw that it was deeply carved with a strange symbol—a cross in the center of a circle—that looked like a letter in some foreign alphabet. The longer she stared at it, the more it reminded her of the witch's mark.

"What is this symbol?" Immanuelle asked, tracing it with her fingertips. Despite the unrelenting heat of the midday sun, the stone was strangely cold.

"It's a sigil," said Adrine, stepping forward. "It's our custom to carve the foundation stones of our houses with them. For luck, prosperity, protection."

"What does this one mean?"

"It's a siphon," said the girl, whispering now though as far as Immanuelle could tell there was no one around to hear them.

"And what is it siphoning?"

Adrine looked reluctant to answer. "Power. From the forest."

"And that one?" Immanuelle pointed across the ruins of the house to another foundation stone. This one was carved with a series of eight overlapping gashes that looked as though they were inflicted in anger.

"A shield," said Adrine. "Meant to repel danger."

Immanuelle didn't need to ask about the marking on the next foundation stone. "The witch's mark."

Immanuelle walked to the last of the four stones, which stood at the far corner of the ruin, nearest the forest. It was capsized and cracked into two large pieces. The girls had to work together, rolling the stones over—as spiders and worms writhed in the newly exposed soil—and push the broken pieces back together. Immanuelle brushed the dirt off the stone to see it clearly, and when she did, Adrine drew back so quickly she nearly stumbled over a fallen rafter.

Immanuelle peered down at the marking, ran her fingers along the cuts in the stone. It looked innocuous enough, just a small hexagon with a series of crosses cut through its center. "What is it?"

"We should go."

Immanuelle frowned. "Why?"

"Because that's a cursing seal," said Adrine in a hiss. "It's meant to do harm."

"But we don't intend any ill will."

"Doesn't matter. Who knows what the sigil's caster intended when they made that mark."

"But it's been years," said Immanuelle, "and the house is long abandoned. There can't be any power left in these stones now."

"Once a sigil is made and a curse is cast, it's done," said Adrine, clearly exasperated with her. "It doesn't matter if a person leaves or dies or forgets; the power that mark was made to represent lives on."

A pit formed in Immanuelle's stomach as she thought about the witches, and the plagues they cast with her blood. "So you're saying that curses live on forever?"

"I'm saying that it's difficult, often impossible, to undo what's already been done. When you make a mark, it's there forever. It can be altered but never fully erased."

If what Adrine said was true, it meant there was little hope of breaking the cycle of the plagues. It seemed that the dark power of the woods would have to run its course. But what did that mean for Honor and Glory and the rest of the blight sick? Would they even survive long enough to see the plague's end?

Immanuelle thought of the prophetic entry at the end of her mother's journal: *Blood. Blight. Darkness. . . . Slaughter.* It was clear that if they didn't find a way to break the curse, then there would be a mortal price to pay. There had to be a way to stop it, and based on everything she'd gathered thus far, her best chance was to decode the sigils, the language of the witches' magic. If the people of Bethel had any hope of defeating Lilith's plagues, they would need to understand them, know what they were fighting against.

Immanuelle slung her knapsack off her shoulder, dug through its contents, and produced a slip of paper and a small nub of graphite. Carefully, she smoothed the blank sheet of paper across the stone and rubbed the graphite back and forth across it, creating the perfect transfer image of the foundation stone. She proceeded to make copies of the next three sigils after that, then collected all of the slips, folded them carefully, and slipped them back into her knapsack for safekeeping. She turned back to Adrine. "How do you know so much about these markings, anyway?"

"They're a part of our language."

"You mean your origin tongue?"

Adrine nodded. "These marks are just words to us. It's the intention behind them that makes the sigils something more . . . something dangerous."

Immanuelle crossed through the ruins of the house and into the narrow stretch of land between it and the Darkwood. A few paces away were the abandoned bones of what might have been an outhouse or a small work shed like Abram's. Beyond that, just a dark, dense stretch of the forest. Its thrall was almost intoxicating.

Immanuelle started toward it and tripped, her boot catching on what she thought was an upturned rock. But when she searched for the source of her near fall, what she found was a small stepping-stone and several more just after it, each of them leading to the sprawling forest beyond the property. Immanuelle followed the path to the feet of two large twin oaks standing side by side, their branches tangling overhead to form a kind of archway. Each of their trunks was carved with matching sigils: one long dash that reached from the start of the first branch down to the roots, the top of which was cut with what appeared to be twenty shorter dashes of varying lengths.

Adrine shook her head. "I don't know those sigils."

"I do," Immanuelle whispered, reaching into the depths of her knapsack. She opened her mother's journal to the page that depicted the cabin where she claimed to have spent the winter. In the foreground of the drawing were two large oaks carved with marks identical to those on the trees in front of her.

Immanuelle edged closer, scuffed her boot through the fallen leaves, uncovering a series of stepping-stones that led into the depths of the Darkwood, to the cabin where her mother endured her last winter. She pressed a hand to the sigil-carved trunk of the nearest oak, half turned to face Adrine.

But the girl merely shook her head. "I'll not go with you. Not in there."

Immanuelle only nodded, a part of her relieved. It was as if she was jealous over the forest, like she wanted its secrets for herself, and herself alone. And so, without so much as pausing to look back, Immanuelle gathered her skirts and stepped past the looming oaks and into the shadows of the Darkwood.

✤

CHAPTER TWENTY-THREE

I made a home in the woods. I thatched a roof and built the walls. And it was there, in a room of stick and stone, that the bargain was struck, and I wouldn't have it any other way.
—MIRIAM MOORE

THE SOUTHERN WOODS were different from those that ran along the Glades. They were thicker, crowded with solemn pines that whispered when the wind moved through their needles. The rest of the world seemed to fall away as Immanuelle walked through the trees. Sunlight dimmed and the shadows thickened, threatening to swallow her up. The path she attempted to follow was quickly devoured by the snarling thicket. She couldn't feel the stepping-stones beneath her boots any longer. And while she knew she should have been afraid, all she felt was a horrible sense of completion. Like she was exactly where she was meant to be.

Immanuelle didn't know how long she walked, but it was nearing midday when she came upon a cabin. One glance at the place and she knew it was long abandoned. She wouldn't have been surprised if its original owners were Bethel's founders, who'd settled in the forest centuries ago. The whole house seemed to stoop on the stones of its foundation, warped and decrepit like an old man leaning on his cane.

In truth, it was less a house than a shanty. It had only one door and one window. The roof was sunken, and the porch was so thoroughly rotten, its blackened planks crumbled beneath her boots. Immanuelle put a hand to the door and pushed it open.

She entered a cramped room that smelled of mildew. To her left sat a side table, its surface cluttered with an arrangement of melted candles. On the far wall, there was a fireplace with a cracked mirror pinned above the mantel, just big enough to house the reflection of a person's face. In the center of the room was a rusted bed frame.

Immanuelle.

She turned, seeking the voice's owner, but instead she found something she'd missed upon first glance. Just to the right of the fireplace was a billowing white cloth, and behind it, a narrow threshold. Raising a shaking hand, Immanuelle drew the shroud away. It drifted to the floor in a cloud of swirling dust motes, revealing a short hallway, lightless, save for a single ray of sunshine that illuminated the room at its end.

Immanuelle reached into her knapsack, withdrawing first her oil lamp, then a single matchstick. She struck the latter alight on the stones of the fireplace, then lit the lamp and turned back to the hallway. The red glow of the flame spilled across the walls as she walked.

At the end of the hall she paused, raising her lamp high to reveal a windowless room, empty save for the circle of ash at its center. Cut crudely into the ceiling above was a small hole to let out the smoke. Scattered throughout the ashes were bones: a mix of hooves and horns, ribs, vertebrae, and, in the midst of the shards, what appeared to be the complete skeleton of a ram—minus the skull.

But it was the walls that drew Immanuelle's attention. They were carved all over with markings, shapes and words that ran together and overlapped, so there was scarcely an inch of the paneling left unmarred.

And the writings had been made by a hand she recognized: her mother's.

The realization hit her all at once. This was the cabin—*the* cabin Miriam had written about in her journal.

Miriam's words crawled like vines across the walls. They repeated the same phrase, over and over: *The maiden will bear a daughter, they will call her Immanuelle, and she will redeem the flock with wrath and plague.*

Immanuelle traced the carvings with a trembling hand, following their path from one wall to the next. The carvings could be separated into three distinct shapes: one on the left wall, one on the right, and another on the far wall between them, where the two marks became one. It took her some time to recognize these shapes for what they were—sigils, just like the ones she'd seen on the foundation stones of the Ward house.

Three shapes. Three . . . *seals.*

Immanuelle stooped to set down the oil lamp, then slid her knapsack off her shoulder and withdrew the slips of paper on which she had copied the foundation stones' sigils. It took her only a few moments to sort through the different symbols until she found the cursing seal. Immanuelle held the paper up to the wall to compare the two marks and found them to be a perfect match in everything but scale.

Swallowing her mounting dread, Immanuelle moved on.

The sigil on the left wall was not a match to any of the sigils carved into the foundation stones. It was a striking twisted shape, looking almost like folded hands or meshed fingers. But despite that, it looked distinctly familiar to her. After a few moments of puzzling in silence—assessing the mark from different angles, tracing the cuts with her fingertips—it came to her. Stooping to one knee, she snatched her mother's journal from her knapsack, flipped through it to the page of her second self-portrait, the abstract illustration she'd sketched in the days after her return from the wood. In the image, she stood naked, arms half wrapped around her modesty, her swollen belly painted with a sigil . . . the same one that was carved into the wall. If the first seal was a curse, then this second was, perhaps, the *conception* of it. A kind of birthing sigil, if you will. A mark of creation.

Puzzled, Immanuelle moved on to the last sigil, the one on the far wall, the only one that she immediately recognized, because she had seen it every day all of her life. It was the same seal that brides wore, carved between their brows—a symbol of union, a binding sigil.

Immanuelle stood up and went over to examine the sigils more closely. She traced the sweeping contours of each carving in turn, moving slowly from one wall to the next: one birthing seal, one cursing seal, and a binding mark between them.

Her blood begets blood. The words from Miriam's journal danced in her mind. She thought back to the night at the pond with the witches, to the start of the blood taint. The first plague, and all of the plagues to follow it, triggered by her first bleed.

Her bleed. Her blood.

They will call her Immanuelle. Her blood begets blood.

The truth struck her like a knife between the ribs.

Lilith hadn't cast the plagues. Miriam had.

And Immanuelle was the curse.

Chapter Twenty-four

We will soon have to choose between who we wish to be and who we must be to carry on. One way or another, there will be a cost.

—From the Last Letters of Daniel Ward

Immanuelle had never been quick to anger. As a child, under Martha, she'd been well schooled in the virtues of patience and restraint; she was more apt to take a slap than to deliver one. But now, as she emptied her lamp, splashing the walls of the cabin with kerosene, an ugly rage ripped through her, as if some animal caged within was trying to claw its way out.

She'd been used.

It was a truth so terrible, Immanuelle could barely conceive it. It was worse than being the harbinger of the plagues, worse than damnation itself. The idea that her mother—for whom she'd spent nearly seventeen years grieving—had never loved her as anything more than a weapon, an agent of her own vengeance.

Immanuelle threw oil across the sigils with blind fury. She snatched the pack of matches from her knapsack and struck one alight, holding it pinched between her fingers as she stared up at the oil-slick carvings.

One for cursing. One for binding. One for birthing.

She flicked the match into the puddle of kerosene a few feet away and a sea of fire washed across the floor. She retreated as the flames rushed down the hall after her, past the threshold, spilling into the front room. In a matter of moments, the building was almost entirely engulfed.

Immanuelle emerged from the cabin in a cloud of ash and cinder. She wasn't sure if she was crying more from the rage or the smoke. She took no comfort in the sight of the cabin burning. A few flames weren't enough to protect her from the truth.

To avenge her lover, Miriam had surrendered her daughter, body and soul, to Lilith's coven. She was their curse made flesh, and everything—the blood and the blight, the darkness and slaughter to come—it was all within her. Miriam hadn't wanted justice; she had wanted blood . . . and Immanuelle had provided. That night in the Darkwood, when she had bled for the first time, she'd unleashed it all. This was Miriam's legacy: one not of love, but of vengeance—and betrayal.

Smoke tumbled through the treetops as the cabin continued to burn. The heat was such that Immanuelle staggered back, the ash on the air so thick it nearly choked her.

But still, she didn't retreat.

In her heart, she knew it made no difference—the cabin on fire, the flames of her own rage roaring from within. None of it would amount to anything more than cinders on the wind. But it felt good, so good, to burn and rage and lose herself to the flames. It was her own personal purging, and in that moment, it was the only comfort she had. She felt almost drunk with it, and perhaps Miriam had as well, all those years ago, when after Daniel Ward's death she'd fled to the Darkwood and struck her deal with the witches. Maybe that devouring rage had mattered more to her than anything else . . . her soul, her daughter, her own life.

But even as Immanuelle's anger boiled within her—even as her rage and guilt consumed her—she couldn't imagine selling her family to the darkness the way that Miriam had sold her.

And therein lay the difference between them.

Immanuelle ran then, fleeing the forest and all of its evils, leaving the burning cabin behind her. Every time she closed her eyes—every time she blinked—she could see the words carved into the walls, the sigils that tied her to the curses . . . and she ran even harder.

After a long, brutal sprint through the thicket, she emerged from the woods and into the light of the setting sun. She brushed the leaves off her skirts and tried to collect herself, picking the twigs from her hair and wiping the last of her tears on her sleeve.

No one could know what she had found in the woods. Not if she wanted to live.

Upon returning from the Outskirts and reaching the Moore house, she found Martha outside, axe in hand, stooped over the chopping block. Without a word of greeting, the elder woman walked to the chicken coop, seized a hen by the throat, and forced it to the block. In one smooth shift of the shoulders, she cleaved its head from its neck. The hen's body scrambled off the stump, wings snapping, claws scrabbling for purchase as it hit the ground.

The Moores usually killed chickens only on holy days, so this was a rare treat, but Immanuelle couldn't muster any joy. The fear in her belly had been replaced by rage since her discovery of the cabin, but now it began to build again as she read the dark expression on Martha's face.

Panic took hold of her: the blight, the girls. Sometimes—on the gravest of days—the Father demanded sacrifice, blood in exchange for a blessing. And perhaps, if they were desperate enough, if one or both of them had taken a turn for the worse . . .

"Honor and Glory—"

"Are fine," said Martha, wiping a spatter of chicken blood off her cheek.

"Then what is the occasion?"

"We have company." Martha lifted the feathered corpse from the dirt. "The Prophet's here, and he's asked to speak to you."

Immanuelle's heart seized. "Did he say why?"

Martha wiped her hands and the axe blade clean on the edge of her apron. "He says he's come for confession. I hear they've been in the Outskirts since dawn—him and his heir—going house to house, letting the sick have their say in case the end comes. So they're here for Honor and Glory." She looked up at Immanuelle. "But I suppose, in his kindness, he wants to hear your confession too."

Her heart began to race, her knees went soft, and she fought with everything she had to temper her mounting panic. Her fear wouldn't save her now. Whatever the Prophet wanted, he'd come to collect. There was no running away, and she refused to cower in the face of what couldn't be changed. Squaring her shoulders, she started toward the farmhouse.

"Wait," said Martha.

Immanuelle paused, one hand on the door's knob. "Yes?"

"Weeks ago, the night you came back from the forest, I was harsh with you. I hope you can forgive me."

Immanuelle swallowed. Her palms were slick with sweat. "Of course."

Martha offered her something almost like a smile. "You scared me when you went into the Darkwood that night. I thought we'd lost you—the way we did Miriam."

"But she came back."

"No, she didn't. When she returned she brought the Darkwood back with her. That's why I was so afraid when you returned . . . but I shouldn't have allowed my fear to make me cruel. That was a sin, and I'm sorry."

"You were only doing what you thought was right."

"Which doesn't mean much if I was wrong," said Martha, and

she nodded toward the farmhouse. "Go now, confess your sins, as I have mine. The Prophet's waiting."

THE PROPHET SAT at the head of the family table, filling Abram's place. He had his hands clasped like he planned to pray, but when Immanuelle entered the room he smiled and gestured to Martha's chair at the opposite end of the table. "I'm glad you're home safely."

Immanuelle sat down. "By His grace."

Across the room, Ezra stood behind his father, shoulders squared, hands clasped at his back. Even though Immanuelle sat in his line of view, he barely registered her presence. And while she knew this was part of their oath—to put the past behind them for his sake and hers—it still hurt to see Ezra look at her like she was little more than a stranger.

The Prophet leaned back into his seat, and its spokes groaned as he shifted. Immanuelle could have sworn he looked a little anxious. His gaze flickered over her, searching as ever, but more tentative than it had been in weeks past, when he'd made no attempt to curb his stare. He nodded toward her knapsack. "What do you have in there?"

"Herbs," she said, hoping the waver in her voice wouldn't betray her. "For my sisters."

"Your grandmother tells me you're quite the nurse."

"I do what I can."

"As we all must," he said.

Upstairs, Glory unleashed a shriek that echoed through the house. The Prophet's smile dimmed at the sound. He turned to Immanuelle and started to speak again, when the back door creaked open and Martha entered with two bloodied chickens, Anna at her heels. They started on dinner, plucking the birds, cutting the vegetables, trying to pretend they weren't listening as they went about their work. A look of irritation flickered over the Prophet's face. He cast his gaze toward the kitchen, raising his voice above the din of clattering pots and pans. "Might we have a moment alone?"

Anna stopped in the middle of peeling a carrot. Strips of orange rind drifted to the floor as she turned to face them. Martha put a hand on her shoulder, and the two of them curtsied and scurried from the room.

The Prophet tipped his head to his son. "You too."

Ezra tensed, then nodded, stepping from behind his father's chair. He brushed past Immanuelle without a glance in her direction and started for the stairs.

As Ezra's footsteps faded to silence, the Prophet's gaze returned to her. He studied her with sharp intent, as if he was trying to commit the details of her face to memory. His gaze was so keen she could almost feel it, like a cold finger tracing along her brow, the seam between her lips, then down her neck to the crook of her collarbones. She froze, afraid that the slightest flinch could betray her for what she was: the plague's harbinger, heretic to the Church, a pawn to witches.

"You're a shepherdess, are you not?"

She nodded. "I tend to my grandfather's flock."

The Prophet raised the cup of sheep's milk—eyeing her above the rim as he drank—then he set it down and licked the froth off his upper lip. "You and I are alike in that. Both of us have our flocks to tend."

"I daresay your calling is greater than mine."

"I wouldn't." The Prophet's gaze hung on her for a moment; then he coughed violently into the crook of his arm. It took him some time to catch his breath. "Do you know why I've come here today?"

"To hear my confession and tell me how to absolve my sins."

"And do you think it's that simple? Do you think sin can simply be wiped away with a few minutes' penance and a sorry heart?"

"Not all sins, no."

"What about the sin of witchcraft?" The Prophet's voice was measured, but his eyes held a malice that almost made her shudder.

Immanuelle fought to keep her face expressionless. "The sin of witchcraft is punishable by pyre purging."

"And have you ever engaged in such a sin?" the Prophet asked, gently, like he was trying to coax the truth from her. "Have you ever conjured spells or curses?"

Immanuelle stiffened. The image of the seals and sigils carved into the cabin walls flashed through her mind. If casting a curse was punishable by death, what was the punishment for being the curse's harbinger? "Of course not."

"Have you kept company with the denizens of the Darkwood, as your mother once did?"

Rage burned through her, but she pushed it down. "I'm not my mother. Sir."

The Prophet stared down at his hands, and there was something odd in his eyes. Bitterness? Regret? She couldn't parse it. "That's not an answer, Ms. Moore."

Immanuelle was terrified to lie, but she knew the truth would damn her. Besides, what were her deceptions compared to those of the Prophet and the Church? If she must lie, it would be for the sake of her life, and the same couldn't be said for them. "I know nothing of the woods or the sins of my mother. I was raised to keep the faith."

The Prophet started to respond, but another fit of coughing cut him short. He hacked into his sleeve for a long while, wheezing and gasping for air. When his fit finally ended, he lowered his arm, and Immanuelle saw a small red stain in the crook of his elbow. "What of lechery?"

Immanuelle stiffened. "What?"

"Whoring, fornication, adultery, lust." He counted the crimes on his fingers. "Surely you know your sins and Scriptures if you keep the faith, like you claim to."

Immanuelle's cheeks warmed. "I know those sins."

"And do you partake in them?"

She should have been afraid, but what welled up within her now was contempt—for him, for the Church, for anyone who would cast stones at others while hiding sins of their own. "No."

The Prophet leaned forward in his chair, elbows on the table, fingers steepled. "So you mean to say you've never been in love?"

"Never."

"Then you are pure, of heart and flesh?"

She began to tremble in her seat. "I am."

There was a long beat of silence.

"Do you say your prayers at night?"

"Yes," she lied.

"Do you mind your tongue and keep vile words off your lips?"

"I do."

"Do you honor your elders?"

"As best I'm able."

"And do you read your Scriptures?"

She nodded. Another honest answer. She read her Scriptures, certainly—just not the ones he was referring to.

The Prophet leaned into the table. "Do you love the Father with all your heart and soul?"

"Yes."

"Then, say it." This was a demand, not a question. "Say you love Him."

"I love Him," she said, a split second too late.

The Prophet pushed back from his seat at the head of the table and stood. He walked down the table's length, stopped beside her chair, and put a hand to her head. His thumb traced the bare spot between her brows where wives wore their seals.

It was all she could do not to bolt from her chair and flee.

"Immanuelle." He turned her name over on his tongue like it was a sugar cube, something to be savored. His holy dagger slipped from the collar of his shirt as he leaned closer, the sheathed blade skimming her cheek as it swung back and forth. "You'd do well to remember what you believe in. I've often found that the soul is apt to wander toward the dark."

Her heart beat so violently she feared he would hear it. "I'm afraid I don't understand your meaning."

The Prophet leaned even closer. She could feel his breath against her ear as he whispered, "And I'm afraid that you do."

"Enough." The Prophet looked up, his hand slipping from Immanuelle's head, as Ezra entered the dining room and edged around the table to her side. "She's answered your questions, and the sun's setting quickly. We should be on our way."

The Prophet's gaze darkened as it fell on Ezra, and Immanuelle wondered if he was even capable of looking at his son with anything other than scorn.

"Let's go," said Ezra, and this time there was a threat between the words.

The Prophet's lips peeled back in a sneer. He started to speak but stopped at the sound of his name.

"Grant . . . the boy is right." Immanuelle turned to see Abram standing on the threshold between the dining room and kitchen. He leaned on his favorite cane—a birch branch with a pommel he'd whittled into the shape of a hawk's head—and his mouth was carved into a thin line. He spoke again, louder this time, though

Immanuelle knew every word was a struggle. "The roads are dangerous . . . at night . . . with the sick lurking."

Immanuelle was so relieved to see Abram in that moment, she could have wept. Gone was the feeble, quiet man who'd reared her. The man before her now stood resolute, his shoulders squared, his jaw firmly set.

She remembered something Anna had once said, how, in the wake of Miriam's death, after Abram had lost his Gifts and the title of the apostleship was stripped from him, he became a ghost of the man he had been before. But now, in this moment, as he stepped firmly over the threshold to stand alongside Immanuelle, it seemed like that man had been resurrected.

Ezra placed a firm hand on his father's shoulder. "He's right, Father. The sick are out of their senses, mad with fever. It's not safe to travel the roads after sunset. We should be on our way. *Now.*"

Immanuelle waited for the Prophet to rebuke them, but he didn't. Instead, he turned his gaze on her again. This time his eyes didn't warm. "These are dark days, that's certain, but the Father hasn't turned his back on us yet. He's watching. He is *always* watching, Immanuelle. That's why we must remember what we believe in and keep to it, if nothing else."

As soon as the Prophet departed, Immanuelle stood, the motion so abrupt her chair clattered to the floor. But she didn't stoop to pick it up. Shaking and without a word, she fled the dining room to the front of the house. Abram called after her as she opened the door and stepped out onto the porch. There, she dropped to a crouch, pressed a hand to the planks to steady herself. She drew several ragged gasps, but the air was thick with pyre smoke and it did little to ease her burning lungs. She could still feel the Prophet's hand at her head, his thumb pressing between her eyebrows, and the memory of his touch alone was enough to make her quake with fear.

"Immanuelle." Ezra stepped outside and closed the door be-hind him. "Are you all right?"

She pushed to her feet, smoothed the creases from her skirts in a vain attempt to collect herself. "You should be on your way."

"Humor me for a moment."

"Why should I?"

"Because this is meant to be an apology."

She frowned. "An apology for what?"

"For being drunk and harsh and careless. For my actions at the pond in the midst of my vision. For hurting you. For behaving more like an enemy than a friend. I don't ever want my actions to make you doubt my loyalty that way. Can you forgive me?"

It was, perhaps, the best apology Immanuelle had ever received. It was certainly the most earnest. "Like it never happened," she said.

Across the pastures and through the rolling smoke, Immanu-elle spotted the Prophet on his horse, waiting for Ezra. There was a gravitas to his gaze, and even at a distance, she could tell he was watching them. "You need to go. Now."

"I know," said Ezra, but he didn't move, just stood there star-ing after his father. It took her a moment to see the expression on his face for what it was: dread. "Do you still believe we can find a way to end this?"

Pyre smoke rolled across the road, obscuring the Prophet from view. "We have to."

CHAPTER TWENTY-FIVE

I often wonder if my spirit will live on in her. Sometimes I hope that it will, if only so I won't be forgotten.
—MIRIAM MOORE

THAT NIGHT, IMMANUELLE dreamed she walked through a field of amber. As far as the eye could see, waves of golden wheat rolled with the breath of the wind. Crickets warbled summer songs; the air was thick and sticky, the sky clear of clouds.

In the distance, two figures moved through the wheat like fish in water. The first, a girl with golden hair and a wicked smile. Immanuelle recognized her from the portrait in her mother's journal: Miriam, her mother.

Walking alongside her, a tall boy with night-dark skin and eyes like Immanuelle's. She knew, without really knowing, who he was upon first glance: Daniel Ward, her father.

Together, the pair waded hand in hand through the wheat, smiling and laughing, enraptured with each other, their faces warm with the light of the rising sun. When they turned and kissed each other, it was with passion . . . and yearning.

Immanuelle tried to follow them through the amber waves, but they were quick and she was slow, and when they ran she stumbled and lagged behind.

The sun shifted overhead, as if pulled by a string. Shadows fell across the plains and the couple disappeared over the bend of a hill. Immanuelle struggled after them, catching the scent of smoke on the wind as night fell.

She heard the muffled rush of flames. Dragging herself through the last of the wheat, Immanuelle peered down at the plains below. There was a crowd some one hundred strong gathered around a pyre. Standing on that pyre, shirtless and bleeding, was her father, Daniel Ward.

A scream broke across the plains. Immanuelle followed the sound to Miriam, who cowered weeping at the foot of the pyre. Like her lover, she was bound, shackled at the throat. She lunged for the pyre, crawling on her hands and knees, the iron brace digging into her neck, but one cruel yank on her chain sent her sprawling, and she collapsed into the dirt again.

Immanuelle didn't want to watch. She didn't want to move, but she found herself descending the hill, the throng parting to make way for her. She came to stand alongside Miriam, in the shadow of the pyre.

The crowds parted again. A man passed through them. It took Immanuelle a moment to recognize him: the Prophet Grant Chambers, Ezra's father. In his grasp was a flaming branch bigger than any torch she'd ever seen. He bore it with both hands, cutting across the field to the foot of the pyre in three long steps.

Miriam clawed at the dirt, shrieking pleas and spitting curses, begging and weeping and swearing on what little she had left to swear on—her life, her blood, her good word—to whatever god could hear her.

But for all of her pleas and curses, the Prophet did not heed her. He lowered the branch to the pyre, and with a roar, the flames stormed through the kindling.

Daniel did not move. He did not flinch. He did not plead the way Miriam did. When the flames chewed up his legs and devoured him, he let loose a single, haunting cry and then fell silent. And as quickly as it began, it was over.

Flesh to bone to ashes.

Immanuelle staggered, stooped, and broke to her knees, hitting the dirt alongside her mother. She clasped her hands over her ears to block out the roar of the flames and Miriam's keening, the jeering of the crowd. Every breath brought the stench of burnt flesh.

Smoke rolled across the flames, too thick to see through. Immanuelle choked, blind in the darkness; the light of the pyre died to little more than the dull glow of an ember in the night.

When the darkness cleared, Immanuelle found herself alone. The pyre was gone, as were the crowds. The Prophet and Miriam were nowhere to be seen. The plains were empty.

Overhead, the moon hung, fat and full.

Immanuelle squinted. In the distance, she could just make out the crude shadow of the cathedral, breaking above the waves of wheat. Immanuelle started toward it, crossing through the empty pastures, traveling east by the light of the moon.

When she arrived at the cathedral, she faltered, standing motionless in the shadow of the bell tower. The doors swung open slowly, and even from a distance, she caught the stench of something raw on the air, all blood and butchery.

Immanuelle climbed the stone steps and entered into a darkness as thick as night. She staggered down the center aisle, hands outstretched, moving from one pew to the next.

A flame flickered to life behind the altar. In its glow, Immanuelle could make out the shadow of a figure, Miriam. She wore a white cutting dress, its folds spilling over the swell of her belly. As Immanuelle drew nearer she saw that she was smiling—a wet gash of a grin. In her right hand she held a broken antler like a dagger, its jagged point dripping blood.

A great shape moved from behind her, like a spider emerging from the edges of its web. Lilith prowled to the front of the altar and hovered at Miriam's shoulder. Upon her arrival, the darkness retreated, and candlelight spilled through the cathedral. And as Immanuelle's eyes adjusted, and the room came into focus, it was all she could do to bite back a scream.

The place was a tomb.

There were scores of corpses, slumped over the pews and crammed into the adjacent aisles, heaped beneath the stained-glass windows and in the shadow of the altar. All of them were mangled and ravaged, limbs twisted, heads skewed, jaws broken open.

Among the throng of the dead were faces she recognized. Judith lay in the pew at her side, her throat slashed above her collar. A few feet away, Martha lay facedown in a puddle of blood. By her side, Abram, his neck twisted on its axis. Cradled in his broken arms was Anna, her lips smeared ink black with blood. At her feet, Glory and Honor lay motionless, as if asleep, but their eyes were open, their mouths agape, as if they'd been struck down in the middle of a prayer. Leah lay stretched across the altar, her pregnant belly carved open like a gutting lamb's. High above her, bolted to the wall with the sword of David Ford himself, was Ezra.

Immanuelle's knees buckled. The floor went soft beneath her feet. She pitched forward, tripping over the cobbles. "What have you done?"

Candlelight played over Miriam's face. That terrible smile of hers widened, like a wound ripping open. She began to laugh. "You know what this is."

Overhead, the ceiling bowed, stones grinding like the cathedral was collapsing in on itself. Immanuelle staggered back, but there was nowhere to run. "Why? Why would you do this?"

"Because they took him from me," Miriam whispered, and at the sound of her voice the candlelight died, plunging the room into darkness. "Blood for blood."

Chapter Twenty-six

A child is a gift greater than any other.
—From *The Writings of the Prophet Enech*

"Get up." Immanuelle woke to the glow of lamplight and the harsh cut of Martha's silhouette in her doorway.

Immanuelle snapped to attention, the memories of the massacre flooding back to her—the bodies, the blood, the slaughter.

"Ezra's here from the Haven."

"Again?" Immanuelle asked, her voice thick and hoarse with sleep. "Whatever for?"

Martha snatched her cloak off its hook on the wall and tossed it to her. "Leah's in labor and she's bleeding badly."

"But she's not due for weeks—"

Martha wheeled to face her. "You knew?"

Immanuelle fumbled with the buttons of her dress. "Yes, but she only told me a few weeks ago. I wanted to let you know, but she made me swear to keep the secret and—"

Martha raised a hand for silence. "Now is not the time for your confession. We need to go to the Haven. I'll need your help at the birthing bed and Leah needs you too."

✤

MARTHA AND IMMANUELLE rushed to the Haven by the light of the purging pyres. Ezra rode ahead of them on horseback, galloping across the Glades. By the time they arrived at the Haven's gate, he was waiting for them. Immanuelle hopped out of the wagon before it slowed to a stop and broke toward him, sprinting through the rolling smoke of the pyres. He ushered them into the foyer and down the hall toward the bridal ward.

Let her live, Immanuelle prayed, to the Father, to the beasts of the Darkwood, to the witches, to whoever was willing to heed her. *Please, let Leah live.*

After a walk that felt leagues long, they entered into a ward Immanuelle didn't recognize. Here, the cries of the blight sick faded to silence and only one voice sounded above the rest. A wet, gargling wail that slapped against the walls and echoed.

Immanuelle's hands began to shake.

"This is as far as I go," Ezra said, and his gaze fell to Immanuelle. "Be strong."

She started to respond, but Martha cut her short. "Tell your father I'm here."

Ezra nodded and, without another parting word, left.

Martha started forward ahead of Immanuelle, murmuring a prayer under her breath as she opened the door. They entered the room together. It was small, all aglow with firelight. The air thick with the scent of sweat and wood smoke. Toward the back of the room, speaking in harsh, urgent tones, were Leah's mother and a few of her older half sisters. Their eyes were bloodshot and almost all of them were weeping.

At the center of the room—crowded by a throng of the Proph-

et's wives—was the bed where Leah lay, writhing. She wore nothing but a thin nightdress, its skirts pulled up to her armpits. Between
her thighs was a dark puddle of blood. Her belly was swollen and
striped with stretch marks that looked like knife wounds, badly
scarred. The child turned within her, and each violent contraction
elicited a scream from Leah that seemed to tear the air in two.

Martha paled. Her gaze turned to Ezra's mother, Esther, who
stood behind the headboard. She wore a long, bloodstained smock
and her hair was pulled back into a fallen bun. It was the first
time Immanuelle had seen her looking anything less than pristine.

"How long has she been like this?"

"Two days."

Immanuelle stared at her, stunned. "You let her labor for *two
days* without calling for aid?"

"Physicians in the Haven were by her side—"

"You should have sent for me sooner," said Martha, a harsh
rebuke.

"I know, but we were only acting on the Prophet's orders," said
Esther, rushing to explain. "He asked if we might . . . *withhold*
information about the circumstances of Leah's condition for a
little while longer."

At once, Immanuelle realized why. He was trying to keep the
birth a secret. Let Leah labor silently, in the confines of the Haven, attended only by personal physicians of the Prophet who
were sworn by holy oath—on penalty of purging—to serve him
and keep his secrets. By withholding that information, he could
expunge the details of the child's illegitimacy and, more importantly, his sin. In a few months' time, he would announce the
child's birth, and no one would question the circumstances surrounding its conception. All would be deemed right and well.

Martha stepped around the birthing table and began her examination. As she worked, Esther moved a damp cloth across

Leah's brow. She paused to whisper something in her ear, and whatever she said was enough to make the girl smile through her tears, if only for a moment. The woman turned back to Martha, lowering her voice to a whisper so quiet Immanuelle had to read her lips in order to understand her. "Were we too late?"

The midwife didn't answer.

"Immanuelle." Leah's swollen eyes split open, and she threw out her hand. "Please, come."

"I'm here," said Immanuelle, breaking forward to take her friend by the hand. "I'm right here."

Leah smiled and a few tears slipped down her cheeks. "I'm sorry. I'm so sorry for what I said last time I saw you. Forgive me. Please. I'm so sorry."

"Hush." Immanuelle brushed a strand of hair from her face. "You have nothing to apologize for."

"I didn't mean it. I don't want to be alone. I don't—" A violent contraction cut her words short, and she grasped Immanuelle's hand so tightly her knuckles popped. "I don't want to be alone."

"You're not. I'm here now and I'm not going anywhere. I promise."

"But *I am* going. I can feel it—" Whatever she was going to say died into a scream. It was plain to Immanuelle that she wasn't herself. Her cheeks were flushed with fever, and when her eyes weren't rolled back into her head, they bore the same frenzy Glory's did.

"It's the fever," Esther hissed, bracing both hands at Leah's shoulders to keep her pinned to the bed. "She's been this way ever since her labor began. No nurse or maid can calm her."

Martha rolled up her sleeves and washed her hands in a basin of water by the window. "That's the way of the plague."

"Will it hurt her child?" Esther whispered, at which Leah loosed another long groan.

Martha cast her a glance so sharp it could have withered an oak tree. Esther fell silent. The midwife walked to Leah's side and pressed her hand to the bare swell of her belly, her fingers shifting over the bruises and stretch marks.

"What is it?" Leah asked, her eyes wild. "What is it?"

Martha paled. "She's dying."

"A girl," Leah said, her eyes rolling back into her head. "It's a little girl."

"We have to save her." Esther cut around the bed to where Martha stood. "She's the Prophet's daughter."

From the far corner of the room, an old woman started forward, leaning on her cane. Hagar—the first wife of the last prophet—raised her voice above Leah's cries. "Cut her."

There was utter silence. Even Leah's screams were swallowed by it. A few of the brides clasped hands over their mouths. The youngest among them bolted to the door.

Immanuelle heard her own voice rattle through the room. "What?"

Hagar's gaze shifted to Martha. "Cut her. Save the child. It's the Father's will."

"No," said Immanuelle, shaking her head. "You can't do that. She'll die."

"My baby," Leah mumbled, out of her senses. "I can hear her heartbeat."

Immanuelle stepped forward, catching her grandmother by the sleeve. "Martha, please—"

"Get me binds," said the midwife, tightening the laces of her apron, "and something she can chew on. A bit of leather, even a wood chip sanded smooth. We'll need the poppy tincture too, for the pain." Her gaze shifted to Immanuelle. "The child comes first. There is no other way."

✤

THE SERVANTS TRANSPORTED Leah to another room, lifting her onto a wide oak table that looked like a wooden altar. Immanuelle stood at Leah's shoulders, whispering stories into her ear as she had done for Honor and Glory.

"It's going to be okay," Immanuelle cooed, pulling a damp strand of hair behind the shell of her ear.

To this, Leah said nothing. She was gone now, lost to the stupor of the poppy tincture, which Martha had administered minutes before. Her bruised belly pulsed in a series of violent contractions, but she was so sedated she scarcely registered the pain.

"Get her out," she slurred. "Just get her out of me. She can't breathe. I can't breathe with her in there."

Martha entered from the hall, her hands still damp with the spirits she washed with. Her eyes met Immanuelle's as she neared the table, scalpel in hand. "Hold her down, if it's the last thing you do."

Immanuelle nodded, bracing her hands on either side of Leah's shoulders.

"This will hurt," Martha said, gazing down at the girl, though Immanuelle wasn't sure that Leah—drugged and drunk off the fever of the blight—was even capable of hearing her, "and it will hurt terribly, maybe worse than anything you've felt before. But you must be still and strong for your daughter, or she'll die."

Leah's head rolled to the side. "Get her out. Just get her out of me."

Martha lowered the scalpel to her hip, just beneath the bulge of the baby. She cut deep and steady, Leah wailing through gritted teeth as she worked the blade.

When she reared and struggled, Immanuelle threw her weight against her shoulders, forcing her down to the table. Opposite her, Esther pinned her legs and a few of the other girls broke forward, grabbing her arms to hold her fast.

All the while, Martha worked with stoic efficiency—hands and forearms bloodied, cheeks glistening with sweat. Immanuelle wanted to close her eyes and plug her ears, shield herself from the screams that rang through the room, but all she could do was watch as the midwife carved the wound wider and wider until it yawned open like a bloody grin.

Leah keened. *"Get her out of me!"*

Baring her teeth, Martha dragged the baby through the wound and into the warm light of the hearth, the slick rope of her umbilical cord slithering after her like a viper.

Leah collapsed to the table, spent, and Immanuelle moved from behind her to Martha, who stood cradling the child, eyes wide, mouth agape.

"She has no name," Martha whispered, hands shuddering around the child's head so violently Immanuelle feared she'd drop her. "She has no name."

Heart pounding in her throat, Immanuelle peered over the folds of the swaddling blanket. The child was small and pink, and her eyes were wide, irises a brilliant blue. She looked like a normal, healthy baby, except for the small cleft that dimpled her upper lip. Immanuelle extended a hand, and the baby grasped her by the finger, cooing a little as she peered up at her.

Leah groaned, fresh tears rolling down her cheeks. The dark puddle between her legs stretched wider and wider.

"No," Immanuelle whispered. "She's not dead. She's breathing. She's all right."

Martha started to shove the child into Hagar's arms, but she refused it, cane striking the floorboards as she backed against the wall. "It's cursed."

"I'll hold her," said Immanuelle, stepping forward to take the child. She cradled the nameless girl against her chest, shielding her from the wandering gazes of the Haven girls and servants who gathered to gawk.

Across the room, Martha worked fervently at the table, her hands shaking as she pierced the needle through Leah's wound, struggling to suture it, to stop the blood from flowing.

"Don't let her see," Esther mouthed from across the room, dabbing Leah's forehead with a cold compress.

So Immanuelle kept her distance, holding that child to her chest in the shadows by the hearth, trying in vain to soothe her. It was only when Hagar, leaning on her cane, whispered, "Ashes to ashes," that she raised her gaze to the table again, and saw Leah sprawled—limp and breathless—her glazed eyes fixed on the ceiling.

Immanuelle clutched the child closer. "No. She's not, is she . . . ?"

"Dead." The word rattled through the room as Martha drew away from the table. She raised her eyes to Immanuelle, and tears moved down her cheeks. "She's dead."

Immanuelle didn't remember who took the child from her arms. She didn't remember crossing through the halls or fleeing the Haven. She only came to when a cold blast of night air struck her across the face like a slap.

All at once, she was on her knees gagging and gasping for breath, her whole body heaving like the blight raged in her too. The tears followed and great sobs racked her, snatching the breath from her lungs.

Immanuelle didn't know how long she crouched there—weeping in the shadows—but she remembered seeing the tops of

Ezra's boots as he stepped down the stairs and catching the scent of him as he wrapped an arm around her shoulders and pulled her to his chest.

He held her as she cried, her face buried in the folds of his shirt, grasping at his hands as if his flesh and bones were her only tether to the world—and perhaps, in that moment, they were.

"You'll be all right," he murmured into her hair, again and again, like a prayer. And as he said it, she began to believe him, began to believe that whatever evil had fallen upon the land, she would survive it. After all, the curse was bred from her. She was it, and it was her. The sin and the salvation, the plague and the purgings, all bound up into one body by a bargain of blood.

Yes, Ezra was right; she would be all right. She would watch all of Bethel burn without sustaining so much as a scratch because Lilith and her legion had no interest in harming their savior, the curse bearer, the soul of the plagues themselves.

She'd been used, betrayed by her mother, sold to the witches. And now—as if her fate wasn't cruel enough—she would watch in silent suffering as everything she loved and cared for was gutted and slaughtered and picked to pieces. Then, once the plagues were finally over, she would remain, a lone survivor amidst the bones and ashes.

❖

CHAPTER TWENTY-SEVEN

I am with you until the end.
—DANIEL WARD

L EAH BURNED FOUR days later. As a wife of the Prophet, she
had a small ceremony and a pyre of her own. Huddled around
the flames was a crowd of mourners, comprised mostly of Leah's
kin, who'd come up from the village for the occasion, and a few of
the wives who'd dared to venture down from the Prophet's Haven. Ezra's mother, Esther, was among them. Most of the mourners stood well clear of the flames with wet cloths pressed to their
mouths, afraid of catching the blight from the ashes.

"It's always the kind ones who keep secrets," said Martha,
squinting into the light of the fire. "Always the kind ones who best
hide their sins."

The pyre logs shifted, and a spray of embers stormed through
the smoke-thick air.

"Leah didn't sin," said Immanuelle. "We took what we wanted
from her, ripped it from her belly, and then we watched her die."

She waited for Martha's retort—a scolding, a slap across the
face—but silence was all she deigned to offer. And the silence was
worse.

Immanuelle shifted her gaze back to the pyre. Through the

bloody glow of the flames, she locked eyes with the Prophet. He stood among his apostles, watching his bride burn. His eyes, like Martha's, were dead.

Something settled deep within Immanuelle. It took her a moment to recognize the feeling. It wasn't the flames of anger stoked, or the cold throes of grief. No, this was something grim and quiet . . . something sinister.

Wrath.

After all, it was he who put Leah on that pyre. If he hadn't lusted for her when she was so young—just a girl doing her penance in the Haven—if he hadn't allowed himself to cow to his own sick depravity, then she would have never fallen pregnant before her cutting. Nor would she have been forced to keep such a horrible secret. If the Prophet hadn't been trying to cover for his own sin, they would have sought Martha's aid far earlier, and if they had done that, then maybe, just maybe, Leah would be alive today. But instead, he let her bleed, let her suffer for his sin. But the blame didn't end with him.

No.

This was the great shame of Bethel: complacency and complicity that were responsible for the deaths of generations of girls. It was the sickness that placed the pride of men before the innocents they were sworn to protect. It was a structure that exploited the weakest among them for the benefit of those born to power.

It made Immanuelle want to scream. Made her want to fall to her knees and carve the dirt with sigils and curses and the promise of plagues. It made her want to tear the cathedral apart, brick by brick. Burn the chapels and the Haven, the great manors of the apostles, set the pastures and farms alight. Her rage was such that she felt it would never be sated unless Bethel was brought to its knees. And that frightened her.

Immanuelle walked, adopting the pace of the other mourners

who circled the outskirts of the fire. Ezra didn't offer his condolences as he fell into step beside her. He didn't say anything at all, and for a little while they just walked in silence, shoulder to shoulder, stalling every few moments to watch the flames. Immanuelle was aware of the gazes that followed them as they went. Martha tracked them from across the pyre. A few paces from her, the Prophet and his brood of apostles stood watching.

Let them talk, Immanuelle thought to herself. In the end, it wouldn't make a difference, and she was certain that the end was coming quickly. Her attempts to break the curse had failed. Her prayers to the Father went unanswered. They had nothing now; there was no one to save them, and no way to keep the coming plagues at bay. Soon darkness would be upon them, and after darkness—slaughter. And sometimes she thought, in light of everything—the lies, the secrets, the killings, the sin—slaughter was exactly what they deserved.

But that was just her anger speaking. That was just the grief.

Bethel didn't deserve this, any more than she deserved to be a vessel of these plagues. There were still innocents living within its borders—Glory, Honor, the people of the Outskirts, men and women who had no choice in their fate. It was for them that Immanuelle had to find an answer to these plagues, a way to stop them. And she'd spent the days after Leah's death searching for just that, knowing that if she failed, Bethel would pay a steep price.

What she needed was someone to turn to, an authority on the dark craft and the ways of the witches. Someone who understood the Darkwood and the secret to containing its power. A person who knew what Miriam had done and had an idea of how to break the curse she cast all those years ago. She needed a witch or, at the very least, an informant who walked a similar path. And the way Immanuelle saw it, there was but one person left to turn to: her grandmother Vera Ward.

She was the true tie between Miriam and the powers of the dark. The same sigils scrawled into the pages of her mother's journal and the walls of the cabin in the woods were carved into the foundation stones of Vera's house. It was plain to Immanuelle, given the path on the cusp of the Ward land, that it was Vera who first led Miriam to the cabin for sanctuary. Vera who saw her through the winter. And, perhaps, it was Vera who first introduced Miriam to the power of the plagues. After all, where else would the wayward daughter of an apostle have stumbled upon such evil? How would she have discovered the ways of witches if not through Vera, a known witch herself?

That was why Immanuelle needed to find her grandmother, to discover if she knew how to stop the plagues that she'd been complicit in creating. Because if anyone knew what Miriam had done in the woods all those years ago, or how to stop it, Immanuelle knew it must be her.

But to find Vera before the next plague struck, she would need to leave Bethel and do it soon. A small part of her wondered whether her departure was for the best. Maybe if she left, the horrors of the plagues would leave with her and everything would go back to the way it was supposed to be. Bethel would be saved.

But something told her that Lilith, in all her power and years of wisdom, would not be foiled so easily. The plagues were intended to destroy Bethel, and a jaunt through the Hallowed Gate wouldn't be enough to end them. She would have to find another way.

Across the fire, the Prophet parted from the throng of his apostles and began to walk alone, wading through the crowds. But his gaze wasn't on the flames.

It was on Immanuelle.

The day of her confession, the Prophet warned her that the Father was always watching, but it seemed that He wasn't the only one. Whenever she was near, the Prophet's gaze fell to her.

At the cathedral, it followed her through the pews. During his Sabbath sermons, she'd often feel as if he was preaching only to her. Even when she was in the privacy of her bedroom, when the night was dark and the house was quiet, his presence seemed to haunt her.

Immanuelle walked a little faster, dropping her voice to a whisper. "How is Leah's baby? I haven't heard any word of her since the night she was born."

"She's alive," Ezra murmured, as if that was the most that could be said for her.

"Is she in danger?" Immanuelle asked, thinking back on that wretched night when Martha announced that the child had no name. She was as good as cursed. "Will they hurt her?"

Ezra took his time with an answer. When he spoke, his voice was so low she could barely hear him above the roar of the flames. "No. I won't let them. She's safe."

"Good."

"You should come to the Haven to visit her. In a few days, once the mourning crowds have left. Leah would have wanted that."

Immanuelle shook her head. "I'm afraid I won't be able to make it."

He stopped short. "Why?"

"Because I'm leaving, Ezra . . . and I need your help to do it."

"I don't understand."

Immanuelle raked a hand through her curls and stared through the flames to the Prophet and his apostles. If the truth got out—if they knew what she was—they'd send her to a pyre like the one burning in front of her. And yet, despite that, she found herself wanting to confess, almost desperate to. Her secrets seemed to eat at her, and in that moment, more than anything else, she wanted to be free of them—if only so she felt a little less alone.

When she finally spoke, it was in a small, tear-choked whisper so strangled and foreign that at first, she mistook her voice for someone else's. "I caused the curses. The plagues are my fault."

"What are you talking about?" Ezra asked sharply.

"I'm not sure you want to know, and even if you do, I'm not sure I can make you understand."

"Try."

She found her voice at last. "Weeks ago, I told you that I'd awakened the curses. At the time I thought that was true, but I was mistaken. I didn't awaken the curses. I *am* the curse."

"I don't understand."

"My mother did something unspeakable in the Darkwood, years ago. She made a deal with the witches, bound me to their magic. She made me a vessel of the plagues. That's why I have to go."

"You're . . . *leaving* Bethel?" he demanded, and Immanuelle found it almost endearing that he seemed more shaken by the news of her departure than he did by her confession about the plagues.

She nodded. "The woman from my census file—Vera Ward, the one with the witch mark—she lives in a village called Ishmel north of the gate. I think it was she who harbored my mother during the months she spent in the wilderness."

"How do you know that?"

"Days ago I went to the Outskirts. While I was there, I uncovered a path on the edge of her property, just a few yards from her house. It led me to a cabin in the woods, the same one my mother spoke of in her journal."

Ezra mulled this for a moment, staring at his shoes. "And you're certain this woman, your grandmother, has a connection to the plagues?"

Immanuelle nodded. "You saw the mark by her name in the census. And I know that she practiced the dark craft. The people in the Outskirts say she was a proper witch, but she fled Bethel before your father had the chance to burn her. I think it was she who taught my mother the ways of the witches. So if I can find her—"

"You can find a way to stop the plagues your mother cast. The plagues she bound to you."

"Precisely."

Ezra was quiet for a moment, turning these ideas over in his head. "Warrants go through the gate's guardsmen. I'd have to approach them with the proposition, days in advance. If I get the warrant into the right hands, there's a chance I could keep it from my father."

"And when the warrant is in their hands, what then?"

"Then the guardsmen have a legal obligation to open the gate for you. The only way that could be thwarted is if my father signed a warrant to annul mine. But he can't do that if he doesn't know the warrant exists."

"So you're saying you can do it? You can get me through the gate?"

"I'm saying I can get you *out* of Bethel. But coming back . . ."

"I know," said Immanuelle, nodding. Bethel's laws were unrelenting. Those who defied Holy Protocol by leaving illegally were deemed hostile foreigners. If Ezra's warrant was revoked, or worse yet annulled, after her departure, she would never be allowed to return again. "I understand the repercussions of my choice to go. Once I leave Bethel, what becomes of me isn't your responsibility. All I ask is that you get me through the Hallowed Gate."

"Why should you have to go? You didn't ask for any of this."

"The plagues were birthed through me and because of that they're my burden to bear, no one else's. You didn't choose to be Prophet, but you have the Sight just the same."

"That's different."

"No, it's not. The plagues are in me like the Sight is in you. It's my sin to atone for. I'm the one responsible for fixing this."

"Then stay. We can fix things together. Between the two of us we'll find a way."

Immanuelle shook her head, watching the flames wash over Leah's bones. "The best thing I can do for Bethel is leave it."

"And what if it's all futile?" Ezra asked, putting words to the question she'd been too scared to ask. "What if you can't find your kin? Or what if you do and she has no way to stop the plagues? What then? You'll be alone out there."

"I'm alone already."

The hurt in Ezra's eyes was unmistakable. "That's not true."

"Listen to me," said Immanuelle, dropping her voice. "You'll be the Prophet soon, and as Prophet you can't continue defying the Protocol in order to protect me."

"Why not?"

"The Holy Scriptures won't allow it. Don't you understand? By the Church's laws, I should be burning right now."

"Damn the Scriptures. I'll do what I want."

"That was the path your father followed, and look what came of it." Immanuelle tossed her hand toward the pyre, to Leah's burning corpse. "You can't allow yourself to rule with impunity the way he did."

"This isn't about him," Ezra snapped, truly angry now. "You said it yourself, weeks ago, he's dying. Soon enough, his bones will be locked in a crypt like the rest of the prophets who came before him. So what difference does it make? The flock, the apostles, the Prophet and his Guard. Let the plagues come and drive them all apart, and then when it's over—when they're burning on their own pyres or rotting in the ground—you'll be safe."

"You can't promise my safety. There's no way for us to redeem ourselves out of reality. Bethel won't change, Ezra. The pyres will keep burning no matter what we do; I know that now. More girls will die. More apostles will rise. More trials will be held—"

Ezra shook his head. "A prophet can't be put on trial. And neither could you, if you bear my name."

It took her a moment to fully comprehend the statement. He'd thrown the offer at her feet so casually, as if he was merely inviting her for an afternoon stroll. "What are you trying to say?"

"You could be First Bride, with all of the allowances that go with the title. You could take up Leah's daughter, raise her in the Haven the way you want. You'd be safe."

Any other girl in Bethel would have wept with joy at the offer, would have lunged at the chance to stand by Ezra's side as his wife and life partner. It was nothing less than a dream. Or at least it should have been. But all Immanuelle could think about was her mother. That life—a life bound to the Prophet, to the Church and the Haven—was what had forced her to flee into the Darkwood in the first place.

"So, you'd have me cut?" Immanuelle asked, barely breathing. "You'd have me stretched across the cathedral altar like a lamb for the gutting? Do you expect me to sit there in that prison of a keep, meek and quiet and minding my tongue? And do what? Pray? Mourn? Pity myself to pass the time, while the plagues rage and ravage everything in their path?"

"We could build another house," said Ezra. "Someplace safe, away from the Darkwood. We'd have the means."

"We'll be lucky if we have ashes and cinders by the end of these plagues. Or have you forgotten what you've seen already? The blood? The blight? Each curse is worse than the last. This is no time for dreams."

"And is that dream such a terrible fate? I'm telling you I can protect you, here in Bethel, if you'll let me. I swear it, on my life."

Immanuelle considered it for a moment, imagined the future she'd have if she chose to stand at Ezra's side. Hers would be a life of finery—filled with good food and smart dresses and the sort of genteel delights she'd dreamed of as a girl. She'd be the wife of a prophet, his *first* wife. She would never be ridiculed or scorned. Never be made to stand alone.

But the longer she dwelled on the thought, the more she realized the folly of it. If she stayed, there would be no goodness or mercy, no Bethel at all. The plagues would destroy everything.

"I don't want your protection," said Immanuelle, and she caught him by the hand. It was then that she realized they had matching scars—his on his right hand, hers on her left—both of the marks cutting through their lifelines. "I want you to help me fix this before the plagues destroy everything. There's still time if you can just get me through the gate."

Ezra gazed down at his hand in hers. He fit his fingers into the spaces between her own.

"Please, Ezra, while there's still time. Forge me a warrant with your seal. Get me through the Hallowed Gate. Bethel's fate depends on it."

She waited for him to refuse her, braced herself for the blow. But then, with a grim nod: "For you, and you only, I'll do it."

Chapter Twenty-eight

I am with child. I know they would take her from me, as they did him. But I will not let them. I would die before I'd do that.

—Miriam Moore

Immanuelle sat at the edge of Honor's bed, gazing out the window to the black stretch of the Darkwood. Three days had passed since Leah's body had burned on the purging pyre. Three days since Ezra had agreed to secure the warrant she'd need to get her through the Hallowed Gate.

In that time, Immanuelle had assembled the provisions she'd need for her journey and prepared to say her goodbyes. She'd resolved herself to going and she was ready for it. She didn't know what the wilds held, or what faced her beyond the gate, but she knew she would find her way.

Immanuelle ran her fingers through Honor's hair, and her bruised eyes split open. She'd awoken for the first time since the sickness struck just a few days prior, though she hadn't said more than two words since.

Though Glory now limped down the halls and joined the family for supper on her better days, Honor was still confined to her bed. Sometimes she shook; other times she wept openly, as if the sickness had taken something from her and she was grieving it.

That night, Immanuelle ate dinner with the Moores for a final time. She noticed every detail, wanting to remember everything. The way Abram toked on his pipe between bites. The dimples in Anna's cheeks when she smiled up at Glory. The gray that threaded through Martha's hair, as pale as spun silver.

After the meal was over and the dishes washed, Immanuelle dismissed herself to her bedroom, where she packed the last of the items she'd need on her journey. She padded the bottom of her knapsack with blankets, grateful for the warmth of the summer that would spare her for a time. In addition to the blankets, she packed a bag of coppers and food—dried fruit, jerky, pale squares of hardtack. Once Immanuelle was finished packing, she threw her cloak over her shoulders and crept downstairs, easing her way through the parlor and into the kitchen.

"You're up late."

Immanuelle stopped dead at the sound of Martha's voice. Her grandmother stood in front of the window, hands buried in the pockets of her skirt, head tipped over her shoulder, cheeks moon bathed. She turned to face Immanuelle, taking in her cloak and boots, the knapsack slung over her shoulder. She nodded toward the clock on the wall above the sink.

"It's almost the witching hour," said Martha, and a bitter smile touched her lips. "Perhaps that's what the Prophet should have named this wretched year. It's more fitting, don't you think? The Year of the Witching."

Immanuelle's hand tightened around the strap of her knapsack. "I want you to know I'm leaving. Before the next plague comes."

The elder woman looked less angry than tired. Her gaze shifted to the window again. "Go back to bed, Immanuelle."

"No."

At that, Martha turned back to face her. Immanuelle braced

for a scolding or even a slap to the cheek, but she simply asked, "What's in your bag?"

Immanuelle tilted her chin, trying to look firm when all she felt was afraid. "Provisions for the road."

Her grandmother drifted closer, her bare feet scuffing across the floorboards as she approached. "Let me see."

Immanuelle took a step back. "No."

Martha didn't ask again. She lashed out, snatching the bag off Immanuelle's shoulder. For a moment they tussled, each of them holding on to a strap, but Martha prevailed, ripping the bag from Immanuelle's grasp so hard she snapped forward and fell into the cabinets.

She rifled through its contents for a few moments in silence, her gray brows knit into a frown. She removed the book of poetry first, gave the first page a passing glance—spotting the holy seal in the corner—then snapped it shut again. Then she withdrew Miriam's journal, and Immanuelle saw the recognition flicker through her eyes like a candle lit. As Martha read her daughter's words—studied her drawings—her eyes narrowed, then filled with tears. "How did you come by these books? Answer me. Now."

"The books were gifts," said Immanuelle, picking every word with care. "Both of them belong to me, and I would like them back, if you would be so kind."

"Kind? You ask me to be kind when you keep secrets like this?" Martha demanded, shaking Miriam's journal so violently a few pages ripped free of the binding and fluttered to the floor. "This is holy treason. Men have died for less."

Immanuelle didn't deny it. It would make no difference anyway. She simply held out her hand. "My bag, please."

Martha turned, shoved the journal back into the knapsack, and hurled it against the door so hard it was a wonder that every

Moore in the house didn't wake at the sound. Coins and crumbs scattered across the floor. A few papers flew.

When Martha spoke again, it was in a harsh whisper. "I dragged you from my daughter's womb. I called your name down from the heavens and pinned it to you. I would have nursed you at my own breast if I could have. And this is how you repay me? With lies and deceit? With witch-work and treachery? By abandoning your family in the dead of night, skulking out of the house like a thief, without so much as a farewell? I didn't raise you to repeat the sins of your mother, or to die on the pyre like your father."

The words struck Immanuelle like a slap, but she said nothing, did nothing except stoop to collect the strewn coins and papers. After she gathered the last of her belongings, she rose to her feet and faced Martha. "I know that I'm not the granddaughter you wanted or the girl you raised me to be. If I were to list my sins, we'd be up half the night, and I'm sorry for that. If I could have been better for you, I would have. But believe me when I say I can't be what you want me to be. I am leaving now to keep people safe."

"There is no safety in sin, Immanuelle. Only despair."

A tear slipped down Immanuelle's cheek, then another. She didn't bother wiping them away. "I know."

"Your mother once said similar things. The day I found her in the arms of that wretched farm boy in the woods, she said she knew, that she understood. But she didn't. You see what became of her, because of her sin and selfishness."

"I'm not my mother. I have never been my mother."

"No, but you are her daughter. You're more like her than you are anyone else, despite all my prayers and efforts, everything I did to keep you from sharing her fate. I see that now. I was foolish to think it could be any other way."

Immanuelle took a half step toward her. "Martha—"

"No." The woman raised a hand, flinching away as if she feared Immanuelle would lash out and strike her. "You've made your choice. But know that if you go tonight, there is no returning. Once you step out that door into the darkness, it's done. No coming home again."

Immanuelle wiped her nose on her sleeve, trying to collect herself. She could barely see Martha through her tears. "I didn't mean to disappoint you." Her voice broke on the words. "I wanted more than anything to make you proud, but I know now that I wasn't meant to do that, and I am sorry. I'm so sorry."

Martha said nothing, but as Immanuelle turned toward the door a sob broke from the woman's lips, and she clasped a hand to her mouth in a vain attempt to muffle it.

In that moment—watching Martha weep—Immanuelle almost broke. She wanted to drop her knapsack right there, repent of her sins, gut a ram on the coming Sabbath to atone. Perhaps it would be enough. Perhaps the plagues would pass and she could begin again, go back to the life she'd led before.

Maybe it wasn't too late.

But then she thought of her nightmare—the church slaughter, corpses strewn across the aisles and slumped in the pews, her loved ones among the dead. If she stayed, she'd forfeit their lives, and the lives of countless others.

She couldn't do that, not for a dream that had died the day Miriam carved her name into the walls of that cabin.

And so, without another word, Immanuelle turned her back on Martha—on everything she had ever known—opened the door, and disappeared into the night.

CHAPTER TWENTY-NINE

With darkness comes sin.
—FROM *THE WRITINGS OF THE PROPHET ENECH*

IMMANUELLE FLED ACROSS the plains, running through the night, finding her way through the Glades by the light of the purging pyres. She and Ezra had agreed to meet at the Haven's gate, halfway to the village proper, along the main road. She pressed a hand to her side as she ran, gasping for every breath, her lungs burning from the pyre smoke. But she kept on, sprinting through the pain, through the black that seemed to thicken with every stride.

It took Immanuelle less than an hour to reach the Haven's gate. Ezra was waiting for her beside his wagon, which was hitched to a dark steed and loaded with supplies.

"I only needed the warrant," said Immanuelle, stunned by his generosity. "You didn't have to provide all of this."

"Of course I did. Getting you through the gate won't mean much if you don't have the supplies you need to survive the wilds beyond it. Now, come along, we should be on our way before the Prophet's Guard patrols. As it stands, we both have warrants to get through the gate, but if my father discovers our plans to escape and revokes them, we'll be in more trouble than enough."

Immanuelle paused, noticing for the first time that Ezra wore a pack like hers on his back. "Wait, *we*?"

He nodded. "I forged warrants for both of us. The wilds are too dangerous to traverse alone." He patted his horse on the neck, and it gave a gruff whinny. "I'll get you as far as you need to go."

"But you're going to be the Prophet someday. This is your home, your flock—"

"Which is why I need to see that you make it to your grandmother. As the Prophet's heir I have as much of a responsibility to end this as you do. From now on, what we do, we do together."

"You've done more than enough already. You don't have to leave everything behind."

Ezra set his jaw. "Weeks ago, I made a promise to help you protect those that couldn't protect themselves. So I'm going with you to find a way to end these plagues. Whether you like it or not."

And so, the two of them started down the long road to the village. Ezra urged his horse onward, and Immanuelle noticed his hands were so tight around the reins, his knuckles were bone white. Immanuelle sat by him, dressed in a dark wool cloak that Ezra had loaned her, the hood drawn low over her brow to hide her face from those they passed in the night.

They were halfway to the village when the cathedral bell tolled.

Immanuelle turned in her seat, straining to see through the darkness. "Did you hear that?"

Ezra nodded, reaching into the back of the wagon to retrieve something.

"Do you think that's for us?" Immanuelle asked. "Do you think they're looking?"

"If they are," said Ezra, turning to face the road again, now with his rifle in hand, "they'll regret it."

The sound of the bells grew louder, the tolls ringing in time to Immanuelle's racing heart. "Ezra. You can't be serious. We can't—"

Ezra snapped the reins, rousing the horse into a full gallop. He yelled above the thunder of the pounding hooves. "I promised you I'd get you through the gate, and I mean to keep that promise."

The woods blurred alongside them, shadows smearing as the horse picked up speed. Ezra peered over his shoulder and swore. "Damn it."

Immanuelle turned, following the path of his gaze to two distant lights that bobbed in the black behind them.

Riders. The Prophet's Guard.

The truth struck her: *Martha.*

She'd seen Immanuelle leave, and there was a Guard post in the Outskirts just ten minutes down the road by horseback. She must have gone to them, must have summoned the Prophet's Guard to drag her back. Martha had betrayed her, and now that the Church knew what Immanuelle had done, the Guard would hunt her down to the ends of the earth to punish her for it. There would be no mercy.

"I hope you said your prayers," said Ezra, yelling above the wind. "Because we'll both have sins to atone for by the time the night's through. Here." He slipped the reins into her hands, and Immanuelle had to brace her feet against the bottom of the wagon just to avoid being ripped off the bench. Ezra climbed into the back of the wagon, rifle in hand. "Hold the reins steady, but keep the horse running. Don't let him slow."

"What are you doing?" Immanuelle asked. The reins chafed her palms so badly she feared they'd bleed. In the dark behind them, the lights burned brighter, bigger, and Immanuelle could make out the shape of a lone rider tearing after them.

Ezra raised his rifle, squeezing one eye shut as he peered down the barrel. He fit his finger over the trigger. "Buying time."

What happened next passed in glimpses. A rider emerged from

the black, cloaked, his holy dagger beating against his breast as his horse charged forward. There was a shout.

A bullet whistled past Immanuelle's head.

Ezra pulled the trigger.

The guardsman behind them fell from his horse and struck the road, motionless, his shattered lantern burning in the dust beside him. Another light in the southern darkness, another rider drawing near. Bullets broke through the black and Immanuelle crouched low, snapping the reins and urging the horse onward.

Ezra fired a few warning shots into the darkness, forcing the riders to fall back, only for the next to emerge from the shadows, rifles raised, screaming orders and curses into the night.

Immanuelle urged the horse onward, but the riders were too fast, and when more lights appeared in the west, she knew that fleeing was futile.

It was over.

"We're not going to make it," she cried above the roaring wind, the reins eating deep into her palms. "There's too many of them!"

Ezra lowered his rifle, climbing over the back of the wagon to the bench. He snatched the reins from her hands and dragged on them hard. The horse reared, and Ezra jumped to the ground before the wagon stopped moving.

"What are you doing?" Immanuelle demanded.

"Getting you out of Bethel." He put the reins in her hands again. "The guardsmen posted at the gate will make sure they open for you. You'll have to get through fast, before the Prophet's Guard orders them shut again. But once you're out, you're safe, at least until my father gives the Guard clearance to pursue you in the wilds."

"Ezra—"

"Ride hard and don't look back for anything. Understand?

There are provisions in the wagon, coins and goods to trade with. If you can make it through the wilds to the towns on the other side, you should have enough to last you through the winter, if need be."

Immanuelle choked back tears. "Ezra. They'll arrest you on treason for firing on the Prophet's Guard. You can't stay here. You can't do this."

"You won't make it to the gate if I don't," said Ezra, his voice hoarse. "The riders are too fast. I can buy you some time."

"But what about the warrant?"

"It's with the guardsmen already. I saw to that days ago. You're expected, so when you approach the gate, it'll open for you. But you have to go. Now."

The thunder of horses' hooves grew louder, drowning the toll of the church bells. In the distance, Immanuelle saw the bright flare of a raised torch sputter to light.

"Go," said Ezra, and he turned to face the riders, rifle raised. When Immanuelle didn't move, he yelled. "Now!"

Immanuelle tossed the reins. The horse charged forward with a start, and they were off again, racing through the darkness, leaving Ezra behind them.

Immanuelle heard a shot, but she wasn't sure who fired. She didn't turn around. She kept her eyes on the road, her hands around the reins.

Don't look back, she told herself again and again, like she was reciting a prayer. *Don't look back. Don't look back.*

Another bullet hissed through the night, this one closer than the first. Then a third.

She peered over her shoulder and saw Ezra stagger, his rifle nearly slipping from his hands. He took two steps forward, one back; then he raised the weapon to his shoulder again and fired into the darkness.

Immanuelle snapped the reins. The village was in view now, and she could see the lights on the gate. She was almost there. Just half a league more. All she had to do was keep going.

Another bullet whistled through the darkness.

This time, Immanuelle didn't turn to look. Lashing the reins, she urged the horse onward, into Amas. A smear of town houses blurred past. The cart rattled across cobblestones and deep ruts in the road. The streets were mostly empty, but the few who were in them leaped for cover as Immanuelle barreled past.

The thunder of hoofbeats grew louder as the Prophet's Guard drew near. Rogue horsemen emerged from adjacent alleys, picking their way through the empty market stalls. In the near distance, she could see the gate, lit with the light of flaming torches.

A bullet whistled past her head.

Immanuelle cracked the reins, breaking for the gate at full speed, determined to make it even if she had to abandon the cart and haul herself over the top of it. Once she cleared it, the horsemen would stand down, as they had no right to pursue her beyond Bethel's borders without a formal warrant from the Prophet. As soon as she was past the Hallowed Gate, she was safe . . . at least for a little while.

The Prophet's guardsmen gained on her. Cries and gunshots echoed through the empty market stall. In mere moments she'd be surrounded. She wasn't going to make it to the gate; she wasn't going to make it out of the market at all. The Prophet's Guard was going to cut her short and haul her back to the Haven for contrition and trial and purging—

Something moved through the night.

Not wind but rather the absence of it, as though all the air was being sucked away. Torches went dark like matches pinched between two fingers. Oil lamps flickered out. Overhead, the moon died and the stars after it, each one winking out like a candle snuffed, until the skies were black. A great blanket of shadow fell over Amas, smothering the village.

The plague of darkness was upon them at last.

In the black behind her, Immanuelle heard riders fall. Rogue gunshots ringing through the darkness. The confused shouts of the Prophet's guardsmen.

It was only by luck and the persistence of her own keen memory that Immanuelle—blind in the sea of night—was able to navigate through the last of the market stalls and out onto the main road. She whispered to the horse, urging it onward into the dark, toward what she knew to be the gate, though the shadows were so thick she couldn't see it.

Then, lights, bobbing in the sea of the black like fireflies. Torches on the gate, the peal of a ram's horn, gears grinding with an ear-splitting screech. By the faint glow of torches newly lit, Immanuelle saw the gate heave open. She snapped the reins a final time, and the horse lunged forward, out of Bethel, and into the dark of the wilderness.

PART III

Darkness

Chapter Thirty

The world is a vast and dangerous place, unfit for the Father's flock.

— From *The Writings of David Ford*

THE MAIN ROAD stretched into the impenetrable black. Immanuelle couldn't see the Darkwood, but she could feel the familiar intoxication of her own unraveling as she delved deeper and deeper into the wilds. Overhead, the sky was dark—no star spatter or the sliver of a crescent moon to light the way ahead. Most of the lamps alongside the road were dark, and the few that were lit held tiny dying flames that flickered violently, threatening to snuff out with even the smallest breath of wind.

There were no traces of life on the road or in the forest that flanked it. No wagon tracks or footprints, no owls roosting in the trees. As Ezra had predicted, the Prophet's Guard had stopped their chase the moment she passed through the Hallowed Gate. She was truly alone, on the dark, wild road. But despite the eerie quiet of the night and her own aching loneliness, she took comfort in the fact that with the onset of the darkness plague, the blight was likely over, since each new plague thus far had signaled the end of the old one. She prayed that meant that Glory and Honor would now be spared. Then she remembered that the final plague was *slaughter*. She could only hope her journey could forestall it.

Immanuelle rode on. The night lapsed on long after its allotted hours were spent, and the black tide of the darkness was almost unfathomably thick. She tried her best to count the hours as they passed, but the unending black took on a kind of timelessness that made any attempt at tracking the time near impossible.

After what felt like a few hours, a drizzling rain began to fall, and it quickly gave way to sloughing sheets of sleet. With no shelter in sight, save for the sparse overhang of the forest's treetops, Immanuelle had nothing but Ezra's cloak to shield her from the torrents of the storm. By the time she came upon the ruins of a long-abandoned monastery, she was soaked to the bone, and the reins had chafed her palms raw and bloody. Knowing she was far too exhausted to continue, she decided to camp there.

The structure was a strange one, built on a berm that overlooked a shallow gulley. It was squat, narrow, and long, like a hallway or run of horse stalls. Stone columns supported a crumbling roof, which was built flat and low and covered in a sprawl of sweetgrass.

Pulling the cart to a stop alongside the ruins, Immanuelle hopped off the seat, untethered the horse, and led him into the structure and out of the sleet. She fed and watered him with provisions from the wagon, then retreated, soaked and shivering, into the far corner of the monastery, while the storm raged on.

When she felt rested enough to keep hold of the reins, Immanuelle roused herself, harnessed the horse to the cart, and set out into the dark again.

After a while, the wilderness pressed closer and the road diverged. One path, the larger of the two, was well cobbled and flanked by streetlamps on either side. It turned east, toward the deep woodland. The other was just a thin lane that looked much like the forest paths that snaked through the Bethelan woods.

Immanuelle went west, to Ishmel.

Brambles and branches tore at her clothes as she traveled down the narrow woodland corridor. The road was rutted with potholes and scattered with all manner of debris. Several times Immanuelle had to hop out of the cart and clear the way before they could pass through. In fact, she spent much of that leg of the journey on her feet, leading Ezra's steed by the bridle. Often, she had to coax the animal through the narrow passages that carved through the wilderness, mumbling calming words and sometimes singing the same lullabies she did to Honor and Glory, just to keep the eerie silence at bay and prevent the poor beast from spooking.

As they journeyed on, the path became progressively steeper and then gave way to a series of winding and treacherous trails that carved around the foothills of the mountains. Immanuelle had never been in the mountains before, and she scorned the dark for depriving her of the chance to see them clearly. She wished, desperately, that Ezra was there with her. It would have been such an adventure, to explore a place like this with him at her side.

She wondered if he was still alive, or if the Prophet's guards had executed him on the plains. Though Immanuelle was no longer in the habit of praying, she prayed for Ezra then. Begged the Father to save him or, if not that, give her the chance to return to Bethel so she could find a way to save him herself. He was too young and too good to die. Bethel needed him. *She* needed him. Because without Ezra, whom did she have left to turn to? Leah was dead and gone. Martha had betrayed her to the Prophet's Guard, and Immanuelle knew that the rest of the Moores wouldn't dare to oppose her. For the first time in her life, she was made to reckon with the idea that she might be truly, and totally, alone.

Immanuelle continued her trek up the treacherous mountain roads—head bowed to the roaring storm winds that swept in from the west, gripping the reins so tightly her fingers locked stiff. As the horse edged its way around a particularly steep crag, there was a loud peal of thunder. The horse lurched forward with so much force he snatched Immanuelle off her feet. They careened around a tight curve in the path, Immanuelle's boots skidding through the frozen muck of the road as she struggled to pull the horse to a stop. But as they raced toward another bend—this one around a cliff so high Immanuelle couldn't see the bottom—the cart's wheel struck a rut in the road. Its back wheels slipped off the cliff's edge, dragging the horse back with it.

The steed gave a scream that echoed through the mountain pass, struggling to drag the wheels of the cart back over the drop-off and onto the road. Immanuelle pulled the bridle with all her might—blisters bursting open as she gripped the leather strappings. But despite her best efforts, the horse began to slip and both of them inched—closer and closer—to the cliff's edge, dragged by the weight of the cart.

Crates of supplies slid off the back of the wagon. There was a long pause before Immanuelle heard the crash as they struck the bottom of the valley, far, far below. The steed skidded back, and Immanuelle sprang forward, releasing her grip on the bridle to unhitch him. Her hands shook, stiff with cold, as she fumbled with the buckles—freeing him from the tacking and traces. The steed inched toward the cliff—pulled by the weight of the wagon—until his back hooves teetered on the edge. A split second before the cart dragged them down, Immanuelle undid the last buckle. The cart lurched off the cliff and crashed to the valley below.

IMMANUELLE MADE THE last of the journey on horseback, riding through the torrents of the storm. The rain came down in sloughing sheets that often gave way to sleet or stinging hail. By the time she saw the lights of Ishmel floating in the distant dark, Immanuelle was so delirious with cold and weariness she wasn't sure she could trust her own eyes. But as she traveled up the road, those distant lights grew bigger and brighter, and she could hear the sound of voices, catch the scent of chimney smoke on the cold night air.

She entered a village in the shadow of a mountain, far smaller than Amas. Here, the dark was not so complete as it was in Bethel. The sky was the bruised blue of deep dusk just before it turns into outright night, and the streetlamps burned bright enough to stave off the shadows. All the houses that lined the streets had shuttered windows and doors bolted closed. To her relief, she saw no sign of the Prophet's Guard.

Immanuelle rode on, through the labyrinth of narrow, packed-dirt streets, until she reached what appeared to be the center of the village. There, she found an inn with large bay windows that glowed with firelight. Every time its doors swung open, a rush of murmurs and the chords of what Immanuelle knew to be a mourning hymn spilled into the streets. Squatting on its stairs was a beggar, broad-shouldered, with bright eyes and a long beard badly matted. He cradled a small drum that looked like a child's cast-off toy. As Immanuelle approached, he began to tap out a rhythm—too fast and sporadic to match the fiddle music that spilled from the tavern.

Immanuelle stooped to place a coin in the cup by his feet. "I'm trying to locate someone . . . could you help me?"

"That depends on who you're looking for," said the man, and his accent was one that Immanuelle had never heard before.

"A woman . . . by the name of Vera Ward." She might have explained that Vera was a soothsayer, hailing from Bethel, but she didn't know whether it was safe to mention such things in a place like this. Certainly, Ishmel seemed devoid of the overt piety that

distinguished Bethel—with its sprawling cathedral and the chapels that stood on its every street corner—but that didn't make it
entirely safe.

The man appraised her by the oily light of a nearby streetlamp;
then he nodded, motioning for Immanuelle to follow him down a
narrow road that snaked east. The beggar led her through a labyrinth of houses, then down a sloping street that wrapped around
a tall hill, until they reached a small, pond-side homestead where
a stone cottage stood.

Immanuelle tethered the horse to a fence post by the road and
started forward. The cottage's windows were warm with the glow
of lit candles, and it was light enough for Immanuelle to distinguish the small symbol painted on the door: It was the shielding
sigil, just like the one carved into the foundation stone of the Ward
house ruins.

She knocked. Waited.

There was a soft disturbance, shadows moving behind cur-
tained windows, the sound of bare feet on wood floors, the click
of a latch slipping out of place.

The door swung open.

A woman stood in the threshold. She was fair-skinned for an
Outskirter, with a dark mane of corkscrew curls and eyes that
were the verdant green of seedlings. She appeared to be Anna's
age, maybe a little older, and she held a basket of laundry perched
on the curve of her hip. But at the sight of Immanuelle, her arms
went slack and the basket hit the porch with a dull *thud*.

"Vera." She said the name with a thick accent. "We have a
visitor."

A figure appeared behind the woman. She was taller, broad-
shouldered, and dressed in a pair of dark men's breeches. She wore
her silvered dreadlocks pinned back out of her face. The buttons of
her work shirt were loose, so that Immanuelle could see the leather

cord around her neck, strung with two holy daggers carved from birch. Her eyebrows were dark and thick—between them, the Mother's mark.

THE TWO WOMEN ushered Immanuelle inside, settled her in front of a roaring hearth before she had the chance to say more than two words to them. The woman who answered the door, who was called Sage, wrapped a thick quilt around her shoulders and prepared her a cup of tea with cream and several spoonfuls of honey. Vera went to tend to her horse and returned a few minutes later, sitting opposite Immanuelle in a large chair. She was an imposing woman—almost as tall as Lilith, dark-skinned and striking in a way that most people weren't. In fact, she reminded Immanuelle of the depictions of the Dark Mother—with her ebony skin and fine-cut features. Her beauty made it hard to look away.

To avoid gawking, Immanuelle turned her gaze to the room. The cottage was larger on the inside than it appeared on the outside. The parlor was tastefully decorated, the floors laid with bearskins, the tables adorned with little trinkets like doilies and candles and books of poetry. The air smelled of yeast and spice, and the remnants of their dinner were still on the table. In an armchair by the hearth, two kittens, one gray, one black, slept blissfully.

Not knowing what to say or what to do, Immanuelle sipped on the honeyed tea in silence.

Vera watched her drink, impassive, near sullen, despite Sage's failed attempts at rousing a conversation. It was only when Immanuelle had finished her tea that Vera finally spoke. "How did you find me?"

"I went to the Outskirts," said Immanuelle, setting her cup down on a delicate pedestal of a side table. "There was a priest there who knew you. He said I might find you here."

"And you traveled alone?" Sage asked, settling herself on a low stool by the hearth. Immanuelle realized, self-consciously, that she was occupying what must have been her seat, and she started to get up, but the woman waved her away.

"I wasn't entirely alone. I had a friend who rode with me through Bethel. He got me through the gate, but..." The image of Ezra standing in the middle of the road, rifle raised, swarmed by the Prophet's guards, surfaced in her reverie. She closed her eyes against the memory, shook her head. "He didn't make it through."

"And what of your family?" Sage asked gently.

"They're still in Bethel."

It was Vera who spoke next. "Do they know that you're here?"

"No."

Vera leaned forward—legs parted, forearms braced on her kneecaps the way a man might sit. "And do they know *why* you left?"

Immanuelle shook her head, rushing to explain herself. "I didn't tell them where I was going or that you're here. I wouldn't have betrayed your privacy that way."

Vera appraised her by the wan candlelight as if trying to determine whether or not she was telling the truth. "Were you followed?"

Immanuelle started to shake her head, then faltered.

Vera's eyes sparked with frustration. "It's a simple question: Were you followed? Yes or no?"

"I was... but only at first. The Prophet's Guard stopped pursuing me as soon as I got beyond the gate. I didn't see another soul on the road until I came upon Ishmel."

To this, Vera said nothing. She stood and took a pipe from its box on the mantel, filled the bowl with tobacco from a pretty tin, and lit up. She fixed her eyes on Immanuelle. Exhaled a mouthful of smoke. "Why did you come?"

"*Vera,*" said Sage, a rebuke cut through gritted teeth. "Maybe you ought to let the girl rest before the interrogation begins?"

"We need to know why she's here."

"Look at her, V. She's yours. She's here for you. Or are you so jaded that you can't see your own kin when they're sitting right in front of you?"

Vera's eyes narrowed behind a veil of pipe smoke.

"Please," said Immanuelle, weary and weak. The quilt around her shoulders felt as heavy as a stone-filled knapsack. "I have no one else. Just let me explain myself, and if you want no part of me after that, I promise I'll leave."

Vera studied her for a long beat. A muscle in her jaw flexed and spasmed. "It's late. Whatever you've come to say will have to wait until the morning. Sage." She turned to her companion. "Prepare the room."

CHAPTER THIRTY-ONE

To be a woman is to be a sacrifice.
—FROM *THE WRITINGS OF TEMAN, THE FIRST
WIFE OF THE THIRD PROPHET, OMAAR*

TUCKED INTO BED, under a thick covering of quilts and bear-skins, Immanuelle lay awake listening to the hushed tones of chatter on the other side of the wall. The conversation between Vera and her companion sounded like the rapid-fire beginnings of an argument, but their hissing whispers made it difficult to distinguish anything more than a few words.

"Dangerous" was one that came up often. "Obligation" was another.

Immanuelle closed her eyes, trying not to cry. She wasn't sure what she'd been expecting to find upon arriving in Ishmel, but it wasn't this. Perhaps she had been naive to expect a warmer welcome. After all, shared blood didn't negate the fact that she and Vera were strangers. Still, Immanuelle had hoped that her arrival would be met with something more than outright coldness. Her disappointment, when coupled with the sting of Martha's betrayal, was almost too much to bear. To be shunned by one grandmother—the woman who had raised her like a daughter—was bad enough. But to be cast aside by another, mere days later, seemed like a particularly cruel punishment.

The night wore on, but she didn't feel tired, due perhaps to the disorientation caused by the never-ending night. Without the rise and fall of the sun, she found that she was often caught in the limbo between waking and sleeping.

To pass the time, Immanuelle let her gaze roam around the bedroom. It was a well-kept place, tastefully decorated, with mirrors and little paintings hanging on the walls. The dozen candles that cluttered the top of the dresser were unlit, but the cast-iron stove in the corner glowed softly, limning the room with a haze of firelight. If the dust on the nightstand was any indication at all, the bedroom was rarely used. This struck Immanuelle as odd, given that it was the second of two in the house.

Eventually, she fell into a fitful slumber—filled with the sort of thin dreams that are prone to fading the moment one becomes conscious again. She didn't know how long she slept, but when she woke, it was to darkness and the smell of fresh-fried bacon.

Immanuelle sat up and slipped out of bed, surprised to see that she was dressed in a thick nightgown, though she had no memory of changing out of her damp travel clothes. There was a knit shawl draped over the headboard, and she wrapped it around her shoulders before leaving the bedroom. The parlor was candlelit, aglow with kerosene lamps and a wrought iron chandelier that dangled from the ceiling by a thick chain. In the far corner of the room, a cast-iron stove, which Sage stood in front of, humming a trilling song that sounded far livelier than any hymn Immanuelle knew.

Sage turned to set a platter on the table and startled at the sight of her. "You're just as soft-footed as Vera. I can never hear when she's approaching."

"Forgive me," said Immanuelle, stalling in the space between the parlor and the kitchen, unsure of where to go or what to do.

Sage waved her off with a smile. "Please, eat."

Immanuelle obeyed, settling herself in front of a large plate of eggs and thick-cut bacon, roast potato, and fat-fried corn cake. She was famished, and she ate like it, but Sage seemed delighted by her ravenous appetite.

"You look so much like her," said Sage wistfully. "I just knew you were Vera's kin the moment I laid eyes on you."

"Are you a Ward too?"

Sage shook her head. "Gods no. Just a road rat like most of those in Ishmel. I don't think I would have ever settled down if I hadn't met Vera."

"And you've been . . ." Immanuelle searched for the right word. "Together, all this time?"

"Eleven years," said Sage, with no small amount of pride. "I suppose you could say we're very well matched."

In truth, Immanuelle wasn't entirely sure what Sage was trying to say, but she thought it might have something to do with the way that the Lovers clung to each other in the woods. Then there was the matter of the spare room, sparse and untouched, and the larger bedroom with two night tables instead of one and a mattress too big for a single person. "I'm glad she found you."

Sage blushed, seeming touched. "Well, that's very kind of you."

Immanuelle sopped up a bit of egg yolk with a piece of fried corn cake. "Where is she?"

"Vera went to a council meeting in the village," said Sage, leaning across the table to refill Immanuelle's mug of tea. "She'll be back soon, I'm sure. She won't want to stay away long. Not while you're here."

A small silence. Immanuelle finished the last of the food on her plate. "Have you been touched by the plagues?"

Sage shook her head, then faltered. "Not in the same way you were. Our waters were only laced with blood for a few days. But we heard stories of the taint that afflicted Bethel. Once we found a woman, naked and mad with fever, roaming the mountain wilds just beyond Ishmel's edge. Her head was cut with that mark your women wear, so we knew she was Bethelan. She died in the village, just a few days after we found her. Nothing the doctors did could ease her suffering. No tincture or herb could touch it." She paused for a beat, frowning at the memory. "But we have not been made to endure the same horrors your people have. Whatever that evil is, it's been largely contained in the borders of Bethel. But Vera thinks there's a chance the contagion could spread to Ishmel, with time."

"She's wise to be cautious."

Sage stood to clear her plates. "Vera is nothing if not that. But I do hope that you haven't mistaken her wariness for malice. I know she's . . . rather harsh at times, but she is happy to see you. I think she's been waiting for you for so long that she doesn't know what to do with herself or how to feel now that you're here. But it'll pass. You two just need a chance to acclimate to each other, that's all."

As if on cue, the front door swung open, and Vera entered. She slipped out of her coat, which, like the rest of her clothes, appeared cut for a man. She took a seat at the table and helped herself to the food Sage prepared. As she ate, she deftly dodged her partner's questions about her morning, only offering nods and the occasional one-word answer when she was forced to speak.

Sage, perhaps realizing this was some subtle cue of dismissal, announced that she was going outside to feed the chickens and clean their coop. With her gone, a long silence lapsed between Vera and Immanuelle, broken only by the roaring of the hearth.

It was Vera who spoke first. "I can't tell who you favor more: my boy or your mother."

It was the first time she'd made mention of Daniel, and the significance of the moment wasn't lost on either of them.

"I always hoped that I favored him," said Immanuelle haltingly. "When I was little, I used to look in the mirror and try to imagine myself as a boy, so I'd know what he might've looked like."

Vera's expression was hard to read. She and Martha were so alike in their stoicism. "I wish I had a portrait to show you, but the Prophet's Guard burned everything I had left of him."

"Not everything," Immanuelle said, and she stood up, walked to the door where she'd dropped her knapsack the night prior, and dug until she found her mother's journal. She carried it back to the table, opened it to the page that contained the portrait of Daniel, then slid it across the table.

Vera took it, her hand shaking some, and stared down at the sketch for a long, long time in silence. "Your mother always had a good hand. This is him, all right. Just as I . . ." She shook her head. "Thank you. It's been a long time since I've looked upon his face."

"What . . . was he like?" Immanuelle said, unsure if it was a question she was allowed to ask. It seemed like such a grave and sacred thing, to ask a mother to resurrect the memory of her dead son. But Vera didn't seem fazed.

"He was a quiet boy. Kind, though he didn't seem like it upon first meeting." Vera smiled down at the picture of her frowning son, traced the furrows in his brow with the tip of her finger. "I like to think that he saw the world for what it was. Most people can't do that. Even prophets are blinded by their own vices. But not Daniel. He saw the truth in everything."

Immanuelle took the book back, pressed a hand to the opposing page, putting pressure on the binding, and painstakingly ripped the portrait out of the journal, then slid it back to Vera. "Here. It ought to be yours."

The woman shook her head. "He's your kin too."

"But I never had the chance to lose him. He was your son. You should have it."

"I have my memories. Besides, this is your mother's work."

"It's okay. Take it, please. As a gift for your hospitality."

"Hospitality," said Vera, and she laughed without a trace of humor. "Hospitality is putting food on the table for a stranger. It's welcoming an acquaintance over for plum cobbler and tea. But this isn't that. This is me doing what I should have done, years ago. I should have waited for you. I should have taken you with me—"

"It's not your fault."

"But it is . . . at least in part."

Immanuelle shook her head and slid the drawing across the table again. "It's yours. Take it."

Vera didn't move. Her gaze became hard again, the way it had been last night. She nodded to the journal. "Who gave you that?"

Immanuelle saw no point in lying now, when she'd come all this way to learn the truth. "It was a gift from two women. Witches that I encountered in the Darkwood."

Vera's expression remained unchanged. She leaned back into her seat. "Why did you come?"

Immanuelle reached for Miriam's journal and opened it to the final pages, with the writings: *Blood. Blight. Darkness. Slaughter.* She slid it across the table to Vera.

The woman stared down at the journal. Immanuelle couldn't parse her expression, but she knew one thing: Her grandmother wasn't surprised.

"You knew," said Immanuelle, so softly she wasn't sure she spoke the words aloud. "You knew about the cabin. You knew about the plagues and the witches and the deal my mother cut with them in the Darkwood. You knew she sold me off."

Vera stared at her, clearly confused. "Miriam didn't sell you to the witches. Your mother loved you. She chose you over everything else. Her home, her family, her life, even her soul."

"That isn't true. I don't know what she told you, or what you think you knew of my mother, but she didn't love me the way you loved Daniel. She made no sacrifices on my behalf. She sold me out. She bound me to darkness before I was even born. My mother bought the plagues with my blood. All she cared about was vengeance."

"Your Mother was trying to protect you. Everything that girl had to give, she gave to you."

"If that's true, why did she cast the curses?" Immanuelle demanded, growing angry now. "I saw the cabin myself. I know what those sigils on the walls mean. If she loved me so much, why would she use me like that?"

"Like I said, she was trying to protect you."

"By making me a weapon? A pawn in Lilith's hands?"

"Miriam was trying to give you the power that she never had. But she was grieving and afraid and sixteen years old and more vulnerable than she knew. Lilith could see that. She perverted Miriam's desire to protect you, preyed on her weakness. I watched it happen. Every time she ventured into the woods, she was a little more mad than the time before. In the end, I think she was more like them than she was us."

"In what way?"

Vera paused before answering, as if to sort through her thoughts. "In life, most of us have the luxury of nuance. We may be angry, but we balance that anger with mercy. We may be filled with joy, but that doesn't prohibit us from empathizing with those who aren't. But after we die, that changes and we're distilled down to our most rudimentary compulsions. A single desire so powerful it trumps all others."

"Like Lilith and her desire for revenge?"

Vera nodded. "Toward the end, your mother became the same way. She was obsessed with protecting you, imbuing you with the power and freedom she so desperately wanted but never had. It was like she lived for nothing else, so she might as well have been dead."

The explanation accounted for Miriam's madness. The writings and sketches in her journal, her singular obsession with the Dark-wood and the witches it harbored. But something still plagued Immanuelle, stoked the flames of her rage. "If you knew all that—if you knew my mother was being manipulated and used by Lilith, driven mad by her grief—then why didn't you do something to stop it?"

Vera struggled with an answer. "Because at the time . . . I was as sick as she was. I'd lost my boy, watched him burn alive on the pyre before my eyes, and his screams, they haunted me like the witches did your mother. But I didn't know Miriam would wield the plagues or bring all of this upon your head."

Immanuelle mulled this for a moment in silence, trying to de-cide whether or not she believed her. "The cabin where she cast those curses, it was yours?"

Vera nodded. "In part. But it belongs to you too. For twelve generations, the women of the Ward family practiced their magic there."

"And is that where you taught her the ways of the witches? How to practice the dark craft?"

"I never taught Miriam anything," said Vera in vehement de-nial. "What little she learned, she learned from Lilith and from the Darkwood itself."

"But why did Lilith bother with my mother in the first place? If she was just a grief-sick girl, then why did the witches even answer her calls?"

"They didn't," said Vera, speaking low now. "The only reason the witches showed their faces to her was because she bore you in her belly. It was your blood running through Miriam's veins that gave her the power to cast those curses. The witches were drawn by you."

Immanuelle's heart stumbled, skipping several beats. "I don't understand."

Vera's voice grew very soft, and for the briefest moment, she stared at Immanuelle with the same tenderness she did the portrait of her son. "Miriam was a brokenhearted farm girl with a vendetta and a vicious temper. And, yes, she carved the sigils, orchestrated the plagues. But the power she siphoned came from you. A babe with the blood of witches running through her veins. All of that nascent power for the taking. You made the perfect vessel."

Immanuelle sat, stricken, in her chair, trying and failing to speak. In her bones, she knew what Vera said was true, but one detail gave her pause. "If I'm nothing more than a vessel to the witches, why was I given the journal?"

"The witches are evangelists before they are anything else. How else could four foreign girls raise armies so large they rivaled the forces of Bethel? How else did they sow the seeds of discord if not by winning the hearts and souls of the Church's flock?"

"So they weren't trying to bait me; they were trying to win my soul?"

Vera nodded. "They want you, Immanuelle—your power, your potential. Lilith would like nothing more than for you to join her, as a sister and servant of the coven. And before the end comes, mark me, they will make you an offer. Invite you into their ranks."

Immanuelle considered the idea, imagined what it might be like to walk the woods alongside Lilith. She would not be made to fight temptation any longer, or grovel at the feet of the Prophet. She would live free of Protocol and punishment—to roam and do as she pleased. "What happens if I refuse their offer?"

"Then you'll share in Bethel's demise."

Immanuelle straightened in her chair. Her hands stopped shaking. Her shoulders squared. For the first time, she looked Vera dead in the eye. "Is there any way to stop them?"

Vera nodded. "There is one way. A powerful sigil to redirect the energy of the plagues. You'd need to carve it into your arm with a consecrated knife."

"Like a holy dagger?"

"Yes, but *only* the Prophet's. You see, a powerful sigil requires a powerful tool to carve it. The blade must be consecrated—imbued with power through prayer or spell casting. There are only a few objects of that nature in Bethel. The Prophet's holy dagger; the sacred gutting knife; and the sword of David Ford, the first crusader saint, which hangs above the altar in the Prophet's Cathedral, are the only ones that come to mind. A point from Lilith's antlers would also suffice. In fact, I suspect that's what your mother used to carve her sigils in the cabin."

"So all I have to do is carve the sigil into my arm with a consecrated blade and then it's over? The plagues will end, and everything will go back to the way it was before?"

"If only," said Vera with a sad smile. "When you carve the sigil, it will drag the power of the plagues back to its origin place: you. Once you've done that—if you're even capable of surviving such a feat—the power of the plagues will be yours to wield as you wish."

Immanuelle paused to imagine it: the blight, the blood, and the darkness, and the slaughter to come, hers to wield as weapons. With it, she'd have the leverage she needed to bring the Church to heel, spare Ezra's life, make the Prophet atone for his sins. She could reign over Bethel if she wanted to, and under her oversight there would be no pyres or purgings. No young girls lying like lambs on the altar for the cutting. No one made to suffer in the squalor of the Outskirts. With power like that, she could raze the

Prophet's Church to the very stones of its foundation. Build Bethel anew.

"What's the cost?" she asked, knowing it would be a heavy one. If there was one thing she'd learned thus far, it was that power was never free.

"It's impossible to say what it will take or when. But know that the price for power like that will be steep. It may claim your life, like it did your mother's, erode your bones and spread through your body like a cancer. Or perhaps it will manipulate your senses, claim your sanity as recompense. Maybe it will steal the life of your firstborn or make you barren. The only certainty is that one day you'll be made to pay for the power you've taken."

"And is there a cure for these . . . afflictions?"

"Perhaps, but that would depend entirely upon what you're afflicted with."

Immanuelle nodded, first to herself, then to Vera. "Teach me how to do it."

Vera laughed outright; the sound was harsh and ugly, almost frightening. Across the kitchen, the oven burned so hot Immanuelle could see heat waves distorting the air around it, and the kettle on the burner began to whistle. Froth spilled from its spout and sizzled on the coals below.

"What's so funny?"

Vera settled herself, dabbing at the corners of her eyes. "The idea that you think that I would damn you to an end like that one." Her smile died, and all at once she was so serious she seemed almost grave. "Bethel has placed its burdens on the shoulders of little girls for far too long. I already lost my boy. I'm not going to lead you to the same fate he met. Certainly not in some futile attempt to save a place that doesn't deserve deliverance."

"There's still hope for Bethel. There are good people there, and if I don't help them, they'll die in the plagues to come."

"Good people don't bow their heads and bite their tongues while other good people suffer. Good people are not complicit."

"There are children there," said Immanuelle, trying to make her see. "Little girls, like my sisters, who are innocent in all of this."

"And I feel for them; I do. But if they suffer it's not because of the witches or the plagues or you. It's because their fathers, and their father's fathers, created this mess. Perhaps you ought to let them answer for it."

"And do what? Stay here with my hands tied? Turn my back on Bethel, my home?"

"If the worst comes—"

"It will."

"*If* it comes, then we go," said Vera. "There are worlds beyond this one, Immanuelle."

"You mean the heathen cities? Valta and Hebron and Gall and the like?"

"More than just them. The world is vast, and you deserve the chance to see it. We can explore it together, the three of us. A family." Vera reached across the table, caught her by the hand, and squeezed. "Let me do what I should have done seventeen years ago. Let me take you with me."

It was a tempting offer, and weeks ago she might have taken Vera up on it. But Immanuelle knew better now. "I can't turn my back on Bethel or on the people there that I love."

"That's what your father said about your mother, years ago, and he burned for it. If you go back to that place, you'll die there, just like he did."

"Bethel is my home. If I were to die anywhere, I'd want it to be there. I'm a part of that place and I won't turn my back on it, or the people that I care about." She snatched her hand away. "I came here to find a way to fix things, not to run away like you did."

Vera flinched at the insult. "Immanuelle—"

"Write the sigil. Teach me how to end this and do it quickly. Please. I'm begging you."

"You know that I can't do that."

"Then I'll go back empty-handed and I'll die without a fight. One way or another, I'll return to Bethel. Either I can return with a weapon, a means of defending myself against the plagues and the Church, or I can go back to Bethel defenseless. But I will return. I have to."

"Their world doesn't want the likes of you. Don't you see that? It doesn't matter what you do, how good you are, or if you save them from the jaws of the Mother herself. You'll always be an outsider to them. You will never earn their favor or their trust."

"This isn't about me."

"But you're the one making the sacrifice," said Vera, nearly shouting now. She reclined back into her seat, ran a hand through her dreadlocks, trying to compose herself. "Let's say I give you the sigil. How can you hope to defeat four of the most powerful witches that have ever walked the earth when you frighten at the sight of your own shadow?"

"I am not a coward."

"Maybe not in the face of certain dangers. I mean, you made it here all by yourself. Braved the wilds beyond Bethel without a single soul to turn to. It's the makings of a hero's legend . . . but I do wonder if that same bravery extends to the other things you fear."

"What other things?"

"Damnation. Ill favor with the Father. Ridicule from the Church. The loss of your soul and virtue and good name." Vera counted each of the strikes on her fingers. "And perhaps, more than anything else, fear of yourself. Fear of your own power. Because that's what terrifies you the most, isn't it? Not the Prophet, not the

Church, not Lilith or the plagues, not the wrath of the Father . . . It's your own power that you're most afraid of. That's why you're suppressing it."

Immanuelle didn't know if she was some sort of seer like Ezra and his father, or if her weakness was so apparent that even a near stranger could recognize it, but she flushed with the shame of being so exposed.

Vera's gaze softened. "If you want to end those plagues, you're going to have to embrace yourself, all of yourself. Not just the virtues the Church has told you to value. The ugly parts too. Especially the ugly parts. The rage, the greed, the carnality, the temptation, the hunger, the violence, the wickedness. A blood sacrifice won't mean much if you can't control the power it affords you. And if you're half as strong as I think you are, the power will be immense. You saw how your mother succumbed to it." Vera tapped the journal. "She was mad out of her senses by the end. And when it's all said and done . . . you may be too. Is that really a sacrifice you're ready and willing to make?"

"Yes," said Immanuelle, without a moment's pause. "I'm ready to see an end to this."

"You really are your mother's daughter," said Vera, and she turned the sketch of Daniel facedown on the table, took up a bit of graphite, and scrawled a small sigil that Immanuelle knew to be the mark of the curse, with a small alteration; a series of forked lines that looked a bit like arrows halved the symbol down the middle. "The plagues were born of your blood. If you carve this mark into your arm, they will return to you."

"That is, if I'm strong enough to harbor them."

"You are," said Vera. "You'll have to be."

Immanuelle parted her lips to reply, but the sound of a woman's scream cut her short. She and Vera were on their feet in an instant, their chairs crashing to the floor behind them. They snatched the lamp off the table and charged toward the door. The darkness beyond it was nearly impenetrable, broken only by three halos of light. In those halos, men, eight of them, with lanterns and torches raised. All of them wore the uniform of the Prophet's Guard. Two had hold of Sage, twisting her arms behind her back, forcing her to her knees even as she kicked and struggled.

One of the guardsmen stepped closer, and in the wan torchlight, Immanuelle recognized him. He was Ezra's older half brother, Saul. The same cruel-eyed commander whom many called the Prophet's favorite son. To her horror, she saw that he now wore Ezra's holy dagger around his neck. A sure sign that he either had, or would, replace him as the Prophet's heir.

"No." Immanuelle broke toward him, toward Sage, but Vera caught her by the arm and dragged her back.

Four of the Prophet's guardsmen raised their rifles in unison, fingers curled over the triggers, but Saul waved them off, his gaze fixed on Immanuelle. "Lower your weapons. We bring the girl back to Bethel unharmed."

✢

Chapter Thirty-two

*He watches me, I know it. In the night, I feel His holy eye
upon me, but I am not afraid.*

—Miriam Moore

D O YOU BELIEVE in the Scriptures of your Father and Prophet?"
The apostle's words echoed through the chambers and carried down the dungeon hall.

"Yes," said Immanuelle.

Apostle Isaac straightened his robes. He was a tall, starved-
looking man with a head that was nearly as pale and gaunt as Lilith's. He looked only half-human, as if—with his robes stripped
away—he could skulk among the forest beasts unnoticed. In one
hand, he held the Holy Scriptures, in the other a small candle that
burned low on its wick. "And do you believe that hellfire meets
those who live in reproach of the Father's law?"

"Yes."

"Have you ever defied the Father's law?"

Immanuelle nodded. "I have."

It had been at least ten days since she'd returned to Bethel and
more than twelve since the Prophet's Guard had stormed Vera's
house, ripped her from the arms of the only loyal family she had
left, and placed her in contrition. But the stagnant dark of the Haven's dungeons made her feel like she'd been there far longer.

Immanuelle tried to sleep to pass the hours, but if her night-mares didn't wake her, then the screams of her fellow inmates did. From the stench of sewage alone, she could tell the cells were crowded to capacity with all of the women and girls held in con-trition under penalty of witchcraft. She'd heard the Prophet's guards murmur about the night raids that had occurred while she was still in Ishmel. In hushed whispers, they spoke of little girls being ripped from the arms of their mothers, homes invaded, doz-ens of women arrested and marched to the Haven under cover of darkness. At long last, the Prophet's wrath was made manifest.

During her imprisonment, Immanuelle had been confined to a remote cell of her own. She had seen no one, save Apostle Isaac, and a few of the low-ranking Prophet's guardsmen, who—every day or so—slipped a bowl of water and a moldy hunk of bread through the bars of her cell. As sick as it was, she had almost come to look forward to these daily interrogations, if only because they interrupted the maddening tedium . . . and the solitude, which was even worse. When she was left alone for too long, time didn't slow so much as it unraveled. And it was in that strange abstrac-tion of timelessness, where the seconds seemed suspended in the torpor of the infinite, that Immanuelle's thoughts turned dark. That thing within her—the maelstrom, the monster, the witch—stirred to life.

It made her feel dangerous. It made her feel . . . ready.

Almost all the pieces were in place. She had the reversal sigil and she knew the tool she'd need to cast it: the Prophet's dagger. Now it was just a matter of securing it, which would be no small feat given her current circumstances. But once she had that blade in her hand, all she needed to do was carve the sigil.

Apostle Isaac drew closer by a half step. "Tell me how you've sinned."

Immanuelle thought back to the beginning of her memories.

To sitting on Abram's knee in front of a roaring fire, a book of Holy Scriptures lying open in her lap. She remembered stringing syllables together into words, and those words becoming sentences, and the sentences then becoming psalms and stories. Another memory surfaced, a summer day, years ago, when she and Leah had paddled in the muddy shallows of the river, swimming in secret. She remembered how free she'd felt the first time she let the current take her.

Immanuelle's chains slithered across the cell floor as she straightened and found her voice. "I lived free—from the Protocol, from the Scriptures, from the Prophet's law. That's my only sin."

The apostle frowned. "Is this your confession?"

"Yes."

"And do you wish to be cleansed of your sin?"

Immanuelle raised her eyes to the apostle's, squinting against the glow of the candlelight. She thought of muzzles and gutting blades, bridal veils and shackles. She thought of little girls lashed bloody for forgetting to fasten the top buttons of their dresses. She thought of purging pyres and the witches who'd died screaming on them, and of heads mounted on the spikes of the Haven's gate. She thought of the Prophet's gaze crawling over her, of Leah writhing and pleading in the torment of her labor until life had left her and she could scream no more. She thought of the reversal sigil, imagined carving it into the bare flesh of her forearm and calling back the plagues.

"I have no sins to cleanse."

There was silence in the cell, save for the distant echo of footsteps, the rhythmic *drip, drip, drip* of the leak in the corner. Here—far below the earth's surface—the water still tasted of brine and metal, the taint of the blood curse lingering.

Apostle Isaac paced from one end of the cell to the other. It was a show, Immanuelle realized, the way he moved, the way he preached the Scriptures and declared her sins. He wanted to plant terror like a seed. "They say you wandered the Darkwood. Is that so?"

Immanuelle lay back against the wet stones, too weak to stand. Hunger gnawed at her like a rat from within, and it was difficult to think past it. "That's true."

"They say you have talked to the demons that dwell there."

Down the hall, the sound of a door grinding open, a girl shrieking for mercy. "I have."

"They say they answer your calls."

"Only sometimes."

The apostle drew closer. "And these creatures, what are their names?"

"You know them already," said Immanuelle. "You say them at feasts and on cutting days. You burn them in celebration. Lilith, Delilah, Jael, Mercy."

The apostle's brows knit together. The candle's flame danced on its wick. "And was it the witches who ordered you to cast the curses? Is it their magic you conjure?"

Immanuelle didn't answer. The truth mattered little in these interrogations.

"You are the daughter of Miriam Moore, is that so?"

"It is."

"Miriam wandered the Darkwood as well. Did she not?"

"She did."

Something like triumph passed through the apostle's eyes. "And is it your mother's god you pray to in the night? Is it her beasts you call to?"

"They weren't her beasts. They belong to no one."

"And yet they obey you."

Immanuelle shook her head. "They heed no one."

At that, the apostle smiled, as if the two of them shared some dirty secret. He drew closer, his boots scuffing across the floor, and dropped to a crouch at her side. "But Ezra heeds your every whim, doesn't he?"

It was the first Immanuelle had heard of him in what felt like weeks. The sound of his name alone was enough to fill her with a heady mix of dread and fear and hope. She wanted to ask if he was still alive, and if so in what condition, but was too afraid for fear of what the apostle's answer would be.

"Ezra always heeds your call, doesn't he?" the apostle asked again, annoyed by her silence. "He had a hand in your schemes?"

Immanuelle didn't know how to answer. If she said no, she would assume full responsibility for all the accusations the apostle leveled against her. The punishment for her crimes would be death by purging, and if she died on the pyre before she had the chance to reverse the plagues, Bethel was all but doomed. But if she answered yes, Ezra could be deemed an accomplice, or even culpable for her transgressions. What would the charge for such a crime be? Conspiracy against the Church, perhaps? Holy treason? The former was a punishment of fifty lashes, the latter death.

But the future prophet couldn't be executed, could he? Would they dare lay the lash upon his shoulders? Or worse yet, send him to the pyre?

A sharp burning snapped Immanuelle to attention and she yelped, snatching her hand away.

The apostle loomed above her, his candle tipped to the side so the hot wax had spilled onto her hand. "Answer the question, girl."

Immanuelle picked her words carefully, scraping wax flakes from the back of her hand. "Ezra is my friend. He heeds me as a friend would."

"And what is the nature of your friendship?"

"He gave me books to read. We talked about poetry and the Scriptures."

The apostle leaned forward, sneering. When he spoke, his breath was hot against her cheek. "Did you lie with each other?"

She stiffened. "No."

Whether the apostle believed her or not, Immanuelle couldn't tell. He stood and turned his back to her, stalking toward the cell door. "You're a sick, sinful girl, do you know that?"

Immanuelle almost smiled in spite of it all. "So I've been told."

The apostle suddenly doubled back to her and tipped the candle once more. Burning wax splattered across her cheeks and she winced. It was all she could do to keep from weeping, but she refused to give him the pleasure.

"I have a surprise for you," said the apostle, stepping aside so Immanuelle had a clear view of the hall. The candlelight's glow illuminated the corridor, and a familiar face soon appeared behind the bars: Martha.

She wore a black wool cloak that she typically reserved for funerals. The hood hung low, casting a shadow over her eyes. "Hello, Immanuelle."

At the sight of her grandmother, Immanuelle straightened, pressing herself against the cell wall so the cobbles cut into her back. "What do you want from me?"

"That's no way to greet the woman who raised you," the apostle chided.

Immanuelle kept her eyes on Martha. Her chains rattled across the floor as she drew back. "She's no kin to me."

A damp wind licked down the hallway. The torch flared and Martha's candle sputtered out. "I was only trying to help you, Immanuelle."

"*Help* me? You betrayed me."

"I tried to save you, as best I was able to."

"You said you'd let me go."

"I did," said Martha, drawing closer. "And I have. That's why you're here in contrition, to be let go. To be released from your sins and forgiven."

Apostle Isaac's lips peeled back into a sneer. He moved toward the door, put a hand on Martha's shoulder. "And so she will be, upon her confession. The Prophet will make sure of it."

Martha trembled so violently her candle rattled on its pricket. In a rare moment of weakness, her eyes filled with tears. When she finally spoke it was not to the apostle, but to Immanuelle. "Honor and Glory weep for you in the night. Anna is broken. Abram is so sick with grief he can barely eat."

Immanuelle squeezed her eyes shut, willing herself not to cry. Her family and her tenderness for them had always been her greatest weakness. Martha knew that, perhaps better than anyone else.

"Tomorrow, at your trial, you must confess to your sins. Admit your guilt so that you can be forgiven and allowed to return home to those that love you. To me. Hope is not yet lost, if you're willing to do that."

Immanuelle laughed at the proposition. If only Martha knew what she was plotting. The sigil she was planning to carve. In the wake of what she was preparing to do, there would be no seat for her at Abram's table. No place for her in Bethel, except bound to the stake of a purging pyre. Once she had a consecrated blade in her hand—whether it be the Prophet's dagger or the sacred gutting knife—she would act. It was only a matter of biding her time. "What if I refuse to repent?"

A tear slipped down Martha's cheek. "Then may the Father have mercy on your soul."

CHAPTER THIRTY-THREE

I have confessed my sins and made peace with my fate. If the
pyre awaits, then let the flames rise. I'm ready.
—FROM THE TRIAL OF DANIEL WARD

IMMANUELLE WOKE ON the floor of her cell to the echo of approaching footsteps. Pushing herself off the bricks, she stumbled to her feet. The cell door ground open, and red torchlight spilled over the walls as Apostle Isaac stepped onto the threshold. "You're to be tried today," he said by way of greeting.

Immanuelle smoothed her skirt over her thighs. Her shackles rattled across the floor as she edged toward the apostle. Two members of the Prophet's Guard stepped in to block her path, but if the apostle was threatened by her, he gave no indication. He raised a gnarled hand, motioning for the guards to stand down. "Let her through."

So, they did. One of them grabbed her by the shackles. The other lowered his torch to the small of her back, so close Immanuelle feared her dress might catch alight and she'd burn to a crisp before she ever laid eyes on her pyre.

"Don't get any ideas, witch."

The guards took a path that Immanuelle didn't know, toward the distant reaches of the Haven. As they walked, the brick walls gave way to corridors hewn through rough stone. Some of these halls were no more than long caves of packed dirt, the ground so soft that cold mud oozed between her toes with every step.

After a while, they came to a door at the end of a corridor so narrow the guards' shoulders brushed the walls as they passed through. Immanuelle struggled up a steep flight of stairs—little more than planks of wood embedded into a wall of packed dirt—to the iron door at its end.

The taller of the two guards stepped forward to open it, and Immanuelle was greeted by a cold blast of clean night air. She swallowed a deep breath, savoring the freshness after all the time she'd spent in the reeking catacombs beneath the Prophet's Haven. Over the course of her detainment, there had been times when she thought she would never walk the plains again. Yet here she was. If this was her last chance now to do so, before the end came, it would be enough. One last night to hear wind in the trees, to feel grass bristle between her toes . . . to live.

But as Immanuelle peered into the endless dark, she realized the plains weren't the same moonlit meadows from her memories.

Oblivion lay before her.

There was no light, save for that of the torches, and the distant darkness was too thick to see through. No moon hung overhead, no stars. Even the fires of the purging pyres appeared to have been swallowed by the black.

As her eyes adjusted to the shadows, she saw odd, nightmarish shapes in the darkness—the glimpse of a strange face, a little girl drowning in the deep, a man-shaped shade that flickered and shifted, beckoning her into the black with a hooked finger.

The guard gave Immanuelle's shackles a cruel yank, dragging her forward, and the shapes in the black disappeared.

"What time is it?" she asked, and the night seemed to devour her words.

"It's a little past noon," said Apostle Isaac. "Tell me, what witch taught you how to cast a curse as powerful as this one? Or did you simply whore yourself to the dark to attain this power?"

Immanuelle stumbled over a rut in the road, stubbing her toe on a rock. "I wrought no curses." Not intentionally, anyway. The real witch-work had been her mother's doing. She was merely the vessel.

The guard lowered his torch to her back again. "Bite your lying tongue, witch. Save your confessions for the trial."

She didn't make the mistake of speaking again.

They walked on. Time passed strangely in the black—as if the seconds slowed—but eventually, Immanuelle spotted lights in the distance. It took her a moment to register the size of the crowd. There were scores of people gathered at the foot of the cathedral, bearing torches and rousing the pyre flames, their faces lit by the glow.

The guards walked ahead of Immanuelle and Apostle Isaac, carving a path through the crowds for them to follow. As she moved through the throng, a chant began, the sound like a hymn without music: "*Witch. Whore. Beast. Sinner. Bitch. Mother-spawn.*"

Immanuelle entered the cathedral and squinted against the light. There were lamps and torches burning on every post, chasing off the shadows that leaked in through the doors and windows. The pews were packed with the throngs who'd gathered to watch the trial. There were the Prophet's brides and village folk, and even a few people from the Outskirts.

Behind the altar stood the seven apostles, and, to Immanuelle's horror, the Moores stood in their shadow, claiming the first row of pews. Anna stood, cloaked in black. She held a damp handkerchief to her eyes, refusing to look at Immanuelle as she passed. Next to Anna, Abram, his eyes bloodshot and flat. Martha stood beside him, dressed in the same dark cloak she'd worn the night she visited Immanuelle in the catacombs. Both Honor and Glory were absent, likely still recovering from the blight.

"Move along," the guard ordered.

Immanuelle staggered up the stone steps to the altar, her muddy feet slipping beneath her. Someone laughed when she fell and bruised her knees on the stairs. The guard shoved the torch closer, mere inches above her shoulder blades, and the flames seared the back of her neck. "Hurry up. You're making a spectacle of yourself."

Pushing to her feet, Immanuelle limped the rest of the way up to the altar, the apostles splitting apart to make room for her. There, she stood before the congregation, head lowered, hands clasped in front of her. She was reminded of how, just a few months prior, on a very different day, Leah had stood in the same spot, back when life still had a little joy.

The doors of the cathedral slammed shut, and it was all Immanuelle could do to choke back her tears. The congregation blurred and doubled before her eyes. They all stared up at her with the same dead gaze, the same scowls and sneers. She knew then that they would vote to send her to the purging pyre, no matter what she said. Their minds were already made up. The trial was just a formality. She'd fought so hard to save them all from Lilith's plagues, and now they would watch her burn. Vera was right—there was nothing she could do to earn their favor. But she had to save them just the same. And to do that, she would have to prove her innocence. Because if they deemed her guilty and damned her to the purging pyre as punishment for her sins, she would never get the chance to cast the reversal sigil.

For Bethel's survival, and her own, she would have to fight for her innocence.

The Prophet emerged from the back of the cathedral and staggered down the center aisle, pausing every few steps to brace himself on the back of a pew and catch his breath. After a long, grueling walk to the altar, he turned to address his flock. "We are gathered here for the trial of Immanuelle Moore, who has been accused of witchcraft, murder, sorcery, thieving, whoring, and holy treason against the Good Father's Church."

The congregation jeered.

"Today, we will hear her confession. We will judge her not according to the passions of our hearts, but by the laws of our Father and Holy Scriptures. Only then may she find true forgiveness. Let the trial commence."

CHAPTER THIRTY-FOUR

If you have any honor, any semblance of kindness or decency,
then spare her. Spare her, please.
                    —THE FINAL CONFESSION OF DANIEL WARD

THE FIRST WITNESS to testify was Abram Moore. He staggered forward, leaning heavily on his cane, his face a picture of pain as he hobbled into the shadow of the altar.

Immanuelle didn't expect him to meet her eyes, but he did. "I'm here to testify . . . on behalf of myself and . . . my wife Martha Moore. Immanuelle is my granddaughter . . . the child of Miriam Moore who died the . . . day Immanuelle was born. She had no living father so . . . I raised her . . . as my own. She bears . . . my name."

"Did you raise her to be what she is?" Apostle Isaac asked, moving toward the altar. He was the apostle who had replaced Abram in the wake of Miriam's disgrace, and Immanuelle could not help but wonder if he relished the opportunity to best his rival once again.

"I raised her to . . . fear the Father," said Abram. "And . . . I believe she does."

There was a collective gasp, but Abram pressed on. "She's just . . . a child."

Apostle Isaac moved to the edge of the altar. He stared down at Abram with a look of such naked contempt, it made Immanuelle cringe.

But Abram didn't waver.

"I would remind you of the words of our Holy Scriptures," said the apostle, speaking slowly, as if he thought Abram simple. "Blood begets blood. That's the price of sin."

"I know the Father's . . . Scriptures. And I know that . . . clemency is extended to those who are not of sound mind . . . or heart."

"She is sound," the apostle snapped. "We spoke at length."

"The girl has . . . her mother's sickness."

"Her mother's only sickness was witchery."

This was met with applause. Men at the back of the crowd raised their fists to the rafters, yelling for blood and burning.

"Sin can be an affliction . . . real as any," said Abram. He turned to appeal directly to the flock. "Sin has come upon us in the form . . . of these plagues, and yet . . . we don't punish ourselves. We don't lay . . . the whip . . . against our own backs."

Apostle Isaac interrupted, "That's because we aren't to blame. We are victims of this evil. But that girl"—he pointed toward Immanuelle with a shaking finger—"is the source of it. She's a witch. She conjured the curses that have ravaged these lands, and yet you would see her walk among us? You would set her free?"

"I would not free her . . . here," said Abram. "I would release her . . . to the wilds. Banish her from Bethel. Let her . . . make a life for herself beyond the wall."

Apostle Isaac opened his mouth to refute him, but the Prophet raised a hand for silence. He brushed past the apostle as if he was little more than a hanging curtain. "Thank you for your witness, brother Abram. We accept your truth with gratitude."

As Abram shuffled back to his seat, the Prophet cast his gaze back to the people, scanning the pews. "Are there others who wish to offer witness?"

A small, thin voice sounded at the back of the cathedral. "There are."

It took Immanuelle a moment to recognize the girl limping toward her, chained and flanked by two of the Prophet's guardsmen. Contrition had not been kind to Judith. She looked like a corpse.

Her auburn curls, which had once been so long they hung to her waist, had been cut into a scum-matted crop as short as a boy's. She was deathly thin, and dirty, dressed in a torn bodice and bloodstained skirts. Despite the cold, she wore no shoes or shawl about her shoulders. Both of her lips were badly split, and when she spoke they began to bleed. "I have a confession to make."

The Prophet nodded. "Speak your truth, child."

Judith stopped at the altar's edge, her gaze pinned to the floor even as she turned to face the flock. She wrung her hands, shackles rattling, and peered up at the Prophet, as if waiting for some kind of cue. When she finally spoke, it was in a lifeless drone, as though she was reciting a catechism or Holy Scriptures. "Immanuelle Moore has defied Holy Protocol. She has cast her charms and worked her evils against the men and women of this Church."

The Prophet appraised her, his expression blank. "And what evidence do you have to charge the accused with these crimes?"

"Her own words," said Judith, her voice wavering. She struggled for a moment, as if trying to remember what she was told to say. "On a Sabbath, weeks ago, Immanuelle said that she liked to walk the woods with the devils, and to dance with the witches naked in the moon's light."

There was a chorus of gasps. People grasped their holy daggers and muttered prayers.

Judith looked to the Prophet again, and Immanuelle saw him

offer her the smallest nod. She turned her attention back to the congregation, spoke in a rush. "When Immanuelle said those words, Ezra Chambers laughed like he couldn't stop. His whole body seized up, the way the sick do when they catch the fever she cast upon us. She seduced Ezra," Judith said, raising her eyes to the Prophet. "She put a hex on your son, using the magic of the Dark Mother to do it. So you see, it wasn't his fault. She forced him to sin."

"I didn't," said Immanuelle, speaking for the first time since her trial began. "I would never hurt Ezra. I'll put my hand on the Scripture and say it. I'll swear it on my mother's bones."

"Your mother has no bones to swear on," Apostle Isaac said, his voice low and lethal. "Your mother's corpse burned on the pyre. Only the ashes of that witch remain."

"Praise be." The flock spoke as one.

Once again, the Prophet raised his hand for silence. "Thank you for your confession."

Judith parted her lips, as if she wanted to say more, but one glance from her husband was enough to quiet her. Head bowed, she returned to her guards, who seized her by the arms. She began to softly weep as they dragged her from the church.

The Prophet paused, his face grave in the flickering torchlight. At last, he spoke. "I would like to call upon my son, Ezra Chambers, to testify to the remarks of our last witness."

Immanuelle's heart froze in her chest.

"Bring my son to the altar."

On his order, the cathedral doors groaned open and two guardsmen emerged from the darkness, Ezra between them. He looked like he'd been beaten. There was a crust of dried blood beneath his nose and bags beneath his eyes as dark as bruises. Through the thin fabric of his shirt, Immanuelle could see dirty bandages wrapped around his chest, badly in need of a changing.

Ezra limped down the aisle and braced both hands against the altar, his breathing ragged. His knuckles were just a few inches from Immanuelle's fingertips, and she wanted nothing more than to take him by the hand. But she didn't dare move.

This was an unexpected turn of events, one with the potential to completely upend her plan. If Ezra was pitted against her—if his innocence was used as evidence of her own guilt—then how could she clear her name without damning him?

The Prophet strode to the front of the altar and stared down at his son. "Is it true that you were in the company of the accused on the fifteenth Sabbath in the Year of the Reaping?"

Ezra shifted his weight. As he did so, his sleeve fell away, exposing the black band of a bruise around his forearm—a twin to the ones around Immanuelle's wrists and ankles. The marks of chains and shackles. "Yes, I was there."

"And is it true that Immanuelle spoke to her doings with the devils that day?"

Ezra's hands trembled slightly. He clutched them into fists. "Many people spoke to many things that day."

"But do you remember her words?"

"I do not."

The Prophet slipped his hands into the folds of his robe. "Our accused has called you her friend. Is that true?"

Ezra hesitated. Immanuelle wouldn't have blamed him if he denied her. Any smart man with the will to live would do so. He could still save himself. "That is true. Immanuelle is my friend, and a loyal one."

At those words, Immanuelle choked back a sob, and Ezra must have heard it because he shifted his hand toward her by a half inch, his knuckles warm against her fingertips. He peered up at her for the first time.

It's all right, his eyes seemed to say, the same words he'd whispered in her ear the night of Leah's death. *You're going to be all right.*

The Prophet circled them. He was close, so close that if Immanuelle had only reached out her hand, she could have seized his holy dagger by the hilt. She was tempted to do it, steal the blade and carve the sigil into her arm then and there. But she knew that if she attempted it, the Prophet's guardsmen would shoot her dead on the spot. No, better to wait. The slaughter wasn't upon them yet. She still had time to spare.

The Prophet dropped to a crouch at his son's side. "Tell me, what is your connection to the accused? What is the nature of your affinity?"

Ezra swallowed hard, shifting his gaze back to his father. He squared his shoulders, as if he was gathering the strength he needed to speak. "I'm guilty of all the charges leveled against me. But Immanuelle is innocent. Any sins or crimes she may have committed were at my instruction, and mine only."

A great, dreadful moan rose from the congregation. Many people wept openly; others ripped their own garments. Children cowered in their mothers' skirts, and some of the more pious men lowered themselves to their knees in prayer.

Their heir had betrayed them.

The Prophet drew himself up to the altar slowly, his robes trailing behind him. "So you're saying that it was you who lured the evil from Immanuelle Moore? You who called it forth?" He turned to point an accusing finger at his son. "All of these plagues have come upon us because of you?"

Ezra nodded. His shoulders rolled beneath his shirt as he shifted his weight against the altar. "Yes. That's true."

"And you manipulated her power to seize the title of prophet, making you a heretic. A *false* prophet."

It wasn't a question, but Ezra answered anyway. "Yes."

His confession elicited a roar of protest. Despair became shock, and shock became fury. The crowd jeered, surging forward, stomping their feet and shouting. The echoes of their cries blasted between the walls. This time, the Prophet let them scream.

"No," said Immanuelle, but her voice was lost below the bedlam of the crowd. In that moment she didn't think of her own innocence or guilt. She didn't think of the reversal sigil or Bethel or summoning the power of the plagues. Her thoughts were only with Ezra, and the grave danger his false confession had put him in. "He's lying. It isn't true!"

Before she could utter another word of protest, members of the Prophet's Guard broke forward to seize Ezra. Grabbing him by the arms, they dragged him back to the cathedral doors.

"Thank you for your confession," said the Prophet. "This trial is adjourned."

CHAPTER THIRTY-FIVE

Sometimes, I think he loves me. Not selflessly, the way that you do, but with a kind of hunger. There is power in that love, but there is malice too. I often wonder what will become of me when that malice manifests.
—FROM THE LETTERS OF MIRIAM MOORE

IMMANUELLE WOKE TO a cold splash of water and a kick to the ribs. "Get up."

Wincing, she cracked her eyes open and peered up at the guard who stood over her. He, like all of the other servants who had come to her cell to question and torment her, wore a mask over his mouth, as if he feared he would catch her evil by breathing. He held an oil lamp that shined so bright, Immanuelle had to squint to keep from being blinded by it.

Without a word, she forced herself off the cold stone floor and stood.

The guard kept her shackled as they walked through the Haven's corridors. Immanuelle tried to memorize the path as she went—*left twice, right once, left three times, right four, pause at the iron door*—but it was futile. The dark made it impossible to discern one hall from the next.

"Where are you taking me?" she asked, hating the tremor in her voice.

The guard didn't answer. They walked on.

With every step, Immanuelle's thoughts drifted, and she was

forced to shift her focus from memorizing the path to simply staying on her feet. Her head swam and her legs felt soft beneath her.
She began to shake, and she wasn't sure if it was the fear or the
hunger or both.

As they moved down the corridors, Immanuelle's thoughts
went to Ezra—his false confession, his sacrifice, all that he'd said
and done in order to protect her. It was a fool's gesture; he must
have known that. She had been doomed the instant she left the
Moore house. But still, despite everything, he had tried to save
her, lying under holy oath to do it, trading his inheritance, his
freedom, his life, for hers. It was a grave sacrifice, and one she
was grateful for. Her only hope was that, if a little luck was still on
her side, she'd have the chance to tell him that before the end.

After a long, silent walk through the Haven, the guard led her
to an empty corridor. At its end stood a wooden door so large, it
spanned the entirety of the wall. It swung open at their approach,
and Esther emerged from it into the darkness of the hall. She was
disheveled, her skirts wrinkled, her bodice sloppily laced. Her
hair fell loose around her shoulders, and her eyes were red and
swollen. As she brushed past them, she gave Immanuelle a look of
so much loathing, a chill carved down her spine.

The guardsman yanked on Immanuelle's shackles, hauling her
forward, and Esther disappeared into the darkness of the corridor. With a sharp strike between her shoulder blades, the guard
shoved her the rest of the way through the portal, and the door
slammed shut behind her.

Immanuelle stalled by the threshold, too afraid to move. She
examined the room before her. At the center of the far wall was a
bed, its mattress big enough for five people. It was mounted on a
massive wrought iron frame, strikingly similar to the craft and
style of the Haven's front gates. Above it hung a large, rusty broad-
sword that looked so old, Immanuelle wouldn't have been sur-

prised to learn its original owner had been one of the Holy War's crusaders. On either side of the blade were windows overlooking what Immanuelle assumed were the plains, though it was far too dark to see more than a few inches past the windowsill.

"It was good of you to come."

Immanuelle jumped and turned to see a man sitting in the far corner of the room, hunched over a small writing desk. There was little light in the shadows beyond the reach of the oil lamp, and it took Immanuelle a moment to recognize him as her eyes adjusted.

The Prophet.

And these, she realized, must be his private quarters.

After a long silence, the Prophet raised his eyes from his paper to study her. By the light of the candle flickering on his desk, she could see the scar carving along the side of his neck. "Normally they cut the curls of the girls who enter contrition. The guards shear them like sheep to keep the lice at bay, but I asked them to leave you be." He stared at her expectantly, as if waiting for her thanks.

Immanuelle didn't offer it.

"Do you know why I've called you here?"

She thought of what Leah had told her, how the Prophet had used her, exploiting her innocence when she was just a child doing penance. Pushing her fear aside, she shook her head.

The Prophet dipped his quill to the inkwell and scribbled something at the bottom of his letter. "Guess."

"I—I don't know."

He frowned. "I was told you were a girl of great imagination. I'm disappointed you have nothing to say."

"I'm tired, sir."

"Tired?" He arched an eyebrow. "Do you have any idea what time it is?"

Immanuelle glanced out the window, to the black of the distant plains. She shook her head.

"It's high noon," he said. "The sun hasn't risen since the night my guards tracked you down. Some believe it will never rise again." He appraised her with a glance, head to toe, and she wondered how many girls had been hurt in this room. "It's hard to believe, even with you standing here before me. A girl with the power to darken the sun, snuff out the stars . . . on a whim."

"I didn't summon the plagues."

The Prophet's eyes glinted. He leaned down to open one of his desk drawers and withdrew Miriam's journal. "Then tell me, what business does an innocent girl have with a witch's spell book?"

The book blurred and doubled before Immanuelle's eyes, and the room began to spin. Her knees buckled, and she staggered backward a few feet before catching herself on the bedpost.

The Prophet shifted his gaze back to his letter. She noted that he was wearing his holy dagger, the very weapon she needed to cast the reversal sigil. If she could but reach out and take it . . . "Do they not feed you down there?"

Immanuelle startled to attention, cast her gaze away from the blade. "Only on the good days."

He motioned to the small bowl of fruit that stood at the corner of his desk. "Eat."

Immanuelle was too hungry to bother with suspicion. She stumbled over to the desk and snatched an apple from the bowl. She devoured it in seconds, then wiped her mouth clean on the back of her hand.

"They're going to sentence you to die tomorrow," the Prophet said casually. "Has Apostle Isaac told you that?"

Her gut twisted, and she tasted apple at the back of her throat. "No."

"Then consider this your warning. Tomorrow morning, you will be sentenced to the pyre for holy treason. After his trial, Ezra will receive the same verdict." He paused to finish his letter. He had a poor hand, and Immanuelle noticed he held his quill wrong, pinching it between his thumb and ring finger. His knuckles bent at odd angles, so that they looked almost broken. "Still, despite the best warnings of my apostles and the Church, I'm of a mind to be merciful. I want to save you." He looked up at her then and clarified, "*Both* of you."

Immanuelle didn't dare to hope. Not yet. There was a catch. There was *always* a catch. "Why would you do that?"

The Prophet didn't answer her. Instead, he pushed away from his desk, the feet of his chair scraping across the floor with a screech. He coughed violently as he stood, and drops of blood flecked his shirt and spattered the floorboards at his feet.

Immanuelle knew enough to know this wasn't the kind of cough that could be cured. His was not a passing bout of grippe or the chill that gets in your lungs when the seasons turn. No, that wheezing bark was nothing less than the gasps of a dying man.

When his fit finally passed, the Prophet wiped his mouth on the back of his hand and started toward her. He drew so close, she caught the scent of blood on his breath.

"I would do it because I care for you, Immanuelle. And I believe that, with time and atonement, we could be of use to each other."

The consecrated blade was mere inches from her grasp. "In what way?"

The Prophet studied his hands. When he lowered his head, she could see the edge of his scar peering above his collar. "In a holy way, through the bond of marriage. If you're cut with my seal, you'll be exempt from whatever punishment they pin to you at the trial. You'll be spared."

It was an odd offer, given the Prophet's state. Why would a dying man care to take her hand in matrimony? Immanuelle couldn't imagine he would survive more than a few months, maybe a year, given Ezra's rapid rise to power. Unless . . . he didn't intend to let Ezra rise to power. A horrible idea occurred to her: What if the Prophet's true plan was to extend his own reign by cutting Ezra's life short? What if he intended to execute his own son?

The shock must have been evident on Immanuelle's face, because the Prophet gave her a reassuring smile that might have been comforting, if it wasn't for the sharpness in his eyes. "Oh, come now. There are worse things to be than a prophet's bride. Here, in the Haven, you'd be safe to live a long life. You'd never know the pain of the pyre's flames. My seal would absolve you completely, and you'd be free to begin again."

An idea surfaced at the back of her mind, as clever as it was revolting. What if she humored the Prophet's plot, agreed to follow him to the altar—let him cut his seal into her forehead and claim her as his own? That night, in the marriage bed, after she'd fulfilled her duty as a bride, when the Prophet was lying spent and prone, she would have the rare opportunity to take up his holy dagger, carve the reversal sigil into her arm, and summon the power of the plagues. If she did that it wouldn't matter what the Prophet's intentions were or what he planned to do to Ezra. All she had to do was act before he did.

"And what of Ezra? You said you'd offer him mercy?"

At the mention of his son, the Prophet's eye twitched. "I did, and I'm a man of my word. After you're cut, Ezra will be absolved of his crimes."

That meant that the Prophet would only enact his plan after her cutting. It meant that she had time. "So you intend to free him, then?"

"Free him?" The Prophet scoffed, looking close to laughter. "I can't do that. As my heir and a former apostle, Ezra took creeds to the Church. Creeds that he subsequently broke when he turned his back on his faith in order to help you. That's an act of holy treason."

And holy treason carried the penalty of death by pyre purging. "How far does your mercy extend if I refuse your offer?"

The Prophet's gaze went dark. "It doesn't extend at all."

Rage boiled in the pit of Immanuelle's stomach. She clenched her fists. He was all but forcing her to the altar in shackles. Either she married him, or she and Ezra burned on the pyre. There was no other alternative.

"You have such a sharp gaze," said the Prophet, smirking. "You do favor her when you look at me that way."

"Favor who?"

"Your grandmother. Vera Ward. Do you know that after your arrest in Ishmel, she followed you on horseback all the way to the Hallowed Gate? She was so exhausted by the time she arrived that arresting her was an act of mercy."

"Vera's here?" Immanuelle whispered, horrified.

"In the flesh, as of a week ago."

"What do you want with her?"

"She's Bethelan," said the Prophet. "The holy seal is carved between her brows. I have an obligation to guide her soul back to the Father's light, which is no easy task given how long she's dwelled in darkness. Besides, I pity her, truly I do. Imagine it, first the poor woman was made to watch her only son burn on the pyre. Now, seventeen years later, it seems her granddaughter—the last of her living blood kin—will share his fate. It's a terrible tragedy."

Immanuelle couldn't breathe. Couldn't speak. All this time she had been so busy chasing beasts and devils, believing that evil began and ended with them. She had been so foolish. True evil didn't lurk in the depths of the Darkwood. It was not in Lilith or her coven, or even in any of the curses they cast.

True evil, Immanuelle realized now, wore the skin of good men. It uttered prayers, not curses. It feigned mercy where there was only malice. It studied Scriptures only to spit out lies. Lilith had known this, and Miriam had known it too. So they'd cast their curses and summoned the plagues. They'd tried to fix things, in their own twisted way, to put an end to all the evil that began with the Prophet and all the prophets who had reigned before him.

"I'll draw it back," said Immanuelle, not knowing if it was even possible. "If you pardon me and Ezra, if you let us leave Bethel with my grandmother, I'll find a way to end the plagues. I'll leave all of you in peace."

"I thought you said you didn't control the plagues."

"No, I said I didn't summon them. There's a difference."

The Prophet studied her for a beat before turning back to his desk. He sat, scribbled his signature at the bottom of his letter, blew the ink dry, then slipped it into an envelope. He tipped his candle, spilling a spot of wax onto the letter's flap, tugged his dagger from the shadows of his shirt, and pressed the hilt's pommel into the puddle, forming the print of the holy seal. "I'm not interested in a hasty fix, Immanuelle. I'm not going to get on my hands and knees and beg you to draw the plagues back. That's not how this works, and it's not what the Father demands. If we are to find a way to end the plagues, we won't do it by delving into the darkness."

"Then how do you plan to stop this? You think cutting me or jailing your son will make any difference? Do you think Lilith and her witches will give a damn about that?"

"No, I don't," the Prophet said calmly. "That's why, if the plagues continue, I'm prepared to raze the Darkwood until there's nothing left but twigs and cinders. The pyres I light will make the holy purges of David Ford look like hearth fires. One way or another, Bethel will prevail and the Father will have His atonement."

Immanuelle's hands tightened to fists. "If it's atonement you want, if that's what the Father truly demands, then why don't you start with yourself?"

A peal of thunder cracked outside, and the dark seemed to thicken, pressing in against the windowpanes.

"What do I have to atone for?"

"I think you know."

"I never claimed perfection, Immanuelle. We all make mistakes."

Rage washed through her. Outside, the wind roared through the blackness. "I'm not talking about mistakes. I'm talking about crimes. You bedded Leah long before her cutting, taking her virtue while she paid penance here, under what should have been your protection. You sent my father to the pyre out of jealousy and spite. You've jailed your own son on charges you know are false. And the dungeons beneath our feet are filled with innocent girls you torture for the crime of having witch marks on their census files. There is nothing you wouldn't do, no one you wouldn't hurt, to keep power in your hands."

The Prophet paled. The little color he had left in his lips and cheeks leeched away, until he stood before her as white and sallow as the witches of the Darkwood. "You're right."

She stiffened. *"What?"*

"I said you're right—about me, my sins, my vices, my shame, my lust, my lies. All of it." He looked at her and cocked his head. "But do you want to know what keeps me up at night? It's not the lies of the Church. It's not my sins, or even my sickness. What keeps me up—tossing and turning and sweating in my sheets—is the knowledge of how fragile it all really is. Bones break and people die. The pyres burn low, barely bright enough to keep the shadows at bay. Forces beyond our walls edge closer, every day . . . and the flock grows restless."

He stared down at his hands, and Immanuelle was surprised to see them shaking. "And who do they turn to in their time of need? Who's responsible for tending their hurts? Who lights the fires that lead them through the night? The Father won't descend from the heavens to care for his children. The apostles return to their wives and beds. The flock fails to account for themselves and so the burden falls to me. *I* am their salvation, and I will do whatever it takes—sin, purge, even kill—in order to ensure their survival. Because that is what it means to be prophet. It's not about the Sight. It's not about kindness or justice or basking in the light of the Father. No, to be prophet is to be the one man willing to damn your soul for the good of the flock. Salvation *always* demands a sacrifice."

Immanuelle stared at him—this man who'd used his lies to make himself a martyr. He thought he was the one who made the true sacrifice, but he couldn't be more wrong.

It was not the Prophet who bore Bethel, bound to his back like a millstone. It was all of the innocent girls and women—like Miriam and Leah—who suffered and died at the hands of men who exploited them. They were Bethel's sacrifice. They were the bones upon which the Church was built.

Their pain was the great shame of the Father's faith, and all of Bethel shared in it. Men like the Prophet, who lurked and lusted after the innocent, who found joy in their pain, who brutalized and broke them down until they were nothing, exploiting those they were meant to protect. The Church, which not only excused and forgave the sins of its leaders but enabled them: with the Protocol and the market stocks, with muzzles and lashings and twisted Scriptures. It was the whole of them, the heart of Bethel itself, that made certain every woman who lived behind its gate had only two choices: resignation, or ruin.

No more, Immanuelle thought. No more punishments or Protocols. No more muzzles or contrition. No more pyres or gutting blades. No more girls beaten or broken silent. No more brides in white gowns lying like lambs on the altar for slaughter.

She would see an end to all of it. She would wed the Prophet, and while he slept in their shared bed, she would take up his dagger, carve the sigil into her arm, and end this once and for all.

"You can cut me if you wish. Chain me to the pyre, douse me with kerosene, and light a match. But it won't be enough to save your life . . . or your wretched soul."

The Prophet flinched, and Immanuelle watched in horror as he raised a hand to grasp the hilt of his holy dagger. When his gaze swept toward her, she staggered back, falling into the edge of the bed. But there was no place to run.

"I have made my intentions plain," he said, and to Immanuelle's relief he released his dagger and retired to his seat at the desk, limping and wheezing as he went. "I have been more than patient with you. But I will make myself clear one last time: Your life, and Ezra's, relies on your decision at tomorrow's trial. I suggest you return to your cell and consider my offer. In the morning, if it's mercy you want, you'll bite your tongue and choose well."

Chapter Thirty-six

I have engaged in lust and lechery. I have delighted in the spoils of the flesh. For these crimes, I will meet my reckoning on the pyres of the purging. I ask for the Father's mercy. Nothing more.

—The Final Confession of Daniel Ward

THE MORNING OF her sentencing, Immanuelle woke with Ezra's name on the tip of her tongue. She had dreamed of him in the night, and as she rose, it was his face that haunted her.

Mere moments after she pushed to her feet and plucked the hay from her curls, one of the Prophet's guardsmen appeared at the threshold of the cell.

"It's time," was all he said. He held a hard square of brown bread through the rungs of the cell door. Breakfast.

Immanuelle shook her head. The thought of taking anything more than a few swallows of water made her feel ill. She smoothed the creases from her skirt with shaking hands. "I'm ready."

They took the short exit, down the corridor and up into the house proper, emerging just off the foyer. It was the route that Immanuelle knew best—and the one she would have taken had she ever had the opportunity to stage an escape. From there, they took a cart through the cold black of the plains, passing the smoking heaps of old funeral pyres, traveling fast beneath the starless sky.

The string of the cathedral lights appeared in the distance.

Immanuelle folded her arms over her chest, a great chill racking her, teeth chattering, her fingers numb with cold.

Today was the day she decided her fate: the Prophet, or the pyre.

Bethel's congregation spilled into the cathedral, filling the pews. The crowd was twice as big as it had been the first session of her trial, and many men and women stood along the walls or sat in the aisles.

When all the pews and benches were filled, Immanuelle took her place atop the altar again, folded her hands in her lap, and lowered her head.

For Ezra, she said to herself, turning his name over in her head. *For Honor. For Glory. For Miriam. For Vera. For Daniel. For Leah. For Bethel and all of the innocents in it.*

The apostles gathered behind her, forming a line along the altar. They were dressed in their most formal attire, thick robes of black velvet, the hems pooling at their feet. As the last of the congregation found seats in the pews or places to stand along the walls, the Prophet entered. He too was dressed in his finest, a robe of rich vermilion so dark it looked almost black. His feet were bare, and as he strode down the aisle, his toes glimpsed from beneath the hem of his robe. "It's time for the accused to testify. Today we will hear her final confession."

Immanuelle's hands shook in her lap. She grasped her knees, her mouth dry and sticky. Raising her head, she peered into the throng of the assembled. There were faces she knew—Esther, sitting in the front row, and the Moores, who filled the pew just behind her—and many others she didn't. The cathedral was crowded with men and women, all of them gazing up at her with the same fear and revulsion with which she had once looked upon Lilith in the Darkwood.

The Prophet turned to face her. "Speak now, and let the truth be known."

Immanuelle squared her shoulders, forcing herself to raise her gaze to the flock. She knew that she had done no wrong, that she had no real sins to confess or be forgiven for. But she also knew that her fate and Ezra's hinged on her confession. What she said next would determine whether they lived to see another day. If a false confession of guilt was what it took to save them both, so be it.

"My name is Immanuelle Moore. I am the daughter of Miriam Moore and Daniel Ward."

Her words were met with silence. Dead, thick, sickening silence.

"I stand before you as a killer, and a liar, and a sinner through and through. I have dishonored my family name. I have dishonored the Scriptures, the Prophet, and the Good Father."

Immanuelle paused, meeting Martha's gaze for the briefest moment.

"I have walked the path of sin," Immanuelle continued. "I have spoken to the beasts of the Darkwood in their foul tongue. I have defied the Father's Protocol and lived in reproach of his reign. I have read in secret. I have seduced men of the Good Faith with my wiles and turned their hearts. I have broken the holy conduct of meekness and modesty and spoken out of turn. I have practiced witchcraft in the shadows. I have befriended evil and shunned the good that's come to me. For these sins, I ask your forgiveness that the Father might—in His mercy—purge my soul of darkness. This is my final confession."

Again, there was silence, save for the rhythmic echo of the Prophet's footsteps as he walked alongside the altar and raised a hand to Immanuelle's head, his fingers tangling through her curls. "Thank you for your witness, child. It is well heard."

The flock said nothing. They waited, openmouthed, hungry for a sentencing. For news of a proper pyre execution, a live purging as the law of the Scripture would demand.

But if it was blood they wanted, they would not get it that day. For their Prophet had other plans. Plans he had made plain to Immanuelle—plans that would see Bethel laid to ruin if it meant keeping power in the palm of his hand.

"The Father has spoken to me through the Sight." The Prophet's hand fell from Immanuelle's head as he moved to stand before the altar. "I have seen his children walk the plains and the woods beyond them freely. I have seen the sun rise above the land and chase away the shadows. I have seen the Father's holy eye upon us once more."

To this, there were shouts of praise and glory.

The Prophet raised his voice above their cries. "But there's a price for the bounty and blessings I've seen."

Apostle Isaac pushed forward, his eyes bright with frenzy. "Whatever price, we will pay it!" He turned to face the congregation. "For the glory of the Father?"

The flock shouted in answer. *"For the glory of the Father!"*

The Prophet raised his hands for silence. Sweat dampened his brow, and the muscles in his neck pulled taut, as if he was fighting to drag the words from his throat. "The Father has demanded that we raze the Darkwood and take dominion over it."

Another cry rose from the flock. There was rapturous applause. A few of the people in the front pews fell to their knees, their hands raised to the heavens.

"To do this," the Prophet pressed on, "to take dominion of what is ours to claim, we must overcome the darkness that resides in every one of us in different measures. We mustn't be afraid to purge it, as David Ford did in the height of the Holy War, when he called the Father's fire from the heavens." He paused a moment for effect. "That is why on the dawn of the coming Sabbath, I will wed Immanuelle Moore and purge her of evil. I will carve the holy seal into her brow. Then—and only then—will the curse be broken."

Immanuelle felt the air shift. There wasn't a single sound. Not the squall of a baby or the whine of a child. Not a breath, not a heartbeat.

"You would offer her mercy?" Apostle Isaac demanded, his face twisted with revulsion. "You would offer this witch a place at your side as a reward for her sins and crimes?"

"I would offer my own life in exchange for an end to these plagues. Whatever the Father demands of me, I will give it, if it means an end to our suffering." The Prophet ran a hand over his head, as if buying the time he needed to collect himself. But when he spoke again, his voice blasted between the rafters. "We have purged, and we have burned, and we are all the worse for it. Sending the girl to the pyre will not end our suffering. She is bound to the Darkness of the Mother, in body and soul, so we must find a way to break that unholy tie. Now I have prayed, lain prostrate at the feet of the Father that He might give me an answer . . . show me a way to dispel this evil that has fallen upon Bethel through her, and He has given me an answer. There is but one way to purge ourselves of the evil this witch has cast: a sacred seal between bride and husband, husband and Holy Father. To atone for her sins, she must be bound to me. It's the only way."

The Prophet turned to face Immanuelle again, his chest inches from the altar's edge. "Do you accept the terms of your sentencing?"

There was silence in the cathedral. The dark pressed in against the windows.

The end was close now.

Immanuelle bowed her head, arms wrapped around her stomach as if to hold her bones together. Raising her gaze to meet the Prophet's, she sealed her fate. "I do."

CHAPTER THIRTY-SEVEN

The last time I saw him he was bound to the pyre's stake, arms pinned behind his back, head hung. He did not look at me. Even when I called his name above the roar of the flames, he did not look.

—MIRIAM MOORE

IMMANUELLE DIDN'T RETURN to her cell that night. Instead, after her trial had concluded, she was surrendered to the Prophet's wives, who ferried her off through the black, back to the Haven and the cloistered quarters where she would remain until the day of her cutting.

It was Leah's room. Immanuelle nearly laughed at the irony of it when she saw her name painted across the rail of the door. The chamber was now sparsely furnished, not a trace of her left. There was a large bed on an iron frame. Beside it was a table that housed a basin, pitcher, and palm-size copy of the Holy Scriptures. Above the bed, a barred window with a padlock on its latch. A candle flickered on a small table by the door, throwing long shadows across the walls.

Immanuelle slipped out of her ragged dress and tossed it into the corner of the bedroom. She retrieved a fresh nightgown from a trunk at the foot of the bed. Exhausted, she climbed under the sheets and drew the blankets up to her chin.

She closed her eyes, trying to block out the howls that echoed through the swirling darkness outside. The plague had a life and mind of its own, and, much like the Darkwood, it spoke to her, whispering against her windowpanes, luring her into the black. She was almost tempted to succumb to it, abandon all the horrors that lay before her—contrition and the cutting knife, the Prophet's wedding bed. Let the darkness make nothing of it all. When the power of the plagues was hers to wield, perhaps she would do just that. Call forth the night, let it drown everything in its wake. It scared her how much she liked the idea, how tempted she was to make it a reality.

The sound of the door creaking open drew Immanuelle from the maze of her thoughts. Before she had the chance to sit up, Esther Chambers slipped into the room.

Ezra's mother wore a long, fog-colored nightdress and robe. Her hair was heaped atop her head and pinned in place with two golden combs. As she stepped into the light of the oil lamp, Immanuelle saw that her skin was pale, her lips colorless.

"They're going to burn my boy," she said. "They're going to send him to the pyre."

Immanuelle opened her mouth to respond, but Esther cut her short.

"They've charged him with conspiring against the Church and holy treason."

"I'm so sorry," Immanuelle whispered.

"I don't want your condolences," she said, the timbre of her voice keen and high like a plucked harp string. "All I want is for you to know that if you let my boy die in the name of your sins, I'll make sure you follow him."

Immanuelle's cheeks burned with shame. "Ezra is not going to die. The Prophet told me that he would be spared. He gave me his word."

"His words mean nothing," said Esther bitterly. "Less than nothing. I don't want to know about false hope and promises. I want to know how *you* intend to save my son. How will you set him free?"

Immanuelle had been careful, so careful, to keep every detail of her scheme a secret. She'd made no mention of her plans to carve the reversal sigil and dutifully played the part of the meek and broken bride-to-be. But with Esther standing there so desperate and afraid, her conscience provoked her to offer some small assurance, enough to let her know that Ezra wasn't alone. "After I'm cut, I have plans to free him. But I'll need your help to do it."

Esther glanced over her shoulder toward the door. When she spoke again, it was in a whisper. "What do you need me to do?"

"Tell me where he is. I need to see him tonight, before his sentencing, so he's ready when the time comes."

"Ezra's in the library with Leah's daughter. The doors aren't locked, but the halls are patrolled by two guards. I can distract them, buy you some time."

"That's all I need."

IMMANUELLE WAITED UNTIL the echo of Esther's footsteps faded to silence before she crept across her bedroom, drew a shawl around her shoulders, and slipped into the hall. She found it odd that there was no bolt on her door—given that only hours before she'd been chained to a cell wall in the catacombs—but then she remembered, she wasn't a prisoner anymore. She was a prize lamb, a treasure, the Prophet's newest bride-to-be.

Besides, he knew she wouldn't run. She was bound to the Haven, bound to her promise—to the Prophet, to the flock, to Ezra. The time for fleeing was over. What was left to be finished would be finished in Bethel.

Immanuelle padded barefoot down the Haven's main corridor, careful to keep to the shadows. When she passed the windows, the darkness rushed to meet her, threatening to break the glass and flood the corridors within. She tried to ignore it, but its call rang through her head like a bell's toll, and she could feel its pull deep in her belly, reeling her into the night.

Halfway down the hall, she paused before a tall stained-glass window, staring into the darkness. "What do you want from me?"

At the sound of her voice, the dark moved like water, rippling and doubling, turning in on itself. Immanuelle raised her fingers to the window, the glass cold beneath her hand. The shadows rose to meet her, and in them she saw a startling reflection. The girl who stared back at her had her features—the same dark eyes and full lips, the firm nose and pinched chin—but every detail was exaggerated, every attribute refined. She was beautiful and keen, and there was a defiant strength in the way she stood, shoulders squared, chin tilted. And there was something in her gaze that made her . . . *more*. It was as if the girl in the darkness was everything Immanuelle had ever hoped to be.

She pressed her hand to Immanuelle's, so there was nothing but glass between them. Immanuelle shifted closer to the window, and the girl in the dark beckoned, almost coyly, to the window's latch. Immanuelle reached for it, and the girl pressed herself to the pane, drawing so close her lips brushed the glass.

Immanuelle pulled the iron handle and the window swung open. A blast of winter wind rushed into the hallway, snuffing the lamps and candles. Night poured through the open window and the corridor went dark.

There was the distant clamor of footsteps. A voice: "Who goes there?"

Turning her back on the darkness, Immanuelle ran—fleeing the guards and the hallway and the girl who haunted the black.

It didn't take her long to find the old cathedral, where the library was housed. Padding across the cold stone floors, she ducked down the hall to make sure the doors were unguarded. The corridor was empty.

Relieved, Immanuelle started forward. She was halfway to the library doors when she heard footsteps. She turned and found a guard standing before her, a long blade hanging on his belt. And he was looking right at her.

"Easy," he said. As he stepped into the torchlight, Immanuelle realized he was one of the men she'd journeyed back to Bethel with. The only guardsman who'd shown her any kindness. His gaze went back and forth between her and the library doors. Then, in a low, urgent whisper, he said: *"Go."*

"Thank you," she managed to stammer, more grateful for that act of mercy than he could possibly know. She turned to the library doors and slipped through them into the darkness.

"Ezra?" she whispered into the shadows. "Are you there?"

There was the scrape of iron on stone, shackles slithering across tile. "Immanuelle?"

She started toward the sound of his voice, weaving between the bookshelves, tripping over toppled stacks. "It's me."

And then he was there, and she was in his arms, and he in hers. They clung to each other in silence, Ezra's hands shifting down her back, each of their bodies fitting into the contour of the other's.

"Are you hurt?" Immanuelle said at last, murmuring the words into his shoulder.

"No," he said, and she could tell he was lying. There was no light to see, but she gingerly lifted the corner of his shirt. She felt the bandages beneath, binding his stomach and chest. They were wet, and when she touched them he hissed.

She sucked in a breath. "Ezra."

"All right," he said, wheezing a little. "I might have had a brief encounter with a bullet or two, but I'm fine. What about you?"

"I'm all right." In truth, she'd sustained a bad beating the first night of her contrition, and several lashings after it, but she wouldn't trouble him with those things. Not now, not when he was so weak, so frail in her arms.

"Why are you here?"

He didn't know, she realized. He couldn't know, of course. He hadn't been there. He hadn't heard her final confession.

"I was sentenced today," she whispered. "I was sentenced, and the Prophet decided to free me."

"How can that be? I haven't even been sentenced yet myself."

"Listen to me." Immanuelle grabbed him by both hands. "About your sentencing, you have to tell them you've repented for your sin. Swear that you will."

"I don't understand."

She heard the echo of footsteps in the distance and ducked instinctively, shifting behind a nearby bookshelf. "I made a deal with your father."

"What kind of deal, Immanuelle?" Ezra's voice was tight. "What have you done?"

"I agreed to take his hand in marriage, to save your life and mine," she said, the words like bile on her tongue. "I'm going to be cut on the coming Sabbath."

"No." Ezra's hands tightened painfully around hers, and in his voice was such revulsion—such *rage*—that Immanuelle flinched away from him.

"It was either the Prophet or the pyre," said Immanuelle, rushing to explain. "He said he'd spare your life if I married him, and I agreed to it—to buy you time, to save you."

"He lied," said Ezra, in a tone so low, his words were barely audible. "That was the deal I made with him. He said if I pleaded guilty he would make sure you survived your sentencing, and he'd set you free."

He'd lied to them both, she realized. His deal had never been about sacrifice—hers or Ezra's. The Prophet claimed he was carrying out the Father's will, but it was power that drove him. The power to purge, to punish, to control. It was all he cared about.

"Immanuelle, you can't go through with this," Ezra said urgently. "He'll hurt you. He'll break you, the way he does everyone."

She closed her eyes, and when she did, she saw a glimpse of that fateful night when the Prophet turned on her mother, and her mother turned on him. "He's not going to lay a finger on me, or on you or anyone else. We'll find a way to stop him, to stop all of this, but I need you alive and well and by my side to do it."

"This is madness," said Ezra. "Isn't it enough just to save ourselves? You got past the gate once; we can do it again. We should run, tonight. I know a way out of the Haven, through the back passages. If you can free me from these chains, we can escape before anyone realizes we're gone. We could make our own way."

Immanuelle humored the idea. She imagined turning her back on Bethel and all of its troubles, running away with Ezra, making a new life for themselves beyond the gate. It was an appealing dream, but Immanuelle knew it was nothing more. Her fate was not that of a runaway.

"Saving ourselves isn't enough," said Immanuelle firmly. "There are other people in Bethel suffering as well, and they deserve better. We have to help them. All of them."

Ezra didn't say anything for a long time. Finally, he asked, "So you're just going to trade yourself? Barter your bones to that tyrant?"

"Yes. That's exactly what I'm going to do. And then, after I'm cut, I'm going to end these plagues once and for all."

"How?"

Immanuelle thought of the sigil, of the sacrifice she'd have to make to bring its power to fruition. "Better that you don't know. That way, if you're ever asked, you can claim ignorance."

Ezra sighed and tilted his forehead against hers. Immanuelle was suddenly aware that this was as close as the two of them had ever been. But all she could think of, as they clung to each other in the darkened library, was how she wanted him even closer.

"I hate this," said Ezra, his breath warm against her face. "I hate that I'm chained up here. That I can't help you. That I'm going to be here in shackles while you're cut by him, claimed by him."

"What's done is done," Immanuelle whispered. "This time, let me help you. Let me fight for you."

Ezra didn't answer as he slipped his arms from around her. His fingers found her face, her cheek, then skimmed down to her jaw, the soft dip of her chin. He traced a fingertip along the line of her bottom lip, then angled closer. He pressed a kiss to her upper lip, then her lower one.

He said, "All right."

PART IV

Slaughter

CHAPTER THIRTY-EIGHT

*I have seen the beasts of the wood. I have seen the spirits
that lurk between the trees and swam with the demons of the
deep water. I have watched the dead walk on human feet,
kept company with the cursed and the crucified, the predators and their prey. I have known the night and I have called
it my friend.*

—MIRIAM MOORE

IMMANUELLE KNELT IN the middle of her bedroom, hands
clasped, dressed in the pale silks of her cutting gown. She was
supposed to be praying, but her thoughts were not with the Father. As she crouched there on the floor, the occurrences of the
past few days flashed through her mind like the bright beginnings
of a headache.

Ezra's sham of a trial had come and gone, as had the sentencing that followed it. Like Immanuelle, he had been indicted on all
counts, but she'd heard no word beyond that. She knew only that
he was still alive and jailed somewhere below in the catacombs of
the Haven. She could only hope they were treating him with more
kindness than they had her. Not that it mattered for much longer.

In the days leading up to her cutting, she had traced and retraced the reversal sigil—in the soft crook of her inner elbow, on
walls and tables, and into the pillows she slept on at night. And
every time she made that mark—committing it to memory over
and over again—she prepared herself for the sacrifice at hand.
The sacrifice she would make the night of her cutting, when she
was called to her husband's bed. She felt there was some poetic

justice in it all. That seventeen years after Miriam had taken up the Prophet's holy dagger, Immanuelle would take up that very same blade and carve the sigil that would reverse the curses her mother had wrought all those years ago.

Tonight, in the wake of her cutting, she would act.

When the Prophet's wives came to collect her, Immanuelle was ready. She walked barefoot through the corridors of the Prophet's home and out to the wagon that awaited her in front of the Haven. She clambered onto the front bench—the other brides piling in behind her—and together they made the long, silent trip to the cathedral.

All the pyres were burning again. The fires had been fed with fresh timber, so the red flames now climbed high, lighting their way.

When they arrived at the cathedral, there were no crowds to greet them. No glowing lanterns. No music or merriment. No fanfare. In this eerie silence, Immanuelle stepped down from the wagon and onto the cold packed dirt of the front drive. She lingered at the threshold of the cathedral as the rest of the brides milled about behind her. Perhaps she ought to have prayed in that moment—to something, to anyone—but all she thought to do was conjure a curse:

Let those who have raised a hand to me reap the harm they sow. Let the shadows snuff their light. Let their sins defy them.

The cathedral door swung open before she had the chance to finish. She was greeted by dancing torchlight, the blurred faces of the congregation gazing at her, expectant. Among the crowd was the Moore family, Martha and Abram, Glory, and Anna, who held Honor cradled to her chest in a nest of shawls and blankets. There were dozens of Outskirters present also, occupying the pews at the back of the cathedral. Immanuelle could only assume they were there as a matter of diplomacy. This was, after all, the first time in Bethel's age-old history that a prophet had wed one of their own. The ceremony was nothing short of historic, and it only made sense that they'd be there to witness it.

Immanuelle walked alone down the center aisle. She took the steps two at a time, the train of her gown trailing behind her, then climbed up onto the altar. The stone was cold and sticky, as though some servant had neglected to sop up the mess of the last Sabbath slaughter.

She stretched herself across the altar, arms spread wide. The Prophet loomed over her, dagger in hand. They exchanged their vows woodenly, Immanuelle muttering the words that would bind her to him—flesh and bone, soul and spirit—forever.

A sacrifice as real as any.

When the proceedings were finished, the Prophet took his dagger from around his neck, wrapping his hand around the hilt. As he lowered the blade to her forehead, Immanuelle didn't flinch.

LATER, THE OTHER wives bandaged Immanuelle in a dark room at the back of the cathedral, tending her wounds with anointing oil that stung so badly tears sprang to her eyes. Blood slipped down her nose as Esther bound her brow with strips of gauze. Her head throbbed as if the Prophet had carved his mark into her skull, not her flesh.

She belonged to him now. She was his, and he was hers. A creed of flesh and blood, a bond she had never wanted.

When she was sufficiently cleaned up, Esther and Judith materialized by her side. Together they led her through the cathedral, past the threshold, and down the stairs to the feast where the Prophet—draped in all his holy robes and finery—sat waiting for her.

If Leah's cutting had been a celebration, this seemed little more than a funeral feast. The guests sat stiffly at the tables, as if they'd been forced there at knifepoint. The Outskirters occupied tables of their own, stone-faced and silent, their unease almost palpable. There was no chatter, no laughter or song. In the distance, the pyres burned high, their flames licking the starless sky, keeping the darkness at bay.

Standing in the shadows at the cusp of the feast, flanked by guardsmen, was Vera. Her head had been shaved, as was Protocol for those in contrition, and she wore a pale garment that looked more like a slip than a proper dress, the fabric far too thin, given the night's cold. She'd lost weight and looked weak, but when Immanuelle locked eyes with her, she squared her shoulders and gave a stern nod as if to say: *It's time.*

The Prophet grasped Immanuelle's knee as she sat beside him, his cold fingers pressing through the folds of her underskirts. "My bride."

Immanuelle gripped the arm of her chair to keep herself from bolting. She shifted her gaze down to the table. Before her, a porcelain plate heaped with blackened vegetables, graying slabs of meat, and a small mug full of mead beside it. She raised the mug to her mouth. One sip for luck, then another for bravery. She'd need both in the coming hours.

Those who were seated at the table watched the Prophet and Immanuelle with what she could only describe as veiled disgust. Their discontent so palpable it hung on the air like a pall.

It was clear that they had expected an immediate end to the plague upon her cutting. But the dark was as thick as it ever was, and the night was unbroken. The seal carved between her brows had not been enough to draw back the plague, as the Prophet had promised it would be.

Halfway through the abysmal feast, the Prophet rose to speak, as if he knew he needed to seize control of his flock before he lost their trust forever. "Through forgiveness, through atonement, through purging and pain, we make ourselves clean. Today, my bride, my wife, Immanuelle Moore, has bled for her sins. She has suffered, and now she is clean."

The flock raised their voices on command. *"For the glory of the Father."*

The Prophet paused to cough into his sleeve. When he spoke again his voice was gravelly. "But my bride isn't the only one in need of grace. Before this day is done, another will be atoned for and forgiven. Another sinner will be cleansed by the Father's mercy." He paused—eyes closed, mouth open—as if he was trying to gather the strength he needed to continue. "Bring me my son."

The cathedral doors swung open and Immanuelle's heart stopped, panic cleaving clean through her. She watched in horror as two apostles ushered Ezra past the cathedral threshold and down the stairs. He staggered, his boots trailing through the dirt as they dragged him to his father. Apostle Isaac forced him to his knees with a well-placed strike between the shoulders. He fell to the ground, his head hanging inches above his father's feet.

"Ezra Chambers." The Prophet peered down at his son, eyes aglow with the light of the purging pyre. "Do you repent?"

Ezra didn't move. He gripped the dirt with both hands, like he was trying to anchor himself. At last he said, "I have nothing to repent for."

"Very well," said the Prophet, nodding. "May the Father have mercy on your soul."

Immanuelle's heart thrashed behind her ribs. She was on her feet in an instant, standing so quickly her chair toppled behind her. "What is the meaning of this?"

No one else moved. No one spoke. No one made a sound, save

for Esther, who cried out with a ragged shriek. But the Prophet didn't dignify her with so much as a glance. His eyes were locked on Immanuelle. Not his son, the guards, or the flock.

Her.

And it was to her the Prophet spoke to when he said, "Take him to the pyre."

The guards didn't make the mistake of hesitating again. They hauled Ezra up by either arm and dragged him to his feet. The Prophet trailed behind them like a shadow as they made their way toward the fire.

"No!" Immanuelle sprang after them, straining toward the guards, toward Ezra, her hands outstretched as if she could snatch him back. She had always known it would come to this, but she'd never expected it to happen so soon. She thought she had a little time, if nothing else, but she was wrong. "You promised Ezra would be spared," she said, though she knew her protests were in vain. "We had a deal!"

"Immanuelle, please." Ezra's voice was tired, resigned. "It's done now. Enough."

Immanuelle didn't heed him. She ran after them, tripping on the hem of her cutting gown as she went.

"You're a tyrant!" She trailed the Prophet so closely, she clipped his heels with her slippers. "You're a liar! You're a madman! You promised me he'd be safe." She caught his sleeve and yanked it so hard she ripped the velvet. *"You promised!"*

The Prophet turned on her then, drew back his hand, and slapped her. Immanuelle fell back, her head spinning, and crashed into a nearby bench. She heard Ezra cry her name again, his voice ringing in her ears.

"We had a deal," she whimpered, pushing herself up from the dirt. Shadows swam before her eyes. She tasted blood. "You promised."

The Prophet stared at the hand he'd slapped her with, as if he couldn't believe what he'd done, what she'd made him do. "I am fulfilling that promise. I told you I wouldn't harm him. That's why I'm going to free his soul and save him from the hellfire."

Immanuelle tried to rise to her feet but staggered. "You gave me your word."

"My word is the Scripture, and the Scripture demands blood atonement." With that, the Prophet nodded to the guards again, and at his bidding, they dragged Ezra to the foot of the nearest purging pyre, his boots carving tracks through the dirt. Once there, they seized his arms and forced him back, flinching as the flames churned and roared before them.

Fire licked across Ezra's back. He cried out in pain.

Immanuelle realized then that the Prophet had never meant for his son to live. He would protect himself above anyone else, even if it meant surrendering his son to the pyre's flames and watching him burn.

The Prophet turned to face his flock. "Sins must be atoned for by blood and burning. That is our oldest and most important law. Blood for blood. Ash to ash. That is what the Father demands, and that's what we will give Him tonight."

"Then take me."

No one heard her above the roar of the purging fire.

But the second time Immanuelle spoke, she was screaming. *"Take me instead!"*

Ezra stumbled to his knees as the guards released him, struck the dirt with a dull *thud*. His shirt was smoking, already singed by the touch of the flames.

And Immanuelle knew then that she had to end it. Either she acted now, or not at all.

She drew forward, moving past the Prophet. "I offer myself as a sacrifice. My life for Ezra's."

To this, there was no jeering, no wails or curses. Every soul in that congregation—man, woman, and child—sat silent, as still as tombstones in a graveyard.

All except Glory Moore, who let out a long, high cry that cleaved the night in two. Abram attempted to fold the girl into his arms, but she thrashed and struggled so violently even Anna couldn't ease her. "No!" she shrieked, and her voice echoed across the plains. *"No!"*

Vera started forward next, attempting to lunge free of her guards, but they dragged her back before she had the chance to do anything more than shout Immanuelle's name to the wind.

In the distant dark, the forest stirred.

Immanuelle forced her gaze back to the Prophet. He stood in her wake, his mouth open, his face bathed red with the light of the bonfire. He looked at his son, bent before the flames, and then he looked at Immanuelle with so much anger she felt the blood curdle in her veins.

"You're my wife before you are anything else."

"I am my own," said Immanuelle, fighting to keep her voice level. "My blood and bones belong to me, and me alone, and I would trade them, on my own authority, to atone for your son's sins. I'll take his place."

The Prophet took a step toward her. "You have no right."

This time, Immanuelle didn't cower. "I have every right. My offering is pure. You can't intercede."

"But you have my seal. You took a vow, *to me.*"

"And now I take another," said Immanuelle. "With the faithful of Bethel as my witnesses, I will go to the altar in Ezra's stead."

The Prophet tried to speak again, but his voice cracked. In his silence, Apostle Isaac limped forward. "Is it true that the girl has not been touched?"

Esther sprang to her feet, even as the wives around her grabbed at her skirts and tried to hush her. "The girl does not lie. She's pure."

"If she is pure," said the apostle, turning to face the Prophet, "then she is a worthy sacrifice."

"No," Ezra rasped. He tried to stand, but one of the guards struck him so hard his legs buckled beneath him, and he hit the ground on his hands and knees. "Don't hurt her. Please. There has to be another way."

"There is." A voice echoed through the dark, and to Immanuelle's shock, Martha stepped forward, moving between tables to the front of the feast. "I'll go in her stead. Spare her."

The apostle appraised the woman, eyes narrow, his upper lip curling with disgust. "You're not pure of flesh."

"No," said Martha, wringing her hands. "But I'm pure of soul. I've said my prayers. I've lived in truth and honor. I've served the Father well, Named generations in accordance to His will. I can take her place. Please."

"Martha," said Immanuelle, and her grandmother met her eyes. She was weeping, great brutal sobs, and she seemed to crumple a little more with each breath she took. "It's all right. I'm ready."

Martha's face went blank, and a few tears slipped down her cheeks, dangling from the point of her chin. She swayed, and she would have collapsed to the dirt if Anna hadn't caught her by the arm to keep her on her feet.

Immanuelle forced her gaze back to the Prophet. This time her voice didn't break. "My life for Ezra's."

For a moment, she thought the Prophet would deny her, seize her by the throat, drag her back to the Haven by her hair, or hang her up in the bowels of that wretched dungeon, where she would remain forevermore. But the Prophet simply lowered his head, hands clasped, fingers locked, as if he was praying. "Take her to the altar."

For the second time that day, Immanuelle found herself ushered into the cathedral and down the long aisle, to the altar at its end. There, in full view of the flock, she stripped out of her bridal gown and loosed her braids. Undressed and unburdened, she climbed onto the altar.

The slip of her bridal gown felt thin and sheer as the wind blew through the doors. Not that modesty mattered much anymore, in light of what she was about to do.

The flock spilled into the cathedral. They didn't bother filling the rows as they had during the trial. Instead, they pressed forward, crushing into the aisle and gathering at the foot of the altar, all of them eager to claim a good spot to witness the sacrifice. Among them, the Moores, weeping and tearing at their clothes. Vera trailed behind them, flanked by guards on either side, expression dead. And then, at the forefront of the crowd—bound and burned and shackled—was Ezra.

Immanuelle had seen broken men before. Men sentenced to die for their sins with nooses around their necks in the town square. She had seen men cradle their dead sons, men with the lash of the whip at their back. Sick or wounded men, men gone mad with rage. But none of them had looked as undone as Ezra did in that moment.

Emerging through the thick of the crowd, the Prophet took his place behind the altar. He moved one hand to the bare slope of Immanuelle's belly and the other to her head, his thumb pressing hard against the seal he'd carved just hours before.

Blood skimmed along the bridge of Immanuelle's nose, pooling in the dip of her upper lip.

She waited for the prayer with her eyes wide open, but it didn't come. They meant to usher her into the afterlife unwelcomed and unannounced, without last rites or prayers for mercy . . . and perhaps that was for the best, given the grave sin she was about to commit. There would be no place for her in the Father's holy halls. No mercy for her in the heavens after what she was about to do.

Apostle Isaac shuffled forward, the gutting knife balanced between both of his hands. At the sight of the blade, fear washed over her. Her heart battered the backs of her ribs and she grasped the edge of the altar to keep herself from fleeing.

The Prophet wrapped a shaking hand around the hilt of the blade. For a moment, he studied it, as if testing its weight. Then his gaze shifted to Immanuelle. "You would really die for him? You would damn yourself?"

She nodded, knowing that the moment was upon her now. There was no turning back. "His sins are mine."

"No." Ezra struggled toward her, fighting his shackles and clawing the floor for purchase. "Immanuelle. Please, no."

The Prophet put a hand to her brow, pressing hard enough to make her seal ache. He raised the gutting knife high above his head.

"Blood for blood."

Chapter Thirty-nine

The maiden will bear a daughter, they will call her Immanu-
elle, and she will redeem the flock with wrath and plague.
—From *The Writings of Miriam Moore*

IMMANUELLE CAUGHT THE gutting knife—one hand wrapped around its hilt, the other around the bare blade—stopping its descent just a split moment before it carved into her chest. With all the strength she had left to summon, she ripped it from the Prophet's hands.

The congregation roared with horror. The guards sprang into action, flooding the aisles, their fingers curled over the triggers of their rifles, which were all trained on Immanuelle. There were simultaneous shouts for them to fire and stand down, but Immanuelle paid them no mind. She raised the gutting knife and slit the sleeve of her dress clean open. Then—in a series of five vicious cuts—she carved the reversal sigil into the bare flesh of her forearm.

Time fractured before her eyes. The pain of the cuts began to build, becoming almost more than she could bear. A series of violent spasms racked her, forcing her to her knees, and as she struggled and writhed in the throes of her agony, the altar began to shudder along with her—stones shifting, its corners crumbling.

Immanuelle tilted her head up, looked toward the cathedral windows, but to her horror the darkness remained unbroken. She

searched the distant sky for signs of daybreak—a glimpse of sunshine, a ray of moonlight, the blue beginnings of early dawn—but
the night was unchanged. The sigil hadn't worked. She'd failed.

The cathedral gave a violent shudder. Rubble ricocheted down
the steps and skittered into the aisles. The floorboards buckled
and the windowpanes rattled in their casings. Overhead, the rafters shifted. Dust and debris rained down. The flock panicked.
Screams rang through the cathedral and children shrieked for
their mothers. A few men fled to the doors, but the rest cowered
in their pews, doing what little they could to shield themselves
and their families from the falling wreckage.

Immanuelle stared down at her bleeding arm, willing the
power of the sigil to work, trying to call the plagues back to her.
But to no avail. Bethel was lost.

The Prophet staggered backward, pale and slack-jawed, stumbling on his robes as he fled behind the altar. The walls began to
shudder more violently, threatening to cave in, and a single word
rang through Immanuelle's mind: *Slaughter.*

As if on cue, the windows of the cathedral shattered, the panes
blasting inward in a storm of glittering stained-glass shards. A
river of darkness rushed into the sanctuary.

And with the night came the legion.

The first of the beasts flew into the cathedral, swarming its
eaves as the flock screamed and cowered below. Fanged bats
roosted in the rafters; a wake of vultures circled viciously above.
Storms of droning locusts spilled in through the broken windows
and ravens rushed through a crack in the roof, cawing and shrieking as they poured into the sanctuary.

The congregation descended into screams and chaos. Some
charged toward the doors; others took shelter in the shadows beneath the pews, desperate to escape the horde swarming overhead. A few of the Prophet's guardsmen raised their weapons,

defending the flock with bullets and bolts. But their efforts were futile. The onslaught raged on.

The land-bound creatures followed the winged legion, rushing in through open doors and shattered windows. There were women helmed with the heads of hounds, spiders as large as lambs that scuttled beneath the pews. The legions of the dead—the blight-struck, the lost souls, the flame-mangled victims of purgings past—staggered down the aisles.

Upon their arrival, the true bedlam began. Mothers fled with their children; men rushed the broken windows and doors only to be barred by the teeming horde that circled the walls and forced the flock back to their pews with bared fangs and hooked claws.

Then the witches entered.

First came the Lovers, Mercy and Jael, walking hand in hand down the center aisle, the hellish throng parting to make way for them. Then Delilah, who scrabbled from a rift in the ground beneath them, emerging sludge slick and wild-eyed, the floorboards rotting beneath her feet as she stood.

The cathedral began to shake again, this time so violently Immanuelle feared the roof would collapse. She searched the shifting crowds, desperate to spot Vera or the Moores, but she couldn't find them amidst the mayhem. The quaking continued. Grown men were thrown off their feet as pews toppled. The Crusader's Sword fell from the wall behind the altar and shattered, mere inches from the spot where the Prophet cowered. Immanuelle tried to cling to the altar but couldn't get a grip on the blood-slick stone, and she tumbled into the aisle below.

A boy stumbled over her. A woman crushed her hand underfoot. She was nearly trampled by an apostle fleeing a snarling wolf, when she felt a hand on her arm, dragging her backward to safety.

Ezra.

Immanuelle heard a deafening roar, and a rafter collapsed,

crashing to the floor where she'd lain just moments prior. It crushed the hapless apostle and the wolf stalking him instead. The force of the beam's fall sent Immanuelle and Ezra sprawling back in a cloud of debris. Ezra sprung to his feet in an instant, dragging her up by the elbow and into the safety of the altar's shadow.

The cathedral stopped shaking, and the legion went still. Ezra drew Immanuelle closer, and the two of them watched in horror as the front doors of the cathedral swung slowly open.

From the shadows of the ever-night, Lilith appeared.

She stood alone on the threshold. Fog seeped through the cracks in her skull and rolled from the black of her eye sockets. Her antlers arched overhead, a bleached-bone diadem. There were screams as she stepped into the cathedral. Grown men cowered on their knees, pleading with the Father as the witch queen passed them by. Barefoot and open-armed, Lilith walked down the center aisle, picking her way through the throng of beasts and ghouls to the altar, where Immanuelle and Ezra sat, frozen. The other witches moved to flank her: the Lovers on her left, Delilah on her right.

Ezra shifted forward to shield Immanuelle, but she caught him by the shoulder, stopping him. "I have to do this on my own," she said.

He didn't back down. "Immanuelle—"

"Trust me. You promised you would."

Ezra worked his jaw, Immanuelle's hand still on his shoulder. Then he nodded, and she released him.

Immanuelle pushed herself off the floor and stood on weak knees, facing the witches in full. For a moment they all surveyed one another in silence. Then Lilith extended a hand.

Immanuelle understood her meaning at once: *Join us, or die with them.*

It was a simple offer, even a generous one. More kind than the fate her mother had met, certainly. Perhaps Immanuelle would be foolish not to take it. After all, the Prophet's flock had been so quick to see her to her grave . . . Would it be so wrong to save herself and leave them to the same fate they would have damned her to?

Immanuelle's gaze tracked across the pews, and she took in the faces of the people gathered there—Anna with Honor on her hip and Glory weeping, Abram and Martha, Vera standing resolute and unafraid, people from the Glades and the Holy Grounds and the Outskirts alike. Some of them were innocent, others complicit; still more were caught in the gray between right and wrong. Few were wholly blameless, and none were free of sin. But there wasn't a single soul in that sanctuary she would condemn to the ruin that now lay before them.

Resigned to her fate, Immanuelle turned back to face the witches. "If this is the end, then I die with them."

There was a shift in the air. The cathedral gave a little tremor and a cold breeze skimmed past the broken windows, stirring up clouds of dust. The darkness thickened, and the few torches that were still lit flickered weakly, doing little to disperse the night's shadows.

Lilith didn't lower her hand.

Instead, in a sweeping gesture, the witch turned to face the flock, surveying the masses with those dead black eyes, taking in the room. Her gaze passed over the Prophet cowering behind the altar, the wreckage and the rubble, the corpses that littered the cathedral aisles.

Then her gaze fell to the Moores. Her hand twisted into a grasping claw.

Anna loosed a little cry, clutching Honor with one hand and drawing Glory into her skirts. Martha threw an arm out to shield them as the witch stepped closer, tears rolling down her cheeks though her expression was stoic. But it was Abram who started forward, limping out into the center aisle to place himself between the witch queen and his family. He stood there, silent and defenseless, leaning hard on his cane. Then, on Lilith's command, a large, bone-faced hound prowled from the ranks of the legion.

It happened so fast, Immanuelle didn't have the chance to scream.

One moment, Abram was standing alone in the center aisle; the next, he was pinned to the floor, the beast's jaws closing around the back of his neck with an ugly, gut-twisting *snap*.

A great roaring filled Immanuelle's ears. Darkness crept in from the edges of her vision, until she saw nothing but Abram's lifeless body sprawled out on the floor. All at once, she was back in the cabin, surrounded by walls carved with plagues and promises. She could see the shadow of her mother, working the curses, carving her fate line by line.

Something stirred deep inside her. The sigil carved into her arm began to burn, bleeding so profusely the blood sloughed off her fingers and formed a puddle on the floor at her feet. A great tremor rattled the cathedral. Immanuelle raised her bloody hands and, with a ragged cry, summoned the power of the plagues.

Delilah was the first to fall.

A red tear leaked from the corner of the witch's right eye, then her left. Blood pooled in the hollows of her ears, droplets dangling from her lobes like little jewels. Delilah sputtered, coughed, then began to choke, retching up mouthfuls of thick black gore with each convulsion. She broke to her knees, twitched twice, then collapsed motionless to the floor.

Blood.

Immanuelle turned on Mercy next. The witch jerked to a halt in the growing puddle of Delilah's blood, swayed a little on her feet, then dropped to her hands and knees, as if pushed by some invisible force. She tilted her head to stare up into the rafters, her back arching to a near spine-snapping angle. With a strangled cry, the witch hurled herself forward, and her brow cracked against the tiles with a sickening crunch that echoed through the cathedral. She raised her bleeding head, leaned back, and struck the floor again, and again, and again.

Blight.

Jael stepped forward next, and Immanuelle turned to face her. The witch stopped beside her lover, looking ready to strike. But before she had the chance, the power of the curse moved through Immanuelle again. With a pass of her hand, a tide of shadows washed across the cathedral floor, lashing around the witch's ankles and clawing up her legs, her chest, her cheeks.

Jael managed a single scream before the writhing blackness devoured her.

Darkness.

Immanuelle stepped forward to pick up the gutting blade from where it lay a few feet from the altar's stairs. She turned to Lilith last and raised the blood-slick blade, cleaving the air between them. "Enough."

Lilith didn't heed her. Undeterred, the witch queen stalked down the center aisle, picking her way past the corpses of her fallen coven. She stopped just short of Immanuelle, so close that the gutting blade's tip nearly pierced into the soft of her belly.

But Lilith didn't flinch.

Instead, she cupped Immanuelle's cheek in her cold, pale hand and pressed even closer, the knife carving deep into her stomach as she tipped her forehead to Immanuelle's. She shuddered violently. Issued a low groan of pain.

The girl peered into the black of Lilith's eye sockets and felt the forest's thrall dragging her to senselessness. The sounds of slaughter died into the hiss of wind in the treetops. Shadows edged in from the corners of her vision and Immanuelle heard the woodland call deep within her, the sound like blood rush in her ears. The witch queen eased her thumb back and forth along Immanuelle's pulse as if measuring the rhythm of her heartbeat, the gesture tender . . . even motherly. Immanuelle could almost imagine the kind of leader she might have been in a time, long ago, before the affliction of her vengeance and bloodlust turned her into the monster she had now become.

Lilith traced a finger along Immanuelle's lips, then caught her by the neck.

A scream tangled in Immanuelle's throat as Lilith ripped her off her feet. Choking, she clawed at the witch's fingers, dangling above the ground as Lilith lifted her higher and higher.

In a panic, Immanuelle raised the gutting knife, slashing blindly. The blade connected first with bone, then flesh, piercing deep into Lilith's shoulder.

The witch queen let out a shriek that shook the church. Fissures raced along the walls and the roof caved inward. Flock and legion alike fled for the doors as the cathedral collapsed around them. Through the mayhem, Immanuelle heard Ezra shout her name, and then his voice was lost to the tumult like everything else.

Immanuelle's vision went blurry. She tried to stay conscious, clawing desperately for a last scrap of strength. With a snarl, she ripped the gutting blade from Lilith's shoulder and raised it high above her head.

This time, her blow struck true.

The blade lodged hilt-deep in Lilith's chest. The witch stumbled forward, crashed into a nearby pew, and sank to the floor. But to Immanuelle's horror, no sooner had she hit the ground than the witch was on her feet again. She braced herself on a nearby pew, caught the gutting blade by the hilt, ripped it from her chest, and hurled it down the center aisle.

For a moment, they stood deadlocked, there in the center aisle of the cathedral. Both of them bleeding and wounded, barely able to stay on their feet. And Immanuelle knew then that the end had come and only one of the two of them would walk out of that cathedral.

Lilith raised both hands.

The wood floors began to buckle and ripple; roots burst free of the cathedral's foundation and slithered—serpentine—down the center aisles. Saplings pressed through the floorboards, growing to maturity in a matter of moments, their branches spreading through the rafters. The crawling roots wrapped themselves around Immanuelle's ankles, coiling so tight she cried out in pain. She staggered forward, struggling to free herself, but she couldn't move.

The sigil cut into her forearm screamed with pain, as if she were being branded. She shut her eyes against it, reached into the depths of herself, and unleashed all that she had to give.

The roots slithered from around her ankles, recoiling back toward the breaks in the floorboards they had emerged from. The trees that sprawled overhead bent double, racked by some phantom wind that swept through the cathedral like the beginnings of a summer storm.

Lilith staggered back, pinned to the altar, as a powerful wind stormed around her so violently the skin on her outstretched hand began to slough away from the muscle, and the muscle from the bone. The witch lashed out with a scream.

The force of Lilith's power ripped Immanuelle off her feet. She careened through the air and crashed to a brutal landing on a heap of upturned roots and floorboards. Her ribs gave a sickening crunch upon impact, and she gasped and struggled, clinging to the cusp of her consciousness.

The wind died to a low wheeze as Lilith pushed off the altar and started toward her, threading through the trees the way she did the night they first met. There was light in her eye sockets now—two glowing motes that moved like pupils and homed in on Immanuelle. Her rage was palpable—it turned the air cold and made the trees shudder. The witch's every step seemed to shake the cathedral down to the crumbling stones of its foundation.

Immanuelle tried and failed to fall back; Lilith was far too quick. The witch leveled her with a single backhanded slap, and Immanuelle struck the floor again. The lights in Lilith's eyes began to dance and multiply, scattering through the black of her sockets like embers from a windblown campfire. She delivered a cruel kick to Immanuelle's ribs, and she screamed at the pain, clawing the floorboards for purchase.

There was a soft click, the sound of a bullet sliding into its chamber. Then Ezra's voice. "Leave her alone."

The witch turned from Immanuelle, faced Ezra in full. He stood in the gap between two pine trees, peering down the barrel of a gun, a finger curled over the trigger.

Lilith started toward him, one hand raised.

The ground beneath Ezra's feet began to ripple, trees and roots sprouting through the gaps between broken floorboards, curling around his legs the way they had that day at the pond. He fired on Lilith, but with the roots dragging at his arms, none of the bullets met their mark.

Undeterred, the witch walked toward him. As she neared, one of the roots coiled around Ezra's neck and ripped him backward so the top of his head nearly touched his spine. He tried to fire again, but a vine wrapped itself around the barrel of the gun and forced it to the floor.

Immanuelle struggled to stand up. The gutting blade was just a few feet away. If she could reach it, she could put the witch down and end this once and for all.

Ezra struggled to speak. "Immanuelle . . . run—"

A bone-faced wolf prowled from behind him, the same one that had taken down Abram, its mouth still slick with his blood. It stalked toward Ezra, jaws slack, ready to lunge, when Immanuelle threw out her hand.

The ground beneath the wolf gaped open, floorboards buckling loose, a landslide of debris tumbling down into a yawning sinkhole. The wolf whimpered, slipped, its claws scrabbling at the floorboards, and plummeted into the void.

Immanuelle pressed to her feet. Every breath sent a bolt of pain through her ribs, but she managed to speak anyway: "Let him go."

At her command the vines slithered from Ezra, and he half crawled, half lunged away from the sinkhole's edge, grabbing for his rifle. He raised it to his shoulder and fired on Lilith again, just as she turned back to Immanuelle. The bullet pierced straight through the crook of her collarbone. Lilith stopped . . . then staggered into a nearby tree. Her knees buckled.

"*Immanuelle!*" Vera stood in the center of the aisle, the gutting knife in her hand. She staggered forward, limping on what looked like a broken leg, and threw it.

The knife careened through the air, flipping several times as it arced overhead. Immanuelle lashed out and snatched it by the hilt a split second before it hit the floor. Then, with a strangled cry, she turned on Lilith and lunged.

The blade lodged, hilt-deep, into the center of the witch's skull. A great crack cleaved the bone, and then, with the softest whimper, the witch queen collapsed.

Spent, Immanuelle crumpled to the floor beside her, gasping

and bleeding, so weak she felt she would never rise again. With the last of her strength, she pressed a hand to the witch's head, smearing the bone with her blood.

Lilith peered at her, chest heaving. Tendrils of shadow eddied from the cracks in her skull, hanging on the air like smoke. One of her antlers snapped and hit the floor. At last, with a shudder that racked the cathedral to the stones of its foundation, the witch went lifeless.

Slaughter.

CHAPTER FORTY

*And on that day, when the dark has passed and the sun has
risen again, the sins of the deceivers will be brought to light
and the truth will emerge from the shadows.*
—THE LAST PROPHESY OF DAVID FORD

THERE WAS SUNLIGHT on Immanuelle's cheeks when she
woke. She opened her eyes and sat up, dizzy and squinting,
struggling to process the scene before her.

The cathedral was in ruins. Half the roof had caved in, and
fallen beams and debris littered the floors. Trees grew from great
gashes in the foundation, their branches stirring when the wind
blew. Survivors wandered the wreckage of toppled pews and broken windows, searching for the wounded and trapped. Strewn
through the rubble were the corpses of beasts, guardsmen, and
the faithful. Among them was Lilith's body, lying limp in the
shadow of the altar.

"Easy." Ezra was by Immanuelle's side, bracing a hand against
the small of her back as she attempted to stand. "You're all right.
You're safe now."

She shut her eyes against the sight of the carnage, feeling
faint and sick. The memories of the battle flooded back to her: the
legions pouring in through the shattered windows, beasts and
demons prowling the aisles of the church, children screaming,
women fleeing, Abram pinned to the floor . . .

Abram. *Abram.*

"Where is he?" Immanuelle demanded, turning to Ezra. "I want to see Abram."

"Immanuelle—"

"I have to see him. Now."

The crowd parted before them, members of the flock shuffling aside to give her a clear view. There, lying motionless amidst the wreckage, was Abram. Glory sat tucked into his waist the way she had as a baby, Honor close beside her, weeping. Next to Honor sat Anna, sobbing into the folds of her skirts. Standing over the two of them, stone-faced and motionless, was Martha. When her gaze shifted to Immanuelle, she offered nothing but a slow shake of her head.

Immanuelle tried to stand. She might have fallen if Ezra hadn't been there to catch her by the arm. She shook him off, dropped to her hands and knees, and crawled through the wreckage to the place where Abram's body lay.

She didn't want to touch him, for fear of unleashing the power of the curses again. So she simply sat there next to him, one hand clasped over her mouth to muffle her sobs.

"Only now do you see the price of sin. Only now do you understand." Immanuelle raised her head to see the Prophet staggering from behind the ruined altar, where he'd hidden during the height of the massacre. He raised his voice, calling out to the crowd: "Do you see the evil this girl has brought upon us? She summoned this darkness, called the coven here. Even now, I see the shadow of the Mother in her eyes."

At this, the survivors of the slaughter murmured among themselves. A few stumbled back toward the walls; others cowered behind broken pews and heaps of rubble. All of them seemed to fear whatever curses Immanuelle would conjure next.

"Look at what this girl has wrought," continued the Prophet, gesturing to the carnage about them. "Look at the ruin she's brought upon us."

"Why don't you bite your lying tongue?" Ezra snapped, stepping forward. "Can't you see she's mourning?"

"That girl mourns nothing but her own demise. She's a witch."

"Maybe," said Ezra, and he looked ready to rip the gutting blade from Lilith's skull and turn it on his father. "But while you were cowering behind the altar, pleading for your miserable life, Immanuelle fought for Bethel. She mastered the plagues and the Mother's darkness, which is more than any prophet or saint has been able to do. She saved us all."

"She didn't save us," spat the Prophet. "She brought this evil here in the first place. She confessed as much to me days ago: These plagues were born of her flesh and blood. All of this is because of her."

He was right. Immanuelle couldn't deny it. Everything—the blood and the blight, the darkness and the slaughter, Leah's death and Abram's—all of it had come to pass because of her. Miriam had died to give her the power to fight back, but all she'd managed to do was hurt the very people she'd wanted to save.

Immanuelle peered down again at her grandfather, choking back a sob. She started to reach for him, then stopped herself, folding her hands into fists so tight her nails cut into her palms. "I'm sorry," she whispered, not to the Prophet, or to the flock, but to Abram. "I'm so sorry."

"It's not your fault." Ezra dropped to her side. "You saved us, Immanuelle. All of us are here because of you."

"Not all of us," she said, her gaze sweeping across the ruins of the cathedral. The Moores weren't the only ones in mourning. There were more dead among the debris and rubble. A guardsman lay slumped over a broken pew, surrounded by the corpses of fallen beasts. The body of an old man she recognized as the candle peddler lay pinned beneath a fallen rafter. A few feet from the peddler, one of the Prophet's brides sat amidst the wreckage, softly singing a lullaby to the lifeless child cradled in her arms.

These were the casualties of a war that could never be won. Immanuelle knew this now. The violence would continue. A new man would claim the title of Prophet. The cathedral would be rebuilt, and the covens of the dead would one day rise again. The war between witch and Prophet, Church and coven, darkness and light, would wage on and on until the day there would be nothing and no one left to mourn.

Was that the fate the Father wanted? Was that what the Mother ordained? Did They send Their children willingly to the slaughter? Could this be Their will?

No.

Gazing around the cathedral—at the corpses crowding the aisles, at Glory sobbing on Abram's chest, at all the suffering and the senselessness—Immanuelle was certain of one thing: There was no divinity in this violence. No justice. No sanctity. All that ruin and pain had been wrought not from the Mother's darkness or the Father's light, but from the sins of man.

They had brought this fate upon themselves. They were complicit in their own damnation.

They did this.

Not the Mother. Not the Father.

Them.

"You ought to burn for this," said the Prophet, whispering now though it was so quiet in the church that everyone could hear him. "Take her to the pyre."

At his command, what was left of the Prophet's Guard broke forward, their rifles raised. But Immanuelle and Ezra were ready. As the Prophet's men backed them toward the altar, Immanuelle sprang for Lilith's corpse and ripped the gutting blade from her skull. Ezra snatched one of the fallen guardsmen's rifles and raised it—peering down the barrel with one eye shut, his finger curled over the trigger.

"Don't make us do this," said Immanuelle, raising the gutting blade. "There's been enough bloodshed today."

There was a chorus of jeers and shouts. A crowd of the survivors pressed into the center aisle. Immanuelle took a step closer to Ezra, the gutting blade raised and readied. She would hack her way to the cathedral doors if she had to. She hadn't come this far just to die at the hands of a mob. But as the throng pressed closer, Immanuelle realized they weren't shouting at her and Ezra.

No. Their eyes were on their Prophet.

Vera was the first to push past the Prophet's Guard, limping between them and Immanuelle. She'd been wounded in the attack; her leg looked broken, there was a deep gash at her hairline, and the left side of her face was slick with blood. But despite the severity of her injuries, her stance was that of a soldier's. "To get to her, you'll have to strike me down first."

More women followed, almost all of them from the Outskirts, placing themselves as shields between Immanuelle and the Prophet's Guard. Glory joined them, elbowing to Immanuelle's side with a fierce cry, and Anna followed after with Honor on her hip.

Martha stepped forward next, much to Immanuelle's shock. "I stand with them."

Esther staggered toward her son and, emboldened by their matriarch, a few of the Prophet's brides followed suit. More joined the ranks. Men of the Outskirts. Leah's mother and older sisters, then other women of the Church after them—little girls no older than Glory, matriarchs who could scarcely walk without the help of their canes. All of them moved forward in unison, flooding the aisle, forcing themselves between Immanuelle and the Prophet.

The Guard faltered, and a few lowered their rifles, unable to point their guns at their wives and mothers . . . their sisters and aunts. Slowly, more and more women, and a few men, stepped forward to join the throng.

A chant began. At first it was little more than a murmur, like the sound of distant thunder. But then the chorus spread through the crowd, rising to the rafters and blasting through the cathedral, *"Blood for blood. Blood for blood. Blood for blood."*

The Prophet cowered in the shadows of the altar, watching in horror as his flock raised their voices against him. They left their pews behind them and spilled into the aisle, surging to the front of the church. *"Blood for blood. Ash to ash. Dust to dust."*

Ezra raised his hand and they stopped dead, like hunting dogs trained to heel at the foot of their master. He turned to Immanuelle. "Give me the blade."

No one moved.

No one uttered a single word. Not a curse. Not a prayer. Not a protest. The whole flock looked on in silence.

Immanuelle's gaze shifted from him to the Prophet. From father to son. She didn't move.

Ezra extended his hand again. "For your father," he whispered. "For your mother. For Leah. For Abram. For us. Let it be over. Let it be done with."

Immanuelle stared at the Prophet, cowering there on the ground, pleading for his life. Then she raised her gaze to Ezra. "Is this what you really want? Is this what you want to be?"

Ezra drew a little closer, stepping with care like he was afraid he'd spook her. "What I want is to make sure this never happens again. I want a world where sins are atoned for. A world where evil men suffer for their wrongdoing."

"So did Lilith," Immanuelle whispered. "So did my mother."

Ezra winced a little at that, like her words cut him. "He deserves to die for what he's done. He would have put a blade through your heart. He killed your father. He preyed on your mother and countless other girls. We can't let him walk free. Blood begets blood."

"The boy is right, Immanuelle." Vera shouldered to the front of the crowd, limping badly. "Think of your father burning on the pyre. Think of the people in the Outskirts, resigned to a life of squalor and suffering because of the greed of this man, and all of the others that came before him. You have a chance to seek recompense for their suffering. So raise the knife and take it."

Immanuelle's hand tightened around the hilt. All at once, she knew what she had to do.

"The world you want can't be bought with blood. You build it with the choices you make, with the things you do. Either we can keep purging, keep the pyres burning, keep hoping that our prayers will be enough to save us—or we can build something better. A world without slaughter." Immanuelle held out the gutting blade to Ezra. "It's your choice. I have no right to take it from you."

Ezra studied the blade in her hand, reached for it, then stopped. "No. You have the only right. The choice is yours, and yours only."

Immanuelle paused, lingering in the shadow of the altar. The Prophet scrabbled at her feet, pleading for mercy.

"*Please.*" He wheezed and hacked like he had to fight for every breath. "*Please. Please.*"

Immanuelle turned to study the faces in the crowd—Anna and Honor, Martha and Glory, Vera and Ezra, people from the Glades and the Holy Grounds and the Outskirts alike. What she did, she did for them, for all of Bethel, for the dream of making their home something better than it was, so that those who followed in their footsteps would never know the heat of a pyre, or the pain of its flames.

A world without killings or cruelty: That was the fate she wanted.

And it was the fate she would have.

Turning to face the pews in full, Immanuelle dropped the blade, and it struck the floor with a clatter that echoed through the cathedral. "Today, we choose mercy."

The flock answered her as one. *"Now and forevermore."*

Epilogue

IMMANUELLE SAT ON the stairs of the Haven and watched the sun rise through the trees. In the days after the attack on the cathedral, she'd spent many a morning on those steps, cradling a cup of tea or a book of poetry, waiting for the sun to climb above the treetops, just to make sure it would. Sometimes, when she was alone, she would peel back the sleeve of her dress, trace the puckered scar of the sigil she'd carved into her arm all those weeks ago.

In her darkest moments, she would hope—even pray—that her recompense would hasten, if only so she wouldn't be made to wait in a state of perpetual dread, under the threat of some faceless affliction she didn't yet know. Better to settle the matter quickly, face her reckoning so she could put all of the strife behind her once and for all. Because if she didn't do that, who would she be? What honor was there in a girl who could fight to save everyone except herself?

"You're drifting again," Ezra said, his eyes on the horizon. He sat close beside her, as he always did when he had the time to. "What's on your mind?"

Immanuelle drew her knees to her chest and gazed out across

the sun-washed plains, watching light flood between the trees. She grasped her forearm, fingertips pressing painfully into the scar of the sigil. So much had changed in the span of a few short weeks. The Prophet's condition had worsened, and preparations for his death were being made. Some of the flock remained loyal to him, but others looked to Ezra as the new leader of the Church and faith. Immanuelle hoped that the tensions between the opposing groups wouldn't implode into a schism—or worse yet a holy war— but whispers emerging from the bastions of the old Church suggested that the matter of the Prophet's succession would only be settled through bloodshed.

But Immanuelle tried not to think about that. Ezra had told her, time and time again, that those troubles weren't hers anymore. She had done her part. She'd saved Bethel from the plagues and all of the evil done in her name. Now it was time for her to let go. "I'm just thinking about how so many things can change and yet stay entirely the same."

Ezra frowned. "Is this about the schism?"

"The schism, the sentencings, the threat of holy war. Sometimes I feel like we're just rehashing the past all over again. I hate feeling that we've gotten this far only to become what others have already been before us."

"We're not repeating the past," said Ezra, "and we're making damn sure no one else will either. You can't lose sight of that."

Immanuelle's gaze shifted west, to the distant ruins of the cathedral. Sometimes, when she closed her eyes, she could picture the slaughter—the bodies strewn through the rubble, the blood smeared across the tiles, Vera with the gutting blade in her hand, Abram lying dead. "It's a little late for that. It seems like I can't keep sight of anything that matters anymore. So here I am trying to pick up the bits and pieces of who I used to be and who I am now, in the wake of all of this."

Ezra raised a hand to her cheek, his thumb tracing over her bottom lip. "I'll take those bits and pieces. Any day, over anything. And when we're stronger, we'll build those bits and pieces into something more."

Immanuelle looked at him and smiled. It was a small thing—a little grin as quick as a flame's flicker—but it was something. It was a start.

Leaning into Ezra's hand, she kissed him. First the pad of his thumb, then his lips, shifting into him as he angled closer, grasping her waist. Immanuelle could have stayed that way with him until the sun pulled high above the horizon line and sank into shadow again. But after a minute, she drew back.

Easing out of Ezra's arms, she pressed to her feet and stepped barefoot off the stairs and out onto the smoke-washed plains. Wind stirred through her curls and tore at her skirts. On the distant horizon, the last pyres of the purging smoldered and died.

"I've thought of a name for the coming year," she said, squinting into the red light of the rising sun. For a moment, she thought she saw Lilith standing on the cusp of the Darkwood, the tines of her antlers tangled in the branches of a birch tree. But it was only a trick of the shadows. The dead were dormant and the woods were quiet. Immanuelle narrowed her eyes and watched as the rising sun crested the treetops. "I think we should call it Year of the Dawn."

--- ❖ ---

Acknowledgments

WHEN I FLIP through the pages of this book, I see the fingerprints of the people who've encouraged and supported me. I owe them my gratitude.

First, I would like to thank my agent, Brooks Sherman. From the start, your vision for this book was bigger and more ambitious than my own, and I'm forever grateful for it. I feel immensely lucky to have such a brilliant collaborator, brainstorming buddy, and loyal advocate.

To my editor, Jessica Wade, who saw the heart of this book and showed me how to hone it. I couldn't have asked for a better creative partner. I'm eternally grateful for your brilliant edits, your passion, and all of the hard work you put into this book. I can't wait to create the next one with you.

I'd like to thank Ashley Hearn, the godmother of my fictional son and one of the most brilliant people I know. You were the first person in publishing to take a chance on me, and none of this would have been possible if you hadn't pulled my book from the Pitch Wars submissions pile.

I'm so grateful to the team at Penguin Random House for championing this book. Special thanks to Alexis Nixon, Brittanie Black, Fareeda Bullert, and Miranda Hill. To Simon Taylor and the rest of my team across the pond at Penguin Random House UK, thank you. I'm immensely fortunate to have so many passionate and hardworking people in my corner.

Thank you to Eileen G. Chetti for the amazing copyedits, Wendi Gu for the whip-smart feedback, and Katie Anderson and Larry Rostant for giving me the book cover of my dreams. Thanks also to Stephanie Koven and the team at Janklow & Nesbit.

To the family that has supported and encouraged my writing, thank you. To my dad for believing in me more than I believe in myself. To my fearless little sister, Alana, who makes a point to keep me very, *very* humble. To my mom—my best friend, and my first (and favorite) teacher who single-handedly instilled my lifelong love of writing. Dedicating this book to you was the least I could do to express my gratitude for the sacrifices you've made to support me, but I owe you so much more.

Since I'm thanking family, I would be remiss not to mention my dumpster kitten, Luna, who is sitting on my lap as I type this. I forgive you for that one time you pulled the books off my shelf and peed all over them. You're the best familiar a girl could ask for, and you have my whole heart. And to my Halloween cats, Midnight and Jet: I adore you both.

To my ride-or-die friend, Rena Barron, who is one of the most loyal and hardworking people I know. Your creativity, unparalleled work ethic, and constant encouragement inspire me every day. I don't know what I'd do without you.

Jacob Woelke, thank you for the laughs, the memes, the movies, and the gas-station snacks. You're one of the best friends I've ever had, and I can't wait to catch up over pancakes when I see you next.

I would also like to thank my friend and first critique partner, Jean Thomas. I'm so grateful for your edits, honesty, and encouragement. You've been by my side through every step of my writing journey, and I wouldn't have it any other way.

To one of my closest and oldest friends, Nicole Schaut. I cut my teeth on the stories we told together as kids, and I'll always treasure them.

I owe a massive thank-you to the writing community. If I were to list all of you by name, these acknowledgments would be twenty pages long. But I'd like to thank Ronni Davis (the living embodiment of a ray of sunshine), the Pitch Wars team, Hannah Whitten, Patrice Caldwell, Sierra Elmore, June C.L. Tan, Deborah F. Savoy, Ciannon Smart, Victoria Lee, Kristin Lambert, Tracy Deonn, Sasha Peyton Smith, Christine Lynn Herman, Mel Howard, S. A. Chakraborty, Roseanne A. Brown, Dhonielle Clayton, Peyton Thomas, Emily A. Duncan, and my black girl magic crew.

I'm so grateful to the incomparable faculty at the University of South Carolina Beaufort, with special thanks to Dr. Ellen Malphrus for her mentorship, as well as thanks to Dr. Robert Kilgore, Dr. Lauren Hoffer, Dr. Mollie Barnes, and Dr. Erin McCoy. To my brilliant Society of Creative Writers, English alumni, and Fiction Workshop cohort—thank you. You were among the first to read this story, and if not for your enthusiasm at that early stage, I'm not sure I would have continued it. I'm especially grateful to my classmates Katie Hart and Bill Lisbon for their friendship and support.

And finally, to the survivors, to the underdogs, to the people who speak the truth when the world tries to silence them: thank you.

The

YEAR
of the
WITCHING

ALEXIS HENDERSON

QUESTIONS FOR DISCUSSION

1. What do you think the Darkwood represents? Is it evil, good, or neutral?
2. How does Immanuelle's desire to know more about her mother drive the narrative, and how does what she learns change her?
3. What is the significance of the seals that the married women in Bethel wear? What do they symbolize?
4. Why do you think the people of the Outskirts were shunned? What is their role in Bethel and the growing resistance within it?
5. Was the violence of the witches justified? Do you think that there was a way for them to achieve retribution without bloodshed?
6. Do you see Ezra as being responsible for (or complicit in) the sins of the Prophet and Church?
7. What is the role of anger in this story? Do you think it was a useful agent of change?
8. Do you think Bethel is redeemable? Why or why not?

Alexis Henderson is a speculative fiction writer with a penchant for dark fantasy, witchcraft, and cosmic horror. She grew up in one of America's most haunted cities—Savannah, Georgia—which instilled in her a lifelong love of ghost stories. Currently, Alexis resides in Columbus, Ohio, where she's learning to cope with the cold.

CONNECT ONLINE

AlexisHenderson.com

 AlexHWrites

Lexish